HOT TEXAS NIGHTS

When they finally stretched out their bedrolls, Shay slipped an arm under Sheridan's shoulders and pulled her close. He lowered his head to nuzzle the side of her neck, to nip the tip of her chin. Then he settled his mouth over hers for a long, lazy kiss.

He braced his weight on one forearm and looked down at her. The deep blue of her eyes looked almost black in the firelight. "Sleepy?"

"Uh-uh. You?"

"No. Guess that nap this afternoon took the edge off."

"Yeah." She lifted a hand and ran her fingers across the muscles of his chest. "So what are we going to do with our time?"

"I can think of a thing or two."

"Really?"

"Uh-huh." He bent closer and ran his tongue over her bottom lip.

Her breath caught in her throat. She swallowed, then said, "I'll give you all night to stop that."

He chuckled, then pressed his mouth to her. When he finally broke the kiss, he drew a steadying breath.

"I want you, Sheridan," he said in a raspy whisper. "I know lying on a blanket in the middle of the desert isn't—"

She pressed a finger to his lips. "It doesn't matter where we are." She grabbed a handful of the slightly curly hair at the nape of his neck and brought his face back down to hers. "Make love to me, Shay," she said, her lips brushing his. "Here. Now."

Books by Holly Harte

DANCER'S ANGEL
TEXAS SILVER
TEXAS JADE
TEXAS INDIGO

Published by Zebra Books

TEXAS INDIGO

Holly Harte

Kensington Publishing Corp.
850 Third Avenue
New York, NY 10022

Zebra Books
Kensington Publishing Corp.

http://www.zebrabooks.com

ZEBRA BOOKS are published by

Kensington Publishing Corp.
850 Third Avenue
New York, NY 10022

First Printing: July, 1999
10 9 8 7 6 5 4 3 2 1

Printed in the United States of America

Dedicated to women healers everywhere

Chapter One

Shafter, Texas
June 1899

Shay Bannigan glanced at the clock on his office wall. *Damn, the stage will be here any minute.* Rising from his chair, he grabbed his hat off the rack by the door, then left his office. After telling his assistant he'd be gone for a while, he stepped outside the building and looked down Main Street with a grimace. When he'd accepted the job as general manager of the Presidio Mining Company, he hadn't realized the silver mines were located in such a remote area of far West Texas. Shafter had sprung up along Cibolo Creek after silver had been discovered in the surrounding hills of the Chinati Mountains more than seventeen years earlier, and as far as Shay was concerned, the town was too isolated—over two hundred miles from El Paso, the closest large city—too backward for a man used to the modern conveniences of San Francisco, and too damn hot.

Shay started walking, flinching at the merciless glare of the sun. *I don't have to worry about going to hell when I die, I'm already there.* Though he'd prided himself on his style of dress by always wearing the latest fashion in men's clothing, living in the arid mountainous region of the Chihuahua Desert for the past eight months had forced him to change his habits. Even working without a tie and in his shirt-sleeves, as he'd taken to doing in recent weeks, didn't provide much relief from the relentless heat. Releasing a weary breath, he headed for the stage line office.

He'd received a telegram from the mine's main offices in San Francisco a few days earlier. Whitaker Stafford, longtime friend and one of the owners of the mining company, sent the telegram, telling him to expect the new company doctor on that day's stage. Since Shay's position as general manager made him the highest-ranking mine official in town, he considered it his duty to personally greet the man.

As Shay continued down Main Street, he heard the rumbling of hooves hitting the hard-packed earth and realized the stage had already pulled into town. By the time he approached the stage office, the driver had climbed down, opened the door, and moved aside to let two male passengers step to the ground.

Shay stopped a short distance away and stared at the men. Recognizing both as local residents, he dismissed them and shifted his gaze back to the door of the stagecoach. The driver had assisted another passenger from the coach, a middle-aged woman wearing a ridiculous hat of what looked like feathers perched atop her short dark-blond hair, and turned to help a second woman, this one younger, wearing a sensible wide-brimmed hat over a wild tangle of shoulder-length, chestnut hair and clutching a wicker basket in one hand. Finally another passenger appeared in the door of the stagecoach. When the man stepped to the ground, Shay frowned at his clothes—a gaudy checked bow tie, white vest, and straw porkpie hat. *Aw hell, don't tell me that young dandy's the new doc?*

Shay moved to where the passengers waited for their luggage

to be handed down from the top of the coach. He stopped beside the last man to exit the stage. "I'm Shay Bannigan, Dr. Kinmont, general manager of the Presidio Mining Company. As soon as you retrieve your luggage, I'll . . ."

The surprised look on the man's face erased Shay's smile of greeting. "You are Sheridan Kinmont, aren't you?" Shay said. "The new company doctor?"

The man opened his mouth to reply, but before he could get any words out, one of the other passengers spoke up. "I'm Sheridan Kinmont," the woman with the chestnut hair said, setting the wicker basket, which Shay realized held a small brown and white wirehaired dog, on the ground. Straightening, she removed her hat and met his gaze.

Shay's eyebrows knitted in a scowl. "No, that's not possible." He gave his head a shake. "You can't be the new company doctor. You're a woman!"

"I'm quite aware of that," Sheridan said, unable to keep the sarcasm out of her voice. This wasn't the first time she'd faced bias against women doctors. From the moment she attended her first class at Johns Hopkins Medical School, she'd met with resistance. And each time she refused to let such outdated attitudes prevent her from fulfilling her lifelong dream to practice medicine. She had hoped things would be different once she returned to the area of Texas where she was raised, but apparently that wouldn't be the case.

She took a deep breath, then said, "I can assure you, it is possible, Mr. Bannigan, wasn't it?" At his nod she continued. "I applied for the job of company doctor, and the mine's vice president, a Mr. Stafford, hired me. I have a letter from him right here." She lifted one arm to indicate the handbag dangling from her wrist. "If you don't believe me."

Shay stared down into her oval face, her thickly lashed indigo eyes momentarily derailing his train of thought. *By all that's holy, a man could lose himself in those incredible eyes. And that hair. What would possess her to cut such beautiful—*The thump of a trunk hitting the ground brought him back to the present with a start. Clearing his throat, he said, "That . . . er . . . won't be necessary."

Sheridan remained silent for a moment as she studied the man standing in front of her. He wasn't handsome exactly, though there was something strongly appealing about his rugged features, the laugh lines at the corners of his full mouth, his sparkling dark eyes—their exact color indistinguishable in the shadows cast by the brim of his hat. He wore a neatly trimmed black-as-midnight mustache, and his equally dark, slightly curly hair brushed well below the collar of his open-necked shirt. He was slightly more than six feet in height, broad-shouldered, and lean but well muscled. Drawing another deep breath, this one to ease the sudden wild pounding of her heart, she forced her gaze back to his face. "Are you sure there isn't a problem, Mr. Bannigan? You don't look or sound happy about my being here."

"I'm not."

She gave an unladylike snort. "Well, at least you're honest."

Shay shrugged. "Nothing wrong with honesty. Too bad you didn't subscribe to the practice when you applied for a job with this company."

Sheridan curled her hands into fists. "How dare you accuse me of dishonesty! I'll have you know there was nothing false in my application. I listed my education and experience working as a physician, and I also provided several letters of recommendation."

"But I bet you didn't tell Whit Stafford you were a woman, did you?"

"My being a woman has nothing to do with applying for a job," Sheridan replied, her control slipping a notch. "I supplied all the pertinent information Mr. Stafford needed in order to make a fair and intelligent decision. And as he should have done, he hired me based solely on my qualifications."

"What about the mutt? Did you happen to mention your dog to Whit?"

"As a matter of fact, I did. In my letter of application. Mr. Stafford didn't have a problem with my bringing Buster."

The dog gave a little yip, as if to emphasize his owner's words.

Sheridan bent to scratch behind her dog's ears. "It's okay, boy, you can get out of there soon." When she straightened, she arched her brows and stared up at Shay, waiting for him to make a decision regarding his next move.

Shay pressed his lips into a thin line, his gaze raking down Sheridan's full breasts, narrow waist, and the flare of nicely rounded hips. A surge of desire flickered to life in his groin. Pushing aside his unwanted reaction to the woman standing before him, he turned to look at a pair of Saratoga trunks, several wooden crates, a half dozen hat boxes, and a collection of satchels sitting behind him. Exhaling an exasperated breath, he said, "Which of these bags belongs to you?"

"All of them."

"All of—sweet mother of God, woman! What the hell do you need with so much luggage?"

"I brought some of my own medical equipment, and one trunk contains my personal belongings. All the rest"—Sheridan waved a hand toward the other female passenger—"belongs to my nurse."

"Nurse!" Shay's eyebrows snapped together in a fierce scowl. "Who said you could bring your nurse with you? The mining company hired a doctor, but our budget won't allow paying anyone else."

"Stop fretting, Mr. Bannigan. I don't intend that the mining company pay one more cent than the salary Mr. Stafford offered me. Poppy is my nurse, so I'll take care of her wages myself."

"Fine. See that you do," Shay replied, then turned and stomped into the stage line office. When he came out several minutes later, he said, "I arranged to have your luggage delivered. So if you ladies will follow me, I'll take you to the house assigned to the company doctor.''

As he moved away from the two women, his thoughts were in a jumble. *A female doctor! How could Whit have done such a stupid thing?* Shay knew firsthand that women weren't cut out to be doctors, and he intended to make sure Sheridan Kinmont's stay in Shafter was short. Damn short! He glanced over his shoulder at the object of his ire. *Whit may have hired you, Sheridan Kinmont, but he sure as hell can also fire you.* Swiveling his gaze back to the street in front of him, Shay started walking.

Sheridan stuck her hat back on her head, then picked up Buster's basket and the one piece of luggage she didn't trust to anyone, her medical bag. As Sheridan turned to look at Poppy and saw amusement in the woman's green eyes, her lips twitched.

Poppy Gilbert reached up to adjust the angle of her hat. ''Seems your new employer is another of those fools,'' she said with a smile, ''who subscribe to the notion that God's plans for the universe didn't include women doctors.'' She smoothed one of the feathers on the newest hat in her collection, frowning when her fingers came away dust covered. ''So, how long will you need to make this one see the light?''

Sheridan chuckled. Poppy was twelve years older than Sheridan's twenty-seven and had worked as her nurse for almost a year. The two had also developed a close friendship during that time, part of which was a long-standing contest. Whenever Sheridan crossed paths with a man who ascribed to the notion that only men should be doctors, the two women wagered on the length of time Sheridan needed to make the man see the error of his ways. If Poppy guessed closest, Sheridan added to the woman's one passion in life—her collection of hats. And in keeping with the current vogue in ladies' millinery, the more garish and overstated the design, the more Poppy loved the hat. But if Sheridan's guess proved closer, she won a two-week reprieve from her choice of domestic chores, using the time to catch up on reading her medical journals.

Sheridan looked up and down the main street of Shafter with a slight frown. Working as a mining company's doctor surely wouldn't keep her as busy as she'd been in Baltimore, so maybe she'd have to change the stakes of their friendly game. Shifting her gaze to the departing Shay Bannigan, Sheridan said, "I'm not sure. His prejudice sounds like it's pretty deeply ingrained. Give me a few days to figure out how deep, then we'll firm up our wager."

Poppy nodded, then said, "Come on, we'd better catch up with him before he decides to put us right back on that stage. I don't know about you, but my behind can't take another callyhootin' ride like the one we just had anytime soon."

"Mine either," Sheridan said with another chuckle. "Those mules must have been half wild. I heard that's how they break wild mules to harness. Hitch a team to a stagecoach and let them run. Now I can vouch for that story." Still smiling, she fell into step beside her friend.

As soon as Shay left the two women in the small adobe house assigned to the company doctor, Sheridan lifted Buster from his basket. As the dog wandered off to explore the house, Sheridan glanced around, then said, "What a mess."

Poppy nodded. "Well, Mr. Bannigan did say this place has been sitting empty for a couple of months."

"Guess we'd better get busy, then," Sheridan replied. "Maybe we can get it cleaned before dark."

"That'll take a miracle," Poppy said, then flashed a grin. Reaching up to remove her hat, she added, "How about we start with the bedrooms?"

Sheridan tossed her hat onto Buster's basket with a sigh. "Fine."

While Sheridan helped Poppy wash windows, sweep floors,

and wax furniture, the two chatted about their journey from
Baltimore and life ahead of them in Shafter.

"Does it feel as good getting home as you figured?" Poppy
said, wringing out a cloth into a bucket of water.

"Home is actually north of here in Fort Davis," Sheridan
replied, thinking of the town sixty-five miles from Shafter where
she was born and raised. "But my grandparents have a ranch
not far from here, so this is almost like being home. And yes,
it's wonderful to be back."

"You don't think you'll miss the hubbub of the city?"

"Maybe some. But I needed to get away, you know that."

Poppy nodded, her expression hardening. "That snake Winston deserves to be flayed alive for what he did to you."

For the first time in many months, mentioning the name of
the man responsible for her seeking the solace of far West
Texas no longer caused a fresh stab of pain in Sheridan's chest.
Already the openness, the clean air, and being close to her
family had begun to heal her wounded spirit.

Sheridan gave Poppy a weak smile. "Maybe he does. But I
did a lot of thinking on the trip here, and maybe I'm partly to
blame as well. Though my parents always encouraged me to
go after whatever I wanted in life, when I got older they also
used to tell me I needed to learn to control my independent
streak—their euphemism for stubbornness—or one day I might
regret my actions. I never gave their warnings much thought.
Until recently."

"You're talking pure foolishness," Poppy replied. "It was
nothing you did that caused your marriage to fail. You're not
the one who lied. Winston is. So don't go thinking that if you'd
stayed with him you could've worked things out. He never
would have changed, and you know it." She narrowed her gaze
at her friend. "You're not thinking of going back to him, are
you?"

"No, of course not, and you're right, I know he'd never
change. Winston is out of my life forever. I haven't decided

yet if I'll go back to Baltimore; however, if I do, it won't be because of him.'' She looked around the room. ''But that's at least a year away. I agreed to be the Presidio Mining Company's doctor, so until my contract expires, this is where I intend to stay.''

Poppy relaxed. Though she wasn't sure she would enjoy living in such a desolate place as Shafter, Texas, she owed Sheridan her life. So wherever Sheridan Kinmont chose to live, she'd be right there with her.

After Shay left the two women at the company doctor's house, he headed straight for the telegraph office. He mulled over what he wanted to say to Whit, then finally wrote out his message.

New doctor arrived today. You must have lost your mind, hiring a female! Suggest you demand her resignation for falsifying her application, then begin immediate search for acceptable male replacement. And while you're at it, take my request for a transfer seriously and find a new general manager.

Shay reread what he'd written. He considered striking the last line, then shrugged and handed the piece of paper to the telegraph operator. Couldn't hurt to try again. Sooner or later Whit would realize Shay was serious and would actually do something about hiring someone to take his place. So far Whit's only response to Shay's monthly request to be replaced had been a pat *You're the best man for the job. Just give yourself more time. You'll get used to living in Texas.*

Shay left the telegraph office, his mouth turned down in a fierce scowl. *Yeah, right! I don't care what you say, Whit, I'll never get used to living in Texas or this godforsaken town.*

Chapter Two

The next morning Sheridan finished putting away the last of her clothes and other personal belongings. When the aroma of coffee drifted to her bedroom, she headed for the kitchen with Buster at her heels.

As Poppy handed her a cup of coffee, Sheridan smiled her thanks, then said, "Where did you get this?"

"Found a can of Arbuckle's"—Poppy nodded at the cupboard—"in there. Way in the back on the top shelf. Whoever lived here before must have missed it when they cleaned out the kitchen."

Sheridan nodded. "Tastes good." She took another sip, then said, "How are you coming with your unpacking?"

"I'm almost done. I have a few odds and ends to take care of, but otherwise everything's put away." She took another swallow of coffee, then set down her cup. "So what are your plans for today?"

"I'm going over to the clinic. If it's anything like this place, it'll need a thorough cleaning. Then later I plan to head over to the mine offices. I want to ask Mr. Bannigan if he knows anyone who has horses to sell.''

Poppy's eyes went wide. ''You're not seriously thinking of buying a horse?''

Sheridan smiled at the shocked expression on Poppy's face. ''Yes, and I also intend to ride the horse. If I have to go see patients who live in the hills around here, I'll need a way to get to them. Besides, I've really missed riding; there was never much opportunity in Baltimore.''

Poppy swallowed, her face going pale. ''I never considered everything here being so far behind the times. It'll be like living in the past.'' She drew a deep breath. ''I . . . uh . . . hope you're not expecting me to ride one of those huge beasts. I'd break my neck for sure.''

Sheridan chuckled. ''Relax, Poppy. I know you've never been on a horse, and I won't make you start now. I'll probably need your services only at the clinic, which is within walking distance. If I need your assistance when I make a house call, we'll figure out a way to get you there. Something that doesn't involve sitting on a horse's back.''

''Saints be praised,'' Poppy replied, the color rushing back to her cheeks. ''Well, I guess I'd better get going. If we want to eat, I need to see about stocking our pantry. Other than the coffee, there's not a bite of food in this kitchen.''

Buster gave a sharp bark. Sheridan looked down at her pet and smiled. ''So you've noticed too, have you?'' Setting her coffee cup on the table, she bent to pick up the little dog. ''Don't worry, fella, you aren't in any danger of missing your supper. Poppy will make sure we have plenty of food by then, okay?''

The dog woofed his agreement.

Poppy chuckled. ''I swear, Buster understands everything you say to him.''

''That's because he's a really smart dog, aren't you, Buster?'' Sheridan replied, scratching the wiry hair under his chin. She shifted her gaze from the dog in her arms to Poppy. "Why don't you go with me to the clinic? I'll do an inventory of the supplies, then you can add what I need to your shopping list."

"Okay. You finish your coffee while I fetch the crates with your medical equipment," Poppy said.

A few minutes later they left the house, each carrying a wooden crate. Buster trotted beside the women, ears perked and dark eyes taking in everything about his new surroundings.

Once Poppy saw the inside of the three-room building that served as the clinic for the Presidio Mining Company, she insisted on helping Sheridan with the cleaning. Two hours later Sheridan assured Poppy she could finish up on her own and shooed her friend out the door as she stuffed a long list of supplies into her hand.

Sheridan walked back into the combination surgery and examination room she and Poppy had just scrubbed, then opened the crates containing her medical equipment and carefully arranged each piece in the glass-fronted instrument cabinet. Next she tackled her office, dusting and sweeping, hanging her diploma on the wall and putting her medical books in the small bookcase behind the desk.

Satisfied she'd done all she could for the time being, she left the clinic and headed up the road toward the mill and the mine offices.

Inside the building she asked where she could find Shay Bannigan and was directed to his office. Finding the door ajar, she didn't knock but peered inside. Shay sat at his desk, shirtsleeves rolled up to reveal well-muscled forearms, the blunt-tipped fingers of his left hand splayed on the desktop in front of him. His right hand held a pen which moved rapidly across a piece of paper. The scratching of the pen's nib and the soft ticking of a clock were the only sounds in the room.

Sheridan studied her new employer for a moment. Sunlight poured into the office through the room's single window, slanting across his desk and making his blue-black hair gleam.

His slightly hunched posture stretched his shirt taut across his shoulders, emphasizing their breadth. She had the sudden urge to run her hands over those broad shoulders, to curl her fingers around his biceps. Sucking in a quick breath at the direction of her thoughts, she quickly shoved such notions aside. This man was her boss, not someone to ogle like a lovesick girl. Determined not to be affected by Shay Bannigan's attractive physique, she lifted her hand to the partially opened door that swung inward at the sharp rap of her knuckles.

The knock brought Shay's head up with a snap, his surprised expression changing to annoyance, which he tried unsuccessfully to mask. Laying his pen aside, he said, "Is there something I can do for you, Miss Kinmont?"

Sheridan longed to correct his form of address but decided she would be wise to ignore his apparent refusal to call her "Doctor." Instead, she said, "I didn't mean to disturb you, Mr. Bannigan, but I wanted to ask if you know anyone around Shafter who might have horses for sale."

"Horses?" Shay's eyebrows pulling together in a frown, he stroked one side of his mustache with a forefinger. "What do you need with a horse?"

She took a moment to rein in her rising temper. "I plan to ride it, of course," she finally replied, hoping she'd managed to take most of the sting out of her voice. "How else am I supposed to visit patients who can't make it to the clinic?"

He folded his arms across his chest. "Do you know anything about riding a horse?"

"I was raised in this part of Texas, Mr. Bannigan. I started riding almost as soon as I took my first steps, so I assure you, I'm an extremely competent rider."

Shay's gaze drifted from the fire blazing in Sheridan's beautiful eyes and the coral flush on her cheeks down to her heaving bosom beneath the tailored shirtwaist and the narrow skirt that hugged her nicely rounded hips.

"Mr. Bannigan, did you hear what I just said?"

Shay snapped back to the present. "Yes, I heard you, Miss Kinmont." Uncrossing his arms, he pushed his chair away from his desk and got to his feet. "I don't know of anyone with horses to sell," he said, moving from behind his desk and reaching out to wrap his fingers around one of her arms. "But I'll ask around and let you—" A sharp bark stopped him in his tracks. Looking down, he spotted the little dog he'd seen the day before, Sheridan's pet, Buster. The dog's wirehaired body quivered, and a growl rumbled in his throat. He looked ready to sink his bared teeth into Shay's ankle.

Shay dropped his hand from Sheridan's arm and took a step back. "What the hell's wrong with him?"

Sheridan bent to scoop the animal into her arms. "He's just trying to protect me."

"Protect you?" His eyes narrowed. "Are you saying I was threatening you in some way?"

Sheridan shrugged. "Apparently Buster thought so."

"That's ridiculous," Shay said, lifting his hand toward the dog. Another growl rumbling in Buster's throat, he raised his head and let out a series of yipping barks.

Sheridan tightened her hold on her pet. "Buster, that's enough." The dog hushed, though he never took his gaze off Shay.

"I don't understand," Shay said, dropping his arm to his side. "I like dogs. We always had one around when I was a kid."

"I'm sorry, Mr. Bannigan. I don't know what to say. Buster was friendly to everybody until—" She cleared her throat. "Anyway, he's become extremely protective of me, especially around men."

Shay wondered at the meaning of Sheridan's statement, but didn't comment. Instead, he said, "Why didn't he growl at me yesterday?"

"I don't know. I guess you weren't close enough to me, or you didn't do anything he interpreted as threatening."

Shay mulled over her words for a moment, then said, "Well, as I started to say, if I hear of anyone with horses to sell, I'll let you know."

"Thank you. I appreciate your help."

Shay bid Sheridan Kinmont good day, then returned to his chair and sat down. He tried to finish the letter he'd been writing but found he couldn't concentrate. He'd always prided himself on being an honest man both in business dealings and on a personal level, so the lie he'd just told Sheridan chafed his conscience. Giving up on finishing the letter, he stared out the window and thought about the woman whose indigo eyes made him weak at the knees and why he'd felt compelled to offer to help her find a horse when he had no intention of doing so.

After a few minutes of self-deprecating musings he pulled himself back to the present. Why the hell was he chastising himself for lying to Sheridan? She wouldn't be in Shafter long enough to need a horse anyway. As soon as he heard from Whit Stafford, Sheridan Kinmont, her nurse, and that damn, yapping dog would be on the next stage out of town.

For some reason, picturing the scenario of the trio leaving Shafter wasn't as satisfying as he'd expected.

Poppy walked down Shafter's dusty, winding Main Street to the adobe building housing the Presidio Mining Company store. Stepping inside, she glanced around, then frowned. While appearing to be well stocked with foodstuffs, bolts of fabric, and a selection of ready-made clothes, the store bore little resemblance to those she'd frequented in Baltimore. She heaved a sigh, knowing she'd just have to make the best of what was available and hope the store's manager could order the rest of the items Sheridan needed.

She approached the man standing behind the counter at the rear of the store. "Excuse me, sir. I have a shopping list I need filled. Could you help me, please?"

Orrin Neilson looked up from the stack of invoices, his eyebrows rising at the sight before him. A hat—at least he thought the bizarre concoction of ribbons and silk flowers qualified as a hat—sat perched on the head of a lady he didn't recognize. If he'd seen this blond-haired, green-eyed beauty before, he certainly would have remembered. Clearing his throat, he said, "I'm Orrin Neilson, manager of the store, and I'd be happy to assist you, ma'am. What can I get you?"

Poppy stared into the totally masculine, deeply tanned face with slightly hawkish nose, square jaw, and kind gray eyes and for the first time in more than twenty years found herself tongue-tied by the mere presence of a man. Her cheeks burning with a blush and her ability to speak suddenly absent, she handed the list to him.

"Hmm, let's see here," he said, perusing the list. "I have most of these things in stock, but I'll need to send to San Antone or El Paso to get the others." He shifted his gaze from the list to the woman on the opposite side of the counter. "Beg pardon, ma'am, but what would you be needing with all these doctoring supplies?"

Poppy started, snapping out of her momentary lapse and finally finding her voice. "They're for Dr. Kinmont's clinic."

"Ah, so the new doctor's finally arrived?" At the woman's nod, disappointment inexplicably dampened his light mood. "Then, you must be his wife?"

Poppy smiled, then shook her head. "Dr. Kinmont is a lady, Mr. Neilson, and she isn't married. I'm Poppy Gilbert, Dr. Kinmont's nurse."

He blinked with surprise, then said, "Imagine that, a lady doctor and a nurse in Shafter." He paused for a moment, then added, "Did your husband come with you?"

Poppy's back stiffened, her cheeks again burning with a flush. "I no longer have a husband. Not that it's any of your business."

Orrin held up a hand. "Hey, don't get your back up, Miss

Gilbert. I just figured a fine-looking woman like yourself had to be married. I'm sorry to hear about your husband."

"Sorry?" Poppy pulled her mouth into a frown. "Why would you be sorry about that miserable excuse for a man? I'm just glad to be shed of him."

"You don't speak very kindly of the dead."

"Dead!" Poppy replied with a snort. "He isn't dead. At least, he wasn't the last time I saw his sorry face." Preparing herself for his reaction, Poppy took a deep breath, then said, "I divorced my husband several years ago."

"Divorced?" Orrin's eyes widened a fraction, then a grin slowly stole over his face. "Let's start over, shall we?" He extended his hand. "Pleased to meet you, Poppy Gilbert. Orrin Neilson, at your service."

Poppy didn't respond for several seconds. As she stared at his hand, an image flashed in her mind—another male hand, this one raised in anger, followed by openhanded slaps turning into tightly curled fists landing blow after blow until she couldn't— Shaking her head to chase the unwanted memories, she tentatively placed her right hand in his. "Thank you, Mr. Neilson," she replied, her voice sounding raspy to her own ears. "It's a pleasure meeting you."

Orrin longed to lean over the counter and kiss the tip of Poppy's slightly upturned nose, but he settled for a brief handshake. He'd seen her painful reaction to his extended hand, how she'd hesitated to touch him, and he refused to do anything to encourage such wariness. He wanted a chance to get to know Poppy Gilbert, not scare her off.

As Orrin filled what he could of Poppy's order, he kept up a litany of questions, hoping to learn more about her, and at the same time get her to relax. After finding out she was originally from Virginia and had spent the previous five years in Baltimore, he said, "How was your trip to Shafter?"

"Long," Poppy replied, a solemn expression on her face,

though her eyes sparkled with amusement. "Sitting on a train seat day after day gets mighty tiresome, and then that unforgettable stagecoach ride from Marfa. Lord-a-mercy, I don't think I'll ever be the same."

"Yes, those wild mules definitely make the last leg of the journey memorable," he said with a smile. "I didn't realize how far it is to this part of Texas until I made the trip from Rapid City five years ago."

"Do you like living here?" she said.

Orrin paused while packing the supplies into several wooden crates. "Took some getting used to, but now I like Shafter well enough." Continuing his task, he chuckled. "The winters are definitely better here than in the Dakotas."

"I'm sure they are," Poppy replied, her lips curving into her first genuine smile.

As he tucked the last package into one of the crates, he said, "These are too heavy for you to manage by yourself. I'll just bring them by when I close up the store. That is, if you have no objection."

"I . . . no, of course not," she said, reaching into one of the crates and removing several items. "I'll just take what I need to fix supper. You don't have to go to the trouble of bringing the rest yourself. Isn't there someone you could send, so you can go home to your family?"

"There's no rush for me to get home, Miss Gilbert. I live alone."

"Oh." Another rush of heat spread up her neck and cheeks. "Well, then, I'll see you later."

"Yes, later," Orrin said in a husky whisper, then watched her turn and leave the store. The sight of her gently swaying backside nearly made him groan out loud.

For the remainder of the afternoon that enticing memory continually appeared in his mind's eye, playing havoc with his powers of concentration.

* * *

Shay opened the telegram, checked the name at the bottom, then scanned the message.

Wasn't aware I'd hired a lady doctor, but don't see why that causes a problem. There are no grounds for dismissal. Never asked applicants for their gender. Wouldn't have mattered anyway. Dr. Kinmont's credentials are impeccable, her references first rate. Suggest you learn to get along with the woman. And for the record, my mind is just fine.

Certain he'd missed something, Shay reread Whit Stafford's telegram. Crumpling the paper with one fist, he scowled out his office window. "Dammit, Whit," he said in a fierce whisper, thoroughly annoyed at his friend for treating him like a spoiled child. *"Learn to get along with the woman."* What a dumbass thing to say!

A few minutes passed before Shay's anger cooled enough to think rationally. Okay, so Whit hadn't responded the way Shay had expected. There still had to be a way to get Sheridan Kinmont out of Shafter—some way to convince Whit that hiring a lady doctor was a mistake.

Shay just had to come up with a plan.

Chapter Three

Several days later Sheridan ran her fingers over the white snip on the velvety nose of the skittish horse while keeping her voice in a low croon. "Easy, Molly, girl. I won't hurt you." She moved her hand to stroke the mare's neck, keeping the motion slow and deliberate. "See there, you can trust me. That's what you need, isn't it, girl? A gentle hand and someone to trust." The horse's responding soft whinny made Sheridan smile.

She'd bought the mare the day before, over the protests of the previous owner, who declared the animal's disposition too nasty for him, let alone a woman. But Sheridan had fallen in love with the dark bay mare at first sight and insisted Molly's so-called nasty temperament was nothing more than the natural independence of her mustang bloodlines. What the horse needed was love and gentle handling, something she was certain the animal hadn't received. Though the man wouldn't admit to using a rough hand with the mare, Sheridan didn't press him and was relieved when he finally agreed to sell Molly.

Since Shay Bannigan never got back to her with the names of anyone with horses to sell, Sheridan had finally started looking on her own. One of the store owners in Shafter had directed her to a small ranch outside of town. As soon as she'd spotted Molly, her search ended. Giving the mare's muscular neck a final pat, she gathered the reins into one hand, then stepped into the left stirrup and swung onto the mare's back.

Sheridan tightened the stampede strings of her hat more firmly under her chin, then directed Molly toward Main Street at a walk. At the Presidio Mining Company offices she pulled the mare to a halt, dismounted, and looped the reins around a hitching rail.

As Sheridan started toward the front of the building, Shay stepped through the door.

Shay's thoughts still on the production report he'd just read, he didn't immediately recognize the woman coming toward him. When her identity registered, he pulled up short. His gaze flickered to the horse standing in the street, then back to Sheridan. Taking in her attire, his eyes narrowed beneath his furrowed brow.

Sheridan closed the distance to Shay, stopping in front of him. Pushing her hat to the back of her head, she offered him a smile. "Mr. Bannigan, I was just coming to your office. I wanted to tell you that I—"

"What the hell are you wearing?"

Sheridan's smile died. Frowning, she looked down at her shirtwaist, split skirt, and boots. then lifted her gaze to meet his fierce glare. "What's wrong with what I'm wearing? I'm dressed perfectly for horseback—"

"No, you're not. That outfit is downright scandalous."

"Scandalous? How can you say that?" If he thought her outfit was scandalous, how would he react to seeing her in the riding clothes she preferred—a pair of buckskin trousers like those worn by her grandmother. Glaring at him, she said, "I'm completely covered, so I don't see the harm in what I—"

"Don't see the harm!" He jerked his hat from his head and slapped it against his thigh. "You're wearing trousers, for God's sake. Surely you're not so dense to think dressing like that won't give men ideas?" He leaned closer and lowered his voice to a silky whisper. "Or maybe that's your reason for wearing such a getup."

She sucked in a sharp breath and crossed her arms over her chest, unaware the movement outlined the fullness of her breasts beneath the thin fabric of her shirtwaist. But Shay was completely aware of the picture she made. Though he tried not to stare, he found he couldn't take his gaze off her bosom. He swallowed hard, willing his body to stop reacting to Sheridan Kinmont—a lushly curved, fiery-tempered woman who, unless he missed his guess, possessed a passion equally as hot.

Sheridan released her breath slowly, hoping to cool her simmering temper. She had the sudden urge to taunt Shay about the buckskin trousers lying in the bottom drawer of her dresser. But realizing he'd probably suffer an apoplexy at the revelation, she managed to ignore the temptation. At last she said, "I am not wearing trousers. This is a split skirt—an acceptable style of female riding apparel back east, I might add—so I can sit my horse astride. And I assure you, any ideas a man might get when seeing me dressed this way would be entirely in his overactive imagination."

Shay couldn't argue with part of her statement; at the moment his imagination was definitely overactive, spinning enticing visions in his head that had him aching with need. Forcing his traitorous body into submission, he remained silent for a moment. Finally he said, "You don't seem to do anything the way you should, do you, Miss Kinmont?"

Sheridan's back stiffened. "What do you mean?"

"Becoming a doctor. Dressing inappropriately. Your hair."

"My hair?" She frowned and reached up to touch a shoulder-length lock. "What's wrong with my hair?"

"A woman's hair was meant to be long, flowing down her

back in a glorious tangle of—'' Shay clamped his lips closed, stunned by the romantic nonsense coming from his mouth and, even worse, shocked to realize his neck burned with embarrassment. Damn, he couldn't remember the last time he'd actually blushed. Clearing his throat, he said, ''Anyway, women weren't meant to wear their hair shorn as short as a man's.''

''For your information, Mr. Know-it-all, bobbed hair was all the rage with the ladies of Baltimore last year when''—she caught herself before she said her former husband's name—''when someone convinced me to cut my hair.''

Shay shook his head. ''Too bad. Whoever convinced you was a fool.'' He took a step closer, then reached up to rub a strand of her chestnut hair between his fingers. ''Hmm, just as I thought,'' he said in a low voice. ''Soft as silk. Wish I could've seen it long.''

Sheridan's breath caught in her throat, her heart pounding a wild cadence. ''I'm—'' She swallowed. ''I'm letting it grow out.''

''Really?'' he replied in a raspy whisper, still fingering the lock of hair. ''I'm glad.'' She saw something hot and potent flash in the depths of his eyes—their color she now knew to be deep brown with tiny flecks of gold. The heat of his gaze seared through Sheridan's clothes, setting her flesh ablaze with need.

She clenched her fists in the fabric of her riding skirt, willing herself to stop reacting physically to this man. He was everything she despised: arrogant, domineering, narrow-minded. There was no room in her life for a man with those qualities—not now, not ever—even one who made her body throb with a craving that she'd never known. Remembering why she had sought him out, she jerked her head to one side, freeing her hair from his grasp.

''As I started to say, I came here to tell you that you don't have to bother looking for someone with horses to sell. I found one on my own.''

Shay's brow furrowed. "That was a fool thing to do. You won't be here long—I mean, you should've waited. You probably paid too much. I could have brokered a better deal for you."

Her head tilted to one side, Sheridan studied Shay's expression. She finally said, "I doubt that, Mr. Bannigan."

"Do you?"

"My grandparents have a ranch not far from here on Alamito Creek. I spent a lot of time there while I was growing up, so I've been around horses my entire life. I'm an excellent judge of horseflesh. I know what a good animal is worth and I'm not easily fooled." Not wanting to continue their conversation in case it escalated into a verbal battle, Sheridan turned toward her horse. "If you'll excuse me, I have some business to take care of."

Before Shay could stop the words, he said, "What business?" He ignored the annoyed look Sheridan flashed him over her shoulder and continued with the first thing that came to mind. "In case you've forgotten, Miss Kinmont, you're the company doctor. Any business of yours is also the mining company's business."

Sheridan swung into her saddle before responding. As she adjusted her hat, she said, "Fine. I'm riding down toward Presidio to find Pedro Zamora."

"Who the hell is this Zamora?" The sharpness of his own words shocked Shay. He shouldn't care who Sheridan chose to see, and his ploy about her business being company business was weak at best. Yet, the notion of her riding off by herself to see another man caused an odd gripping sensation in his chest.

"He's a *curandero*. A healer. I asked some of the Mexican families in town where I could locate the closest *curandero* and they told me where to find Señor Zamora. I want to ask him what healing plants I can get from him if I can't find—"

"Healing plants!" Shay said in a near shout, the tightness

in his chest momentarily forgotten. "I thought you're supposed to be a real doctor, not some kind of charlatan relying on bogus folk remedies."

"I am a real doctor, Mr. Bannigan. I'll have you know, I graduated near the top of my class at Johns Hopkins," Sheridan replied, valiantly trying to hang on to her temper. "But modern medicine hasn't found cures for all illnesses and injuries. There are still times when using the old ways are warranted, and, I might add, they're often a more effective treatment."

Shay didn't respond. He just gave her a sour look as she turned her horse around, then touched her heels to the animal's sides. While he watched horse and rider trot away from him, inspiration struck. He mulled over the idea taking shape in his mind, then a smile slowly replaced his scowl.

Whit obviously needed proof in order to agree to replace Sheridan, and Shay intended to do just that. He'd get Whit to Texas, then present a list of irrefutable evidence—beginning with the woman's use of healing plants. Relieved to have finally hit on a workable plan, he began to mentally compose the words for another telegram to Whit.

Shay continued to watch Sheridan until she disappeared from view. Settling his hat on his head and pulling the brim low on his forehead, his smile broadened. *Enjoy your time in Shafter, Miss Kinmont, because it'll soon be coming to an end.*

That statement should have brought him immense satisfaction. After all, getting a new company doctor was what he wanted. But in reality his reaction to Sheridan's imminent departure fell far short of his expectation. His smile fading, he refused to contemplate the reasons for his lackluster response. Instead, he vowed to confine his thoughts of Sheridan to her inadequacies as a doctor and proving her unfit to stay on the company payroll. Fully aware the temptation of Sheridan Kinmont as a female would be difficult to resist, he shored up his resolve to do exactly that, then turned and headed for the telegraph office.

* * *

As Sheridan left Shafter behind, the surrounding hills rang with the constant shouting of male voices and the ringing of iron-rimmed wheels striking the rocky road connecting the mine and town. Glancing around, she spotted the source of the noise: a procession of ore-laden, metal-lined wagons and the muleteers shouting commands at their teams of big mules. Though she had been in Shafter only a few days, she'd already learned that in order to extract the silver from the chunks of rock, the ore had to be brought to the stamp mill in town, where it would be crushed by steam-driven rollers.

She soon left the mountains behind, dropping down onto the flat terrain of the Chihuahua Desert. As she headed south toward the Rio Grande and the town of Presidio, the heat of the day rose from the ground in shimmering waves.

Sheridan drew in a deep breath of the hot, dry air, then sighed. Being back in Texas felt wonderful. She hadn't been sure how she'd feel once she returned, not after living in the East for most of the past ten years. While attending first college, then medical school, and then working as a doctor, she'd always missed Texas. And though she enjoyed her infrequent visits with her family, she'd always been eager to return to the East. At first she'd been eager to go back to Baltimore because of her studies, then because of her work as a doctor, and finally because she wanted to return to Winston.

She frowned, her light mood slipping. She'd still be in Baltimore, enjoying her life as a doctor, if not for Winston Taylor Collingwood III. The low-down snake had lied to her. When she and Winston started keeping company, he'd eagerly accepted her invitation to attend meetings of the National American Woman Suffrage Association. Then, during the months of their engagement, he'd professed to agree with her views on the women's movement, constantly saying he admired her dedication to such a worthwhile cause.

She gave a snort of laughter. What a fool she'd been, believing all the drivel he'd spouted during their engagement, allowing her to think he'd have no objection to her continuing the fight for women's rights once they were married. Too bad he hadn't shown his true colors until after their wedding. But, of course, she now knew that had been his plan all along.

Thank God, Winston and his deceitful, tyrannical ways were out of her life forever. She still vividly remembered the look on his face when she announced her plans to seek a petition for divorce. Thinking of herself as a divorcee still astounded Sheridan, but Winston had left her no other choice. There was no way she would remain married to a man who'd used her devotion to the women's movement to his own end. First by hoodwinking her into marriage with false promises, then, after she became his wife, by forbidding her contact with what he considered little more than a group of old biddies with nothing better to do than stir up trouble.

She could still see Winston—impeccably dressed as always, narrow shoulders thrown back and small chin jutted forward—when he announced she wasn't to attend another suffrage meeting. The memory of his obviously rehearsed speech made her grit her teeth. *The gall of that scrawny little weasel!* She burst into sudden laughter. She'd never thought of his small stature in such negative terms before. Wondering what had brought about the change, her thoughts drifted to Shay Bannigan. Now, there was a prime example of what a male physique should look like. Broad shoulders, narrow waist, muscular arms and chest. She sighed. *I wonder what those arms would feel like wrapped around—*

The heat of a blush flooded her neck and cheeks, halting the direction of her thoughts. She shouldn't be thinking of Shay in those terms, especially since he'd freely admitted his intolerant attitude about women doctors. But no matter how much his outdated ideas rankled, she couldn't deny the wild tingling in her body every time she came within ten feet of the man.

She straightened in the saddle, steeling her resolve to ignore Shay and her unwelcome reaction to him. She'd signed a contract to be the Presidio Mining Company's doctor, which she fully intended to honor, and Shay Bannigan could do whatever he pleased—as long as it was nowhere near her. Then once she fulfilled her contractual obligation, she'd leave Shafter to look for another position back east, maybe in Baltimore, but more likely in New York or Boston. Until that time came, she could only hope Shay would keep his distance and his opinions to himself.

Her decision should have restored her flagging spirits, yet the opposite proved to be more accurate. Kicking Molly into a lope, Sheridan tried to put everything from her mind and simply enjoy the afternoon, the scenery, and the ride. Not an easy task when the increasingly appealing Shay Bannigan continued to invade her every thought.

Sheridan left Pedro Zamora's house late that afternoon, her saddlebags filled with an assortment of dried plants and herbs which she'd purchased from the old *curandero*. Señor Zamora had also been gracious enough to share some of his *recetas*— recipes for remedies—with her, which she'd carefully written in a notebook for future reference.

Many of the remedies he spoke of during their visit were familiar to Sheridan. Both her grandmother, Karina Tucker, a half-Mescalero Apache medicine woman, and her mother, Jade Kinmont, who'd been trained by Sheridan's grandmother as well as a Mexican *partera*—midwife—were highly skilled in using plants and herbs and had taught Sheridan all they knew about healing. Sheridan could have gone to one of them for a supply of plants and herbs, but both her parents and grandparents were in Denver, visiting her brother. Instead of waiting for their return, she'd chosen to locate the closest *curandero*. Besides, as her father, Dr. Eli Kinmont, had often said, it never hurt to talk to someone else about healing. All doctors, he'd explained, whether formally trained or self-taught, had unique stories to tell about their experiences treating patients, and as a healer she should never stop trying to learn something new—advice she'd never forgotten.

As Sheridan rode into Shafter, her thoughts dwelled on her family. She hoped her parents and grandparents would be returning soon. The four had already left for Colorado by the time she arrived in West Texas, and she was eager to see them. When Eli and Jade Kinmont and Rafe and Karina Tucker learned she'd been hired as the company doctor in Shafter, they sent her a telegram offering to postpone their trip. But in Sheridan's reply she insisted she'd need some time to settle into her new job, so they should go ahead with their plans. Then, once they recovered from their trip to Denver, they could all get together. Thinking of the possibility of her family coming to Shafter, she wondered what they'd think of Shay. Her lips pressed into a firm line, she scolded herself for letting him sneak back into her thoughts. She tried to concentrate on something else, but visions of Shay sitting with her family around the dinner table, laughing at something her father or grandfather said or roughhousing with her cousins' children, kept popping into her head.

For heaven's sake, the rational part of her brain shouted, stop thinking about that man! He'd be nothing but trouble. He might be trouble, replied the emotional part of her brain in a sultry whisper, but you know he'd be worth every minute. After her failed marriage she'd vowed never to become involved with another man since that gender's word couldn't be trusted. But after meeting a rogue named Shay Bannigan and experiencing the incredibly strong stirrings of desire, she feared her promise would become more and more difficult to keep.

Chapter Four

Two days after Sheridan's appearance at the mine offices to announce she'd bought a horse, Shay left the dining hall in the company-owned boardinghouse. As he hurried toward the clinic, anticipation thrummed in his veins. He refused to consider that his anxiety had more to do with seeing Sheridan Kinmont than his reason for heading down Main Street at a near run—the plan he'd devised to get her replaced.

In response to his second telegram, Whit Stafford had agreed to come to Texas, though with his busy schedule he wouldn't be able to make the trip for at least a month. In preparation for Whit's eventual arrival, Shay had already set his plan into motion: to be present whenever Sheridan treated a patient, so he could gather firsthand evidence against her. Since he couldn't abandon his responsibilities as general manager, he'd hired a man, Boyd Smith, to keep an eye on the comings and goings at the doctor's clinic. Smith had just sent word that a patient had recently entered the clinic, and Shay intended to be there as well.

Just outside the clinic door the sight of Sheridan's dog lying next to the stoop brought Shay to an abrupt halt. When Buster spotted him, the little dog leapt to his feet, hackles raised, and a warning growl rumbling in his throat.

Shay took a step closer to the dog, then slowly bent forward and held his hand toward Buster. "Look, you little piss-willy," he said, taking care to keep his tone light and friendly. "What do I havta do to convince you I'm not a threat to you or your mistress?" He waited patiently while the dog gave him the once-over. Maybe he was planning to send Sheridan packing, along with her flea trap of a dog, but he sure as hell had no intention of hurting her. There were a lot of things he'd like to do to Sheridan, but physical force definitely wasn't part of the erotic fantasy playing havoc with his mind.

As Buster's whiskers brushed Shay's fingers, the dog's growl grew fainter, until the rumbling finally stopped. After a moment Buster took one last sniff, then returned to the shade cast by the building and flopped down in the dirt. Resting his muzzle on top of his paws, his gaze remained fixed on Shay.

Shay shrugged, wondering if he'd made any headway with Sheridan's feisty pet. Somehow he doubted he had. *Well, at least he didn't sink his teeth into my hand.*

Shay opened the door of the clinic and stepped inside. The building's rock walls kept out some of the afternoon's oppressive heat, but not much. There was no one in the waiting room, so he proceeded to the examination room. That, too, proved empty, so he turned toward the last room, the one used as an office.

As he pushed the partially opened door inward, Sheridan looked up, surprise evident in the depths of her blue eyes.

Sheridan swallowed hard, trying to calm the sudden wild beating of her heart at the appearance of the man who filled her thoughts more than she cared to admit. "Shay . . . um . . . I mean Mr. Bannigan, what are you doing here?"

Shay crossed the threshold, looking around with a frown. "I thought you had a patient."

"How would you know whether I had a patient or not?"

"That's not important. What happened to the woman who was here a few minutes ago?"

"Señora Lara wasn't a patient. She came to talk to me about her husband. As soon as she returns from the company store, I'll be going home with her so I can examine Señor Lara."

"Fine. I'll accompany both of you."

Sheridan stared at him through narrowed eyes. "Why are you so bound and determined to annoy me?"

"Annoy you?" Shay replied with a grin. "Lady, I'm not trying to annoy you. I just want to make sure you're doing your job."

"And what does that mean?"

He tugged on one side of his mustache, then exhaled heavily. "You're going to see an employee of the mining company. The welfare of all mine employees is my responsibility, so it's my duty to see that they're taken care of properly. And in order to do that, I need to witness firsthand how proficient you are as a doctor."

"Did you do the same thing with my predecessor?"

"No, of course not. The previous company doctor was a—" Shay nearly said "man" but stopped himself just in time. "That is, he'd already been here for several years when I arrived in Shafter last November, so there—" Ignoring the piercing glare of the indigo eyes leveled at him, Shay cleared his throat, then turned toward the door. "I'll wait in the other room."

Her lips pressed together in a thin line, Sheridan pushed a lock of hair away from her face. "If you insist on going with me, I can't stop you," she said to his back. "But, I'm warning you, I won't put up with any interference while I'm examining my patient."

"Fair enough," Shay said over his shoulder. He stepped

through the doorway and pulled the door closed behind him with a soft click.

A few minutes later Señora Lara, a small woman with huge dark eyes and an easy smile, returned to the clinic.

"You are ready to go with me, *Doctora* Kinmont?" the woman said from the doorway to Sheridan's office, sending a quick glance in Shay's direction.

"Yes," Sheridan replied, picking up her medical bag and stepping into the waiting room. When Shay moved to stand next to her, she said, "I hope you don't mind, señora, but Mr. Bannigan will be accompanying us."

The woman's dark eyebrows rose into delicate arches. "No, I do not mind. The señor is welcome in my home."

Sheridan let out a relieved breath, then smiled. "Good. Then, let's get going."

On the walk to the Lara house, Shay remained quiet, content to listen to the occasional talk between the two women. Though the day was sunny and hot, the heat didn't seem to bother him as much as it normally did. Wondering what accounted for the difference, his gaze landed on Sheridan. Was her presence somehow responsible? He scowled, shoving such a foolish notion aside and forcing his gaze back to the path in front of him.

At last the three arrived at a row of small rock cottages crowded together on a hillside west of town. Señora Lara stopped at the door of the last house and turned to Sheridan.

"Hector does not know I went to see you," Señora Lara said in a quiet voice. "He keeps telling me he will be fine, that he does not need to see a doctor. But I worry so much about him."

Sheridan placed a hand on the woman's shoulder and squeezed. "You did the right thing."

Inside the house Sheridan paused to let her eyes adjust to

the dim interior. The room was neat though sparsely furnished, with a fireplace at the far end, one door leading into what Sheridan assumed would be the kitchen, and a second opening into a short hallway. Señora Lara returned from putting her purchases away, then indicated Sheridan should follow her down the hall.

The bedroom Hector Lara occupied was also extremely small, the bed taking up nearly the entire room. The only other piece of furniture was an old dresser, with a cloudy mirror hanging above it.

"I am back," Josefa Lara said, moving to the side of the bed and bending to place a kiss on her husband's cheek.

When Hector opened his eyes and spotted the couple standing behind his wife, his smile of greeting froze. "Who did you bring with you?" He tried to push himself to a sitting position. "Señor Bannigan, is that you?"

"Yes, Hector, but don't get up. I . . . uh . . . heard you weren't feeling well, so I came to see how you're doing."

The man dropped back onto the mattress, his dark gaze shifting to the woman holding a black bag. "And the señorita, who is she?"

"This is *Doctora* Kinmont," Josefa said, clasping her hands together at her waist. "I stopped by her clinic and asked her to come see you. Señor Bannigan was there when I returned from going to the company store, and he asked to accompany us."

Hector's heavy eyebrows pulled together in a frown. "I told you I am fine, Josefa. I just need to rest. You should not have brought the *doctora* here."

"*Sí*, I know what you told me, but I am so worried about you. No matter how much sleep you get, you are always exhausted and your breathing does not improve." She unclasped her hands and placed one atop his work-roughened fingers. "Please, Hector, let *Doctora* Kinmont examine you."

After a moment Hector's chest rose and fell with a heavy sigh. "*Sí.* For you, *querida,* I will allow it."

Sheridan placed her medical bag at the foot of the bed, then withdrew her stethoscope. As she examined Hector, she asked him questions about his health.

At first he tried to evade answering her, but when Josefa freely offered the information, he finally gave in and told Sheridan what she wanted to know.

"How long have you worked as a miner?"

"I came here soon after the mine opened in 'eighty-three. I worked for a few months, then returned to Mexico long enough to marry Josefa and bring her back with me. I have been a miner ever since."

"When did you start feeling short of breath?"

"I am not sure. Maybe a few months ago."

"And is that when your exhaustion began?"

"*Sí,* it was about the same time."

After Sheridan asked a few more questions and completed her examination, she carefully placed her medical instruments back in her bag. Then she turned to Hector and said, "I hate to have to tell you this, Señor Lara, but I believe you're suffering from a disease of the lungs called pneumoconiosis."

"I have never heard of this disease," Josefa said. "Where would Hector get such an illness?"

"From working in the mines. The coal miners back east have suffered with another form of this disease for years. There, it's called black lung. Here I believe it's referred to as miner's consumption."

Josefa gasped. "You are certain, *Doctora* Kinmont?"

Sheridan nodded. "If we were back east, I might be able to confirm my diagnosis with more sophisticated medical equipment. Unfortunately in this part of the country, that isn't possible. But the gray tinge of his skin, his shortness of breath, and the fact that he's worked as a miner for so many years all support my conclusion."

"How does working as a miner cause this disease?" Hector said.

"All types of pneumoconiosis are caused by constantly breathing irritants—in the case of miners, it's the mineral and metallic particles in the dust—that accumulate in the lungs and cause the shortness of breath you're experiencing."

"But there is something you can give him?" Josefa replied. "Something to make him better?"

Sheridan drew a deep breath then exhaled slowly. This was the hardest part of being a doctor, a task she hadn't gotten used to and probably never would. "I wish I could give him something, señora. But I'm afraid there's no cure for miner's consumption. The only thing that can be done is to try to stop the progression of the disease. Which means ending your exposure to mining dust."

"Are you saying I should quit my job?" Hector said in a strangled voice.

"Yes, I'm afraid that's exactly what I'm saying. To prevent your lungs from absorbing any more dust, you should stop working in the mines immediately."

"No, that is out of the question. I have a family. A wife, a son, and two daughters. Who will support them if I quit my job?"

Josefa started to answer but was cut off by a voice coming from the doorway. "I will, Papa."

Sheridan turned toward the door. A boy of thirteen or fourteen stood in the doorway, a muscle in his handsome bronze face working with the emotion he was obviously trying to control. His straight black hair brushed shoulders already beginning to show signs of a well-developed physique.

"Enrique!" Josefa said, moving toward the boy. "How long have you been standing there?"

"Long enough," he replied, taking a step into the crowded room. "Do as the doctor says, Papa. Quit your job." He turned to look at Shay. "Mr. Bannigan, I will take my father's place in the mines."

Before Shay could respond, Josefa said, "No, Rique, you cannot do this. You are only fourteen. You are still in school, and you know how much we want you and your sisters to get an education."

Enrique shrugged. "I won't need more schooling to work in the mines. And boys younger than me are working there. Isn't that true, Mr. Bannigan?"

Shay could feel Sheridan's gaze boring into him, but he refused to look in her direction. "Yes," he finally replied. "Some of our employees were twelve and thirteen, maybe even younger, when they started working for us."

"That's an outrage," Sheridan said. "How can you allow children to work for you?"

Shay finally allowed his gaze to meet Sheridan's. "I can't say as I like it, Miss Kinmont, but it's the way of the mining business. When we can't find enough older employees, we hire whoever is available and willing to work."

"Well, I won't allow this boy to work in the mines," she said, laying her hand on Enrique's shoulder. Sheridan looked at Hector, then at Josefa. "If you'll permit me, I'll try to find a job for your son. Work he can do after school or on Saturdays."

Josefa swallowed hard, then said, *"Gracias, Doctora* Kinmont. We would be most grateful. And I, too, will look for work."

"Josefa, no," Hector said. "I do not want you working. A man should take care of his family."

"And you did, *amor mío,* for many years. Now my turn has come to help support our family."

As Sheridan and Shay prepared to leave the Lara house a few minutes later, Josefa accompanied them outside.

"I want to thank you again, *Doctora* Kinmont, for coming to see Hector."

"De nada," Sheridan replied, pleased the Spanish she'd been taught as a child came back so easily. "I just wish I could have given you better news." She reached over to give Josefa's hand a squeeze.

"Sí, I do too. But we must accept whatever God wills."

Sheridan gave Josefa's fingers another squeeze before releasing her hand. "I'll come by to see Hector again in a few days. But if he becomes feverish, let me know right away. His lungs have been weakened by the disease and could easily become infected."

Josefa nodded. "I will let you know."

"Bueno. I'll be in touch soon about a job for Enrique." Sheridan smiled, then turned and started down the path leading to town. She heard Shay murmur his good-bye, then he fell into step beside her.

The two walked in silence for a while, then Sheridan said, "Have there been a lot of cases like Hector Lara's?"

"Some. I don't know how many."

"Deaths?"

"One since I've been here. According to the mine's records, there have been others over the years."

Sheridan nodded but didn't respond.

After a moment Shay said, "I wish there were some way to keep our employees from getting miner's consumption. But anytime you drill into rock, there's going to be dust, and I don't see how that can be prevented."

"No, I don't either. But if I can find Enrique Lara a job, at least I'll have kept one person out of the dust-filled air of the mines. He deserves a better fate than that."

Shay didn't reply. He had mixed feelings about the issue. He hated that miner's consumption was a risk faced by all men choosing to work in the mines. Even so, he still had a job to do, which meant keeping three crews of miners working around the clock to extract chunks of ore from the mine shafts. As he'd told Sheridan, he didn't like hiring young boys and avoided doing so whenever possible. But at times there had been no other choice.

He remembered Sheridan's outraged expression when Enrique offered to take his father's place, then glanced over at her with a frown. Did he have something else to worry about? Would Sheridan stir up trouble among the miners over their working conditions? *God, I hope not. I've already got more than I can handle.* Between watching her every move as a doctor and keeping up his normal responsibilities as general manager, there would be time for little else.

He inhaled deeply, then released a weary sigh. *Damn you, Whit, for not getting me out of this living hell!*

Sheridan turned their heads and said, as if to say the into pillow to sleep. She sighed, then wished him a good-bye, then he slid into her bedside too.

"We may well sit in silence for a while, don't you?" he said.

"Have there been a lot of these? Did they ever shake—"

"—me. I don't know how long."

"—nothing."

"One since I've been here. A co-relative of the mine's people, they've here been alive since the years."

Sheridan pushed me dark. "No good."

After a difficult stay, said, "No, but there were some way to keep the conflicts down, making miners complaining. But anyway, goodnight. I go wash them. I came to see that, and I don't say how they'll be managed."

"Well, I can't believe she'd made Enrique? I'm afraid I'd have nearly gotten them out of the mine, tired of of the miner. He's always a miner. You think that—"

"No, I don't agree. He's just never. Like an entry tired. He thinks that many were complaints of me, are ignores, by all well as morning to work in the mines. Even so, he still had a job to pay their more and thought of that a center of things, work they should.

She choose to extract chunks of ore, but that, side-she times by that chambers was more like sitting in place, as for as not

Chapter Five

By the time Shay had left Sheridan at the clinic and returned to his office, he realized his trip to the Lara home hadn't gained him one scrap of evidence to present to Whit. He knew there wasn't a cure for miner's consumption, so as much as he hated making the admission, he couldn't fault Sheridan's handling of her visit to Hector Lara.

He dropped his hat on a hook near the door, then moved behind his desk and sat down. Running a hand through his hair, he heaved a sigh. He should tackle the pile of paperwork on his desk, but he couldn't summon the ambition. His mind persisted in dwelling on a more interesting topic. Sheridan Kinmont.

Maybe I didn't get anything this time, Doctor *Kinmont, but just as surely as you have the most incredible blue eyes, I will.* The corners of his mouth tipped up in a smile. *Yessiree, it's only a matter of time, and I can be a patient man.* Sooner or later Sheridan would do something to confirm his staunch opinion about her gender becoming doctors. He'd seen firsthand how a female doctor performed under stress—her emotional reaction to dealing with an illness, her total inability to remain calm during a crisis—and he intended to prove Sheridan Kinmont fit that mold.

Several days after Sheridan's visit to the Lara house, she sat down to eat supper with Poppy. "This looks great," she said, helping herself to a piece of fried chicken. After taking a bite, she looked across the table at her friend. "I was right. The chicken's wonderful. Your cooking always did put mine to shame."

"You'd do all right," Poppy replied. "If you practiced more."

Sheridan swallowed another bite of chicken, then shook her head. "I disagree. You just have more natural ability. No matter how much I practiced, I'd never get fried chicken to taste this good."

Poppy smiled. "It's the spices. An old family secret, passed down for generations."

"The only thing passed down in my family are ways to make use of plants and herbs. Which ones are edible and how to fix them. And the only recipes I learned were for salves and tonics." Sheridan pushed what was left of the chicken leg around on her plate. "For as long as I can remember, all I wanted to do was become a doctor. I had little interest in anything not related to medicine, like learning how to keep house or sew or"—she flashed a smile at Poppy—"cook."

"Well, there's certainly nothing wrong with that. Being able to treat sick and injured folks is a lot more important than whether you're good at keeping house, sewing, or cooking."

"Well, maybe you're—" Buster's sudden bark and a simultaneous knock on the front door halted Sheridan's reply. Laying her fork aside, she pushed away from the table and rose. "I'll get it."

As she headed across the room, a yipping Buster followed at her heels, his little body quivering with each excited bark. Glancing down at her pet, Sheridan gave him a stern look. "Buster, that's enough." The dog immediately hushed, though his stub of a tail continued wiggling in a furious rhythm, his dark eyes sparkling with anticipation.

"Good boy," she said, reaching for the door. Finding Enrique Lara standing on the porch, she smiled. "Enrique, what a surprise." Her smile faded. "Has something happened? Is your father—"

"Papa's condition is the same, *Doctora* Kinmont. I came here to thank you for getting me a job at the company store."

"You worked today?"

"*Sí.* I am going home now, but first I wanted to thank you."

"That's not necessary, Enrique. Mr. Neilson needed help, and I knew somebody who needed a job." She shrugged. "It was easy."

"Maybe, but my parents are extremely grateful, and so am I. If there is some way I can repay you, you will let me know?"

"As I said, I didn't do anything special."

"You found a way to keep Papa from going back to the mine. That is very special to my family, and I will do whatever I can to show my gratitude."

"But that's—"

"*Por favor, doctora,* if there is something I can do, you must tell me."

Sheridan stared down into the boy's face, seeing the honesty reflected in his dark eyes, the determination in the firm set of his full mouth. "All right. Poppy Gilbert works as my nurse, but she also does most of the work around here, and at the clinic as well. To relieve her workload, I could use the occasional assistance of a strong back at the clinic." She glanced over her shoulder at Poppy, who smiled her approval, then she turned back to Enrique. "How about helping me at the clinic after school lets out for the day? I'd need you for about an hour, maybe a few times a week.''

Enrique bobbed his head. ''School will be out for the summer soon. Señor Neilson wants me to work more hours then, but I can work for you too.''

''As long as working for me doesn't jeopardize your job with Mr. Neilson. You work out a schedule with him, then let me know which days will be best for you to come to the clinic, *bueno?*''

''*Sí*, I will talk to him tomorrow. *Gracias, Doctora* Kinmont, *gracias.*''

''*De nada.* Now you'd better get home before your mother starts to worry.''

He nodded, then bent to scratch a patiently waiting Buster. After fussing over the dog, he straightened, murmured good-night, then turned and headed down the street.

Once Sheridan had returned to the table, Poppy said, ''That boy is really special. So proud and mature for his age. You did a nice thing, agreeing to let him pay off a debt that doesn't exist.''

Sheridan nodded. ''Yes, Enrique is special. If having him work for me saves his pride, I don't see the harm. Eventually I'll try to convince him he's paid off his debt and get him to take wages from me.'' Sheridan fell silent for a moment. ''Besides, what I told him is true. You should have your work-load lightened.''

''I don't mind working hard, and I enjoy what I do.''

''I know that, Poppy. But all you do is work. You need some time for yourself, some time to relax and do something besides working at the clinic all day, then coming here and doing all the cooking and more than your share of the housework.''

Poppy dropped her gaze to her plate, a blush staining her cheeks. ''Maybe I would enjoy a few hours to myself.''

Sheridan blinked, then stared at her friend for a few moments. This wasn't the first time she'd suggested that Poppy worked too hard and needed time away from her duties. So what had brought about her sudden acquiescence? Since Poppy made no offer to explain, Sheridan chose not to pursue the subject, knowing her friend would tell her when she was ready. Still, Sheridan couldn't help wondering at the reason behind Poppy's secretive smile.

The following week Enrique kept his word and showed up at the clinic several days after school. He never fussed about the chores Sheridan assigned him, tackling each task with all his strength and concentration.

Sheridan enjoyed those hours with the boy, often wishing she could spend more time just talking to the bright, courteous young man. But his obvious dedication to his job kept her from asking more than a few questions once she explained what she wanted him to do. She always inquired about his family, in particular his father's health, but then left him to carry out that day's chore.

One afternoon, while Enrique finished whitewashing the walls of Sheridan's office, he said, *"Doctora* Kinmont, can I ask you a question?"

Sheridan removed the old sheet she'd draped over the bookcase, then looked at the boy. "Certainly."

"Do you think I could go to college?"

Her hands stilled in the task of folding the sheet. "Of course you can. Do you know what you want to study?"

Enrique didn't answer immediately, then in a low voice he said, *"Sí,* I want to study law."

Sheridan smiled. "A lawyer. I think that's wonderful. Do you know what college you want to attend?"

He shrugged. "I was never certain I would be able to go to college, so I never thought about which one."

"You have a few years to decide, though it's never too early to begin making plans." She finished folding the sheet and laid it aside, then said, "I know a little about the colleges back east. I researched a number of them before I chose to enroll at Johns Hopkins. The brother of my former hus—uh . . . someone I used to know is a lawyer. He went to Georgetown University, but there are other fine law schools. We can discuss them sometime if you'd like."

"I would like that," Enrique replied. "But college is very expensive, isn't it?"

"Yes, it can be. But there are ways to help with the cost, like getting a scholarship."

"You know about these scholarships and how I could get one?"

"I know a little about them, and I can find out more if you're interested."

He nodded. "Can we talk about this tomorrow? I don't have to work for Señor Neilson, so I could come here after school."

Sheridan chuckled at his enthusiasm. "Sure, tomorrow's fine, unless I have patients. They must come first."

"*Sí*, I understand," he said, then turned back to his work.

Several hours later, just as Sheridan prepared to leave the clinic for the day, she heard the front door open. Since Poppy had the afternoon off, Sheridan left her office and went into the waiting room.

"Can I help you?" she said to the burly man standing just inside the door.

The man pulled his hat from his head, revealing a thatch of carrot-colored hair. "Aye, if yer the new doctor, then I'm hoping ye can." He rubbed one of his big hands over his heavily freckled face, then exhaled a long breath. When he met Sheridan's gaze, she saw wariness and pain in his bright green eyes.

"Yes, I'm Dr. Kinmont. What can I do for you, Mr.—"

"Finlay, ma'am. Ian Finlay. I'm the blacksmith for the mines, and I—" The clinic door opening halted whatever the man was about to say.

Sheridan shifted her gaze to the door. Frowning, she watched Shay enter, shut the door behind him, then move to one side of the waiting room. When he didn't say anything but just gave her a nod, she squashed her annoyance and turned her attention to the man standing in front of her. "You were saying, Mr. Finlay?"

The man swallowed hard, then said, "I wasna paying attention to what I was doing a while ago. I was thinking about me wife. She's arriving on tomorrow's stage after spending the better part of the past three months visiting our families back in Scotland, and I—" He cleared his throat, a flush turning his neck and cheeks a red nearly as bright as his hair. "Anyway, with me mind otherwise occupied, I got careless when I took a piece of metal out of the forge. I dunna know what happened, but I guess I must've dropped the blasted thing. The next thing I remember is hearing the clang of metal hitting the anvil, and then me nose gets a whiff of burning fabric and me thigh feels like it's on fire."

For the first time Sheridan noticed the scorch mark on the right thigh of his trousers. "Come into the examination room, and I'll have a look."

Finlay turned and started toward the door she indicated, then stopped in front of Shay. "It was me own stupid fault, Mr. Bannigan. I won't let it happen again, ye have me word."

Shay nodded, then said, "Your preoccupation is understandable." He stole a quick glance in Sheridan's direction. "It happens to all of us at one time or another, don't worry about it. Just take care of that burn. And next time be sure to wear your smithy apron."

Finlay nodded, another flush coloring his face. "Yes, sir. I always wear me apron, but like I said, I just wasna thinking clearly today." With that he moved past Shay and entered the examination room. Sheridan followed behind him. She stepped over the threshold and started to close the door, but something kept the door from shutting all the way. She looked down to find Shay's booted foot planted in the doorway. When she opened her mouth to protest, the warning expression on his face halted her words. Lifting her chin, she shot him a furious glare, then released her grip on the door and marched across the room.

"You'll need to remove your trousers, Mr. Finlay, then take a seat on the examination table."

Once he'd followed her instructions, Sheridan examined his burn, taking care not to probe the reddened patch of skin with too much pressure. "The burn doesn't appear to be too serious. Though I'm sure it's paining you a great deal."

"Working around a forge all me adult life, I've suffered worse. But, aye, me leg's causin' me a fair amount of pain."

"There are some small pieces of fabric from your trousers stuck to the wound, which I'll need to remove. I promise to be as gentle as I can, but the procedure still may cause you some discomfort. Afterward I'll clean the burn, then apply a soothing salve and a dressing."

From where Shay leaned against the doorframe, he watched Sheridan treat her patient. As much as it galled him that his efforts to gather evidence against this woman had hit another roadblock, he had to admit she knew how to make her patients feel at ease. She kept her touch gentle, her voice soft and soothing. and she explained everything she did in easy-to-understand terms. He noticed other details about her as well—details having nothing to do with her rapport with patients. Like the way the reddish tint in her hair caught and reflected the sunlight coming through the room's window. Or how she pursed her lips in concentration, revealing a tiny dimple beside her mouth, a dimple he had the sudden urge to kiss.

He stifled a groan, uncomfortable with the direction of his thoughts. Why did Sheridan have to look so damn competent, when he knew the truth about female doctors? And why did he find her so damn appealing, when she was nothing like the women he preferred?

Shay suddenly needed to distance himself from the woman he found entirely too tempting. Pushing away from the doorframe, he said, "You should rest that leg for a day, Ian, so take tomorrow off. And give my best to your wife." Not waiting for a response, he cast one last look in Sheridan's direction, then wished he hadn't. Though he hadn't meant to give her more than a cursory glance, he couldn't pull his gaze from hers. Staring into those mesmerizing indigo eyes, something wild and throbbing ignited in his veins. He couldn't move, breathing became difficult, as though the air had been sucked from his lungs, and his groin ached with a longing he'd never known.

After several seconds that seemed more like hours he managed to shake himself out of whatever kind of stupor he'd fallen into, then turned and hurried from the clinic. Outside the building he paused on the stoop and wiped a trembling hand over his damp face. *Damn, what the hell happened in there?*

Only one explanation came to mind that made any sense: He needed a woman—apparently worse than he'd thought. He stepped off the stoop and started up the street, frowning at the reminder of another reason he found living in Shafter so unpleasant. In San Francisco he'd had his choice of female companions, women who knew he wasn't looking for a permanent or even long-term relationship, and who were more than willing to settle for mutual enjoyment for whatever time they had together. Shay grunted with disgust. Moving to Shafter had swiftly brought such liaisons, and thus his sex life, to a standstill.

After Ian Finlay left her office, Sheridan cleaned up the supplies she'd used, her thoughts shifting to Shay Bannigan and how he'd once again showed up at the clinic right after a patient arrived. Well, she now knew the truth about that little mystery. It turned out he didn't possess a sixth sense or even uncanny timing; he got his information from the man he'd hired to watch the clinic.

When Sheridan first learned the truth, her temper had sky-rocketed. She'd nearly marched to Shay's office and confronted him, prepared to demand he call off his watchdog. But when the worst of her fury began to recede, she realized the folly of such a tactic. An angry confrontation would only add fuel to Shay's already considerable prejudice against her, a biased opinion she wanted to reverse, not feed.

The wise choice, she'd concluded, would be to keep quiet. She had nothing to hide, and as long as neither Shay nor his hired man interfered with her duties as company doctor, she planned to ignore both of them. Easier said than done, considering she found herself growing more and more attracted to Shay with each passing day. Just thinking about the look they'd shared before he left the clinic caused the same reaction. Her breath caught midway in her throat, a wild tingling shot up her spine, and a dull ache swirled low in her belly.

She closed her eyes and clenched her teeth until the fever in her blood cooled and her body relaxed. Such sensations were foreign to Sheridan. Even though she'd been married and experienced desire, she'd never reacted to Winston with such immediate intensity, even in their most intimate moments, the way she did to just a look from Shay Bannigan. She heaved a weary sigh, wondering why the one man determined to get her fired also had to be the one who made her body come alive with a desire she'd never known.

After whispering a prayer to both the white man's God and the Great Spirit of her Nde ancestors, asking for the strength to get her through the coming year, she left the clinic.

Chapter Six

During the next several weeks Shay watched Sheridan treat an assortment of illnesses and injuries, but he witnessed nothing of significance to add to his report. And with Whit due soon, Shay began to wonder if he'd have enough evidence by the time his friend arrived. He hadn't altered his opinion of women practicing medicine, but for reasons he couldn't fathom, Sheridan had yet to display behavior typical of lady doctors.

Shay opened the folder lying on his desk, the one containing the notes he planned to hand over to Whit. He hadn't written much. He'd cited his personal views on women being unfit to become doctors—their frailty, lack of rational ability, and propensity to be too sensitive and too emotional made it impossible for them to carry out the responsibilities of such a position. He'd also noted her visit to a Mexican *curandero*, including her admission of her intent to use concoctions made from herbs and plants if she thought them necessary. Beyond those two entries the evidence he'd hoped to compile was decidedly lacking.

As he contemplated the situation, a knock sounded on his partially opened office door. He looked up to find Boyd Smith standing in the doorway, hat clutched between hands gnarled from years of hard work.

"Didn't mean to interrupt, Mr. Bannigan," the older man said, his tanned, deeply grooved face resembling a relief map, his thinning white hair plastered to his head.

"You're not interrupting, Smith, I was just—never mind. Was there something you wanted to tell me?"

Smith bobbed his head once, then replied, "The lady doc's got herself another patient." He lifted a hand to scratch his bristled jaw. "I'd say the man was hurtin' some too."

As Shay rose from his chair and moved around to the front of his desk, he said, "Why would you think that?"

"Cuz he was practically doubled over, grabbing his middle and squealing like a pig, while a couple of men helped him from the mill over to the clinic."

Shay bit back a grin, not because one of his employees was in pain, but because this could be the opportunity he'd been waiting for. Snatching his hat from the rack, he turned to Boyd. "How would you like the rest of the afternoon off?"

Smith narrowed his pale blue eyes, giving Shay a wary stare. "I thought you wanted me to watch the clinic until the doc leaves for the day."

"Normally I do. Starting tomorrow morning you can go back to your usual hours. But I'll take over for the rest of today."

"Whatever you say," Smith replied, settling his worn hat back onto his head. "Yer the boss."

Shay hurried over to the clinic, anticipation making his heart hammer in his ears and his strides longer than usual. When he stepped into the doctor's clinic, he found the waiting room empty. He hesitated until he heard voices coming from the examination room, then turned in that direction. He carefully pushed open the door and peered inside.

A man he recognized as Noah Thompson, one of the engineers at the stamp mill, lay on the examination table. A sheet covered his legs and lower anatomy barely enough to protect his modesty. Poppy stood at Noah's head while Sheridan examined his lower abdominal area.

Shay didn't think his entrance had been noticed, until Sheridan looked up from her work and briefly met his gaze. There had been no surprise on her face, only a slight tightening of her mouth in what he assumed to be resignation. When she finished her examination, she pulled the sheet up to the man's chest, said something Shay couldn't hear to Poppy, then moved across the room to where he stood.

"What's wrong with Noah?" he said in a low voice.

"Mr. Thompson has appendicitis."

He frowned. "Noah's my best engineer. I can't afford to have him missing work."

"Well, I'm afraid you'll have to figure out a way to get along without him for a while."

"You're sure it's his appendix?"

Sheridan took a deep breath to quell her rising irritation, then said, "Yes, I'm sure. Aside from his other symptoms which made me suspect appendicitis, the localized tenderness in the right lower quadrant of his abdomen confirms my diagnosis. I need to operate immediately, so if you'll excuse us"— she grabbed his arm and tried to turn him toward the door— "Poppy and I need to get started."

He refused to move. "I'm not going anywhere."

Sheridan tightened her grip. "Yes, you are. You can wait in the other room."

"No," he replied, shaking off her hand. "I intend to stay in here."

"Have you ever watched a surgery?"

"No, but—"

"Then you don't need to start now."

"Dammit, Sheridan," he said in a low snarl. "I'm staying and you can't stop me."

She tipped back her head to stare into his face. The determination she saw reflected in his dark eyes and in the hard set of his jaw told her he wasn't going to be swayed. "Fine, but you'll have to wear a gown."

His eyebrows snapped together. "What?"

"It's imperative to keep a sterile operating field so the patient isn't exposed to harmful organisms. That means using sterilized instruments and dressings and wearing surgical gowns."

Shay stared down at her for a moment, then finally said, "All right, fine, I'll wear one of your damn gowns."

Sheridan had to bite her bottom lip to keep from grinning at his resigned expression. Turning to Poppy, she said, "Get an extra gown from the cabinet. Mr. Bannigan will be observing."

After Sheridan explained to Noah what she intended to do, she washed her hands, donned a surgical gown, and pulled on a pair of rubber gloves.

She instructed Poppy on how much anesthetic to administer, then gathered the instruments she would need from a cabinet. When the patient fell into an opiate-induced sleep, she arranged the sheet and several towels so that Mr. Thompson's lower abdomen was exposed, then reached for a scalpel.

Shay stood several feet away, on the opposite side of the table, where he watched Sheridan's every move, looking for a telltale sign to indicate incompetency. But her instructions to Poppy were issued in a calm voice, her hand rock steady as she moved the scalpel into position over her patient's skin.

Sheridan glanced up. "Ready?" When Poppy gave her an affirmative response, she turned her gaze on Shay. At his tight-lipped nod she shifted her attention to her work.

Shay watched the tip of the knife move closer and closer to its target, his gut knotting with each descending inch. When Sheridan applied pressure on the scalpel, allowing the blade to slice into skin, Shay swayed on his feet. He squeezed his eyes closed, aware that a cold sweat had broken out on his forehead. Determined to remain, he opened his eyes. A thin line of blood identified the location of the incision Sheridan had made. As the flow of blood increased, darkness started to close in on Shay's field of vision.

He gave his head a shake and swallowed once, then again. But it was no use. With a groan, he clapped his hand over his mouth, turned, and bolted from the room.

Poppy chuckled. "Did you see the color of his face? Strangest green I ever did see."

Sheridan smiled. "It was an odd shade, wasn't it? The way he was moaning when he charged out of here, he's probably outside, emptying his stomach."

Poppy used a sponge to soak up the blood around the incision. "And he thinks women aren't fit to be doctors."

"Like a lot of men, Mr. Bannigan still believes in the way things were fifty years ago."

"Humph," Poppy replied. "What ridiculous beliefs. Men thinking female nurses are fine because we keep our proper place, always acting docile and submissive. But let a women study medicine, and all that changes. She suddenly thinks her opinions are as good as a man's." As she reached for another sponge, she made a sound of disgust in her throat. "Men can be such idiots."

"Now, Poppy, don't get cross-legged," Sheridan said, using one of her friend's favorite expressions.

"I'm not losing my temper." Poppy drew a deep breath and exhaled with a sigh. "I just get so blasted frustrated. I don't understand why men can't accept the fact that women are capable of doing a lot more than they think we are."

"I know, and I agree," Sheridan replied.

"You agree about what?" a raspy voice asked from the doorway.

Sheridan glanced up to see Shay, his face as white as the surgical gown he wore, moving into the room on unsteady feet.

"Are you sure you're up to coming back in here?" she said,

shifting her gaze back to her patient and searching inside the incision for his inflamed appendix. "Ah, there is it."

Shay watched her poking around in Noah Thompson's insides and swallowed the bile rising into his throat. Praying his stomach would stay down this time, he finally said, "I'll be—" He swallowed again and took a deep cleansing breath. "I'll be fine."

She gave him a nod but didn't look up. In a matter of moments she'd removed the enlarged appendix and prepared to close the incision. When she reached for a needle, she caught a glimpse of Shay's face. If possible, he looked even paler than he had a few moments earlier.

"Mr. Bannigan, the operation is over, so why don't you take a seat in the waiting room?"

He looked at her through glazed eyes, then managed a jerky nod and turned toward the door.

Once he'd left the room Poppy quickly closed the door, then returned to Sheridan's side. In a low voice she said, "He may have backward views and a squeamish stomach, but at least he wasn't afraid to come back in here and finish watching the operation."

"Uh-huh," Sheridan replied, concentrating on the stitches she was taking to close the incision.

Poppy watched her work for several minutes, then said, "Something just occurred to me. We never established the terms of our wager concerning Mr. Bannigan. Or have you decided he's a lost cause?"

"No, I'm not giving up on him. But something in his past had a serious effect on his trust in women doctors, so he'll definitely be a challenge." She paused to consider a time frame. "Let's say a month from now."

Poppy's eyebrows rose sharply. "Just one? You're really being optimistic. I wouldn't have been surprised if you'd said you wanted twice that long."

Sheridan chuckled, making the final knot in her neat line of stitches. "Gee, thanks for the vote of confidence, Poppy," she said, though there was no sting in her words. She snipped the thread, then laid the needle and scissors on the tray with her other surgical instruments. "I'm still willing to wager a new hat of your choice against three weeks of no household chores."

"Three weeks, huh?"

"You agree he's going to be a tough one to convince, right?"

Poppy nodded, silently considering Sheridan's words. Finally she said, "Okay, if those are the terms you want, you've got a bet."

Sheridan nodded. "Bet." All the while she dressed her patient's incision, she mulled over her decision to wager with Poppy. In the past they'd played their betting game as much for the fun of the competition as for the chance to convince a man of the error in his bigoted thinking. But this time she couldn't help wondering if she'd agreed for a different reason. Just the thought of spending the needed time with Shay Bannigan in order to change his biased views sent a shiver of anticipation up her spine—a shiver having nothing to do with her usual reasons for making a wager.

Though she'd already acknowledged her strong attraction to Shay, she had no intention of becoming involved in a personal relationship with the man. So why didn't that squelch her reaction to spending more time with him? Forcing her thoughts back to her work and her patient, she refused to examine the possible answers to that question.

Once Mr. Thompson had awakened from the anesthetic and Sheridan gave him a dose of medicine to ease his pain, she headed for the waiting room.

Shay sat in one of the several chairs arranged on one side of the room, his head resting against the wall, eyes closed. Sheridan moved to stand in front of him.

"That was brave of you, Mr. Bannigan."

He opened one eye and looked up at her. Letting his eye

drift closed again, he said, "Yeah, I was a regular knight in shining armor."

She bit her lip to hold in a chuckle. "Don't be so hard on yourself. A lot of students in medical school get sick or pass out the first time they watch an operation."

He grunted. "I doubt any of them are thirty years old, for cripes sake."

This time Sheridan couldn't stop a giggle from slipping out. He opened both eyes long enough to give her a sour look. Immediately she sobered. "Sorry."

When he merely shrugged, she said, "Why don't you go home and lie down for a while?"

"Can't. I've got work to do."

"Certainly there's nothing that can't wait until tomorrow, is there?"

Shay sighed. "I guess not." After a moment he opened his eyes, then slowly pushed out of the chair and got to his feet. "I'm still feeling kinda queasy, so I think I will go lie down."

"Good. Here, let me help you get that gown off, then you can head for home."

"Thanks, I'd appreciate it."

After Shay left, Sheridan wondered if his embarrassment over his weak stomach would put an end to his constant invasion of the clinic whenever a patient arrived. Turning toward the examination room, she doubted he'd give up that easily.

Since Noah Thompson would have to remain at the clinic for several days before Sheridan would risk having him moved, she and Poppy arranged a schedule to take turns staying with him.

Sheridan had taken the first shift, while Poppy went to their house to fix something to eat and take a nap.

Several hours later Poppy arrived back at the clinic to relieve Sheridan. "I left your supper in the warming oven."

Sheridan nodded. "Thanks." After going over her instructions for Noah Thompson's care, she said, "I'll be back by midnight. After I eat and change clothes, I'm going to check on Mr. Bannigan. If you need me, send someone to his house.''

"The man saw blood and puked," Poppy said. "It's that simple." She stared at Sheridan for a moment, lips pursed in a thoughtful moue. "Or do you think he has something more serious?"

Sheridan dropped her gaze, her face burning with a blush. "No, but I ... um ... just thought I'd make sure he isn't suffering any long-term effects. The stomach can be touchy sometimes and—"

"Okay, okay," Poppy said, her eyes sparkling with laughter. "Whatever you say. If you want to see Shay Bannigan, you don't need to explain your reasons to me." She waved a hand toward the door. "Now, go on. Get out of here."

"Just let me check on Mr. Thompson one more time," she replied. "Then I'll be on my way."

By the time Sheridan headed for the small house occupied by Shay Bannigan, full darkness had fallen, the silvery glow from a nearly full moon providing enough light for her to see her way through town.

As she approached the house, she watched him rise from a chair and step into a shaft of moonlight at the edge of the porch. He was barefoot, his hair mussed, and his clothes rumpled. His shirt, unbuttoned and pulled from his trousers, hung open to reveal a strip of naked flesh with a mat of dark hair in the center of his chest. The moonlight turned his face into an enticing study of planes and angles and emphasized the breadth of his shoulders and the muscles of his arms and thighs. Sheridan stared at him, remembering a statue she'd seen in a Paris museum. But that stone sculpture hadn't made her head spin or her pulse quicken. Only this man, this very real man, had done that.

Shay couldn't believe his eyes. Once he'd recovered from

his bout of sickness, his thoughts had been filled with Sheridan Kinmont. But he hadn't expected the woman he couldn't get out of his mind to appear at his house. "What are you doing here?"

Sheridan had to draw several deep breaths before she could get any words through her tight throat. "I . . . um . . . I wanted to see if you had recovered."

"I'm fine. I did as you said and lay down for a while. Now I'm right as rain."

"Good," Sheridan replied, taking a step closer. "Have you eaten anything?"

"Yeah, after I took a bath." Noticing she held something against her left thigh, he said, "What's that?"

Sheridan lifted her arm. The moonlight reflected off the bottle in her hand. "I brought you something. Brandy." She offered him a smile. "For medicinal purposes, of course. I thought if you were still feeling queasy, a glass of brandy would help settle your stomach."

Shay stared at her for several seconds, nearly overwhelmed with the urge to haul her up onto the porch and into his arms, then plant a kiss on her mouth. He drew a steadying breath and exhaled slowly. "As I said, I'm fine, but I could still use a drink."

When she held the bottle out to him, he wrapped his fingers around hers and pulled her up the two steps and onto the porch. At her startled expression, he said, "Why don't you come in and join me?" In a silky whisper he added, "Or are you a teetotaler?"

Sheridan ignored what his voice did to her insides and replied, "I drink spirits on occasion, so, yes, I'll join you. But just a small glass. I have to go back to the clinic later, and I'll need a clear head."

"Of course," he responded, her statement dousing the heated thoughts swirling in his head. This woman was a doctor, and he couldn't allow himself to forget that fact. He had no business thinking of taking Sheridan inside his house, of kissing her senseless, of pulling off her clothes and burying himself in— He bit back a groan, his manhood painfully aroused and throbbing against his trousers.

His teeth gritted, he willed the desire humming in his veins to cool. At last he said, "On second thought, let's stay out here, where it's cooler." He indicated the pair of chairs on one side of the porch. "Have a seat while I fetch some glasses."

Sheridan nodded, then moved to the farthest chair and sat down, determined not to let Shay see her disappointment when he returned. She shouldn't care that he'd revoked his invitation into his house, but inexplicably she did.

Chapter Seven

Sheridan accepted the glass of brandy from Shay, murmured her thanks, then watched him move to take a seat on the top step of the porch rather than on the chair beside hers. She took a sip of the liquor, waiting for him to speak. When he didn't, she said, "If everything goes well, Mr. Thompson should be able to return to work in a few weeks."

"Any chance things won't go well?" Shay said.

"There's always a chance of infection. But I took all the necessary precautions, so I expect his recovery will be uneventful."

"You'd better be right," Shay replied, his voice muffled by his glass. He took a healthy swallow of brandy, sending liquid fire down his throat and causing a hitch in his breathing. He sucked in a deep breath, the air hissing through his clenched teeth. The burning in his gut quickly gave way to a soothing warmth, loosening the tightness of his muscles and making him relax.

Sheridan decided not to pursue the meaning of his comment

but shifted her gaze to the moonlit hills surrounding the town. After a moment she said, "I'd forgotten how peaceful it is here."

Shay grunted in response.

"You don't like Shafter, do you, Mr. Bannigan?"

He took another gulp of brandy before replying. "What's to like?"

"Just what is it you find so objectionable?"

He gave a snort of laughter. "Lord, where should I begin?"

She shrugged. "Start wherever you want."

He flashed a disgusted look over his shoulder. "I was being facetious."

"Fine, but you still dislike living in Shafter, and I'd like to know why."

Shay ignored her statement, took another drink of brandy, then said, "Let me ask you something, Miss Kinmont. After living back east, in a real city with all the modern comforts, how do you like being stuck in a backward little town in the middle of nowhere?"

Sheridan tucked away the scrap of information he'd revealed about his views on life in Shafter, then rose from the chair and moved to the steps. After taking a seat next to him, she said, "I'll admit life here is much slower and less advanced than in Baltimore, but I'm really glad I accepted this job and came home to Texas. I love the fresh air and the solitude of the mountains, the sound of cottonwood trees rustling in the wind." She looked up at the night sky. "Being able to see the stars."

Shay had trouble concentrating on Sheridan's words. Swallowing hard, he silently warned his body not to react to her closeness or the intoxicating scent of her skin. *God, she smells like vanilla.* He leaned away from her, resting his shoulder against the porch railing in an attempt to distance himself from the temptation of Sheridan Kinmont.

To his disappointment, changing his position provided little relief. He cleared his throat, then said, "What about the isolation? The lack of modern conveniences? Or the god-awful heat?''

"Isolation? There must be over a thousand people living in Shafter. I don't call that being isolated. Shafter may be remote, but eventually all the modern conveniences will arrive. I can wait. And as for the heat, it's not so bad.''

"Not so bad! It's hotter than blue blazes, and summer's just started.''

Sheridan chuckled. "If you think it's hot now, then you surely wouldn't want to leave these mountains and head down onto the desert.''

"You're right, I wouldn't,'' Shay responded, certain the only reason he'd leave the mountains would be his return trip to California.

A few minutes of silence passed before he spoke again. "You said you were raised in this part of Texas?''

"Yes, north of here in another mountain range. The Davis Mountains.''

He stretched his legs out in front of him and crossed one ankle over the other. "Tell me about your life.''

Sheridan turned to look at him through narrowed eyes. She couldn't help wondering if his request stemmed from mere curiosity or if it was for some nefarious purpose. Finding nothing in his moonlit face to support the latter, she shifted her gaze back to the surrounding hills. "I was born in the town of Fort Davis, in the house my grandfather built for my mother after she was hired as an assistant to the army surgeon at the Fort Davis military post. Daddy is a doctor in town and—''

"Ah, so he's the one behind your becoming a doctor.''

"Not in the way you think. Daddy was a big influence on my decision to become a doctor, but he never pushed me into following him into medicine. Actually my mother's abilities as a healer influenced me just as much. Even when I was just three or four years old, I was fascinated with healing. From then on, all I ever wanted to do was become a doctor.'' She paused to draw a deep breath. "Graduating from Johns Hopkins with a medical degree two years ago fulfilled my lifelong dream."

"What was it that you said about your mother? She used to be a healer?"

She nodded. "She still is. Like me, that's all Mama ever wanted to do. In fact, that's the reason she met Daddy. She found him after he'd fallen in the mountains, then took him to her house and treated his injuries with remedies she learned from both my grandmother, a Nde medicine woman, and Paloma Diaz, a highly skilled Mexican *curandera.*"

Shay's brow furrowed. "What's a Nde?"

"The native people called Mescalero Apache by the white man. But their true name is Nde, which means 'the people' in their language."

"If your grandmother is Indian," Shay said, "then that would make you . . ."

"Part Indian? Yes, that's true," she replied, lifting her chin and waiting for him to make some derisive comment. When he didn't, she relaxed and said, "My grandmother, whose Nde name means Silver Eagle, is also a mixed blood. Her mother was Nde and her father was Spanish. Even though the amount of Nde blood I carry has been diluted with each generation to only a small percentage, I'm proud of my heritage."

"Your mother was the one who taught you about using plants and herbs?"

"Mostly. But my grandmother taught me as well. She's past seventy now and no longer travels great distances to treat patients, as she once did. But she's still a highly regarded healer throughout this part of Texas."

"What about your mother? Does she still see patients?"

"Yes. When Daddy proposed to her, he asked her to be his wife and his medical partner."

Shay's eyebrows rose. "Really? Your father agrees with using plants and herbs as bona fide medical treatments?"

She chuckled. "Not when he first met Mama. He said it took him a while, but she eventually changed his mind. Oh, he still firmly believes in modern medicine, but he also thinks there are times when the old ways are needed.

"In the office Mama and Daddy share, sometimes he treats patients with modern medical techniques, sometimes Mama uses the ways she was taught, and other times they collaborate and use a combination of treatments."

Shay remained silent for a few moments, now understanding why she became a doctor and the basis for her belief in the use of plant and herbal remedies. But in spite of his having a better grasp of what made Sheridan Kinmont tick, the additional knowledge did nothing to change his opinion about lady doctors.

He studied her profile for a moment, watching her raise her glass and take another small sip of brandy. Then he said, "Ya know, your drinking liquor surprises me. I would've figured you to be part of the temperance crusade."

"Just because I worked as a suffragist to improve women's rights doesn't mean I have anything against strong drink. The only way the two causes are related is that liquor is often the reason husbands abuse their wives. Shutting down saloons won't stop those men from imbibing. They're unable to control their need for liquor and would still find a way to get what they crave. What must be changed are the divorce laws. Some states have passed reforms, extending grounds for divorce to include cruelty, drunkenness, and abandonment. But to protect all women in abusive marriages, the rest of the states must follow suit."

Shay pursed his lips, smoothing a thumb and forefinger over his mustache. A suffragist. Well, that certainly explained a lot about the prickly woman sitting beside him. "So," he said at last, "what brought on this interest to try to change divorce laws? Did some woman in your family suffer abuse at her husband's hand?"

She sent him a fierce glare. "My interest started after I treated several women who were married to abusive husbands. But not all abuse is physical. There are other ways men try to control their wives. Like continually attempting to browbeat her until she complies with his wishes, or threatening to make retribution if she doesn't follow his orders."

"I bet you've had no trouble converting others to your cause. You sound real adamant on the issue. And the bitterness in your voice is a good touch. Really lends a ring of truth to your arguments, like you've experienced that kind of relationship firsthand."

Her fingers clutched the glass of brandy more tightly, her voice dropping to a soft whisper. "I have."

"What?" Shay straightened his spine with a jerk. "Are you saying some son of a bitch treated you that way?"

She took a deep breath, then exhaled slowly before replying. "Yes. My former husband."

"Your former—you were married?" That piece of information was the last thing Shay expected to hear. Though divorce wasn't unheard of, and was becoming more common, her admission genuinely shocked him.

Sheridan turned to look at him. The moonlight wasn't strong enough for her to make out his expression, but she expected his features bore a look of astonishment. Or maybe his face displayed the more common reaction both she and Poppy received when someone learned they were divorcees: disgust. Her back stiff, she said, "Yes, I was married, though only for a few months. But of course the length of a marriage doesn't make any difference to most people. The fact that I'm divorced is enough to earn the typical less-charitable reaction. Like yours."

"Like mine? I don't know what you're talking about." Not giving her time to explain, he said, "Your being divorced doesn't bother me. If two people can't get along, I think they're better off getting divorced, though my parents would probably disown me if they heard me make such a statement, good Irish Catholics that they are. I'm just surprised to hear some fool wasn't smart enough to know how to keep a beautiful woman like you happy." Shay clamped his lips shut, surprised by the words spilling from his mouth.

Sheridan gave him a weak smile. "That's kind of you, Mr. Bannigan. Unfortunately Winston would say I was the one who couldn't make him happy. That I was the one who refused to make our marriage work."

"What happened, if you don't mind my asking?"

She took a deep breath and exhaled slowly. Shifting her gaze back to the hills, she began speaking. "I met Winston soon after I returned from Europe. I went there to continue my medical studies for a year right after I graduated from Johns Hopkins. Anyway, Winston claimed he fell in love with me at first sight and wanted us to do everything together. He even started going with me to my suffrage meetings, claiming to share my passion for women's rights. He told me I was noble for trying to make a difference and commended my dedication to the cause. A few months later he proposed. I accepted, but because I was trying to get established as a doctor, I insisted on a long engagement. Winston wasn't happy about my terms, but he reluctantly agreed.

"We were married in Baltimore at Thanksgiving last year. My entire family made the trip. We had such a wonderful reunion," she said with a sigh. The corners of her mouth turning down, her fingers tightened even more on her glass. "Since I had just taken a new position at the hospital, Winston and I had only Thanksgiving weekend for our honeymoon. He said he didn't mind, but I later learned he resented my job taking precedence over the lengthy wedding trip he felt he deserved." Her frown deepened. "Turns out he resented a lot of things."

Shay reached over and gave her shoulder a gentle squeeze. "If this is too painful, you don't have to talk about it."

"No, it's okay." She lifted her glass and swallowed the last of her brandy. "Right after our wedding Winston insisted we spend as much time as possible with each other. Since we were newlyweds, he said we shouldn't be separated any more than necessary and asked me not to attend my suffragist meetings. I was naive enough to be swayed by such a romantic notion, so I agreed.

"Then, a few weeks later, he started spending more and more time at his club. When I realized he'd apparently forgotten his speech about us spending time together, I told him I would be resuming my work for women's rights. He gave me a haughty look and announced I was no longer allowed to attend suffragist meetings. I was stunned and asked him what he meant by 'no longer allowed.' He said a man has every right to tell his wife what she can and can't do, and he no longer wanted me to be part of the women's movement. I believe his exact words were 'I refuse to tolerate my wife meddling in a crusade doomed to failure.'

"Needless to say, I was floored by his change in attitude. If he found suffragist meetings so repellent, I couldn't understand why he'd bothered going to them before our wedding. I'll never forget his answer. He laughed and said going to those meetings was just part of his pursuit of me. Once he'd captured his prize, he no longer needed to pretend interest in such a worthless cause. A woman's only right, he stated, was to obey her husband's bidding without complaint."

"Pompous jackass," Shay said under his breath.

Sheridan blinked, then glanced over at him and smiled. "Exactly. I called him something similar, along with a few other more colorful names to let him know exactly what I thought of his behavior." She chuckled. "You should have seen the look on his face when I told him I was moving out; it was priceless."

"You just left. You didn't try to work it out?"

"What was there to work out? He wasn't going to change his opinion, and I refused to be the wife of any man who ordered me around as if I didn't have a brain of my own. I immediately started packing my belongings. When I walked out the door half an hour later, he sputtered something about when I came to my senses, he'd be willing to take me back." She gave an unladylike snort. "I came to my senses all right. I stayed up the entire night, going over the days and months since we'd met. Looking back, I couldn't believe what a fool I'd been, that I should have known better. But the night I left Winston, I saw what I'd missed for so long. From the moment we met, his behavior had been nothing more than a manipulative charade to get what he wanted. In retrospect, I realized I'd been so flattered by his attention, so thrilled by his claims of sharing my devotion to women's rights, I never saw him for what he really was."

"You were right to leave him," Shay said.

Sheridan nodded. "I filed a divorce petition several days later. Winston was furious. I'm sure he thought I'd come crawling back, begging for his forgiveness. And when he found out otherwise, his male pride took a terrible beating."

Shay remained silent for a few moments, then said, "Has it been rough? I mean, folks finding out you're divorced can't be easy for you."

"Some people have treated me fine, but the others"—she shrugged—"well, they've said some awful things to both Poppy and me, sometimes to our faces but mostly behind our backs."

"So Poppy's divorced as well?" When Sheridan nodded, he said, "You seem to be taking all of this in stride, but how's Poppy dealing with how you're treated?"

"After the hell of a marriage she went through, a little name-calling is nothing compared to her husband's fist."

Shay sucked in a sharp breath. "Fist? My God, did her husband beat her?" Of all the vile things a man could do, hitting a woman ranked worst in Shay's view.

"She's one of the women I mentioned. The reason for my

interest in divorce reform. So, to answer your question, yes, Poppy's husband was a cruel, sadistic man, always using physical force to get her to do what he wanted. The first time I met her, she had a black eye and a broken arm, courtesy of her husband's rage.''

"Bastard," Shay muttered.

"Anyway, I tried to convince her she had to get away from him before he did permanent damage, or, worse, killed her. Thank the Lord, she finally took my advice. After I helped her get a divorce and get on her feet, she told me she'll always be beholden to me for saving her life. I tried to convince her she was overreacting, but she wouldn't listen. She went to nursing school while I was in Europe. Then, when I returned, she insisted on becoming my nurse, and she's been with me ever since."

"That's why she came here with you, because of a debt of gratitude?"

"Yes. Poppy says she plans to stay with me until I marry again." She made a sound somewhere between a snort and a laugh. "I keep telling her that isn't going to happen. I refuse to become involved with another man, not when the entire lot can't be trusted any further than I could throw one of their sorry hides."

Shay didn't respond. Though he didn't like being lumped in with all other men, he realized his current mission made him a prime example of why Sheridan considered men untrustworthy. He was surprised to realize the idea bothered him more than a little.

After a few minutes of silence Sheridan took a deep breath, then turned to look at Shay. "That's enough about me. Now tell me about you."

Chapter Eight

Shay glanced over at Sheridan and shrugged. "Not much to tell. I was born and raised in San Francisco, fourth of my Irish immigrant parents' six kids and the youngest of two sons. My folks didn't have much, but they worked hard to make sure us kids never went without. After I finished school, I wasn't sure what I wanted to do with my life. I'd always had an interest in studying law, so when Harvard offered me a scholarship, that settled my immediate future."

"A scholarship to Harvard?" Sheridan said. "Pretty impressive. You should talk to Enrique Lara. He told me he wants to study law."

"I doubt I'd be much help. I didn't get a law degree. Truth is, I never even graduated. I left Harvard after a year.

"Well, you could still talk to him about applying for a scholarship."

"I suppose," he replied.

When he didn't continue, Sheridan said, "So why didn't you finish college?"

"I had no idea law school would be so boring. Studying tired old torts and stuffy case law, and always writing those damn briefs." He groaned, a shudder racking his shoulders. "Makes my skin crawl just thinking about it. Anyway, I went back to San Francisco and started looking for work."

"Is that when you began working in the mining industry?"

Shay shook his head. "My first job was on the docks, unloading ships. In two years time I'd worked my way up to a management position. That's when I met Whit Stafford. He was part of a group of investors in a corporation that owned the shipping company as well as a number of other businesses, and he wanted me to come to work for one of their mining companies. I told him I knew nothing about mines, but he said that didn't matter. The board of directors wanted someone with management skills, and he thought I was just what they were looking for.

"I worked in several of the corporation's other mines in California and Colorado, then last year Whit told me I'd been selected to take over the general manager position of the Presidio Mining Company. I'd heard talk around the corporate offices about the silver mines in Shafter, but I didn't know exactly where it was located, and Whit, damn his hide, never volunteered the information before I left."

"So have you forgiven him yet?" Sheridan said.

"What do you mean?"

"Well, as much as you hate Shafter, I figure you must've been real upset with Mr. Stafford once you got here."

Shay frowned. "I thought sending me to Shafter was strictly a business decision made by the board of directors, but once the stage pulled into town—yeah, you could say I was upset with Whit. The truth is, I was angry as hell. I even considered the idea that his sending me here was part of some sort of crazy scheme he'd cooked up. He knew I'd always lived in the city and wouldn't take kindly to being in such a primitive setting, so far from civilization. He claims that isn't true, that in fact he warned the other members of the board that I probably wouldn't be happy here, but they wouldn't listen. In the end Whit gave in to their pressure. The vote was unanimous.'' He fell silent for a moment, then added in a low voice, ''Sometimes I wonder if he told me the entire truth.''

''Why don't you ask him to move you somewhere else?''

He gave a bark of laughter. ''I have. Numerous times. Every month since I got here, I've sent him a telegram asking to be replaced. I don't care what job they find for me as long as I'm in San Francisco. But his response is always the same. Give yourself more time and you'll get used to Shafter.''

Sheridan thought about that, then said, ''Is there a woman waiting for you in San Francisco? Is that why you're so eager to go back there?''

He flashed her a grin, his teeth sparkling in the moonlight. ''No, not a *woman*. Women. Lots of women are waiting for my return. Sweet-smelling, even-tempered, totally feminine women.'' He sighed. ''And I miss every last one of them, even the ones I haven't met.'' ·

Sheridan's chest suddenly felt tight, and a knot formed in her belly. What did she care if Shay Bannigan had every woman in San Francisco, or in all of California for that matter, eating out of his hand like a trained bird? She didn't care, she told herself, not one damn bit. But if that were true, why didn't her disclaimer stop the ache in her chest from intensifying into full-blown jealousy? She squeezed her eyes closed for a second, trying to compose herself. *This is ridiculous. You can't be jealous. You barely know this man.* Determined not to think about the flock of San Francisco women awaiting Shay's return, she opened her eyes and turned toward the man she found so disturbingly attractive.

When Sheridan opened her mouth to speak, he suddenly leaned toward her and captured her lips with his. She gasped at the contact, her initial surprise at his actions quickly giving way to a wonderful warmth tingling in her veins. Lifting one hand to encircle his neck, she curled her fingers into the thick black hair at his nape.

Shay nibbled at her mouth, used his lips, his teeth, his tongue to acquaint himself with her taste, her silky warmth. Needing to deepen the kiss, he changed the angle of his head, wrapped an arm around her, and pulled her against him. As he settled his mouth firmly atop hers, the hardened tips of her breasts brushed his chest, causing a low groan to rumble in his throat.

He wanted to crawl inside Sheridan. He wanted to devour her. He wanted to have her naked and breathless beneath him. Somewhere in his feverish brain he realized this was a kiss like none he'd ever known, a kiss that could easily lead to an entire litany of unbelievable pleasures. Sheridan Kinmont was proving to be much more than he'd anticipated.

Sheridan's head reeled, her senses swamped with the scent, the feel, the taste of Shay Bannigan. She'd never experienced anything even close to the powerful desire surging through her body. Certainly Winston had never created such an inferno. Only the man kissing her—a man who objected to her chosen life's work, a man who was no more trustworthy than the rest of the male population—caused her to react with such intensity. She wanted Shay Bannigan to continue kissing her, to touch her, to pull her clothes off and— Shocked by the direction of her fertile imagination, she came back to reality with a jolt.

When Sheridan pulled her mouth from his, Shay moaned but didn't try to stop her from pushing out of his embrace. "What is it?" he said, his voice a raspy pant.

"I . . . um . . . I need to get back to the clinic." She ran a hand through her hair, then straightened the bodice of her dress. When her palm brushed over her breast, she bit her lip to hold in a gasp. She couldn't believe how sensitive her nipples were, how just the light brush of her own hand had aroused her even more, intensifying the throbbing between her thighs. How would she react if Shay's hand touched— Stifling another gasp, she scooted farther away from him, then struggled to her feet.

"I really do have to be going," she said, unable to meet his gaze. "Poppy is probably wondering what happened to me." Sheridan prayed that what had just taken place wouldn't be written all over her face by the time she arrived at the clinic.

Shay also got to his feet. "I'll walk with you."

"No, that's not necessary."

"Well, if you're sure." At her nod he said, "Thanks for the brandy."

Sheridan nodded again, then handed him her glass. Murmuring good night, she turned and headed down the street.

Shay watched until she disappeared from view, his still-aching body reminding him that something remarkable had just taken place. He scowled at the moon. No matter how desirable he found Sheridan Kinmont, he couldn't allow himself to think of her as anything other than a doctor who would soon be out of work. Once that happened, she'd be heading out of town and out of his life, so daydreaming about anything else between them was a waste of time.

Though he knew he was right, he wondered if he'd be able to follow his own advice.

When Sheridan returned to the clinic, Poppy took one look at her, opened her mouth to say something, then wisely clamped her lips shut. Sheridan could have hugged her friend, grateful she wouldn't have to explain where she'd been or how she'd acquired the fiery flush burning her cheeks. Instead of grilling her with questions, Poppy gave her a rundown on Noah Thompson's condition, then left the clinic.

After Sheridan checked on her patient, she went into her office and took a seat behind her desk. Releasing a long sigh, she rolled her head from side to side, hoping to ease the tension in her neck and shoulders. Though she tried to concentrate on completing some paperwork, she found her thoughts drifting to Shay Bannigan and the kiss they'd shared.

She finally gave up and leaned back in her chair. The lamp on her desk casting a flickering yellow glow around the room, she stared at the shadows dancing on the wall. Though she told herself to stop thinking about Shay, he persisted in filling her thoughts. One thought in particular bothered her. She couldn't figure out why he'd kissed her. The two of them usually engaged in verbal battles whenever their paths crossed. So his sudden change in behavior struck her as odd. She mulled over the situation for a few minutes but came up with only one explanation that made sense: He'd kissed her merely because of her proximity. Since he no longer had his usual pick of female companions, he'd simply settled for the woman closest at hand. She grimaced. Her conclusion wasn't the least bit flattering but undoubtedly the truth.

Unfortunately she couldn't make the same claim—that she'd returned his kiss solely because of his convenient proximity. Though she wasn't sure of the exact reasons for her enthusiastic response to his kiss, his being convenient definitely wasn't one of them. Closing her eyes, she recalled everything about those few moments. The smooth texture of his mouth, the silky hair of his mustache brushing her upper lip, the unexpected intensity of her response. Just thinking about the kiss they'd shared made her ache with need. Swallowing a groan, she pushed away from her desk and got to her feet. She moved to the window and stared out into the night.

She shouldn't be thinking about kissing any man, especially one like Shay Bannigan, who had no use for lady doctors. The corners of her mouth lifted in a weak smile. At least he'd been honest about his philandering ways. Still, one instance of honesty wasn't reason enough for the two of them to become more than business associates. After her painful experience with Winston, she'd made herself a solemn vow: Never place trust in a man. Based on the way she'd reacted to Shay's kiss, she realized she was facing her first real test at keeping that promise. And it wasn't going to be easy.

After considering possible solutions, she decided there was only one viable course of action. Stay away from Shay as much as possible and hope her attraction to him would fade with time.

Over the following days Sheridan and Poppy continued their care of Noah Thompson by taking turns spending the night at the clinic, sleeping on a cot they moved into Sheridan's office. After a week passed, with her patient recovering nicely and displaying no complications from his surgery, Sheridan made arrangements for him to leave the clinic. Noah would continue his convalescence in his room at the clubhouse—a company-owned boarding house for single male employees—though she warned him he wasn't to return to work without her approval.

Later that afternoon Shay dropped by the clinic as he'd done every day since Noah's surgery. He found Poppy working at the small desk in the waiting room. When he nodded and started to move past her desk, she informed him Mr. Thompson had been moved to his own living quarters. He nodded, then asked to speak to Sheridan.

"Sorry, Mr. Bannigan, but you'll have to wait, she's with a patient." When Shay took a step toward the examination room door, she added, "I wouldn't be going in there if I were you. Dr. Kinmont's patient is a woman."

Shay swung back to face Poppy. "Really. Who?"

"Mrs. Finlay."

"Ian Finlay's wife?" At Poppy's nod he said, "What's wrong with her?"

Poppy's chin came up, her hands clenching into fists atop her desk. "I wouldn't know, and even if I did, that's privileged information between Dr. Kinmont and Mrs. Finlay."

Shay didn't bother arguing the point. Instead, he nodded toward the chairs on the opposite side of the room. "I'll just wait for Miss Kinmont, if you don't mind."

Poppy lifted a shoulder in a shrug. "Won't bother me none."

A few minutes later the examination room door opened. A buxom young woman with dark brown eyes and golden-brown hair stepped through the doorway. Sheridan followed her into the waiting room.

"Thank you, Dr. Kinmont," the woman said, tucking a small packet of something into her handbag. "Ian was right. Yer a fine doctor."

Sheridan smiled, then said, "Just do as I told you, and you'll be fine."

Mrs. Finlay returned the smile, nodded at both Poppy and Shay, then left the clinic.

When Sheridan went back into the examination room, Shay followed her, closing the door behind him.

"What's wrong with her?"

Sheridan swung around to face him. "Why is it you have to know what ails every person who comes here?"

"You know why. Now tell me. What's Mrs. Finlay's problem?"

Sheridan hesitated a moment, then said, "It's of a personal nature, and I don't think she'd appreciate having you know why she came to see me."

Shay closed the distance between them and reached out to wrap his fingers around her upper arms. "I won't say anything."

Sheridan stiffened at his touch, but she didn't respond.

"Listen," Shay said in a tight voice. "We've had this discussion before. I have every right to know the health condition of my employees and their families. Now, talk."

Sheridan's lips remained sealed.

"Look, if Mrs. Finlay has something contagious, the others in town are at risk. I can't afford to have some disease cripple my work force.

"You're overreacting."

"I don't think so. Dammit, just tell me what Mrs. Finlay has, so I can take measures to prevent an epidemic."

"An epidemic?" Sheridan replied with a snort. "That's absurd."

Shay glared down at her. "Then convince me otherwise."

Though Sheridan hated breaching a patient's trust, the contrary man gripping her arms left her no alternative. "All right," she said with a sigh. "But you don't have to worry about an epidemic. Honeymoon cystitis is not contagious."

Shay's brows knitted into a deep frown. "What the hell's that?"

"Painful urination caused by excessive sexual activity."

"Excessive—" Shay dropped his hands from her arms and took a step back, a sudden fiery heat creeping up his neck. He cleared his throat, then said, "Didn't she just return from a trip to Scotland?"

"Yes, a little over a week ago," she replied, thoroughly enjoying his discomfort over their discussion. "Apparently she and her husband are still celebrating her return, making up for the months they were separated." Seeing Shay's cheeks turn a dull red, she couldn't resist adding, "When a couple is overzealous in their lovemaking, especially after a long period of abstinence, or, as the name implies, during their honeymoon, unfortunately this painful condition can result. Would you like me to tell more about how sexual relations cause—"

"God, no!" He turned away, mortified to realize the burning of his face and neck was a blush. "Believe me, you've said more than enough."

Sheridan smiled at his back.

Shay didn't speak for a moment, trying to compose himself. Her talk of sexual activity reminded him of the kiss they'd shared a week earlier and how much he'd like to kiss her again. In fact, kissing her was just one of the things he'd like to— Forcing his thoughts away from such tantalizing images, he took a deep breath, then said, "I do have one other question. What's the treatment for Mrs. Finlay's . . . er . . . problem?"

"I suggested she and her husband resist being intimate for

a few days. And I gave her some dried mallow. Drinking mallow tea frequently will help ease her pain.''

"Mallow?" Forgetting his embarrassing blush, he swung back to face her. "Another of your old-fashioned plant remedies?''

"Yes. If she follows my instructions, the mallow tea will help cure her condition.''

His forehead furrowed. "Humph, so you claim.''

"Yes, so I claim, because it works. Now, unless you have something else you want to say, I'd appreciate your leaving. I have work to do.''

Shay glared down at her, his irritation fizzling out and being replaced by the first stirrings of desire. *Damn those indigo eyes. One look into their incredible depths and I'm on the verge of forgetting my own name.* Straightening his shoulders, he jerked his gaze away from her mesmerizing eyes. "I've said all I want to say. For now.'' Giving her a curt nod, he turned on his heel and started toward the door, "Good day, Miss Kinmont.''

"It's Dr. Kinmont," she called after him. "When are you going to acknowledge that I'm a doctor?''

Shay waited until he'd stepped outside the clinic and closed the door before responding to Sheridan's parting words. "I'm not, Miss Kinmont," he said under his breath. "I'm not.''

Chapter Nine

Two days later Sheridan stopped by the company store on her way to the clinic. Stepping inside, she approached the counter with a smile. "Good morning, Mr. Neilson. Enrique said you have a package for me."

Orrin returned her smile. "Yes, ma'am. The last of your medical supplies came in yesterday afternoon from San Antone. It's in the back room. I'll fetch it right now."

While Sheridan waited for Mr. Neilson to return, she wandered around the store, her thoughts also wandering. As happened all too often, her mind picked Shay Bannigan as the topic to ponder. Ever since the night they kissed, she'd hoped he had reached the same conclusion as she—that they needed to keep their distance from each other. Apparently he hadn't, since he continued to show up at the clinic just minutes after each patient arrived.

The jangling of the bell over the door pulled Sheridan from her musings. She turned to see a young woman, a wool shawl wrapped around her shoulders, entering the store. Sheridan frowned, wondering why anyone would wear a heavy garment on such a warm day. Shrugging off her curiosity, she moved closer to the woman and extended a hand. "I don't believe we've met. I'm Sheridan Kinmont, the new company doctor."

The thin woman turned to look at Sheridan, a startled expression on her angular face. Staring at Sheridan through wary pale-green eyes, she clutched her shawl more tightly over her bosom. After several seconds she tentatively reached out and placed a work-reddened hand in Sheridan's. "Pleased to meet ya. I'm Betsy Pringle."

Sheridan nodded, then said, "Beautiful day, isn't it?"

"Hadn't noticed," Betsy replied, glancing out the storefront window. "But I reckon it is."

After a moment of silence Sheridan said, "Have you lived in Shafter long?"

"A little over a year. My husband, Lenny, works in the mine. Before we came here, he worked in the silver mines in Colorado." Her eyes took on a glazed look. "I liked Colorado. So peaceful and green." She exhaled with a sigh. "But Lenny had to go and lose—uh, I mean, he . . . um . . . decided it was time to move on."

"Change can be good. That's why I moved here."

"Are you married?" Betsy said, lifting one hand to push a lock of drab brown hair off her forehead. The movement allowed her shawl to fall away from her arm, revealing several ugly bruises just above her elbow.

Sheridan's stomach tightened. "No, not anymore."

"Not anymore? Did yer husband die?"

"No, he's still alive. At least he was when I left Baltimore. I divorced him."

Betsy's mouth dropped opened and her eyes went round.

Ignoring the woman's surprised expression, Sheridan pointed toward the bluish-black bruises above her elbow. "Betsy, what happened to your arm?"

Betsy snapped her mouth shut and jerked her arm back under her shawl. "Nothing. It was just my own clumsiness. I fell."

Sheridan lowered her voice to a gentle whisper. "Betsy, you don't have to lie to me. You couldn't get those kinds of bruises by falling. I think someone grabbed your arm." When Betsy didn't respond, Sheridan dropped her voice even more. "Was it your husband?"

Betsy clutched her shawl even tighter. "I said I fell."

"I heard what you said, but I don't think you're telling me the truth. I can help you, Betsy. I'll help you get away from your husband and start a life on your own. Lots of women have done the same thing, and you can do it too."

The woman didn't reply but simply stared, her eyes filled with distrust.

"Betsy, at least let me take a closer look at your bruises. I'd like you to come to the clinic with me."

"That ain't necessary. They're only bruises. They'll fade just like all the—" She clamped her lips shut and turned away.

"I want to be your friend, Betsy. At least let me make sure you aren't seriously hurt."

After a moment Betsy inhaled a ragged breath. The offer of friendship was too good to dismiss. She glanced around to make sure they wouldn't be overheard, then met Sheridan's gaze before saying, "If I let you look at my arm, ya can't tell Lenny. You gotta promise me you won't tell Lenny."

Sheridan swallowed the bile rising in her throat. "I promise, Betsy. I won't say anything to him."

Betsy's fingers flexed several times in the woolen fabric of her shawl. She glanced around the store again, then said, "Okay, I'll go with ya."

Sheridan smiled, relief rushing through her. "As soon as Mr. Neilson returns with my package, we'll walk over to the clinic."

Betsy swallowed, then bobbed her head in agreement.

* * *

A few minutes later Sheridan ushered Betsy into the clinic. As she performed her examination, she found only a sore rib to add to the obvious bruises on the woman's arm.

"How often does your husband do this to you?" Sheridan said once Betsy had slipped back into her clothes.

"I told you, I fell. I'm real clumsy that way. Always tripping and bumping inta things."

"Betsy, you can lie to me all you want, but I can tell your bruises weren't caused by a fall. They were made by someone wrapping their fingers around your arm, someone a lot bigger and stronger than you."

The woman didn't reply, her lips pressed into a grim line, her gaze fixed on a point over Sheridan's right shoulder.

After a moment Sheridan said, "I meant what I said at the store. I do want to be your friend, so if there's anything I can do to make things better for you, I hope you'll let me know."

Betsy's gaze flickered to Sheridan's face, then skittered away. "I appreciate yer concern, but I don't need no help."

Sheridan sighed. "If you change your mind, you know where to find me."

Betsy slid off the examination table, then reached for her shawl. Settling the garment around her shoulders, she said, "I need to be going now." She moved to the door then paused. "Thank you, Dr. Kinmont, for yer kindness."

"You're welcome. Take care of yourself, Betsy."

Sheridan watched the young woman leave the room, hoping she would be able to keep herself safe. Having seen similar circumstances in Baltimore, she prayed Betsy Pringle would stop denying the truth and seek help. If she didn't—Sheridan repressed a shudder—next time her injuries could be far worse.

* * *

Later that afternoon Shay returned to town after visiting one of the mines to find a telegram on his desk. Dropping onto his chair, he quickly read the message, then crumpled the piece of paper and tossed it across his office. "Dammit, Whit, why can't you just do what I asked?" His friend had sent word that his departure from San Francisco had been delayed for at least several more weeks. The telegram hadn't gone into any detail, stating only that a crisis at one of the company's other business interests required his immediate personal attention. Somehow Shay doubted the reason for the unavoidable delay was as urgent as Whit wanted him to believe.

Shay sighed, then pushed away from his desk and got to his feet. He needed some fresh air—even if breathing the air of Shafter was like sucking the fires of hell into his lungs.

Once he stepped outside he halted, uncertain where he should go. Glancing down Main Street, he noticed a woman approaching and then entering the clinic. His decision made, he headed in that direction. As he neared the clinic, he spotted Boyd Smith coming toward him. "I saw her, Smith," Shay said.

Smith nodded, started to turn away, then turned back. "By the way, while you were at the mine this morning, another woman came to the clinic. She and the doc came walking up the street together."

"Really? Do you know the woman's name?"

"Ain't never seen her before. She weren't in the clinic more than a few minutes."

"Well, thanks for telling me."

"You bet," Smith replied, then retraced his steps to his observation post across the street.

When Shay entered the clinic, Poppy was nowhere to be seen, so he moved toward the examination room. He'd barely opened the door when Sheridan's voice stopped him.

"Hold it right there, Mr. Bannigan. You can't come in here."

He released a weary sigh. "How many times are we going

to have this conversation, Miss Kinmont? You have a patient and I—"

"I recall our conversations quite vividly," she said, grabbing his arm and escorting him back to the waiting room. "But my patient is female, a female who's with child. And no matter what you say, I won't allow you to be in the same room while I examine her."

Shay frowned, realizing the truth to her statement. "Okay, then I'll wait out here. And leave the door open a crack. If anyone else comes in, I'll make sure they don't disturb you."

Sheridan stared up at him for several seconds, her brow furrowed. She finally gave him a nod, then turned on her heel and went back to her patient.

Shay moved a chair closer to the examination room door and took a seat. Though he couldn't make out all the words, he heard the murmur of Sheridan asking her patient questions and the woman's softly spoken answers. After a short span of silence he heard the rustle of cloth, followed by the occasional creak of the wooden floor or a delicate metallic clink and Sheridan's hushed voice. Though again her exact words were indistinct, Shay had the impression she was explaining each step of her examination, a technique he realized was meant to relax and reassure the patient.

The near silence soon lulled him into a trancelike state, allowing his thoughts to drift.

His mind wandered backward in time, to the night he and Sheridan had sat on his porch, drinking the brandy she brought him. He recalled the moonlight splashing over Sheridan's oval face, the way she'd responded to his kiss. He shifted on the chair, his groin growing heavy with need. As much as he tried, he hadn't been able to banish the memory of kissing her from his brain.

Maybe he should reconsider his decision not to try to kindle a relationship between the two of them. After all, she was divorced, not an innocent maid, just the type of woman he would have pursued in San Francisco. And based on her reaction to his kiss, he suspected she possessed an extremely passionate nature. That brought a smile to his lips. Yes, Sheridan Kinmont was probably a real tigress in bed..

The sound of Sheridan's voice, louder now, filtered to him. He listened with half an ear, content to resume his musings about how she would behave in bed. Then something in the conversation between the two women caught his attention. Bracing his forearms on his thighs, he leaned closer to the door.

"Are you asking about ways to prevent conception, Mrs. Townsend?"

"Yes, Dr. Kinmont, that's what I'm asking. It seems like all my husband has to do is look at me and I'm with child. I hope you don't misunderstand. My husband and I love our children, but after this one, we . . . we would prefer not having any more."

"With three children and another about to make his appearance," Sheridan replied, "I can certainly understand your desire to limit the size of your family. So if you're certain, I can explain several methods that work well to prevent pregnancy."

"Yes, I'm certain, but first I need to ask you another question." She dropped her gaze to her clenched hands, then took a deep breath. "My husband and I have heard that preventives damage a woman's health." She shifted her gaze back to meet Sheridan's. "Is that true?"

"I've heard such reports as well, but let me assure you, that is not true. In fact, many of today's doctors, myself included, believe more harm is done to a woman's health, both physically and mentally, by not limiting the number of children she bears."

Mrs. Townsend nodded, then said, "Good, then we'd like your advice on what method we should use after I have this child."

"Is your husband willing to do his part in preventing another pregnancy? Or will you be taking sole responsibility?"

A blush bloomed across the woman's cheeks. "I know some

men want no part in this. They think if a woman wishes to keep herself from getting with child, it's her duty to do something about it. But not my Harry. He's willing to do whatever you think best, provided''—her blush deepened—''provided you don't tell us we have to abstain.''

Sheridan gave the woman a gentle smile. ''Don't worry, I wasn't going to suggest abstinence. Of course, that is the one method that never fails; however, there are others that also provide excellent odds against pregnancy. Your husband could use condoms, or you could use sponges, douching syringes, or a vaginal shield. I'll explain how each method is used, then you and your husband can decide which would be best for the two of you.''

Shay jumped to his feet, the rest of the conversation between the two women fading to a dull buzz in his head. He began pacing the length of the waiting room, unable to believe what he'd just overheard. Sheridan was actually discussing methods of preventing pregnancy with a patient. He considered himself worldly and knowledgeable, yet he'd never spoken, nor had he heard others speak, so frankly about a subject many considered taboo. He pivoted and started back across the room, his mind nearly numb with shock.

A few minutes later, when Sheridan and her patient entered the waiting room, Shay had stopped his pacing and stood staring out the room's small window. Keeping his back to the women, he waited until after Sheridan bade Mrs. Townsend good-bye before moving.

''That was quite a lecture you gave in there,'' he said, turning to face her. ''Just how did you become such an expert on preventives?''

Sheridan's eyebrows pulled together in a frown. ''I wasn't lecturing. I was simply giving a patient the information she requested. And I'm a doctor, in case that fact has slipped your mind, whose primary duty is to look after the health of my patients. And if some of them want to use preventives to limit the size of their families, I support their decision and see nothing wrong in openly discussing their options.''

"Humph," he replied, then silently chastised himself for not coming up with a better response.

"I suppose you're one of those backward thinkers who believes women are breeding machines, producing as many children as nature allows without complaint.''

"No, I didn't say that. I've seen what having too many children does to a woman. But I just don't know how appropriate it is for you to be having discussions about something so . . . well, private.''

Sheridan crossed her arms over her chest, her eyes flashing with ire. "I agree, preventing conception is an extremely private and personal matter. Women who want to control the size of their families need someone to give them honest answers. So if speaking with a doctor isn't appropriate, where would you like those women to get the answers they desperately need?''

Shay didn't immediately respond, then finally said, "I . . . uh . . . I guess talking to a doctor is probably the best option.'' He stared at Sheridan for a moment. "Do most doctors share your views about this?''

Sheridan shook her head. "Just like the American public, doctors are split on the issue. Some are against controlling family size and have tried to extricate themselves from the issue. While others, like myself, believe it's important to address all our patients' needs to the best of our ability. And if that means giving advice on preventing contraception to the patients who ask, then we don't have a problem with doing so.''

When Shay didn't respond, she said, "Have I explained my stance on this to your satisfaction, or do I need to go over something again?''

"No, you've stated your reasons clearly enough.''

"Good. Now, if you'll excuse me, I have work to do.'' Before he could respond, she turned and left him standing in the middle of the waiting room.

Shay didn't move for several minutes, still mulling over their conversation. *Why does this situation keep getting more confusing?* What Sheridan Kinmont said and did should be emotional and illogical—the reason he damn well knew made women unfit to become doctors. Though her conduct with her most recent patient had at first seemed to fit that mold, he had to admit, the argument she'd tendered for her actions made perfectly good sense. Even so, would Whit and the others on the board of directors think it appropriate for the company doctor to discuss ways to prevent conception with her patients?

Shay contemplated that question on his way back to his office.

Chapter Ten

Leonard Pringle opened the door to the small stone house he and his wife shared on the edge of town, then stepped into the dim interior. Not seeing his wife in the main room, he scowled. "Betsy, where are you?"

Betsy rushed into the room, drying her hands on her apron. "Sorry, Lenny, I didn't hear ya come in. I was just startin' supper."

Lenny shoved his dinner pail at her, studying her through narrowed eyes. "Who'd you see today?"

Betsy clutched the dinner pail against her waist. "I went to the company store, like ya told me to."

He waved a heavily muscled arm in a dismissive gesture. "I mean after ya left the store. One of the men on my shift had an errand to run this morning, and he told me he saw you walking down Main Street with some woman."

"Oh, her," Betsy replied in a whisper.

"Yeah, her." He folded his arms over his chest. "Who the hell was she, Betsy?"

Betsy considered her options. There were only two, neither of which offered much hope. She could make up a story and pray Lenny never found out she'd lied, in which case he'd fly into a rage. Or she could tell him the truth, which still might rile his temper, since he'd warned her numerous times to stay away from folks in town.

She decided to take her chances with the truth and said, "She's the new company doctor, Sheridan Kinmont."

"And what were you doing with the new doc?"

"I met her in the company store. She saw my arm and wanted me to go to the clinic so she could examine me."

Lenny's square face turned beet red. "What! And just like a trained dog you trotted along beside her?" Not waiting for an answer, his voice rose even more. "I wanna know what the hell you told her?"

"Nothing, Lenny, I swear. When she asked how I got the bruises on my arm, I told her I'm real clumsy and I fall a lot."

"And she believed you?"

Betsy dropped her gaze to stare at the room's threadbare carpet. "Dr. Kinmont said a fall couldn't have caused my bruises." Before Lenny could respond, she said, "I told her she was wrong, that I fell and hurt my arm." She worried her bottom lip with her teeth. "But, I—I'm not sure I convinced her."

Lenny grunted, then moved to one of the worn, overstuffed chairs and sat down. He didn't like the idea of his wife getting too friendly with anyone in town, especially a woman. When women get too friendly, they start telling each other things they have no business talking about. He stroked his stubbled jaw. But maybe this time he should make an exception. Maybe Betsy should get better acquainted with the new doc. Deciding he'd have to think about that awhile, he glanced up at his wife, who still stood clutching his dinner pail. "Why ain't you fixing supper? I've been working hard all day while you were lollygagging in town, and I'm hungry."

Betsy turned and bolted from the room. For the moment she was almost giddy with relief that he'd accepted her explanation without further comment. But as she hurried to get supper ready, she couldn't help wondering if he'd let the matter drop.

Orrin Neilson walked beside Poppy, enjoying the balmy evening air but, even more, his companion. Poppy had consented to take a walk with him, something of a milestone in their relationship since she'd refused all his previous invitations.

"Are you getting used to living in Shafter?" Orrin said, wishing Poppy would allow him to take her hand but knowing she wasn't ready for anything physical—even holding hands.

She tipped her head to one side and flashed a brief smile up at him. "Not having the conveniences I was used to in Baltimore gets mighty frustrating and turns me into a real fussbox at times. But I'm adjusting well enough."

"Yes, I'd say you are," he replied, unable to resist brushing a lock of hair away from her face. His fingers tingling from their brief contact with her cheek, he watched her eyes widen and her lips part with surprise. "You're a lovely woman, Poppy Gilbert," he said in a raspy voice. "Truly lovely."

Poppy blinked, her pulse increasing to double time. Acting on an instinct she thought she'd lost, she reached up to run her fingertips over his whisker-roughened jaw. "And you're a sweet-talkin' man if ever there was one," she responded, giving his cheek a playful pinch. She sucked in a quick breath and dropped her hand, unable to believe what she'd done. Though her actions were meant in jest, she couldn't halt a chilling panic from gripping her middle. Would he react in anger? Would he extract punishment?

Orrin saw the color drain from her face, the fear leap into her eyes. His chest aching, he carefully took one of her hands in his. "It breaks my heart to see you so frightened," he said, lifting her hand to his mouth and kissing the backs of her knuckles. "I swear to you, Poppy, I'll never lay a hand on you in anger."

She pulled her hand free of his grip. "That's what he used to say," she replied in a stilted whisper. "Each time he beat me, he begged for my forgiveness, promising he'd never hit me again." She drew a quavering breath. "He broke every promise he ever made."

Orrin didn't have to ask who *he* was. He knew. His fury at the bastard who'd once been her husband nearly strangled him. He took a deep breath and exhaled slowly, willing the bloodlust pounding in his veins to cool. At last he said, "I know you don't trust me yet. I understand that. But I also hope you'll give me the opportunity to prove I'm a man of my word." When she didn't reply, he said, "I'm starting to care about you, Poppy, more and more each day. Please say you'll give me a chance."

Poppy couldn't speak around the enormous lump in her throat. Staring up into Orrin's gray eyes, she wondered why such a kind, decent man would be interested in her. Surely he could find a woman who wasn't emotionally scarred by her past, one who wouldn't flinch every time he made a move to touch her. For reasons she couldn't fathom, he'd set his cap for her. Swallowing hard, she finally managed a jerky nod.

Orrin grinned, silently thanking the powers that be. When he opened his mouth to speak, the clatter of hooves on the hard-packed ground halted his words. He turned toward the sound to see a burro trotting down the street, a group of bare-footed children running behind the small animal.

"What in the world?" Poppy said, her brow furrowed at the strange sight.

"You're witnessing one of the favorite pastimes of the local children," Orrin replied with a smile. "They like to catch and ride the burros that roam through the area."

"Really? Why would they want to do such a thing?"

Orrin shrugged. "Why not? There isn't much to occupy a child around here. So what's the harm in—"

"That's exactly my point, the children coming to harm. Won't they get hurt chasing and trying to ride a wild beast?"

"The burros aren't that wild, and besides, the children have been riding one kind of animal or another since they could walk. There's really very little danger." Noting the disbelief on Poppy's face, he said, "Well, sure, once in a while one of the burros gets a little too frisky and tosses a youngster to the ground. But they don't have far to fall, so the child just picks himself up and climbs right back on, no worse for the wear."

Poppy frowned, shifting her gaze back to the children. The group had finally surrounded the burro and forced the animal to a halt. As one child, a boy of eight or nine, hauled himself up onto the burro's back, Poppy held her breath. The boy threaded his fingers in the stiff black mane, then used his bare heels to gently nudge the dusty animal into motion.

The burro lifted his gray head, gave one loud bray, then took off down the road in what looked like a bone-jarring trot. The other children followed behind, kicking up a small cloud of white dust that drifted back to where Poppy stood beside Orrin.

"See, there's nothing to it," Orrin said, then leaned over to brush the dust from his trousers.

"I guess you're right," Poppy replied, shaking the fine layer of dirt from her skirt. She stared after the departing group of children, heard their enthusiastic shouts and high-pitched giggles. "They do seem to be having a wonderful time." A bright smile stealing over her face, she turned to look up at Orrin, her green eyes twinkling with humor. "And the burro is awfully cute."

He chuckled. "Reckon he is," he said, thinking he'd never seen a sight more lovely than Poppy Gilbert's face when she smiled.

* * *

Several days later Sheridan strode toward the clinic, her mind occupied with the visit she'd just made to the Lara house. Hector's slightly improved condition had pleased her. Obviously, staying out of the mines and getting extra rest had proven beneficial, though she knew neither would cure his diseased lungs. His plea to allow him to return to work still rang in her head. She understood his need to have something to occupy his mind, to have something to do rather than lying around day after day. Though she knew working in the mines was out of the question—he'd be shortening his life even more—she still sympathized with his feelings of helplessness. Even so, she hadn't been able to come up with an alternative. Wishing she knew of something he could do that wouldn't worsen his already failing health, she glanced up Main Street.

The stamp mill loomed in the distance, and beyond the huge adobe structure she could see the building housing the mine offices. She stared thoughtfully at the smaller of the two buildings for a few seconds. Deciding to make another stop before returning to the clinic, she picked up her pace.

When Shay looked up from his work to find Sheridan standing in his office doorway, his heart gave a strange little lurch. Dismissing his reaction as one of surprise, he laid his pen aside and sat back in his chair.

"Miss Kinmont, to what do I owe this unexpected visit?"

Sheridan ignored his condescending tone and replied, "I wanted to speak to you about Hector Lara." Noticing the pile of paperwork on his desk, she quickly added, "Unless you're too busy to spare a few minutes

"I can always make time for you." He nodded to the chair in front of his desk. "Have a seat and tell me what's on your mind."

Sheridan moved to the chair and sat down. "Señor Lara's

condition has improved to the point where I think it would be beneficial for him to find something to occupy his time."

"Are you saying his condition isn't fatal after all?"

"No, unfortunately his improvement is only temporary. He may remain this way for a while, but eventually his condition will begin deteriorating." She fell silent for a moment, then said, "I wish I had my mother's and grandmother's psychic abilities. Then maybe I'd know if a cure for miner's consumption will be found in the near future."

"Psychic abilities?" Shay's gaze narrowed. "What are you talking about?"

Sheridan wondered if she'd made a mistake by speaking her thoughts aloud. Before she could make up her mind, Shay spoke again.

"Sheridan, tell me what you meant by psychic abilities."

He'd never called her by her first name before, and the effect was startling. Her pulse quickened and her belly clenched with need. Pushing her reaction to the back of her mind, she took a deep breath before speaking. "Both my mother and grandmother have visions, though Gran's are usually stronger and more distinct than Mama's."

"Visions? Are you talking about seeing into the future?"

Sheridan nodded. "Not all their visions predict the future, but some do. Gran had visions about Granddad before they actually met, and Mama had visions about finding an injured man in the mountains. That man became her husband and my father."

Shay shot a fierce glare at her. "You're making this up."

"No, I swear it's true. The Nde believe visions are direct communications from the spirits." At Shay's confused expression, she added, "Sort of messages from their gods. Not all Nde have visions, so those who do are generally held in high esteem by the others in their band. Though, of course, if some members of the band don't believe what another saw in a vision, there can be trouble. Like charges of witchcraft."

"This time you're kidding, right?"

Sheridan shook her head. "My grandmother was accused of being a witch when other Nde refused to believe what she said the spirits revealed to her in her visions. She was taken before the council of Nde leaders, found guilty of witchcraft, and sentenced to die. She was hung by her wrists over a fire, but thankfully Granddad got to her in—"

Shay held up a hand. "Whoa, hold it right there. This has gone on long enough. Listen to the bizarre notions you're spouting. Visions. Witchcraft. Death by fire." He shook his head. "You really expect me to swallow all of that?"

"Yes, I do," she replied with a weak smile. "To someone who isn't familiar with the Nde life way, I'm sure it does sound unbelievable. But I give you my word, everything I've told you is the truth."

Shay stroked one side of his mustache, mulling over her response for a few seconds. At last he said, "Okay, let me get this straight. You're telling me both your mother and grandmother have visions, which are communications from the spirits and sometimes predict the future. But you don't get these messages. Is that right?"

Sheridan sighed. "Yes. Since my mother's visions have never been as strong as my grandmother's, I've come to the conclusion that because the Nde blood has grown weaker in each generation of our family, our psychic abilities have also diminished. The most I've ever experienced is an odd feeling that something was going to happen. Premonitions, I guess you could call them, though they've never been about anything of much consequence."

Shay nodded thoughtfully but didn't reply. The more he learned about Sheridan Kinmont, the more intriguing she became. After another long silence he finally shook himself out of his reverie. "Guess our discussion got a little sidetracked. So let's get back to your reason for being here, which is . . ." He stared at her, his eyebrows lifted in anticipation.

"I was hoping you could help Señor Lara. He is becoming very depressed and I'm concerned the depression will grow worse. He needs a reason to get up each day, a reason to make him feel like he's contributing to the support of his family. He needs a job. But it can't be in the mines because of the dust. And it can't be too strenuous, or a full-time position. He shouldn't work more than one or two days a week."

"Are there any other requirements?" Shay replied with a snort.

"I know that's asking a lot, but this is important to Hector's pride as the head of his family."

Shay considered her request for a moment, then said, "I suppose he could work as a drayman. Around here there's always a need for an extra hand to drive a team of mules. Lara could haul wood to the mill or take a load of silver up to the train station in Marfa. Would that meet with your approval?"

The dazzling smile on Sheridan's face struck him like a fist in the gut. He could no longer breathe normally. A sudden dizziness made his head spin, and desire roared through his body like wildfire.

"Yes," she replied, apparently unaware of his reaction. "That would definitely meet with my approval. Shall I tell him, or would you like to?"

He shifted in his chair, managed to drag air into his lungs then had to clear his throat before he could make any words come out. "I . . . uh . . . I guess I should be the one to tell him. I'll go out there tomorrow after I've had a chance to find out where he's needed."

Sheridan rose from her chair. "Thank you, Mr. Bannigan, I appreciate your help."

Shay also got to his feet and stepped around his desk. "Don't you think you should call me Shay?"

She stared up at him for a moment, her indigo eyes pulling him into their snare. Shay wanted nothing more than to wrap her in his arms and kiss her senseless, but he made no move to do so.

She swallowed, then said, "All right." Her voice was slightly raspy. "Thank you, Shay."

"That's better," he said, dipping his head toward hers. Just before his lips reached their destination, a knock on the partially opened office door make him jerk upright. "Dammit," he said in a soft mutter.

Sheridan touched her fingertips to his lips, humor dancing in her eyes. "I quite agree," she whispered, then turned to leave.

He watched her sweep through his office door, desire once again playing havoc with his good sense, then shot an exasperated look at the man now standing in the doorway. "What the hell do you want, Orrin?" he said, somehow managing to keep his voice below a bellow.

Orrin rubbed a hand over his jaw to hide a grin, then stepped into the room. "You asked me to stop by so we could go over last month's report on the company store. Don't you remember?"

Shay huffed out a breath. "Oh, yeah, right." He waved to a chair. "Come on in."

Orrin took a seat, then watched Shay move back behind his desk and sit down. When Shay made no effort to speak, Orrin said, "Looks like the ladies from Baltimore have made another conquest."

Shay's eyebrows snapped together. "What are you talking about?"

Orrin chuckled, then crossed one ankle over the opposite knee. "Love, my good man, love is what I'm talking about. I realized this morning that I'm falling in love with Poppy Gilbert, and from the look on your face just now, I'd wager you're about ready to take the plunge."

"Don't be ridiculous," Shay replied. "I'm not falling in love with Sheridan Kinmont."

Orrin held up his hands in surrender. "Okay, whatever you say."

Though Shay managed to forget Orrin's statement during the rest of their meeting, the notion popped back into his mind as soon as the man left his office. He slumped against the back of his chair to contemplate the situation. Was Orrin right? Was he falling in love with Sheridan?

A few seconds later he gave a snort of laughter. Not likely. Hell, he'd admit he loved women—there was nothing he loved more than women, they were the joy of his life—but he'd never actually been *in* love with one. And he didn't intend to start just then.

He gave his head a fierce shake. No, whatever Orrin thought he saw, the man was clearly mistaken.

Shay picked up his pen, then opened one of the folders on his desk, determined to forget the other possibility—it was simply too ludicrous even to consider.

Chapter Eleven

The next afternoon, when Betsy Pringle didn't find Sheridan at the clinic, she nearly panicked. Fearing Lenny's reprisal if she didn't follow his orders, she finally tracked down the company doctor at the men's clubhouse. Mr. Bryant, the manager of the boardinghouse, told her Dr. Kinmont was visiting a patient, then indicated she could wait in the front parlor.

Half an hour later Sheridan entered the room. "Betsy, what a surprise. When Mr. Bryant said someone was waiting to see me, I couldn't imagine who . . ." Her gaze skipped over Betsy in a quick visual examination. "You didn't . . . um"—she hated playing along with Betsy's story, but for the time being she saw no other alternative—"fall again, did you?"

Betsy got to her feet. "No, I just wanted to talk to you, if ya have a few minutes."

"Certainly. I need to get back to the clinic, so if you'd like to walk with me, we can talk on the way."

As Betsy walked beside Sheridan, the woman made no offer

to speak for several minutes. Finally Sheridan said, "Are you sure you're okay?"

Betsy stared straight ahead, her bottom lip caught between her teeth. Finally she released a long sigh, then said, "I'm fine, but I've been thinking about what ya said the other day. Ya know, about the bruises on my arm not being caused by a fall?" She turned to look at Sheridan. "And I wanted to tell ya you were right."

Sheridan stopped, then reached over to touch Betsy's arm. "Who caused these bruises?"

Betsy swallowed hard, wishing Lenny hadn't made her promise to say her next words. "My husband." Before Sheridan could reply, she rushed on. "But you gotta understand. Lenny didn't mean nothing by it. He—he had reason to be angry with me. And sometimes when he gets like that, he forgets how strong he is, that's all."

"Do you really believe that, Betsy? Do you really believe a man's superior strength makes it okay for him to hurt a woman?"

"It's his right. I'm his wife," she replied in a small voice.

"Yes, you're his wife, but that still doesn't give him the right to inflict physical pain on you, even in anger. A wife is not a possession, Betsy. A wife is a human being who should be treated with decency and respect. And she especially should never have to endure bodily harm from a man who supposedly loves her."

"Lenny does love me," Betsy said, her chin lifting to a defiant angle. "And I love him."

"Yes, I'm sure you do," Sheridan replied with a sad smile. "But loving each other still doesn't give him permission to hurt you, no matter how angry he gets." As many times as she'd heard that same claim from the women she'd met in Baltimore, she would never understand their rationale. How could a woman continue loving a man who used her to physically vent his anger? And, more perplexing, why did she stay with him after he displayed such violent behavior? Those questions had plagued her for years. Now she'd met Betsy Pringle, another example of how women in such miserable situations stubbornly clung to their incomprehensible views about marriage.

Sheridan shook herself out of her musings, then exhaled a weary breath. "Was there something else you wanted to tell me?"

"No, I . . . uh . . . felt like I owed ya the truth." Betsy remained silent for a few seconds, then blurted out, "I don't want nobody else to know what I told ya. I mean, about Lenny hurting my arm. That ain't nobody else's business."

"Of course it isn't," Sheridan replied. "I won't tell anyone. You have my word." She frowned. Something about Betsy's tracking her down just so she could admit she'd lied about her bruised arm seemed suspicious, but she couldn't put her finger on what disturbed her. Thinking she was being overly skeptical, she decided Betsy's actions were simply the woman's way of reaching out for a friend, nothing more.

Sheridan forced her lips into a smile and said, "I haven't had the opportunity to meet many women since I arrived in town, so I was hoping we could become friends." She knew she couldn't make Betsy leave her husband—that had to be Betsy's decision—but in the meantime, offering friendship would be an appropriate course of action.

"Friends?" Betsy said, her eyes going wide. "Ya mean, me and you?"

Sheridan nodded. "You're welcome to stop by the clinic anytime. If I'm not busy, we can talk, or maybe one day we could have a picnic lunch down by the creek."

"I'd like that, Dr. Kinmont."

"Why don't you call me Sheridan? Friends should call each other by their first names, don't you agree, Betsy?"

Betsy murmured her agreement, then quickly turned away,

not wanting Sheridan to see the relief on her face. She smiled.
Certain Lenny would be pleased by her efforts.

Over the next several weeks Sheridan settled even more
into a routine. She split her time at the clinic between seeing
patients—always with Shay hovering nearby—talking and
laughing with Enrique while he did the chores she assigned
him, and getting to know Betsy Pringle, who'd taken her suggestion and stopped by at least twice a week.

Whenever Betsy paid a visit, Sheridan said little and tried
to ignore the fresh bruises the woman occasionally sported.
Since she let Betsy do most of the talking, she learned a great
deal about the Pringles during those visits.

Lenny and Betsy were originally from Ohio, both coming
from rather meager beginnings. Lenny had always dreamed
big, boasting of his plans to become rich, a man everyone
would look up to. With few prospects in Ohio to fulfill his
dreams, he shifted his focus to striking it big in the silver mines
of Aspen, Colorado. So he married sixteen-year-old Betsy and
the two headed west in the spring of 'eighty-eight.

Unfortunately Lenny's visions of Aspen—staking a claim
for his own mine, then just scooping out the silver-laced ore
for instant wealth—bore no resemblance to the reality of silver
mining. The mines were owned by large companies that hired
employees to work long hours for wages that would never gain
him the riches he craved. Though bitterly disappointed, he went
to work in one of the mines, more determined than ever to find
a way to reach his goal in life. He worked at one mining
company for several years, then moved to another because, as
Betsy claimed, he wasn't appreciated for his abilities.

In 1893, when the price of silver dropped sharply, all the
mines in Aspen abruptly closed, putting a great many men out
of work. Lenny and Betsy moved around Colorado for almost
five years, but Lenny found no permanent employment to his

liking. Then he heard about the silver mines in far West Texas. Seeing another opportunity to resurrect his youthful dreams of immense wealth, Lenny and Betsy set out again, their destination Shafter.

Sheridan didn't interrupt Betsy's narrative of her eleven-year marriage to Lenny, absorbing what the woman said as well as what she didn't. The picture Betsy painted of her husband wasn't at all flattering, though Betsy seemed unaware of how she'd portrayed him, which added to Sheridan's already biased opinion of Leonard Pringle. She suspected he hadn't told Betsy the truth about his frequent changes in employers, but she kept such thoughts to herself. Instead, she tried to convince Betsy, by carefully worded hints, that a marriage where the husband physically hurt his wife was never acceptable, that there were alternatives for women stuck in what they viewed as a hopeless situation.

Though Betsy listened politely whenever Sheridan brought up the issue, the pinched expression on her face spoke loudly of her true feelings on the subject. As soon as Sheridan finished speaking, Betsy would nod, then change their conversation to the one topic she never tired of—town gossip.

"I heard some ladies talkin' in the company store about a party the Shannons are gonna have this Saturday night," Betsy said to Sheridan late one morning during one of her visits. "They even hired some Mex musicians to play music for dancin'."

Sheridan looked up from the patient chart she was working on. "Yes, I heard that too." James Shannon was a successful businessman who owned and operated the stagecoach line between Shafter and Marfa, a town forty-five miles to the north. He and his wife enjoyed hosting parties and often opened their home to a group of their friends.

"Wonder who's gonna be there? Betcha there'll be lotsa rich folks from Marfa or maybe even El Paso."

"I haven't seen the guest list, but Mrs. Shannon told me it

won't be a formal occasion. She decided to have a party at the last minute and her husband is indulging her whim. I doubt they asked anyone from out of town on such short notice.''

''Yer invited?'' When Sheridan nodded, Betsy's eyes went wide. ''I always wondered what the inside of their house looks like. Bet it's filled with fancy furniture from back east, all kinds of expensive paintings, maybe even real crystal and china.'' She sighed dramatically.

Sheridan chuckled, turning her attention back to the patient chart on her desk. ''If I go Saturday night, I guess I'll find out.''

''Oh, but you gotta go,'' Betsy replied, her voice rising sharply. When Sheridan glanced up again, this time with her eyebrows knitted in a frown, Betsy lowered her voice to add, ''I—I didn't mean to sound pushy. But I ain't never been inside a fancy house like that. Probably never will be. So since yer invited, well, I was kinda hopin' that maybe you'd tell me what it was like.''

Sheridan stared at Betsy for a moment, then finally smiled. ''Sure, if I decide to go, I'd be happy to tell you.''

By the time Saturday came, Sheridan still hadn't made up her mind about going to the Shannon party. Poppy and Orrin would be attending, and although they invited her to go with them, she declined, not wanting to intrude on their evening. Though the idea of staying home alone didn't appeal to her either, she thought that would be best.

She bade Orrin and Poppy good-bye, then wandered around the house, looking for something to occupy her time. When nothing held her interest for more than a few minutes, she glanced at the clock and made a quick decision.

After a hurried bath Sheridan selected a pale blue dress with a tailored skirt and wide lapels on either side of a lace bodice. When she left her house a few minutes later and started down the street, the soft strains of music drifted to her on the warm evening breeze. As she drew closer to the Shannon house, the festive music increased in volume. The enticing rhythm of Mexican guitars shook off the last of her misgivings about attending and put her in a jovial mood.

Sheridan's knock was answered by a young woman assigned the task of directing guests through the house to the rear yard. There she found perhaps a dozen couples standing or sitting in small groups beneath a grove of large cottonwood trees. Lanterns hung from the trees and other places around the yard to bathe the area in a soft yellow light. Spotting the Shannons on the far side of the yard, Sheridan started toward them, exchanging greetings with some of the other guests on the way.

After the Shannons welcomed Sheridan and introduced her to the couples she didn't already know, she moved off to mingle. Though being the only unaccompanied guest initially made her feel awkward, the open warmth of the others soon banished her discomfort.

She was deep in conversation with several of the ladies—their husbands having opted to go inside for a game of euchre—when she happened to glance toward the house. A man stood on the top step of the porch. Though his face was hidden in the deep shadows cast by the porch roof, she had no trouble recognizing him—even though he wore a suit, wing collar, and four-in-hand tie. Her heart racing and her breath lodged in her throat, she watched Shay descend the steps.

One of other women made a comment which she couldn't discern over the thundering of her blood against her eardrums. Finally the tittering of feminine laughter jerked her back to the present. Her cheeks burning, she turned her attention to her companions again, hoping the muted lantern light would camouflage her flushed face.

The rest of the evening alternated between moments of relaxed conversations and wild bouts of nervous anticipation, the latter—much to her self-disgust—the direct result of Shay

Bannigan's presence. In retrospect she should have known he would be there. As the highest-ranking mine official in town, she'd heard he was invited to nearly all social functions. But even if she'd remembered that bit of information sooner, would the possibility of his being there have changed her decision about attending the party?

She wasn't at all certain of the answer, which she found greatly disturbing. After the fiasco of her marriage to Winston, she'd learned several valuable lessons. Men couldn't be trusted, and never allow herself to become involved with a man who believed he had control over everything she did. Remembering those lessons, and their consequences, hadn't been a problem until her arrival in Shafter. Based on the seemingly effortless way Shay exerted control over her, in particular her libido— his mere presence igniting and stoking a firestorm of desire— she wondered if what she'd learned had been for naught. Catching a glimpse of him across the yard, his head thrown back in laughter, his dark eyes glittering in the lantern light, she turned toward the house. If she didn't leave the party immediately, she feared she'd do something to cause them both embarrassment.

Shay had watched Sheridan's every movement from the moment he stepped onto the Shannons' rear porch and caught sight of her. He hadn't meant to be so captivated, but once he saw her in the prim and proper blue dress, the high collar nearly brushing the underside of her chin, the slim skirt hugging her softly rounded hips, he couldn't keep his gaze from seeking her out every few minutes. Such behavior wasn't his norm. He'd always been one who met a woman, dawdled awhile— enjoying what she gave him and, in turn, seeing that she received equal enjoyment from their liaison—then moved on to a new feminine diversion, leaving no broken hearts in his wake. He'd certainly never been consumed with only one woman. But ever since he'd met Sheridan, the patterns of his past were slowly but surely falling by the wayside.

From the corner of his eye he watched her flit from one

group of guests to another, like a bird flying from branch to branch in a tree. Her dress looked like it would be much too warm, though she didn't appear to be suffering. He lifted his glass to his mouth to hide a sudden grin. Beneath the prim and proper facade Sheridan displayed that night, he had no doubt, beat the heart and spirit of a real wildcat. He liked that about her—he liked that a lot.

He lowered his glass, then frowned into the contents. *Damn, I'm doing it again. Thinking crazy thoughts about her.* Downing the last of his beer in one swallow, he headed for the refreshment table and a refill. As he moved across the yard, he spotted Sheridan making her way to the porch. She stopped to talk to Mrs. Shannon, turned to wave at several other women, then disappeared into the house. He refilled his glass from the beer keg, his gaze glued to the door. Several other people went into the house and returned a few minutes later, but Sheridan was not one of them. Wondering why she left so early, he suddenly remembered the visit he'd had earlier that day from one of the mine employees. He'd planned to discuss that visit with Sheridan during the course of the evening, but ridiculous notions about her clothes and what lay beneath them had banished the thought from his head. And now she was gone.

He set his untouched glass of beer on the nearest table, then went searching for his hosts to bid them good night.

As Shay approached Sheridan's house, he saw the sudden flash of a match through a window, followed by the muted golden glow of lantern light. Grateful she'd gone home after leaving the Shannon party, he hurried up the steps and onto the porch.

Sheridan started at the knock on her door. Expecting some sort of medical emergency, she shushed Buster's excited barking, then hurried to open the door.

The last person she expected to find standing on her porch was Shay Bannigan.

"Mr. Bannigan, is something wrong? Has someone been hurt?"

"You agreed to call me Shay, remember?" he replied. "And, no, there's nothing wrong. But there is something I need to speak to you about."

Sheridan eyed him for a moment, then finally stepped aside. "Come in."

Shay moved into the room, then loosened his tie and unfastened his collar button. As Sheridan closed the door, he bent down to try to coax Buster closer. The dog stopped growling but wouldn't budge.

"Buster, go lie down," Sheridan said. When the dog trotted away, she shifted her attention to Shay. "Now, what's this about?"

Shay straightened. "I was paid a visit today by Leonard Pringle. Seems he isn't too happy with you, Miss Kinmont."

Sheridan's gaze narrowed. "Really? I've never met the man."

"No, but you know his wife. Pringle says you see her several times a week."

"Yes, that's true."

"He also said you're putting all kinds of newfangled ideas in his wife's head. Talking to her about leaving him, about getting a divorce."

"The man hits her, for God's sake, Shay. What am I supposed to do, sit around and wait until he kills her?"

A muscle in Shay's jaw ticked. "You have proof he hits her?"

"I've seen the bruises myself, and Betsy admitted her husband is responsible. But she refuses to leave him."

"Whether she stays married or not is none of your concern. I demand you stop interfering in their marriage."

"You demand?" Sheridan said in a harsh whisper, moving closer. "You can't demand I do or not do anything."

"The hell I can't," he replied in a near roar. Lowering his

voice to a fierce growl, he added, "You work for me. Or have you forgotten that in all your women's suffrage recruiting?"

"I wasn't trying to recruit Betsy Pringle for women's suffrage." She took another step closer, her face just inches from his. "I was simply trying to make her understand that she doesn't have to stay with her husband, that women can get out of marriages like hers, that they can survive on their own."

Shay inhaled what was meant to be a calming breath. But Sheridan's scent filled his lungs, making his head reel and his groin ache with need. "I don't care what you were trying to do," he finally managed to say, his voice now a raspy croak. "I want it stopped." He watched her tongue come out to wet her lips. He squeezed his eyes closed for a second, trying to control his reaction to the infuriating yet equally desirable woman standing in front of him. After a moment he said, "Do you understand me?"

Sheridan didn't respond; she couldn't. She just stared up at him with widened eyes, her palms damp, breathing erratic, and a coil of heat swirling low in her belly. Trying to ignore her body's reaction to this man, she summoned the strength to speak. She opened her mouth, but before she could get any words out, she found herself pressed against Shay's chest, her lips fused to his.

Chapter Twelve

For a fleeting moment Sheridan wondered if she'd initiated the kiss. Pressing her lips to his certainly had crossed her mind, but she didn't think she'd actually acted on the impulse. Yet, she didn't remember Shay making the first move either. Deciding it didn't matter which of them originated the kiss, she gave herself over to Shay's masterful mouth and the incredible sensations swamping her body.

She leaned closer, looping her arms around his neck and pressing her breasts against his chest. She felt a rumbling sensation where their bodies met, then heard the resulting moan. Whichever of them made the sound, she couldn't be certain. The only thing she did know for certain was she didn't want the kiss to end.

She pressed herself even closer to his hard body, wanting to crawl inside his skin. When he lifted his head a few seconds later, she moaned a protest.

"Shh, it's okay," he murmured. When she quieted, he kissed her eyes, her temple, then trailed a line of soft kisses down her cheek. After placing a quick peck on her chin, he returned to her lips. Using his tongue, he teased her mouth open, then slipped between her parted lips.

Sheridan gasped at the contact, changing the angle of her face to allow him better access. His tongue played a tantalizing game, plunging into her mouth followed by an immediate retreat, then repeating the pattern. The mock sex act stirred a wild heat between her thighs, intensifying with each stab of his tongue.

Raw need ripped through her, more intense than she'd ever experienced. She should have known it would be this way with Shay. From the moment they met, he made her react in ways completely foreign to her. He could instantly infuriate her, but as he'd just proven, he could also turn her into a brazen hussy, making her cling to him like the barbs of a cactus spine.

Her head spinning—a combination of Shay's kisses and her line of thinking—she suddenly jerked free of his intoxicating mouth and pushed out of his arms.

The combined rasp of their labored breathing filled the air. Finally he said, "What is it?"

"I—" She drew in an unsteady breath. "I can't breathe."

He chuckled. "Yeah, me too." He lifted a hand and ran the backs of his knuckles down her cheek. "You're so beautiful. All flushed with desire." He brushed her bottom lip with his fingertips. "I want to do more than kiss you."

She forced her gaze upward to meet his, her mouth tingling where he'd touched. The blazing heat in his dark eyes exuded a desire more potent than any she'd ever witnessed. No man had ever looked at her that way. The wild throbbing between her thighs returned, stronger than before.

She couldn't imagine why she'd first thought Shay wasn't handsome. His rugged features had always held a strong appeal for her, but now she found him not only handsome on a physical level but even more appealing on an emotional— Her eyes went wide. *Oh, my God, I'm falling in love with him!*

She squeezed her eyes closed for a few seconds. *This can't be happening! I swore never would be too soon for me to want another man in my life.* When she opened her eyes and looked up at Shay, her stomach dropped to her feet. Never had arrived; she wanted this man.

She stared up at him for a silent moment. The conclusions she'd just reached defied all logic, but she knew them to be true. Inhaling a deep breath, she made a decision she hoped she wouldn't live to regret. Unable to speak around the lump of emotion clogging her throat, she reached for his hand, then turned and led him across the room.

As Shay followed Sheridan through her house, curiosity mixed with the desire still pounding in his veins. When they entered a darkened room, she dropped his hand and moved away from him. He kept his breathing shallow while he waited in agonized silence. A few seconds later he heard the scratch of a match, smelled the pungent odor of sulfur, then watched the flaming tip of the matchstick move to the wick of a lamp. As Sheridan replaced the glass chimney, a soft golden glow filled the room. A bedroom, he realized, allowing himself to finally breathe normally.

When she turned toward him, he swallowed hard. Fear and anticipation warring inside him, his gaze scoured her face, searching for some sign of her intentions. He hoped she wanted him as much as he did her. Surely, that's why she'd led him to her bedroom. But what if he'd misread her reaction to the kisses they'd shared in the other room? Or what if she changed her mind and ordered him to leave? Seeing nothing in her expression to indicate an affirmative answer to either of his questions, his fears eased a little.

Still, he had to know. He had to hear her say the words. He took a step closer, then said, "If you're not sure about this, say so now and I'll leave." He drew a labored breath. "But once this goes any further, I might not be able—"

Sheridan's fingers pressed against his lips. "Shh. You can stop fretting. I'm sure."

Shay searched her face once more. Seeing only the reflection of his own desire, he planted a firm kiss on her lips, then reached for the row of buttons running down the front of her dress. As he tried to work the tiny buttons free of their holes, he was dumbfounded to realize his hands actually shook. *Damn, you'd think this is my first time.* Glancing up into Sheridan's eyes, the trust and need shining in their deep blue depths sent a shock wave rocketing through him. For reasons he couldn't grasp, she made everything fresh and new for him, almost as if what was about to happen were truly his first time.

A few minutes later, as Shay stretched out on the bed beside a naked Sheridan, he could remember only bits and pieces about removing her clothes and even less about how he'd gotten out of his. He recalled tussling with the buttons on her dress, then finally parting the lace bodice to find the swell of her bosom staring him in the face. The next thing he remembered was watching her step out of her dress and petticoat, pull her chemise over her head, and shimmy out of her drawers. Then somehow his clothes had melted away, until he stood facing her, wearing not a stitch and painfully aroused.

Sheridan had smiled at his erection, dropped onto the mattress, and sent him a come-hither look. With a growl rumbling in his throat, he hadn't hesitated to accept her silent but blatant invitation.

Now, as he gathered her into his arms, his body hummed with a need like none he'd ever experienced. As he ran a hand down her back, then onto her hip, he wondered if he'd be able to satisfy her, or would she find his carnal knowledge lacking? A shudder racked his body. He'd never worried about pleasing a woman in the past. He'd always been confident of his abilities with the fairer sex, never having left one of his previous partners disappointed. So why the sudden self-doubt? The answer had to be the woman making mewling sounds against his neck. He frowned at the direction of his thoughts, then quickly shoved them aside. More pressing matters required his attention and his complete concentration.

After a silent prayer asking for help should an unexpected need arise, Shay lowered his head and settled his mouth atop Sheridan's. She moaned, pressing closer, one of her hands trapped between their bodies, the other clutching a handful of hair at his nape. She rotated her hips against his, bumping his engorged sex. He bit back a groan, then offered another quick prayer, this one for the strength not to lose control.

Sheridan had never experienced such blinding desire. Being both a physician and a formerly married woman, naturally she was familiar with how the human body became aroused and the mechanics of sexual intimacy. But her knowledge fell far short of the reality of the moment. What was happening to her bore little resemblance to what she'd learned in medical school or as Winston's wife.

Shay nibbled along her neck, one hand busy exploring the silky skin of her belly, the delicate ridges of her ribs, then moving up to test the weight of one breast. His thumb rubbed over the hardened tip, making the nipple tighten even more. Her head dropped back, a moan vibrating in her throat.

He shifted position, lowering his head to her breast. When his mouth replaced his fingers, she gasped, the erotic rasping of his tongue over her sensitive nipple almost more than she could bear. And when he switched his ministrations to a gentle suck, her body jerked in response, feeling the tug of his mouth much lower on her body, on another sensitive nubbin of flesh. She whimpered, rubbing her hips against him in an effort to ease the ache between her thighs.

Shay released her nipple, then lifted his head to stare into her flushed face. "You're incredible," he said in a husky whisper. "We've barely gotten started, and already you're hotter than a Chinese firecracker and I'm about to burst."

She laughed, a lazy, throaty sound that wrapped around his

heart and squeezed. God, how he loved to hear her laugh. Though startled by the revelation, he realized the truth of his thoughts. He'd never tire of hearing her laughter or looking into her lovely eyes. She might try his temper to the limit, but— His manhood jerked against her belly, reminding him that he'd spent enough time daydreaming.

He bent to nuzzle her neck. "That discussion we had about you talking to your patients about preventives, do you practice what you preach?"

Sheridan's brow furrowed. "What? I don't know—" Her mind suddenly cleared. "Oh! Um, yes, I do. Not that I've had occasion to . . . I mean, I think we should take the necessary precautions, don't you?"

"I'm always in favor of being cautious." He ran his tongue around the rim of her ear, then grinned when she groaned. "But since I didn't anticipate this, I'm afraid I came here unprepared. So you'll have to provide the means."

Sheridan closed her eyes for a second, willing the desire pounding in her veins to cool. "I—I can't." When Shay's head snapped up, disbelief registered on his face, she said, "I have several varieties of preventives at the clinic, but I don't keep anything here." At his scowl she added, "There was no need before tonight."

Her admission, though a relief because she didn't make a habit of inviting men into her bed, also brought disappointment. He wanted to bury himself deep inside her. He wanted to feel her inner muscles squeeze around his hardened flesh. He wanted to thrust into her time and time again, then empty himself while crying out her name. He bit the inside of his cheek to halt such thoughts.

After taking several seconds to compose himself, he lifted one hand to push a lock of hair off her face. "Don't look so worried," he said. "There are other ways to gain relief without running the risk of pregnancy." Seeing her confused expression, he smiled. "Don't tell me you're so naive that you don't know what I'm talking about?'' When she didn't respond, one dark eyebrow arched. ''Really? Well, let me enlighten you.'' He bent closer and whispered in her ear.

Sheridan's face flamed with heat at his frankness. When he lifted his head, she stared up at him, her mind envisioning what he'd said, her body restless for him to put his words into action.

Shay trailed his fingers down her throat, over one breast, across her belly, then stopped at the soft curls at the apex of her thighs. ''I know you're aching, but I can give you the relief your body desperately needs. What will it be, Sherry?''

She blinked. He'd called her Sherry. The only person to try shortening her name had been a would-be beau soon after her move to Baltimore. Immediately hating the nickname, she'd quickly rectified the situation, telling him in no uncertain terms that he'd be wise to dispense with the name since she wouldn't tolerate being called anything other than Sheridan. Yet oddly enough, Shay using that same nickname didn't rankle; in fact, hearing him call her Sherry sounded right. His fingers moving a fraction lower chased thoughts of nicknames and former beaus from her head.

Instantly the throbbing just inches below his hand rekindled, then rapidly escalated. She swallowed hard. ''Yes,'' she said in a strangled whisper. Her hips came up off the mattress in agreement. ''Please, yes.''

Shay eased his fingers through the patch of springy dark chestnut hair, then lower. As his fingers skimmed over her woman's flesh, he clenched his teeth against the urge to shout with joy. She was damp and smooth as silk, and touching her was pure heaven. Holding a tight rein on his own need, he carefully opened the soft petals of flesh to find her clitoris already swollen with desire. As he rubbed his fingers over the sensitive bud, she gasped, her hips bucking upward.

He crooned to her, whispered words meant to both soothe and encourage. He dipped his hand lower, then slipped a finger into her warmth. His breath catching in his throat, he squeezed his eyes closed for a moment. *God, she's like hot silk.* He thrust his finger into her several times, mimicking what he longed to do with another part of his anatomy. She groaned again, more guttural this time, the rhythm of her breathing changing.

"Shay, please," she said in an agonized whisper. "I can't . . . I can't take—you've got to—"

Shay bent to press a quick kiss on her mouth. "Shh, it's okay. I'll take care of you. Just relax." Continuing the thrust-and-retreat pattern with his finger, he used the pad of his thumb to rub her clitoris. She sucked in a sharp breath. Her body went rigid for a split second, then her hips began a feverish thrusting motion against his hand.

Sheridan could barely think. Her mind, along with her body, had been given over to Shay's control. His magic fingers played her as skillfully as the finest musician played his chosen instrument. She couldn't begin to understand how a man she'd known for only a few weeks could be so in tune with her body's needs, knowing exactly where and how to touch her almost before she did. The idea that Shay Bannigan possessed such knowledge astounded her. Yet, she couldn't deny that he did, and the results were frankly spectacular.

"Don't fight it, Sherry," he murmured, his lips brushing hers in a soft kiss. "Let yourself go."

The rhythm of her hips increased. Throbbing heat continued to build in her belly and between her thighs where his fingers worked her slick flesh. The sensations soon became too much for her raw nerve endings, for her overstimulated system. She couldn't take much more of the pleasure-torture he continued to inflict. Then just as she opened her mouth to beg him to stop, her orgasm started. She gave another sharp gasp, her back arching, heels digging into the mattress. She continued to thrust her hips against Shay's hand until she fell back on the bed with a groan. Physically spent and mentally dazed by the strength of her release, she lay in a senseless sprawl for several minutes.

When her breathing returned to normal, she turned her head

to look at Shay. He'd rolled onto his back, an arm draped across his eyes. As she watched him, a muscle jumped in his jaw.

"Shay?" When he didn't respond, she levered herself up onto one elbow. "Is something wrong?"

He pressed his lips together, the corners turned down. "Now, there's an understatement."

"I don't know what you mean," she said, rolling toward him. When her hip encountered something sticky, she froze. "What the—?" Frowning, she looked down at the sheet. As understanding dawned, her brow cleared. "Oh."

"Yeah, oh!" he said, lowering his arm but unable to meet her gaze. "I've never been so humiliated in my life."

Sheridan rolled onto her side, ignoring the cool wetness beneath one hip. She placed a hand on the center of his chest, tunneled her fingers into the patch of silky black hair. "There's no need to be embarrassed."

He turned his tortured gaze on her. "You don't know what you're talking about. You're not the one who couldn't wait, who couldn't control your lust, who spilled yourself like an inexperienced boy when the woman next to him reached her orgasm."

"I admit, there's no way I could know what that's like. But you shouldn't take this so hard." When he didn't respond, she said, "Has this happened to you before?"

"God, no! That's never happened to me. Do you hear? Never!" His jaw clenched, he closed his eyes.

Sheridan didn't reply; she had no idea how to ease his obvious distress. Before she could come up with something to say, he spoke again.

"I've always made sure I satisfied the woman first, then took my own pleasure. For me, that's as natural as breathing." He opened his eyes and stared up at the ceiling. "But a few minutes ago, when you got closer to your peak, something happened to me. I don't know what it was, but suddenly I could no longer hold back. It was like your pleasure became my pleasure, and

I couldn't separate the two. Then when you reached your orgasm, I—'' He swallowed, then let his eyelids drop closed. ''I did too.''

The agony Sheridan heard in his voice touched her heart. Though she didn't think the situation was nearly as bad as he'd painted it, she kept that thought to herself, unwilling to poke more holes in his already deflated ego. After a few moments of silence she said, ''Has it been a long time since you've been with a woman?''

''Considering what I told you the other night, do you have to ask?''

''Well then, that's the answer. Because of your abstinence, you became overstimulated and that's what caused you to ejaculate when I—'' Her face burning, she cleared her throat. ''When I . . . you know.''

Shay turned his head on the pillow and looked at Sheridan. Momentarily forgetting his embarrassment, he managed a smile. ''You can't say it, can you?''

Her chin came up. ''I don't know what you're talking about.''

''Sure you do. You can't say 'when I reached orgasm.' ''

''Of course I can.''

One eyebrow arched. ''Okay, then say it.''

Sheridan licked her suddenly dry lips. She was a doctor, for God's sake, and she'd never had a problem speaking frankly. Of course, she'd never had occasion to discuss her own sexual activities, since Winston had made it clear the topic wasn't one to be discussed, even between husbands and wives. Taking a deep breath, she looked Shay straight in the eye and said, ''When I reached orgasm.''

Something hot flickered in his gold-flecked dark eyes, a flash of intense heat that seared a path of liquid fire through her body. Clamping her thighs together, she dropped back to a prone position on the mattress.

Shay saw her reaction—dilated eyes, increased breathing, throbbing pulse at the base of her throat—and realized how lucky he was to have found such a passionate woman. Though he considered reaching for her and bringing her to another climatic peak, he thought better of the idea in case his body decided to betray him a second time.

Instead of touching her in an intimate way, he settled for reaching for her hand and lacing his fingers with hers. Resting their joined hands on his chest, he closed his eyes, surprised at the contentment such a simple gesture brought him.

Sheridan lay quietly beside Shay, contemplating her new-found feelings for him. She'd never figured to fall in love with a man who had such biased opinions about female doctors. In fact, she hadn't figured to fall in love at all, but there was no predicting the ways of the heart. If their relationship was meant to be, then she'd have to change his mind about her chosen profession.

She looked over at him. His face was relaxed, his dark hair and mustache gleaming blue-black in the lamplight. "Shay?"

"Hmm?"

"Can I ask you something?"

"Uh-huh."

"Why are you so against women becoming doctors?"

Chapter Thirteen

Shay didn't respond to Sheridan's question for a long time. Finally his chest rose and fell with a deep breath, then he said, "My sister, Clare, died because of her doctor. A completely unqualified, totally inept woman."

Sheridan's heart cramped at the pain and bitterness in his voice. "I'm so sorry, Shay. After losing a family member, being angry at the doctor is a natural reaction. Especially when it's a situation where nothing can be done to—"

"You don't understand. Clare could have been saved. If that quack woman hadn't insisted on performing a procedure she knew nothing about. If she'd called in another doctor like she should've done when Clare took a turn for the worse, instead of going into hysterics, my sister would still be alive."

"Shay, you don't know that. No one does."

He turned his head to glare at her with tortured eyes. "Don't tell me what I know, dammit. I talked to a number of doctors after Clare's death, and they all told me she could have been saved."

"Hindsight is always perfect. Have you forgotten that? Besides, not one of those doctors was there treating your sister. They don't know all the circumstances, whether there were complications. Their saying she could have been saved is unfair and, in my opinion, grossly incompetent. You shouldn't blame your sister's doctor, when—"

"That doctor was also my sister's best friend," he said in a fierce whisper. "And all the woman could do was stand around crying and wringing her hands, while Clare slipped away."

Sheridan eased her fingers from his grip, then smoothed a lock of his hair off his forehead. "Have you considered the possibility that perhaps there was nothing more she could do?"

Shay gave a snort of disgust. "Naturally you'd stick up for one of your kind."

"I'm not sticking up for anyone. I don't even know the specifics of your sister's illness or what her doctor did to treat her." When he opened his mouth, she sent him a warning glance to halt whatever he planned to say. "And I don't want to know, since that won't change anything. You have to realize that even with the best medical care, sometimes it's not enough to save a life. Modern medicine still has a long way to go." She paused for a moment, then said, "There's something else you need to understand, Shay. Doctors aren't God. We don't have all the answers. We're human beings just like you, with the same frailties, the same flaws. And unfortunately, because we're human, we make mistakes."

He grunted. "Yeah, mistakes that cost lives."

She nodded. "That's true. Sometimes a doctor's mistake does result in losing a patient, something that can happen to any doctor, man or woman. Gender has nothing to do with it."

"The hell it doesn't!" His eyebrows pulled together in a fierce scowl, deep grooves bracketed his mouth. "The woman who treated Clare had no business becoming a doctor or practicing medicine. She was overemotional, irrational, and the sole reason my baby sister's dead.''

Sheridan didn't respond immediately but waited for Shay's fury to subside. When the harshness of his features eased, she said, ''In medical school, students are instructed to keep their emotions out of their work. That's a necessary part of becoming a doctor but also extremely hard to do. Some medical students, both men and women, have difficulty learning how to control their feelings.'' She ran her fingertips down one of his cheeks, the stubble of his beard a gentle rasp against her skin. ''Staying emotionally detached is especially difficult when the patient is a friend or relative. Maybe that's why your sister's friend reacted the way she did. Maybe she hadn't yet mastered keeping her personal feelings at bay, a situation compounded by the fact that she was treating a close friend.''

Shay's scowl deepened. He didn't want to hear justifications for the woman's actions. He didn't want to know there might be an acceptable explanation for her behavior. He wanted to continue nursing his anger over the wastefulness of Clare's death, to continue venting his fury at the senseless loss of his youngest sister's life. Yet, when he closed his eyes and summoned the memory of his last view of Clare—no longer a young woman with sparkling eyes, freckled nose, and mischievous grin, but pathetically thin, pale, and drawn, laid out in her coffin—the usual accompanying wrath didn't rise to its normal raging boil. Instead, his anger rose no higher than a low simmer, his once-intense pain of loss replaced by a dull ache.

When Shay finally spoke, his voice was raw with the myriad emotions running through him. ''I'd better go before Poppy comes home.''

''Poppy! Oh, Lord, I forgot about her,'' Sheridan said, jerking to an upright position, then scooting off the bed. ''She could arrive any minute,'' she mumbled, snatching her underclothes off the floor and pulling them on with jerky motions. ''How would I explain . . ." She waved a hand to encompass where Shay sat on the edge of the mattress.

Shay chuckled. "A naked man in your bed?"

Heat crept up her face, making her cheeks sting. "She'd be shocked."

He rose and reached for his clothes. "We're both adults. With adult needs. Poppy should understand that."

Her blush burned even more at his blunt words. Keeping her gaze averted from his, she said, "I doubt she would, given her opinion of men. She's more likely to think you took advantage of me."

Shay halted his efforts to get dressed, one foot poised above a trouser leg. "I hope you're joking."

She found a robe and slipped her arms into the sleeves before responding. As she tied the belt around her waist, she said, "Only about you taking advantage of me. She knows I wouldn't go to bed with a man unless I wanted to. But I definitely wasn't joking about her low opinion of men."

"But she's seeing Orrin Neilson," he said, hopping on one foot while trying to stick the other foot into the corresponding trouser leg.

She glanced over at him and smiled. "Do you need help getting dressed?"

The frown he shot her nearly made her laugh. Clamping down on the urge, she said, "I was shocked when she told me about Orrin. That's a real milestone for her."

"Her marriage was that bad, huh?" he replied, finally corralling his trousers and successfully getting his legs into the appropriate openings.

Sheridan's smile faded. "Yeah, it was." Forcing her mind back to the present, she said, "Anyway, I'd rather not have Poppy find us in such a . . . well . . . intimate situation."

He nodded, shrugging into his shirt. "You planning to tell her about us?"

"I don't know. Is there an us?"

He moved around the bed and stopped in front of her. Raising a hand, he tucked a chestnut curl behind her ear. "Do you want there to be?"

She stared at the strip of hair-covered chest visible in the opening of his unbuttoned shirt. She inhaled a deep breath, filling her lungs with his scent. Swallowing hard against the urge to press her face against his heated skin, her brow furrowed. "It's probably not a good idea."

"Really?" he murmured, lowering his head until his lips grazed hers. "And why's that?"

"Because I can't . . . I can't think when you're close to me."

"Ah." He licked her bottom lip. "So you don't like not being in control."

She shook her head. "I swore I'd never let another man try to control me," she said in a ragged whisper. "Now, stop teasing and kiss me."

Shay chuckled then dipped his mouth lower and complied.

Midmorning on the following Monday, Sheridan closed the medical book she'd pulled from the shelves behind her desk. Resting her head against the back of her chair, she sighed and wished she could concentrate on her work. But ever since Shay's visit to her house on Saturday night, her mind persisted in wandering at every opportunity.

She kept thinking about her unbelievable response to him. A sudden heated throbbing started between her thighs. Closing her eyes, she tried to turn her thoughts to something else. But nothing stopped her mind from conjuring up memories of Shay lying beside her, of his intimate touch, of her body reacting with such wild abandon. She squeezed her thighs together, waiting for the ache to ease.

Thank goodness Poppy hadn't returned earlier that night. Sheridan smiled, imagining the look on her friend's face if she'd arrived home and found Shay Bannigan in her bed.

Though Poppy might not have said anything in Shay's presence, she certainly wouldn't have minced words after his departure.

Poppy probably would have shaken a finger at her, then said she never thought she'd see the day when Sheridan would do anything to get out of a few weeks of chores—even take a man into her bed. If Poppy had made such accusations, she would have done so in jest, a deliberate act meant to provoke a reaction. After all, she and Poppy were close friends, and Poppy knew she'd never do such a thing.

Her eyes popped open. But Shay didn't! Though he had no way of knowing about her bet with Poppy, what if he believed she had an ulterior motive for leading him to her bedroom? What if he thought she'd taken him to her bed to sway his opinion about lady doctors?

She groaned. She was half in love with a man who might think she'd used her body as a bribe. *I knew I shouldn't have gotten involved with him. Men are nothing but trouble, and I'd be better off without—*

A knock on her office door jarred her back to the present. Releasing a long sigh, she straightened and called for the person to come in.

The door opened and Betsy Pringle stuck her head into the room. "I ain't interrupting nothing important, am I?"

"I was just—" She couldn't admit the truth, that she'd been daydreaming about Shay being in her bed and the possible repercussions. "Never mind. Come in and have a seat."

Betsy settled into the chair in front of Sheridan's desk. "What was it like?" When Sheridan just stared at her, she said, "Saturday night?"

Sheridan's back stiffened. "What about it?"

"The Shannon party. I was just talkin' to Poppy and she said ya went." She leaned forward. "So, tell me. What was it like?"

Sheridan relaxed her tight muscles, relieved Betsy hadn't been asking about what happened later Saturday night. "I'm afraid I didn't see much of the house. Mrs. Shannon held the party in the backyard, so I passed through the house only when I arrived and again when I left."

"Oh." Betsy slumped against the back of her chair, the glow of excitement faded from her eyes.

"I'm sorry I didn't get the chance to see more."

Betsy tried to smile but with only partial success. "That's okay. Maybe you'll go to their house some other time, and then you can tell me all about it."

"Betsy, why's it important for you to find out what the inside of the Shannon house looks like?"

The woman dropped her gaze to where she held her hands clasped in her lap. "I wanna know cuz Lenny keeps telling me we'll be rich someday. Richer even than the Shannons. And when that happens, I gotta know what kinda things to put in the house Lenny says he's gonna buy us."

Sheridan nodded, then stared thoughtfully at Betsy for a moment. Finally she said, "How's your arm? Are you in pain?"

Betsy lifted her gaze to meet Sheridan's, one hand moving to the spot beneath the long sleeve of her dress, the place where Lenny had twisted her arm. "I'm fine," Betsy replied, though Sheridan thought she detected a wince in her expression as she rubbed her latest injury.

"If you need something for pain, let me know. I have some liniment that will help."

"Thanks, but I don't need nothing. Like I told ya, my arm's fine. It'll get better, just like all the—" Betsy bit her lip to still the rest of her words. Clearing her throat, she rose from her chair and said, "I gotta go now. I got things I gotta do."

Sheridan also got to her feet. Remembering Shay's warning about interfering in the Pringle marriage, she carefully chose her next words. "If you ever want my help, for any reason, you know you can count on me, don't you?"

She thought Betsy was going to respond. Instead, she just nodded, her lips pressed together in a thin line.

Sheridan followed her from her office into the waiting room. "Come back when you have more time."

Betsy nodded again, murmured a hurried "Bye," then left the clinic.

After Sheridan closed the door, Poppy said, "Do you think she'll ever leave her poor excuse for a husband?"

Sheridan turned to look at her friend. "I don't know. She listens to me, but always with a mutinous look on her face. So I'm not sure I'm really getting through to her."

"I was that way once. Not listening to anything anyone else told me. Thinking I had to stay with my husband no matter how bad it got."

Sheridan nodded. "I hate seeing another woman put herself through such misery."

"Me too. But no matter what you tell her, she won't leave until she's ready."

"Yes, I know," Sheridan replied with a sigh. "I just hope she doesn't wait too long."

The following afternoon Enrique arrived at the clinic, a bright smile curving his full mouth.

"*¡Hola!,* Enrique," Sheridan said. "This is a surprise. You aren't supposed to work for me until tomorrow."

"*Sí,* I know, *Doctora* Kinmont," he replied, pulling his battered hat from his head. "This afternoon I am working for Señor Neilson. I came into town a little early so I could stop here first. I wanted to tell you that Papa went to work yesterday. He drove a wagon load of wood to the mill and said he got only a little tired. Not like when he worked in the mine."

Sheridan smiled. "That's wonderful, Enrique."

"Mama and I want to thank you for finding a job for Papa. He is much happier now."

"It was my pleasure. I'm just glad I could help." Her smile

faded. "But you and your mother understand what I told your father about working, don't you?"

"*Sí*, we understand. Even though he has improved enough to work again, we know that does not mean he will be cured."

Sheridan nodded. "I'm sorry, Enrique. I wish it could be different."

He swallowed, a muscle working in his cheek. "So do I," he finally said in a soft voice. Regaining his composure, he settled his hat back into place and tugged the brim down low on his forehead. "I must go now. Señor Neilson said he would give me additional responsibilities today, so I do not want to be late."

Enrique's maturity continued to amaze Sheridan. At fourteen, he was more grown-up than many adults. As he turned to leave, she said, "Oh, by the way. There's something I've been meaning to tell you. You should talk to Mr. Bannigan about becoming a lawyer. I recently found out he attended Harvard's law school."

"Mr. Bannigan is a lawyer?"

"No, he left before he graduated. He had his reasons, which I'm sure he'll explain to you. But he can also answer a lot of your questions, like how to get into law school and how to apply for a scholarship."

"You think he will talk to me?"

Sheridan gave him an encouraging smile. "If you ask him, yes, I'm sure he'd be happy to."

Enrique stared up at her from beneath his hat brim for a few moments. At last he nodded, determination evident in the set of his jaw. "*Bueno*, then I will ask him."

Sheridan finished drying the few dishes she'd used for her supper, then wondered what she should do to fill the rest of the evening. Orrin had asked Poppy out to supper, then the two planned to play whist with a couple they'd befriended at the Shannon party.

There were a number of chores awaiting her attention: One of her skirts needed a button sewed on, several of her shirtwaists needed ironing, a stack of medical journals needed to be sorted. Dismissing all those tasks, she finally settled on taking Buster out for some exercise.

"Come on, boy," she said to the dog. "Let's go for walk."

Buster gave an excited yip, then hotfooted it to the door, nails clicking on the wooden floor, his stub of a tail wagging in a furious rhythm.

Sheridan chuckled, then opened the door. Buster shot past her, leapt off the porch, and raced down the path. Stopping in the middle of the road, he turned to look back at the house, then barked his encouragement.

"I know. I know. I'm hurrying," she said with a smile. When she reached him, she bent to give him a scratch under his chin. "Okay, so which way should we go?"

The dog gave another sharp bark, did a canine-type pirouette in the dusty street, and took off at a trot. Sheridan followed at a more leisurely pace. She'd gone less than a hundred feet when she realized the direction Buster had chosen. She stubbed her toe and nearly fell. Regaining her balance, she stopped to consider her choices. She could call Buster back and cut over to another street, or she could stay on this one.

Though she wondered at her sanity, she started walking, following her dog down the street that led straight to Shay Bannigan's house.

Chapter Fourteen

When Sheridan approached Shay's house and spotted him sitting on the top step of his porch, she again wondered at her sanity. She should be steering clear of the man, not purposely taking a walk down the street where he lived. She still believed what she'd told Shay the previous Saturday night, that continuing their relationship wasn't a good idea. She couldn't, she wouldn't, put herself through another nightmare like she'd endured with Winston. Yet, she found herself powerless to stop whatever was happening to her.

For a moment she blamed Buster for choosing the route of their walk. Then, just as quickly, she repositioned the blame precisely where it belonged—on her own shoulders. She could have changed direction as soon as she realized where Buster was leading her, or at any time afterward. But she hadn't.

The truth was, she did want to see Shay. She'd thought of little else since he left her house Saturday night. And even though she knew she'd be wise to turn and run like hell in the opposite direction, she couldn't make herself heed her own advice. The prospect of seeing Shay was too strong a temptation, one she couldn't ignore.

Shay watched a dog pass in front of his house, then stop to hike his leg on a bush. He stared at the dog for a second, then his eyes went wide. *Damn, that looks like Buster.* Wondering if Sheridan knew her dog was running loose, Shay got to his feet. As he started down the steps, he glanced up the street and nearly missed the last step. Suddenly rooted to the ground, he watched Sheridan walk toward his house and stop at the edge of his yard, his mouth as dry as the dust under his feet.

Before Shay could work up enough spit to speak, Sheridan smiled, then said, "Cat got your tongue, Mr. Bannigan?"

He licked his lips, then swallowed, the smoky quality of her voice making his belly clench with a flare of desire. Shaking off his sluggish reaction, he said, "If you're looking for your dog, he went . . ." He looked up the street, then frowned. "Damn. He was right there by that bush. I saw him lift his leg and take a p—er, that is, he—well, you know what I mean."

Sheridan chuckled. "Yes, I know about male dogs. And no, I wasn't looking for Buster. We were taking a walk."

As Shay moved toward her, he said, "I see. And you just happened to walk by my house?"

When he came to a halt in front of her, she replied, "Sort of. Buster started in this direction, and I just followed."

"So I have that mutt of yours to thank for this visit?"

She smiled at the disappointment she heard in his voice. "I suppose that's true. When I realized where he was heading, I considered calling him back, but then I . . . I decided not to."

"You wanted to come here?" He reached out and ran his fingertips down the side of her neck. "You wanted to see me?"

Her shoulders quivering at his touch, she opened her mouth to respond, then clamped her lips shut. For the first time in her life she wasn't sure she should speak the truth. She'd never had a problem being honest, but this time she wondered if doing so would be going too far. Maybe this was one of the times her parents had warned her about. Maybe she was being too brash, too independent. Such behavior had never seemed inappropriate in the past. She'd spent her entire adult years living under the philosophy she'd adopted as a child—do what you want and to hell with the consequences—and she'd never had reason to question her convictions. Until then. She looked up at Shay, saw her need mirrored in his dark brown eyes, and felt herself falling deeper under the spell that had been cast over her. Swallowing hard, she finally managed a jerky nod.

He chuckled. "Seems that cat has your tongue now." He ran his fingers down her cheek, then across her mouth. Bending his head until the silky hair of his mustache brushed the side of her face, he said, "I can think of a few ways to cure that." In a wickedly softer voice he murmured his list of suggestions into her ear.

Sheridan's eyes widened at his graphic words, her face burning with a flush—not of embarrassment but anticipation—her heart speeding up to beat double time. She leaned toward him, the tightened tips of her breasts grazing his shirt and the hard muscles beneath. The depth of her need for this man and how quickly her heart had become involved frightened her. Her doubts of a moment before returned. Perhaps she had acted rashly and should rethink the situation. Drawing an unsteady breath, she said, "Shay, maybe I shouldn't have come here. Maybe this isn't—"

"Shh," he said against her temple, wrapping his arms around her waist and pulling her close. "We're adults with adult needs, right? And we both want you to be here, so stop analyzing and let whatever happens happen, okay?"

Several seconds passed before he felt the top of her head bobbing against his jaw, a gesture he recognized as a nod of agreement. He squeezed his eyes closed for a second and eased out the breath he hadn't realized he'd been holding.

He moved his hands to her upper arms, then held her away from him. "Shall we go inside, where we can be more comfortable?'' he said, his gaze glued to her face, watching for her reaction.

She swallowed, drew a deep breath, then exhaled slowly. Looking him square in the eye, she said, ''As I told you, I hadn't planned on coming here, so I'm not prepared.''

His brow furrowed. ''Prepared?''

''Did I misunderstand what you just whispered in my ear? I thought you said you wanted me naked in your bed. If that's the case, we need some kind of contraceptive. I hope you're better prepared than I am.''

Her candid statement made Shay's mouth twitch with amusement. He never thought he'd find such a blunt woman to his liking, but he'd been wrong. In fact, if he wasn't careful, this *liking* he had for Sheridan Kinmont could turn into something stronger—a whole lot stronger. He already wanted her more than he'd ever wanted a woman. He frowned. Hell, he hadn't had a woman in recent memory, so his wanting Sheridan shouldn't be a surprise. But aside from desiring her, he'd never found a woman as intriguing or as— Sheridan shifted, bringing the foolish notions tumbling around in his mind to a halt. Clearing his throat, he said, ''You didn't misunderstand, and yeah, I'm prepared.''

He released his hold on her arms, then turned so they stood side by side. Placing a hand on the small of her back, he urged her toward the house. ''Come on, let's go inside,'' he said, shortening his stride to match hers. ''Would you like some brandy? I still have the bottle you gave me.''

Sheridan glanced up at him, her brow crinkled. ''Am I going to need the fortification of liquor?''

Shay came to a halt, then threw back his head and laughed. ''Not at all. I just thought a glass of brandy might relax you.'' When his laughter faded, he stared down into her mesmerizing eyes. ''On second thought, I don't want you to have any brandy. When I make love to you, Sherry, I want you stone-cold sober.''

As they continued toward the house, his last words echoed

in Sheridan's head. A throbbing heat ignited in her stomach, then moved lower to settle between her thighs. She walked beside him in a daze, her senses on full alert, every nerve ending tingling with anticipation. How a man could make her want him so easily, or so fiercely, went completely beyond her understanding.

When she stepped up onto the porch, she abruptly stopped. "Wait," she said, swinging around to face the street. "Where's Buster?"

Shay turned. "Last time I saw him, he was sniffing around a cactus across the street." He squinted into the fading evening light. "Yeah, there he is," he said, pointing to a large prickly-pear cactus. "If he'll behave himself, he can come inside."

Sheridan shot him a peeved look. "Buster's well mannered. He always behaves himself."

Shay lifted a hand in surrender. "Hey, I was just going by personal experience. He took an instant dislike to me, so I wasn't sure what to expect. Go ahead and call him."

When Buster came running up onto the porch, then sniffed Shay's boots without so much as growl, Sheridan said, "See there, he likes you now."

As Shay opened the door for Buster and Sheridan, he said, "I hope you're right." Not wanting to figure out why he cared whether Sheridan's dog liked him, he stepped over the threshold into the dim interior of his house.

Sheridan waited for her eyes to adjust, then glanced around the room. The house was similar to hers, the stone walls holding much of the day's heat at bay, the furnishings austere though adequate. There were several framed photographs sitting on a table along with a leather-bound book, but from where she stood she couldn't make out the subjects of the photos or the book's title. Other than Shay's hat hanging on the wall by the door, she saw nothing of a personal nature in the room.

Buster finished his own investigation of the house, then moved to the rug in front of the fireplace. Turning in a circle several times, he finally lay down, dropping his muzzle onto his front paws.

Sheridan smiled at the dog. "Good boy." His tail wiggled once, then he sighed and closed his eyes. Keeping her voice low, she said to Shay, "See, I told you he'd be—" A pair of male arms wrapping around her from behind made her forget what she'd started to say.

"God, I love how you smell," Shay murmured, pressing his lips to the side of Sheridan's neck and filling his lungs with the scent of vanilla. "Let me make love to you."

She turned in his arms, then rose on her toes to press a gentle kiss on his mouth. "Yes," she whispered. The flare of heat in his eyes dissolved the last of her apprehension over her forward behavior.

In his bedroom Shay lit a lamp on the dresser, then moved to the bed and tossed back the covers. When he turned back to Sheridan, she stepped into his arms. Praying there wouldn't be a repeat of his embarrassing first intimate encounter with her, he tried to push such thoughts aside and captured her mouth with his.

They helped each other undress, then resumed kissing, this time lying face-to-face on the bed. "You're incredible," Shay said, pushing a wavy tendril of chestnut hair off Sheridan's face. "You make my head spin. Are you sure we didn't have that brandy we talked about? All of a sudden I'm feeling tipsy."

She chuckled. "No, we skipped the liquor, but I feel the same way." She moved her mouth closer to his, and ran her tongue over his lower lip. "You're a talented kisser. Did you know that, Mr. Bannigan?" Not giving him a chance to respond, she said, "Of course you do. A man with your experience would surely know all the secrets of kissing." Pushing aside the surprising jealousy her statement spawned, she settled her mouth firmly atop his.

Shay groaned, wrapped an arm around her, and hauled her flush against him. Her tightened nipples pressed into his chest, the soft hair between her thighs cradled his throbbing erection. He loosened his grip enough to run his hand up and down her back, the silky texture of her skin further fraying the already precarious hold he had on his control. He wanted to touch her everywhere, press his lips to her heated skin, taste her woman's flesh. He wanted to do everything imaginable to the woman in his arms, but he doubted he'd get very far down the list before giving into his own need. And he couldn't risk another episode of humiliation by waiting.

As he pulled his mouth from hers, Sheridan moaned in protest. "More," she said in a voice she didn't recognize as her own.

"Give me a minute." Shay rolled away from her, then got out of bed and moved to the dresser.

"What's wrong?"

"Nothing," he replied, opening one of the drawers.

She pushed herself up onto one elbow. "Then, what—" When he turned and she saw what he held in his hand, she smiled and dropped back onto the mattress. "Glad you remembered. I was thinking about other things."

As he returned to the bed and sat down on the edge of the mattress, he chuckled. "I promised to provide the protection, didn't I?"

"Uh-huh," she replied, reaching out to run her fingers down the length of his spine. A shudder racked his shoulders.

"Hey, stop that. I'll never get this damn thing on if you don't keep your hands to yourself."

"Want some help?"

"No," Shay said in a near shout. Lowering his voice, he added, "Uh, thanks, but I can handle it."

Her whispered "Maybe next time you'll let me handle it" sent a shock wave through his system. No woman had ever asked to help him don a condom, and even if one had, he never would have agreed. Yet, for a fleeting moment the idea of Sheridan's hands pulling the rubber shield over his engorged—

He bit back a curse, then turned his attention to finishing a task he'd done countless times but now found awkward and intimidating.

When he'd finally managed to sheath himself, he turned and stretched out on the mattress beside Sheridan. He had hoped the diversion of finding and putting on the condom would take the edge off his raging desire, but as was proving to be the case ever since Sheridan Kinmont's arrival in town, nothing worked out as he expected. As soon as his fingers touched her naked flesh and he kissed her pliant mouth, he knew he wouldn't last much longer. Moving his hand lower, he slid his fingers between her thighs. He had to make sure she was ready to accept him, because waiting was no longer an option.

He found her hot and slick, her hips lifting to meet his intimate touch, her clitoris already swollen. God, she was incredible. Exhaling a relieved breath, he pressed one more kiss on her lips, then rose to his elbows.

"I can't wait any longer," he murmured, pushing her onto her back, then moving onto his knees between her parted legs. He leaned forward, carefully opened her, then eased just the tip of his sheathed organ inside. Taking a deep breath, he pushed, slowly sinking his hardened flesh into her body. Her inner muscles clenched around him, wringing a groan from his chest. "Forgive me. I don't want to hurt you, but I—" His hips jerked forward, finishing his slow descent in one clean thrust.

Sheridan gasped. Not from pain, but from an unbelievable sensation of completeness. Wrapping her arms around his neck, she tried to pull his face down to hers, but he resisted. He held himself perfectly still, a muscle ticking in his tense jaw. "Relax, Shay," she whispered. "You didn't hurt me. "In fact, you feel wonderful." To illustrate her words, she lifted her hips off the bed and rotated her pelvis against his.

He didn't react for a second, then he blinked, the tension easing from his face. Another groan rumbling in his chest, he moved slightly, a tentative thrusting motion of his hips. He drew a ragged breath, then dropped his head and pressed a quick kiss on her mouth. "Better hang on, Sherry, this could be a hard ride."

Shay hadn't been kidding, Sheridan realized a few moments later as she wrapped her legs more firmly around his hips and tightened her hold on his neck. His hard thrusts intensified, pounding against her in a frenzy, until he cried out. The rhythm of his hips increased even more, pushing her deeper into the mattress. Then he abruptly froze. Head thrown back, nostrils flared, his body's only movement was the throbbing of his climax deep inside her. After a moment he released his held breath with a moan and collapsed atop her.

A few moments passed before he could move or speak. "Good Lord," he finally said in a breathless whisper. "I may not survive." Levering himself off her, he rolled to the side. His weight braced on one elbow, he stared down into her face. "What have you done to me?"

A devilish smile curving her lips, she lifted a hand and ran her fingers over his stubbled cheek. "I'm not sure, but I wish you'd do it to me."

Shay laughed, shaking his head. "You're a wonder. An absolute wonder."

She gave one side of his mustache a playful tug. "You're not so bad yourself."

"Not so bad, huh?" he said, leaning down to nibble on her lips. "I'll have to work on that."

Sheridan didn't reply; she couldn't, not after he'd taken possession of her mouth in a mind-drugging kiss and his hand moved down her belly and between her thighs.

He knew exactly how to bring her to the height of pleasure, rubbing her heated flesh with his skilled fingers. With each stroke the throbbing intensified. Her hips moved faster and faster, lifting to push against his hand, her body seeking relief. Just when she thought she couldn't stand the pleasure-pain for another instant, her release began. She said his name, a combination sob and shout, her body convulsing with wave after wave of incredible sensation.

"Yes, Sherry. I'm here," he whispered. "That's it, darlin'." He pressed a kiss to her temple. "That's it."

She continued thrusting her hips upward in rhythm with his fingers, then arched her back off the bed and went still. She held that position for several seconds, then dropped onto the mattress with a long sigh.

Shay bent to kiss her slack mouth, then rolled onto his back and pulled her into his arms. After a few minutes of peaceful, sated silence he said, "A lifetime of making love to you wouldn't be enough."

As soon as the words left his mouth, Shay's eyes went wide with shock. What the hell was wrong with him? He'd never spouted such nonsense in his life. Before he had time to analyze the reason for his statement, Sheridan's voice broke into his musings.

"I hope that wasn't meant as a marriage proposal." Before he could gather his thoughts and respond, she continued. "Because I don't intend to get married again." She yawned against his chest. "But that doesn't mean we have to stop seeing each other."

"What?"

She pushed away from him so she could see his face. "You're not looking for a permanent relationship, right?" At his curt nod she swallowed the disappointment she hadn't expected to feel over his response, then said, "Well, neither am I. So as long as we're both in Shafter, I don't see why we can't enjoy each other."

"You're suggesting we become lovers, a sexual relationship with no commitments, no promises?"

"Sure, why not? As you pointed out earlier, we're both adults with adult needs." Watching his face scrunch up in a fierce scowl, she said, "Is something wrong?"

"No, everything's fine," he replied, though he wasn't sure he'd spoken the truth. Something about her suggestion didn't sit right. Normally he would have jumped at the offer, thrilled to have found a woman with such an open attitude, but as he'd discovered, *normal* wasn't a word he associated with his dealings with Sheridan. Listening to her baldly state the ground rules for a relationship exactly as he'd done a number of times in the past had inexplicably rubbed him the wrong way. His reaction didn't make sense.

Not unless he'd fallen in love with her.

His body stiffened at the notion of being in love with Sheridan. Forcing himself to relax, he decided that wasn't the case. His unsettling reaction to Sheridan's proposition had to be because he wasn't used to women openly discussing sexual affairs.

Yeah, that had to be it. Glad he'd hit on a solution that made sense, he decided to accept what Sheridan offered. They would be lovers for as long as she stayed in Shafter. Then, just like with all the women in his past, their affair would end, she'd move on, and he'd forget her.

He glanced down at the woman now dozing in his arms, an unfamiliar pain clutching at his chest. At least, he hoped he'd be able to forget her.

Chapter Fifteen

Later that night Sheridan lay in her own bed, unable to fall asleep. Her conversation with Shay about their immediate future kept running through her mind. She didn't regret what she'd told him—she had no intentions of remarrying. Men couldn't be trusted, and she refused to risk another debacle like her first marriage. That's why her suggestion to become lovers with no commitments had been the perfect solution. However, a part of her balked at the idea of a physical involvement with Shay because there was one complication—her heart was involved as well. She'd fallen in love with him.

Her common sense told her the best thing for both of them would be for her to rescind her suggestion. Yet, her romantic side wouldn't give up so easily. Having experienced the blazing passion that sparked so easily between them and admitted to herself that she loved him, she refused to void the deal the two of them had struck. Still, she knew there would be a price to pay for ignoring her better judgment. When the time came, leaving Shafter and Shay might well be the hardest thing she'd ever done.

She finally drifted into a fitful sleep, her dreams alternating between erotic snippets of Shay making love to her and painful glimpses of her bidding him a final good-bye.

Late in the afternoon a few days later, out of boredom more than necessity, Sheridan decided to go through her medical supplies at the clinic and make a list of items to order. The day had dragged by, a frustration for Sheridan, since she would have welcomed the distraction of a constant stream of patients. Unfortunately in a town the size of Shafter, that didn't happen. Instead, she'd spent most of the day thinking about the previous evening and the hours spent in Shay's bed—hours she wouldn't soon forget.

Shay had invited her to have supper with him in the boarding-house dining hall, where many of the mine employees ate their meals. Her initial awkwardness at receiving the curious stares of the other diners quickly faded. Shay's relaxed smile and warm gaze made her forget there was anyone other than the two of them in the dining hall.

He told her more about his family—the fights he'd had with his brother as a boy and how close they'd become as adults, being overprotective when his sisters started accepting male callers, playing baseball with his many nieces and nephews. His obvious love of family struck a familiar chord in Sheridan and made her wonder why he'd never married. Unable to quell her curiosity, she spoke her thoughts aloud.

Shay didn't seem upset by such a personal question. Rather, he shrugged, then said, "Marriage isn't for me. I like my freedom too much." He flashed her a grin and added, "Besides, variety's what gives life all its flavor. Isn't that the old adage? So I can't imagine why I'd want to tie myself down to just one woman."

Sheridan stared at him for a moment, the words on the tip of her tongue to tell him she could be the one woman to change his mind. Just in time, memories of her failed marriage resurfaced and halted what would surely have been a mistake.

After they finished their meal, they went for a walk, ending up along the bank of the creek. There, beneath the leafy canopy of tall cottonwood trees and near the babbling waters of the creek, Shay drew her into his arms and kissed her. His mouth touched hers, gently at first, then became increasingly more demanding, seeking and finding her heated response. Widening his stance, he pulled her flush against him, the hard ridge of his arousal digging into her belly. She rose onto her toes, pressing closer, her tongue dipping into his mouth to elicit a rumbling groan in his chest.

He pulled his mouth free, his breathing harsh in the cool night air. "Much more of that, and I'll haul you to the ground and have you right here."

Sheridan's shoulders rippled with a quiver of excitement. "Hmm," she said, rubbing her nose in the open neck of his shirt. "Sounds interesting. Shall I help you undress?"

He chuckled, slapping her hands away from the buttons of his shirt. "No, Sherry. As appealing as the idea might be, I can wait. I don't want to take you here, sprawled in the dirt, in shadows so deep I can't see the expression on your face. I want you in my bed, your naked skin flushed and glowing with lamplight, your eyes gleaming with passion when I touch your breasts. I want to watch your reaction when I push my fingers through the lovely bush between your thighs and find the sweet nubbin hiding there. I want to see your face when your body convulses with your climax." He lowered his head to run his tongue over her lips. "Do you have any idea how much watching you excites me?"

She swayed on her feet, a moan vibrating in her throat. She swallowed, then said, "I—I'm not sure."

Shay chuckled again. "Well, you will, Sherry. You definitely will."

A shout from somewhere outside the clinic brought Sheridan's daydreams of the previous night to an abrupt halt. Drawing a ragged breath, she closed her eyes and willed her heart to stop its wild pounding. She couldn't believe how she'd reacted to Shay's kisses, his touch, his intimate possession of her body. And now, just thinking about the time she'd spent in his bed, she again ached with need, longing for the incredible moment when Shay made her lose control. She opened her eyes with a start, her lips pulled into a frown.

No, she hadn't broken her vow to never let a man control her. Shay wasn't controlling her actions—well, not entirely. He did know exactly how to arouse her to heights she'd never known, how to make her cry out her pleasure when she reached her peak. But just because he controlled her sexually, that didn't mean he also had control over the rest of her life. Hoping her conclusion was correct, she pressed her lips together with determination. One thing for certain, she'd have to take care not to confess she loved him—such an admission would definitely give him the control she didn't want to relinquish.

She drew a deep, steadying breath, then dragged her attention back to her task. After checking the last cabinet, she made a final notation on a pad of paper, then closed the cabinet door. Hearing voices coming from the waiting room, a wave of relief washed over her. Thank God, something to keep her mind off Shay.

She glanced around the examination room. Satisfied everything was in order, she moved to the washstand in one corner of the room. As she picked up a cake of soap, she heard the door open.

"Dr. Kinmont," Poppy said. "There's some folks here who'd like to see you."

"Thanks, Poppy," Sheridan replied, working the soap into a lather. "Send them in."

She heard Poppy murmur something to the patients in the outer room, followed by muffled footsteps and the swish of fabric. Rinsing her hands, she called over her shoulder, "I'll be right with you."

Towel in hand, she turned from the washstand. "Now, what can I—" Sheridan's mouth dropped open. "Mama! Daddy! What are you doing here?"

Jade and Eli Kinmont looked at each other, then chuckled. "Obviously you didn't know we were coming," Eli said.

"No, of course not. How would I—" Sheridan smiled at the man whose dark blue eyes were so similar to hers. "Ah, you still think I might acquire Gran's and Mama's psychic abilities, and that was another test."

"Busted," Eli replied with another chuckle, crossing the room to pull his daughter into his arms.

When he released her and moved aside, Jade stepped forward to hug Sheridan. Pressing a kiss on her cheek, she said, "Your father's just teasing you, honey. If the spirits were going to send you visions, I'm sure they would have done so long before now."

"Yes, I agree. How's Erik? When did you get back from Colorado? And why didn't you send word you were coming to Shafter?"

"Your brother's fine. He sends his love," Eli replied. "We've been back for several weeks. And we didn't send word because we didn't know we were coming. We were on our way to your grandparents' ranch, then"—he looked over at his wife—"at the last minute we decided to stop here first."

"Gran and Granddad are okay, aren't they? Going to Denver wasn't too much for them, was it?"

"They're fine," Jade said, moving to look around the room, "The trip was tiring for all of us, especially Mama and Papa, but they've recovered by now. We're going to visit your grandparents so I can help Mama prepare some of the medicines we use." She stopped in front of the glass cabinet containing Sheridan's medical equipment. "Eli, doesn't this examination room remind you of ours?"

He moved to stand next to his wife, one arm slipping around her waist. "Only some of our daughter's equipment is more modern than ours, *roja*." At forty-nine, Jade's mahogany hair still possessed the brilliant red highlights he'd found so fascinating when they first met. Her fire-filled hair and her fiery nature were the reasons he'd given her the nickname *roja,* Spanish for "red."

Sheridan heard the love in her father's voice, saw it in his expression, and suddenly wished she had someone who talked and looked at her like that. Shaking her head to clear such foolish notions, she said, "How long can you stay?"

"Just until tomorrow afternoon," Jade replied. "I sent word to your grandmother that we'd arrive by week's end, and I don't want to worry her by staying here any longer."

Sheridan nodded, moving close to her parents and looping an arm through her mother's. "Well, I'm so glad you decided to—"

The door to the waiting room burst open, allowing Poppy's outraged voice to filter into the room. "Now see here! I told you, you can't go in there. Dr. Kinmont is—"

"And I said, if Sheridan has a patient, then I'm—" Shay stumbled to a halt, his eyebrows knitted in a frown. His gaze skipped from Sheridan to the two other people in the room, a middle-aged couple he didn't recognize, then back to Sheridan.

Though Sheridan was annoyed at Shay's highhandedness in gaining entrance into her examination room, her blood quickened at the sight of him. Forcing aside her reaction to his presence, she said, "Did you need something, Mr. Bannigan?"

His frown deepened. "No, I thought you had a patient."

"I was just talking to my parents."

"Parents?" Shay blinked, his cheeks warming with a flush. "Sorry, I . . . uh . . . didn't mean to barge in."

"No harm done," Sheridan replied. Turning her gaze on her parents, she said, "Mama, Daddy, I'd like you to meet Shay Bannigan, general manager of the Presidio Mining Company." She shifted her gaze to Shay. "And, Mr. Bannigan, these are my parents, Eli and Jade Kinmont."

Shay cleared his throat, then took a step toward Eli. Sheridan's father matched him in height and was obviously fit for a man who had to be in his fifties. His gold-streaked light brown hair was heavily sprinkled with silver, his eyes nearly the same deep indigo as Sheridan's. Extending his hand, Shay said, "Pleased to meet you, Mr. Kinmont."

After Eli gripped his hand and offered a greeting, Shay turned to Jade and found the source for Sheridan's beauty. Jade Kinmont was indeed a lovely woman, slender and smooth skinned, her hair several shades darker than her daughter's with only a strand or two of gray and eyes an unusual silver-flecked green. Shay tipped his head in acknowledgment and said, "Mrs. Kinmont, it's a pleasure meeting you."

"The pleasure is mine, Mr. Bannigan," Jade replied, glancing at Sheridan, then at Shay, then back at her daughter. The air between them crackled with tension. But not from anger, Jade mused. Could this man be the reason the spirits had brought her there? Perhaps Shay Bannigan would be the man who faced the monumental task of convincing her daughter that men could be trusted, that it was safe for her to love again. Based on the heated looks the two exchanged, Jade felt certain she'd reached the correct conclusion.

"I apologize again for barging in," Shay said, shifting his narrowed gaze to Sheridan. "But your daughter didn't mention she was expecting you."

"Sheridan didn't know we were coming," Eli replied. "We were on our way to Sheridan's grandparents when Jade had another vis—" He flashed a quick glance at his wife. "That is, Jade had a sudden longing to see Sheridan, so we made a detour to Shafter.'' He smiled at Shay. ''You know how it is, Bannigan. When the woman you love gets a whim to do something, there's no way you can refuse her.''

Shay grunted but made no comment.

''Well,'' Sheridan finally said to break the silence. ''Let me show you two around the clinic.''

''If you'll excuse me,'' Shay said, ''I need to get back to my office.''

''Of course,'' Jade replied. ''Will you join us for supper, Mr. Bannigan? I'm planning on fixing the meal, since I know Sheridan isn't fond of cooking.'' She smiled at her daughter. ''Sorry, dear, but you know it's true.''

Sheridan laughed. ''You're right, Mama. I'm all thumbs in the kitchen. If it weren't for Poppy, I'd probably live on tinned fruit and vegetables.''

Jade's smile widened. ''As a child, all Sheridan wanted to learn was how to use plants and herbs to cure, and as she got older, all she thought about was becoming a doctor. She never cared about learning how to do household chores, especially cooking.'' She turned back to Shay. ''Anyway, Mr. Bannigan, if you're free this evening, you're more than welcome to join us.''

''Why don't you be my guests for supper in the company dining hall? Then you won't have to cook after your long trip.''

Jade glanced at her husband. When he nodded, she said, ''That's kind of you, Mr. Bannigan. We accept.''

Sheridan stood a few feet away, her gaze jumping back and forth between her mother and Shay. What was her mother doing? She couldn't recall her mother ever inviting someone she'd just met to supper. Remembering her father's slight falter when he explained their reason for coming to Shafter, her gaze narrowed. She was sure he'd started to say their decision was the result of her mother having another vision. Since he had no way of knowing she'd already told Shay about her mother's psychic abilities, naturally her father would be cautious in his choice of words around a stranger.

Her curiosity piqued about what the spirits had revealed in her mother's visions, she couldn't wait for the two of them to have a few minutes alone.

After Sheridan took her parents on a walking tour through town, they headed for her house. Since Poppy had left the clinic soon after Shay's arrival, Sheridan had hoped to invite her to join them for supper. But when they arrived at her house, the only occupant was an excited Buster. A note on the table said Poppy wouldn't be back until late.

"I wish you could stay here with me," Sheridan said once she'd shown her parents around the small house and Eli took Buster outside.

"That's all right, honey," Jade replied. "We'll be fine at the boardinghouse." Since Sheridan didn't have an extra bedroom, Shay had graciously offered her parents the use of one of the rooms normally reserved for company officials.

Jade turned from watching her husband throwing a stick for Buster in the front yard. "Mr. Bannigan certainly is a nice man." She studied Sheridan's face, searching for a reaction to her innocent statement. The sudden splash of color on her daughter's cheeks and the darkening of her eyes to a blue-black gave Jade the answer she sought.

"Um, yes," Sheridan replied, dropping her gaze from her mother's penetrating stare. "Shay is nice."

"By the way, what did he mean when he barged into the clinic? Something about when you're seeing a patient?"

Sheridan sighed, then sank into a chair. "From the moment I arrived here, Shay has made no secret of the fact that he doesn't think women should be doctors. He tried to get me to resign, but I refused. Ever since then he's been my shadow, watching over my shoulder while I treat patients—except my lady patients, of course, when I ban him from the examination room. He's even gone as far as hiring a man to watch the clinic and notify him whenever a patient arrives so he can be there to make sure I don't do something wrong."

Jade studied her daughter for a few moments, wondering if she'd misinterpreted the reason for the spirits sending her to Shafter. Maybe she'd been wrong to think Shay would have a place in Sheridan's future. She turned to look out the window again. Watching her husband, she remembered the first time she saw him. The day she found him lying hurt along a mountain trail. Treating Eli's physical injuries had been an easy task, but his tortured soul required much more care and took considerably longer to heal. Pursing her mouth thoughtfully, she realized that not only did Sheridan need Shay, but he needed her as well: to help him overcome his bias against women doctors. Satisfied with her conclusion, she swung back to face Sheridan. "I'm sure you can convince him he's wrong. You're an excellent doctor."

"Thanks, Mama, but I don't know if I can. He lost a sister because of an incompetent doctor who happened to be a woman. I'm not sure I, or anyone else, can change his mind."

Her voice low, Jade replied, "Love changes a lot of things."

"Love?" Sheridan eyed her mother, her brow furrowed. "Mama what did the spirits reveal in your visions about me?"

"What makes you think I've had visions about you?"

Sheridan's frown deepened. "Because Daddy said you decided to come see me after you had another vision."

Jade smiled. "I figured you'd catch his little slip. What your father said is true. We did come here because I had a vision while we were traveling. But you weren't in it. At least, I didn't see you." She closed her eyes, trying to recall that vision. "I thought I knew what the spirits were trying to tell me, but now . . ." She opened her eyes and shrugged. "Anyway, my latest vision was little more than shadows. Images of people that weren't fully formed. Then, just before the vision faded completely, the haze cleared and I saw Buster. I decided if the spirits showed me your dog, the vision must have something to do with you. That's why I told your father I wanted to stop here before going to see your grandparents. I had to make sure you were all right."

"You thought something had happened to me?"

Jade shook her head. "The vision didn't give me the impression that you were hurt." Not wanting to get into what she now believed to be her real reason for coming to Shafter until she knew if her speculations about Shay were correct, Jade decided to use an explanation she felt certain Sheridan would accept. "But after I saw Buster, the indistinct images in my vision frightened me, and since your father and I were so close to Shafter, I didn't want to take any chances."

Sheridan nodded but didn't comment. She knew both her mother and grandmother took what the spirits revealed to them seriously, and she'd learned at an early age not to question what either of them said they saw or heard in their visions— no matter how bizarre the descriptions sounded to her.

Chapter Sixteen

Though Sheridan feared supper with Shay and her parents would be nerve-racking at best, to her surprise, she soon discovered she'd worried needlessly. Shay acted the charming host, easily carrying the conversation and making her parents laugh at his stories, all the while embedding himself deeper into her heart.

"I'm afraid I don't know much about the mining business," Eli said to Shay after dessert had been served. "Can you explain it in terms a simple country doctor like me can understand?"

Shay leaned back in his chair. "We use the amalgamation process to extract the silver, which isn't all that complicated. Once the ore is dug out of the mine, it's hauled to the mill here in town, then crushed by steam-driven rollers. After water and mercury are mixed with the crushed ore, the entire mass is shaken to disperse the mercury, then heated. In the final stage the slag is removed and the silver poured into bars."

Eli nodded. "You're right. That doesn't seem as complicated as I'd imagined."

"The process sounds fascinating," Jade said. "You must enjoy such interesting work, Mr. Bannigan."

"I do. If you'd like, I'd be happy to take you on a tour of the mill sometime tomorrow. We'll steer clear of the boilers since it's too dangerous, but I can show you the rest of the operation."

"Thanks," Eli replied. "We'd like that. We have to leave by early afternoon, so how about in the morning? Around ten?"

"Fine," Shay said, pushing away from the table and getting to his feet. "Now, if you don't mind, I'll say good night. I'm sure you and Sheridan have a lot more catching up to do." He shook Eli's hand, then nodded to Jade. "I'll see you in the morning."

"We'll be there," Eli replied.

Shay nodded again, then shifted his attention to Sheridan. The heat in her indigo eyes almost made him forget propriety and do what he longed to do: sweep her into his arms for a sizzling good-night kiss. During the entire evening he'd ached to kiss her, to touch her, to claim her as his. Tamping down the urge to brush her lips in a brief kiss, he managed a murmured good night, then turned and left the dining hall.

As Shay walked away, Jade studied Sheridan's expression. Placing a hand on her daughter's arm, she said, "Honey, if there's something on your mind, you know you can talk to me about anything."

Sheridan blinked, then a brief smile flickered across her face. "Am I that transparent?"

Jade chuckled. "Not to everyone, but you are to me. Do you want to tell me what's going on between you and Shay Bannigan?"

Sheridan fiddled with her napkin. Though she'd always shared everything with her parents, this time she just couldn't bring herself to admit the truth. Finally she said, "Shay and I didn't get off on the right foot when I first got here. But recently we agreed to see each other socially after we reached an understanding.''

"An understanding?'' Eli said.

She nodded. "After what Winston did to me, you know how I feel about men and marriage. Shay also has no plans to marry. He enjoys women too much to ever settle for just one. So we agreed to some rules.'' She lifted her chin and met her mother's gaze. "No promises. No expectations. Just enjoy each other's company for as long as we're both in Shafter.'' She shrugged her shoulders. "Simple.''

"I see,'' Jade replied, not certain she did. Had she been wrong to think her daughter and Shay might have a future together? Glancing over at Eli, whose shrug told her he was equally confused, she said, "Well, if you ever need someone to talk to, I'm a good listener.''

"I know, Mama, and thanks,'' she replied, then put a hand over her mouth to cover a yawn. "I hope you don't mind, but I think I'll go home.''

"Patient keep you up late last night?'' Eli said.

Sheridan hoped the room was dark enough to cover the fiery blush warming her cheeks. "No, I just had trouble sleeping.''

Jade pushed her chair away from the table. "We should turn in too,'' she said. "It's been a long day.''

Eli helped his wife from her chair, then moved around the table to assist Sheridan. "Would you like me to walk you home?''

"That's not necessary, Daddy. I'll be fine.''

Eli nodded, then extended an arm to each woman and escorted them across the dining hall. When they stepped outside, Jade said, "What a lovely evening.''

"Hmm,'' Eli replied. "The cottonwoods remind me of the evenings we used to sit on the patio at your parents' ranch.''

"I loved the sound of the breeze ruffling the leaves overhead,'' Jade said, smiling at the memory. "Mama and Papa used to—oh, Sheridan, I nearly forgot. Your grandparents' anniversary is next week, and I wanted to ask if there's any chance you could come to the ranch to celebrate with us."

"As much as I'd love to see Granddad and Gran, I can't promise I'll be there. Do you think they'll be upset if I miss their anniversary?"

"Of course not, honey. We all know how important your job is to you, so they'll understand."

When the trio arrived at the boardinghouse, Jade turned to Sheridan and said, "Will you be able to join us for Mr. Bannigan's tour of the mill?"

"I don't know. Depends if I have patients to see."

"We'll stop by the clinic on the way to his office," Eli said. "If you can't go with us, we'll come back before we leave town."

Sheridan nodded. "I wish you didn't have to leave so soon."

"I know, honey," Jade replied. "So do we. Next time we'll make plans to stay longer."

After Sheridan said good night and started home, she stopped partway up the street and glanced back at her parents. She could see their shadowy figures in the light cast from one of the boardinghouse windows. As she watched her father pull her mother into his arms, then lower his face until their shadows merged with their kiss, a sharp pang clutched at her heart.

Determined to stop longing for a love like her parents shared, Sheridan pressed her lips into a firm line, then turned and resumed walking up the street. With every step she tried to persuade herself the convictions she'd adopted weren't wrong—that love and marriage didn't have a place in her future. Yet deep inside, a tiny bubble of hope refused to listen to her arguments.

The following morning Eli and Jade arrived at Shay's office promptly at ten.

Shay greeted them warmly, then said, "Will Sheridan be joining us?"

"Afraid not," Eli replied. "Poppy said a patient arrived just before we got to the clinic. We'll have to proceed without her."

Shay nodded, then pulled the brim of his hat down lower on his forehead, but not before Jade caught the flash of disappointment in his dark eyes. The man might be a confirmed bachelor, a ladies' man who held outdated views on women doctors, but intuition told her he was still the man her daughter needed. And unless Jade had misinterpreted her observations of both Sheridan and Shay, she also sensed they cared for each other. But whether they cared enough to chase the ghosts from their pasts remained to be seen.

After Shay finished giving the Kinmonts a tour of the mill, Eli stopped to speak to one of the engineers while Shay escorted Jade outside.

"I want to thank you again, Mr. Bannigan," she said, "for showing us through the mill. Eli and I appreciate your clearing what I'm sure is an extremely busy calendar to make time for us."

Shay chuckled. "I can always use a reason to get away from the stack of paperwork on my desk."

Jade smiled, then turned to look down Main Street. "Shafter is certainly nothing like San Francisco."

"You've been to San Francisco?"

"Once, a few years ago. I imagine it's bigger and busier than when Eli and I were there."

"I suppose it is," Shay replied, sweeping his gaze over the small, dusty town.

"I've been lucky enough to visit a number of large cities, but I much prefer the slower life here in this part of Texas, even if it means doing without some of the fancy modern conveniences."

Shay started to respond, then snapped his mouth shut, appalled by what he'd nearly said. Damn, he'd almost defended

Shafter's lack of amenities! Where the hell had that thought come from? The town was still as backward, still as remote, still as hot—okay, hotter than it was on the day he'd arrived. Yet for some reason, what he disliked about the place didn't bother him nearly as much. The idea that he was actually getting used to Shafter crossed his mind, making him twist his face into a scowl.

When the silence continued to stretch between them, Jade said, "I hope you don't think I'm interfering, Mr. Bannigan, but there's something I want to say to you about my daughter."

Shay snapped out of his musings and shifted his gaze to Jade. "What about her?"

"I'm sure you've discovered how, shall we say, spirited Sheridan can be."

Shay lifted a hand to smooth one side of his mustache, his mouth curved in a faint smile. "Yes, I learned that on the day she arrived."

"From the time she was just a child she always possessed a willful, independent nature. Once she made up her mind to do something, her father and I just looked at each other and cringed, then crossed our fingers that whatever she wanted to do wouldn't end in disaster." She chuckled. "You might find this hard to believe, but she isn't as impetuous as she was as a girl. My point is, Mr. Bannigan, don't let Sheridan's headstrong ways fool you into thinking she doesn't have a kind and loving heart."

Shay mulled over her words for a moment, then said, "Did Sheridan say something about me? Is that why you're telling me this?"

Jade gave him a sheepish smile. "Actually I'm the one who brought you into the conversation I had with her. I wasn't trying to pry, but I sensed—well, that doesn't matter. Sheridan admitted you two butted heads when she first arrived. But she also told me you're now seeing each other socially." She paused for a moment to gather her thoughts. "I know my daughter could use the occasional guidance of a firm hand on the reins of her temperament, but I'd hate to see someone try to break her wonderful spirit in the process. She needs to be handled like a skittish mare, with a firm but loving and gentle touch." She tipped her face up to meet his gaze. "Am I making any sense?"

Shay stared down at her, trying to figure out whether she meant to warn him off or offer encouragement. Unable to decide about her motive, he finally said, "Yes, I think you are."

Before Jade could say anything more, Eli joined them. After he thanked Shay again and the two men shook hands, Eli and Jade said their good-byes then headed back to the clinic. Shay watched the couple walk away and finally turned toward the mine offices.

As Eli and Jade prepared to leave Shafter an hour later, Eli looked over at his wife and said, "What's your opinion of Bannigan?"

"I like him," she replied.

"Even though he's a philanderer?"

"People change when they fall in love." She sent him a dazzling smile. "You should know that."

Eli stared at Jade for moment, remembering how bitter and irritable he'd been when they first met and how Jade's love and devotion helped him shed the pain from his past. He finally returned her smile. "Yes, I know what love can do, *roja.*" He moved closer and pressed a quick kiss on her mouth. "Are the spirits predicting our daughter and Shay Bannigan will fall in love?"

Jade sighed. "I'm not sure. The spirits are being stingy with what they reveal to me."

"Well, if he turns out to be the man who can handle Sheridan without dampening her independent nature *and* love her, then all I can say is Shay Bannigan has both my profound pity and my deepest gratitude."

Her mood lightening, Jade chuckled. "I agree."

* * *

The following day Betsy Pringle showed up at the clinic complaining of pain in her side. When Sheridan examined the woman, she found a long purple bruise on the lower part of her rib cage.

"How did this happen, Betsy?"

"Just me bein' clumsy again," she replied, though she wouldn't meet Sheridan's gaze. "I . . . uh . . . stumbled and fell against a table."

When Sheridan opened her mouth to reply, Shay's voice drifted to her from the waiting room. "Betsy, will you excuse me for a minute?"

At the woman's nod, Sheridan said, "You can go ahead and get dressed," then turned and crossed the room. As she reached for the knob, the door opened to reveal Shay on the opposite side. Her mouth pulled into a frown, she put her hand on his chest and pushed him backward. Stepping through the doorway, she shut the door behind her, then said, "You can't go in there." Before he could reply, she grabbed his arm, turned him around, and practically shoved him to the other side of the waiting room.

"Who's in there?" he said, stumbling to a halt and shaking off her hand.

"Betsy Pringle. She says she fell and hurt her ribs but I don't believe—"

"Dammit, I told you to stay out of their marriage."

"I know what you said, but—"

"Just leave it alone, Sheridan. You've got no business interfering in people's marriages."

"Even when a husband strikes his wife?"

The muscles of Shay's jaw worked. "Look, I'm not saying I condone any man lifting a hand to a woman. But this is still none of your concern."

"If a doctor can't stand up for an injured patient and try to correct the situation, then who can?'' Before Shay could respond, she turned on her heel and started back toward the examination room.

He caught up with her just as she reached the door. His fingers gripping her elbow in a gentle but firm hold, he forced her to look at him. "I mean it, Sheridan," he said in a gruff whisper. "Keep your nose out of the Pringles' marriage. If she's not happy, then she'll have to be the one to do something about it."

Sheridan stared up into his dark eyes, her heart pounding in a wild rhythm from his nearness, the scent of his heated skin making her light-headed. Knowing he was right about the decision being Betsy's, she finally released a long sigh. "Fine," she replied in a low voice. "I won't say anything to her about leaving her husband."

Shay studied her face, trying to gauge the sincerity of her response. Finding nothing suspicious in her expression, he relaxed his tense muscles. When she tried to pull free of his grasp, he tightened his fingers on her arm. "Wait. Can I see you tonight?"

Though Sheridan wanted to tell him no—out of spite for maneuvering her into backing down on her stand about Betsy Pringle—she couldn't bring herself to refuse. "I have plans for supper, so it'll have to be later."

"Your house?"

She glanced over at Poppy to make sure they weren't being overheard. Shifting her gaze back to his face, she lowered her voice even more. "No, I'll come to yours."

Shay longed to haul her close and kiss her senseless, but he resisted the urge. Releasing her arm, he murmured, "Until later," then took a step back. Loud enough for Poppy to hear, he said, "Good day, Miss Kinmont," turned, and started toward the door. As he passed Poppy's desk, he nodded, then stuck his hat on his head and left the clinic.

Sheridan stared at the front door until she felt Poppy's gaze.

Snapping out of her daze, she drew a fortifying breath, then went back into the examination room.

"Sorry for the interruption," she said, hoping Betsy didn't notice the huskiness of her voice. "Now, where were we?"

"I was tellin' ya about falling and hurting my side."

Sheridan frowned. "Are you sure that's what happened, Betsy? I thought we'd gotten beyond your making up stories."

The woman dropped her gaze to her lap, nervously twisting her hands together. "I did hurt myself when I fell, but I didn't really stumble. Lenny shoved me." She looked up, a glint of defiance in her pale green eyes. "But he had every right to. I didn't have supper on the table quick enough to suit him, so he grabbed me and gave me a shove."

Sheridan had to bite her tongue not to try again to persuade Betsy to get out of her marriage. Instead, she went to one of the cabinets and removed a glass jar from one of the shelves. Holding the jar out to Betsy, she said, "Rub this salve on your side twice a day. It should help with the soreness. If you're not feeling better in a couple of days, come back and I'll wrap your ribs."

Betsy accepted the jar with a nod. As she slid off the examination table and stood, she said, "You still got that Mex kid workin' for ya? I ain't seen him around here lately."

"Enrique?" Sheridan replied, swallowing her annoyance at Betsy's insensitive referral to the boy. "Yes, he works a couple of afternoons a week."

"I saw him at the company store the other day. Guess he still works there too, huh?"

Sheridan nodded. "Mr. Neilson says Enrique has been a real help to him."

"So what's he do at the store?"

Sheridan gave Betsy a quizzical look, wondering at the woman's sudden interest in Enrique. Remembering the woman didn't have any other friends, she decided Betsy was just making conversation. "He does a lot of different things. Makes deliveries. Stocks shelves. Sweeps the floors. Locks up after the store closes."

"But Mr. Neilson is there when he locks up, right?"

"I don't think so. Why?"

Betsy shrugged. "No reason. I'm just surprised Mr. Neilson lets anybody lock up his store. Reckon that means he trusts the kid."

"Yes, he does," Sheridan replied, turning her attention to setting her supply cabinet to rights.

"Well, I gotta go. Lenny'll be wanting his supper as soon as he gets home. Bye, Dr.—I mean Sheridan."

"Good-bye, Betsy," she said. "Be sure to use that salve."

Betsy murmured an affirmative reply, then started toward the door of the examination room.

Sheridan opened her mouth to add another piece of advice, then she remembered her conversation with Shay. Fear for Betsy's safety almost made her speak out anyway, but she finally clamped her lips shut.

Ever since she'd taken up the cause of women's rights, she'd never held back speaking out against any form of injustice to women. And as for Betsy not wanting to leave her husband, she'd faced the same resistance before. She'd continued counseling those women, hoping to convince them they could break the cycle of violence in their marriages, that there were alternatives. She eventually succeeded with many of those she tried to help. But with the others—women she hated to think about for fear they hadn't survived their husbands' violent behavior—her efforts failed.

She balled her hands into fists. She didn't want to add Betsy Pringle to her list of failures. Closing her eyes against the anguish that thought caused, she wondered why she told Shay she wouldn't say anything to Betsy. As the answer to her pondering formed, her eyes popped open.

She loved him.

"Oh, God," she said with a soft groan. *If this is what love does to a person, I don't think loving Shay is a good idea.*

Chapter Seventeen

By the time Sheridan headed for Shay's house later that night, she'd come to another realization: Regardless of whether loving Shay was a good idea, she couldn't change how she felt. In spite of his infuriating demands and his strong bias against women doctors, she loved him.

"Heaven help me, but I do," she muttered to herself, moving up the steps of his house. As she started across the porch, she warned herself to take care not to reveal her feelings. If she thought loving Shay wasn't a good idea, she dreaded finding out what would happen if she confessed her love. Lifting a hand to knock on the door, she decided he'd probably throw her out on her ear, or, worse, laugh in her face.

When the door swung open and Shay's mouth curved into a smile of welcome, her painful musings scattered like dust in a windstorm.

"Come in," he said, stepping aside to let her enter. After she moved past him, he looked outside. "Where's the mutt?"

"I left him home." Noticing the look on his face, she said, "You're not disappointed that I didn't bring Buster, are you?"

"No. I just wanted to see if the little piss-willy is really getting used to me."

"That's not a very nice name to call my dog."

Shay chuckled. "It's only an expression. I didn't mean anything by it." He closed the door, then turned to look at her. "Besides, you've got to admit, he was a growling terror around me. Hell, I thought he was gonna take a chunk out of my leg."

"I told you, he was just being protective," she replied, moving farther into the room and taking a seat on the sofa.

"You also told me Buster doesn't like men." When she didn't respond, he said, "What happened to make him that way?"

Sheridan glanced up, watching him move to sit down next to her. Finally she said, "My family has always had dogs, and I missed not being able to have one of my own while I attended college and then medical school. I planned to get a dog as soon as I settled into a routine as a doctor. But then I returned from Europe and met Winston and accepted his proposal." She inhaled a deep breath and released it slowly. "Anyway, a couple of months before my wedding, Buster showed up on my doorstep one day. He was dirty and hungry, so I took him in and started looking for his owners. When no one claimed him after a few weeks, I was relieved, because by then I didn't want to give him up. Winston tried for days to talk me out of keeping Buster, but then he finally dropped the subject."

"Did he do something to the dog?"

Sheridan frowned. "I don't know. I never saw him do anything. Buster and Winston tolerated each other, I guess is the best way to describe their relationship. I didn't think much about it because I knew Winston had never had a dog and getting used to having one around would take time. But a few months after our wedding, Buster suddenly started growling whenever Winston got near him. I knew something had happened, but Winston claimed he'd only scolded Buster for getting muddy paw prints on our new hallway carpet. But I doubt just a scolding would make Buster react the way he did."

"And the dog hasn't liked men since?"

Sheridan nodded. "He was okay around men he already knew, like Daddy and Granddad. But he's real skittish around men he doesn't know."

"Like me?"

"Yes, but I told you, he's getting used to you. Dogs have a sixth sense, an instinct, I suppose, that tells them when they aren't liked. Buster's a smart dog. He already knows you like dogs, or he wouldn't have stopped growling at you. He's still wary. But he'll be your friend as soon as he's convinced you're no threat to him or to me."

Shay scooted closer to her. "So when he stops being such a piss-willy, then I'll know we're friends?"

She chuckled, the husky sound sending a ripple of desire zooming through his body. "Yes, I guess that's what I mean."

As he lowered his face to hers, he heard her breathing hitch, saw the wild beat of her pulse at the base of her throat. "Then I look forward to being Buster's friend." His voice dropping lower, he ran his fingertips down the side of her neck. "But right now I look forward to being a whole lot more than a friend to his owner."

Sheridan made a sound in her throat, something between a whimper and a moan. Goose bumps popped out on her arms and a tight knot of heat formed low in her belly. She looped her arms around his neck and lifted her mouth to meet his.

Her fingers fisting in his hair, she let her eyes drift closed, giving herself over to the mastery of his kiss. He rubbed his lips against hers, gently at first. then increasing the pressure until she opened her mouth to him. His tongue plunged inside, tasting her, teasing her, tightening the knot of heat in her belly.

When he withdrew his tongue, she took the initiative and pushed her tongue into his mouth, wrenching a groan from deep in his chest. He pulled her tighter into his embrace, forcing her breasts to flatten against his hard muscles. As she continued to duel with his tongue, her breathing became more erratic, her need quickly increasing to an all-consuming fire in her blood.

She finally wrenched her mouth from his. "I . . . can't . . . breathe." Gulps of air punctuated her words.

Shay managed a shaky chuckle. Resting his forehead against hers, he said, "Yeah, me too." When his breathing slowed to nearly normal, he lifted his head and stared down into her passion-filled eyes. "I want to make love to you, Sherry."

A shiver of anticipation raced up her back. Unable to speak past the tightness in her throat, she nodded.

He smiled, then pushed himself off the sofa and got to his feet. Shocked when his knees nearly buckled under his weight, he closed his eyes, willing his strength to return. *God, my legs are actually shaking.* Once he recovered from his momentary weakness, he opened his eyes and offered his hand to Sheridan. He pulled her up next to him, then without saying a word led her to his bedroom.

The dimly lit room's open window allowed a cool breeze to ruffle the curtains, then waft across the turned-down bed. As Sheridan pictured herself on the crisp white sheets, Shay poised above her, another shiver rippled over her. She turned to look up at him and saw the raw need reflected in his dark eyes.

Their clothes quickly became a jumbled pile in the middle of the floor. Kicking his last piece of clothing to one side, Shay reached for her. His arms wrapped around her waist, he toppled backward onto the bed, a laughing Sheridan landing on top of him.

"Impatient, are you?" she said.

"Yes," he replied, running his hands down the smooth length of her back to cup her bottom. "Something else is impatient too," he said in a husky whisper, flexing his hips to press his erection more firmly against her belly.

She laughed again. "You're terrible."

He lifted his head from the pillow and brushed her lips with his. "No, I'm not. I'm good. Damn good, and you know it."

She pressed a kiss to his chin. "Do I? Well, I do know one thing. You're definitely not modest."

"That's right," he murmured. "I know women, and I know how to please them."

His words sent a sharp pain through Sheridan's chest. Ignoring the sudden spurt of jealousy, she tried for a lightness in her voice. "Well, if you're so knowledgeable, how about putting your claim to the test?" She wriggled her hips, rubbing against his hardened length.

A growl vibrating in his throat, he rolled them until their positions were reversed. "At your service, Sherry," he said, his heated gaze boring down into hers. He lifted a hand and brushed a lock of chestnut hair off her cheek. "You know we're wonderful together." As he lowered his face closer to hers, he whispered, "I'm the best lover you'll ever have." Hot on the heels of that statement came an astounding revelation. He couldn't stand the idea of another man replacing him as Sheridan's lover. Stunned by the direction of his thoughts, he quickly banished them as absurd.

Sheridan didn't doubt Shay's boastful words for one minute, but rather than add to his already enormous self-esteem, she said, "More bragging. My, you are full of yourself, aren't you?"

"For the moment," he replied with a low chuckle. "But soon"—he brushed a gentle kiss on her lips—"you'll be the one who's full of me."

His fierce possession of her mouth halted her hoot of laughter. Looping her arms around his neck, she pulled him closer, arching her back to press her aching breasts against his chest. She dug her heels into the mattress and lifted her hips in a silent plea for relief.

He finally pulled his mouth away from hers. "Easy, Sherry," he said, shifting to run his tongue down her neck. "Give me a minute to catch my breath." Shoving himself up onto his hands and knees, his gaze moved from her flushed face to the rise and fall of her breasts, then on to the triangle of dark chestnut hair.

He swallowed hard, nearly overwhelmed by the urge to push her legs apart and bury himself in her heat. Somehow he finally managed to wrestle his need into temporary submission, allowing him to concentrate on Sheridan's pleasure.

His hands skimmed down her body, cupping and lifting her breasts, caressing the concave satin of her stomach, stopping less than an inch from the enticing hair-covered mound shielding her sex. Scooting farther down the mattress, he pushed his fingers through the silky nest of hair and found her clitoris. He rubbed the bud of flesh with the pad of his thumb and heard her breath catch. Bending forward, the tip of his tongue flicked out to replace his fingers. This time she gasped his name, her body going rigid.

"It's all right, Sherry. Don't tense up on me. I just want to love you."

Before she could form a reply in her muddled, passion-drugged brain, he touched her again with his tongue. This time he slowly licked her, repeated the motion, then twice more. She couldn't think, couldn't get enough air into her lungs. Her fingers clutched at the sheet on either side of her hips, the knot of heat in her belly growing larger and hotter. She'd never experienced anything approaching the sensations storming her body, nothing had ever felt so good. Until he closed his lips around the swollen nubbin and sucked.

She cried out, her hips bucking up at the incredible streak of wildfire zinging through her body. The intimate pull of his mouth stoked her need into a white-hot flame. As her hips moved faster and faster, the pressure continued to build between her thighs, moving ever closer to the crest of her release. Her head thrashed on the pillow, her fists tugging and twisting the sheet at her sides, her breathing harsh gasps for air.

Shay gentled his sucking and changed to a rhythmic flicking of his tongue. Sheridan's sharply inhaled breath ended with her moaning his name.

"Yes, darlin', yes," he murmured between flicks of his tongue, moving one hand to slip a finger inside her. God, she felt incredible, her tight passage hot and slick. Praying he could remain in control, he continued his ministrations, laving her swollen clitoris with his tongue, mimicking the sex act with his finger.

Sheridan couldn't take much more, her nerve endings raw, her body clamoring for relief. Then abruptly she cleared the final obstacle of her quest. Holding her body rigid for a moment, a loud humming sound filled her head. Then sobbing Shay's name, she exploded with her orgasm.

She continued the thrusting motion of her hips, her breathing growing more ragged until she pushed up one final time, then dropped back onto the mattress with a long, rasping sigh. Her muscles quivered from exertion, and her fingers ached from clutching the sheet, but she'd never been more content.

After a moment Shay shifted, pressed a kiss on her inner thigh, then sat back on his heels and looked down at Sheridan. Her eyes were closed, her cheeks flushed, her breasts heaving with her labored breathing. She was incredibly lovely, incredibly passionate, and she was his. But only for the time being, he reminded himself. A temporary diversion in his life, just like all the women in his past.

The notion that he would eventually grow weary of Sheridan and end their relationship, letting her down gently as he'd always done, hit him like a punch in the gut. Sheridan was different. She would never bore him, but challenge him at every turn with her quick mind, fiery temper, and mile-wide independent streak. And then there was her passion. He bit his lip to hold in a groan. He'd have to be dead not to appreciate her passionate nature. She was definitely a rare gem. He closed his eyes for a moment, his throat clogged with an emotion he didn't recognize. Would he really be able to end their relationship when Whit finally came to his senses and fired her? Could he just turn his back and let her walk out of—

"Shay? Shay, are you all right?"

He blinked several times. "What?" His mind finally registering her words, he said, "Yeah, I'm fine."

"You had the strangest look on your face. Are you sure you're all right?"

Shay ran a hand through his hair, then nodded. Flashing a crooked smile, he said, "What about you?"

His smile eased her apprehension. "Terrific." She stretched, her lips curving into a smile.

He chuckled. "You look like a contented cat. All that's missing is the purring."

Her smile broadened. "If I could, I would." Her gaze met his. "You were right. Despite your deplorable lack of modesty, you are a wonderful lover."

He leaned forward to trace circles around the aureole of one breast with a fingertip. Smiling when the distended nipple tightened even more, he said, "That'll teach you not to believe what I tell you."

"Maybe," she replied in a throaty whisper, trying not to squirm under his touch. "Aren't you going to . . . I mean, don't you need to—will you stop that?" She tried to shove his talented fingers away from her breast. "I can't think straight when you're doing that."

His chuckle grew into a full-fledged laugh. Giving her nipple one last gentle pinch, he said, "Okay, I'll stop. For now." He pushed her knees farther apart, then shifted his position until he knelt between her thighs. Just as he leaned forward to join his flesh to hers, he halted his movement, cursing under his breath.

"What is it?"

"I almost forgot." He started to get out of bed. "I'll be right back."

She grabbed his arm. "Wait. You don't need a sheath this time. I took care of it before I left home."

He stared down at her through narrowed eyes. The thought of slipping into her warmth with no barrier between them sent a wild surge of apprehension through his veins. "You're sure you're protected?" At her nod, a slow grin deepened the laugh lines at the corners of his mouth. "Then let's let her rip."

As he joined their bodies with one smooth thrust, Sheridan's giggle ended with a soft gasping of his name.

"Bend your knees," he said in a low voice. She immediately complied, a flare of desire darkening her eyes.

He flexed his hips, pushing his throbbing member farther into her welcoming passage. When she lifted her legs and wrapped them around his waist, the new position allowed him to sink even deeper. Certain he'd never felt anything as wonderful, a guttural groan vibrated in his chest. As her inner muscles stretched to accommodate the intimate intrusion, gripping him in a slick, velvety heat, the need to seek his release soared. "Dear God," he whispered through clenched teeth, his blood roaring in his ears. Hoping he'd last more than a few seconds, he leaned forward and braced his weight on his forearms.

After drawing a deep, steadying breath, he began moving his hips in a slow thrusting motion. Sheridan quickly matched his rhythm, lifting her hips from the mattress to meet each of his downward thrusts. She sought his mouth with hers, kissing, licking, nipping at his lips until he finally jerked away from her.

"Easy, Sherry," he said in a breathless voice. "I'm on the edge as is it."

"Then I want to take you over it," she replied, her breathing as labored as his. Moving one hand down his muscular back, over a taut buttock, then beneath one hard thigh, she found her target. As she cupped his testes, he inhaled sharply, his body going rigid above her.

She relaxed her fingers but didn't remove her hand. "Am I hurting you?"

"Uh-uh," he finally managed to reply between gasping breaths.

"Good," she murmured. Tightening her hand just a fraction, she waited for him to make the first move.

A moment later the stiffness left his spine and he resumed his thrusting movements. As his breathing grew more labored and his hips moved in a faster rhythm, Sheridan whispered, "Kiss me, Shay."

He turned his head, his mouth finding and settling over hers. The kiss wasn't gentle, his lips wild and demanding. Just as he slipped his tongue into her mouth, she gave his testes a gentle but firm squeeze.

Shay jerked his mouth from hers. "Holy Christ!" Head thrown back, nostrils flared, veins bulging in his neck, he tried valiantly to cool the fever in his blood. But his efforts proved futile. Sheridan's boldness had severed the last strand of his quickly fraying self-control. With a primitive cry he thrust into her with a frenzied pumping of his hips, then went still. As he climaxed deep inside her, he moaned against her neck.

After several seconds he drew a ragged breath, then rolled onto his side. Completely drained, he lay next to Sheridan in a sated stupor, pondering what had just happened. He considered himself a knowledgeable and experienced lover, always in control, always able to curb his body's need for release. But with Sheridan, the rules had changed. She had turned him into a wild man, pounding into her like a lust-crazed youth who climaxed after only a few thrusts.

He closed his eyes and sighed. Why the hell had Whit asked him to be the general manager of the Presidio Mining Company? And, even more disturbing, why had he taken the job? Another thought crossed his mind, making him scowl. If he hadn't come to Shafter, he wouldn't have met Sheridan.

The two dozed for a few minutes, then Sheridan came awake

with a start. Searching her mind for what had roused her, she rose from the bed and started sorting through the pile of clothes on the floor.

Shay rolled onto his side, propped his head on one hand, and watched her. "We made quite a mess, didn't we?"

As she stepped into her drawers, she flashed him a smile. "Guess we were in a hurry, huh?"

"I'll say," he replied, returning her smile. "Need any help?"

"No. I haven't found my other shoe, but it has to be"—she reached under the bed—"ah, here it is." With hurried motions she jerked on the last of her clothes, then pulled on her shoes.

"What's the big rush?"

"I have to go home."

He sat up and swung his legs over the edge of the mattress. "Is something wrong?"

"I don't think so. But just in case, I'm going home."

"Sheridan, what's going on?"

Her gaze found his. The concern in his dark eyes touched her more than she cared to admit. "All of a sudden I had this feeling that something is going to happen. I need to be home in case someone is looking for me."

"What's going to happen?"

"I don't know. It was just a feeling."

He stared at her for several moments. "Is this one of those premonitions you told me about?"

She nodded. "I was half asleep, when a strange sensation woke me. It was nothing specific, kind of a nagging feeling that something was about to happen." Realizing how bizarre her explanation must sound, she shrugged. "Anyway, it's late, so I'd better head for home."

Shay got to his feet. Deciding to dispense with his underdrawers, he scooped his trousers off the floor. "Do any of these feelings ever turn out to be false alarms?" he said, stepping into a trouser leg.

She mulled over his question for several seconds. "Not so far."

As he escorted her to the front door, he finished buttoning his trousers. "Sleep well, Sherry," he murmured before pressing a firm kiss on her mouth. Lifting his head, he added, "And let me know when you find out the meaning of this premonition of yours."

She nodded, then turned to leave. Though she wasn't sure he believed her, she knew something was about to happen. She just didn't know what.

Chapter Eighteen

Early the next afternoon Sheridan left the post office and had started back to the clinic, when a man approached her on the street.

"You are the *doctora, sí*?" he said, jerking his hat from his head and running a hand through his straight black hair.

"*Sí*, I'm Dr. Kinmont," Sheridan replied, taking in the man's appearance. Of medium height and whipcord thin, his dust-covered clothes indicated he'd ridden long and hard. "What can I do for you, señor . . ."

"Gurza. Francisco Gurza. I need your help, *Doctora* Kinmont. Some of the people in my village are *muy malo*—very sick. I rode to Presidio late last night, looking for a doctor. But the people there say the new *doctora* in Shafter is the only one for many, many miles."

"I thought Presidio County had appointed a county physician."

"This is true. But I was told he is not scheduled to arrive until next month."

"What's the name of your village?"

"It is called Polvo."

Sheridan nodded. "I've heard of it. It's downriver from Presidio, isn't it?"

"*Sí,* about twenty miles. *Doctora* Kinmont, you will help my people, *por favor?*"

Sheridan nodded. "I have some things I need to take care of first, but, yes, Señor Gurza, I'll go to Polvo. Walk with me and tell me about the illness that has struck your village, then I want you to get something to eat and find a place to sleep.

"No, I will ride with you."

"*Gracias,* but you're staying here. You're in no condition to make another long ride." When he opened his mouth, she held up a hand to silence what she knew would be a protest. "Señor Gurza, was your family ill when you left Polvo?"

He shook his head. "I have a small farm up the canyon from the village. My wife is there with our four children. They were fine when I left, but what if the illness has reached them by now? What if they are calling for me? I should be—"

"If your family has taken ill, I promise I'll take care of them until you return. I know this hard for you, but, please, listen to me. As a doctor, I'm telling you it's important not to let yourself become ill by pushing yourself too hard. Rest for at least a day, then leave for home, *bueno?*"

Sheridan watched the emotions pass over his swarthy, weather-beaten face: anger, fear, then finally resignation. Putting his hat back on his head, he sighed. "*Sí,* I will do as you say."

After Francisco Gurza told her what he could about the illness plaguing the tiny community of Polvo, he went in search of something to eat and she headed back to the clinic. She explained the situation to Poppy while gathering the supplies she needed. "Do we have more aspirin powders?"

"No," Poppy replied. "The last order I placed hasn't come in."

"Well, I'll just have to make do with what I have. Will you put these in my medical bag, please?" She handed Poppy the bottles and packets of medicines she'd taken from the storage cabinet. "I need to go to the mine offices and tell Shay I'll be out of town for a few days."

"He'll probably get all hot and bothered."

Sheridan chuckled. "Maybe he will be angry, but that's too bad. There are sick people who need me, and I intend to treat them. Besides, he should calm down when I tell him you're capable of handling most medical problems while I'm gone."

"If he doesn't," Poppy replied, "don't you turn into a cross-patch."

"Don't worry. I have no intention of losing my temper." At Poppy's snort, Sheridan added, "Okay, so I might, but only if he pushes me too far."

Shay's reaction to Sheridan's announcement wasn't entirely what she expected. After she explained the circumstances, he expressed concern for the mine employees not having a doctor, then accepted her statement about Poppy's competence without comment. He stared at her for a moment, then said, "Is this what your premonition was about?"

She pursed her lips, contemplating his question. "I hadn't thought about it. But, yes, it probably is."

Shay's next statement came as a surprise. "I'll go with you."

The idea of having Shay with her sent a warm glow over her body, which she quickly shook off. "That's not necessary. The people I'm going to see aren't mine employees, so there's no need for you to watch over my shoulder. Besides, Polvo is at least forty miles from here across some pretty harsh desert country. And I plan on riding through the night, stopping for only a couple of hours. Surely a city boy like you wouldn't want to spend that much time sitting in a saddle."

Though being called a city boy rankled, Shay let the comment pass. He considered himself a decent horseman, though he hadn't been on a horse's back more than once or twice since leaving California, and he hadn't spent an entire day in the saddle in years. Even so, he'd already made up his mind. "You shouldn't make the trip alone," he finally said. "And since Poppy is staying here in case someone needs medical attention, I'm the logical choice."

Sheridan stared up at him long and hard. "You'd better be absolutely certain. Because once we start across the desert, I'm not bringing you back if you decide the trip is too much for you."

Shay drew an X on his chest with one blunt-tipped finger. "Cross my heart, Sherry. No matter what, I won't change my mind."

She remained silent for a moment, then huffed out a breath. "Okay, fine. Go pack some clothes and get yourself a horse, then meet me at my house in an hour."

"Yes, ma'am," he said, flashing her a smile and a smart salute before turning on his heel to carry out her orders. He bit the inside of his cheek to hold in a laugh at the shocked expression on her face.

Sheridan closed her gaping mouth, then turned to follow Shay from his office. Though certain he didn't know what traveling across the desert could entail, she looked forward to his company on the journey.

After picking up her medical bag from the clinic, she stopped to get Molly at the stable where she boarded the mare, then headed home. She packed one small satchel with several changes of clothes, filled a canteen, and stuffed as much food as she could into her saddlebags before changing into her most comfortable riding clothes. Her final task was retrieving her rifle and revolver. Though she hadn't fired either gun in a long time, they were both in prime condition. She'd never forgotten what her grandfather had taught her, not only how to shoot, but also the importance of always keeping her firearms clean and oiled. After checking and loading each gun, she put two boxes of cartridges in the satchel containing her clothes, then slipped the pistol in its holster and strapped the belt around her waist. She checked through her supplies one last time, stacked them by the front door, then sat down to wait for Shay.

Buster hopped up next to her on the sofa. "Hey, boy," she said, scratching his head. "I'm gonna miss you. You behave for Poppy, okay?" His woof made her smile. "I knew I could count on you to—" The sound of an approaching horse caught her attention. Giving Buster one last pat, she rose and went to the door.

From the doorway she watched Shay rein a big gray to a halt in front of her house, then dismount. She studied the gray for a moment. Pleased to see Shay had good taste in horseflesh, she turned her attention to the man coming up the walk. He wore a leather vest, white shirt tucked into a pair of snug-fitting denim trousers, and scuffed boots. Startled at how his appearance affected her, she resisted the urge to place a hand over her pounding heart. Somehow his casual attire made him even more appealing. Shoving her sudden spurt of desire aside, she turned to pick up her gear.

As Shay moved up the porch steps, Buster charged outside to greet him. "Hi, Buster," he said, smiling when the dog didn't growl but danced around his feet. Crouching down to pet the wiggling dog, Shay said, "Guess we're friends now, huh?" Buster's answering bark made Shay laugh. "So do you get to go with us?"

"Not this time," Sheridan responded from the doorway.

Shay gave Buster's head a final pat, then straightened. "Sorry, boy, guess you havta stay—" Catching sight of Sheridan, his jaw dropped open. *Sweet Mother of God, what the hell's she wearing?* Snapping his mouth closed, his initial shock gave way to a much stronger emotion. As she started past him, he grabbed her arm. "Wait," he said, his voice a soft snarl. "You don't expect me to make this trip while you're wearing that getup, do you?"

She lifted her chin to stare up at him. She knew he'd object to her buckskin trousers but wore them anyway. "I don't expect anything from you." She twisted sideways, trying to pull her arm from his grasp. "Now, let go—"

"My God, there's a gun strapped to your hip!"

"Your powers of observation simply astound me," she replied in a silky whisper, a false smile plastered on her face.

He narrowed his gaze. "Don't get smart-mouthed with me, Sheridan, or I'll—"

Her smile disappeared. "You won't do anything," she said in a clipped voice. Successfully jerking free of his hand, she sent him a scathing glance. "For the record, yes, I'm wearing this getup because I want to be comfortable for the long ride ahead of us. And, yes, there's a gun strapped to my hip, because in this part of Texas, you never know when you might need to shoot a snake, or a varmint, or a man who's pissed me off one too many times."

Shay stared down at her, a muscle ticking in his clenched jaw. The sizzling fire in her glare reminded him of another kind of blaze he'd seen in those dark blue eyes: the smoldering inferno he could ignite with just a touch or a kiss. Abruptly his fury cooled. Sheridan Kinmont was a hell of a woman, like none he'd ever known. His lips twitched, then pulled into a smile. "I think you're bluffing, Sherry. I don't think you'd really shoot the man who makes you scream with pleasure."

When she didn't respond but continued to glare at him, he dipped his head until his mouth nearly touched hers. "Can we kiss and make up?" he whispered, flicking the tip of his tongue over her bottom lip.

Her shoulders quivered with a shiver of pleasure, but her voice remained frosty when she said, "Are you going to make any more derogatory comments about my clothes?"

He shook his head, the movement brushing his mustache over her lips. "Kiss me, Sherry. Kiss me so I know you've forgiven me."

His softly spoken words shattered the last of Sheridan's

resolve to be unaffected by his nearness and dissolved the last of her temper. With a groan she pressed her mouth to his and forced her tongue between his lips.

Shay's groan echoed hers. Grabbing her shoulders, he pulled her flush against his chest and deepened the kiss. Ready to haul her inside and strip those indecent though extremely erotic buckskins off her body, the whicker of one of the horses brought him back to the present. Lifting his head, he loosened his grip and looked down into Sheridan's flushed face. "I think we'd best leave right now, otherwise . . ."

She took a deep breath, knowing exactly what he meant. If they didn't leave immediately, they'd end up in bed, maybe for the rest of the day. Repressing another shiver, she finally said, "Yeah, we'd better get going."

Several hours later Sheridan and Shay had wound their way out of the Chinati Mountains and started their journey across the Chihuahua Desert. Shay pulled his hat from his head and wiped a shirt-sleeve over his forehead. "Damn, it's hot," he muttered, glancing up at the sky. *And still three or four hours of sunlight.*

As he settled his hat back on his head, he looked over at Sheridan. Wondering why she didn't appear to be affected by the temperature, he recalled what she'd told him when he complained about the heat. *If you think Shafter is hot, then you wouldn't want to leave the mountains and head down onto the desert.* Pondering her statement, he gazed around him at the clumps of grass and scrubby plants dotting the bleak landscape. Heat rose off the hard-packed ground in shimmering waves. Well, Sheridan was right. Shafter could be called downright cold compared to the furnacelike temperature of the desert. Determined to make the best of the situation, he turned his thoughts to more enjoyable topics. Like the surprising beauty of the cactus blooms scattered across the terrain, or Sheridan in her body-hugging buckskin trousers. Though the latter didn't make him feel any cooler—in fact, thinking about Sheridan's choice of clothing had the opposite effect—she was undeniably better food for thought than the desert heat.

By the time they stopped to rest the horses, the sun had started to slip below the horizon, and the air was already noticeably cooler. When Shay commented on the change in temperature, Sheridan said, "It'll drop a lot more between now and sunrise. Even on the hottest days of summer, desert nights can get pretty cold."

He nodded but made no comment, surprised to realize he found the fickle nature of the desert oddly appealing. He scowled into the twilight. Where the hell had that thought come from? Deciding the heat had temporarily scrambled his brain, he followed Sheridan's lead and loosened his horse's cinch, then led the gray to the small spring several yards away. Once the gelding had drunk his fill, Shay hobbled him near Sheridan's mare to graze on a large clump of grass.

When he returned to Sheridan's side, she handed him something wrapped in heavy paper. "Here," she said. "I made us sandwiches. Eat, then you'd better try to get some sleep. I want to start out again in a couple of hours. That should get us into Polvo by daybreak."

"Thanks," he replied, taking the sandwich from her.

They ate in silence, washing down the hurried meal with water from their canteens. After taking turns moving into the deeper shadows to take care of their personal needs, they spread blankets on the ground.

As Shay pulled off his boots, Sheridan said, "Be sure and check your boots before you put them back on. Otherwise you might have an unpleasant surprise."

Shay turned to look at her but saw only the pale oval of her face in the rapidly falling darkness. "Like what?"

"Scorpion," she said with a yawn. "Their sting isn't fatal, but it's still a nasty experience."

He scowled. "Great," he muttered, setting his boots aside, then stretching out on his back.

Shortly after midnight Sheridan roused Shay from a surprisingly deep sleep. He sat up, rubbed his eyes, then reached for his boots. Remembering Sheridan's warning, he took care to turn each one upside down and give it a shake before pulling it on.

A few minutes later they were back on the trail, a three-quarter moon providing a pale silver light and casting eerie shadows over the desert terrain.

Near sunup they arrived in Polvo, a collection of less than a dozen adobe buildings on a flat stretch of land not far from the Rio Grande. As they rode down the town's single street, the wind kicked up, sending a reddish-colored cloud of dust billowing around them.

Sheridan closed her eyes against the stinging bits of sand and decided the town's founders had selected an appropriate name: *Polvo* means "dust" in Spanish. When the wind gust subsided, she opened her eyes, and squinting against the glare of the rising sun, checked each building for any sign of activity.

She finally spotted a woman outside one of the houses, then reined her horse in that direction. As she dismounted in front of the adobe house, she called to the woman. *"Buenos días, señora."*

The woman dropped the bucket she carried, then whirled around, surprise evident on her round face. A hand pressed to her ample bosom, she said, *"Buenos días."*

Sheridan moved closer. *"¿Habla usted inglés?"*

"Sí, I speak English."

"My name is Sheridan Kinmont, señora. I'm the doctor from Shafter. And this"—she nodded toward Shay who moved to stand next to her—"is Shay Bannigan, the general manager of the Presidio Mining Company. Señor Gurza told me about the illness here."

The woman bobbed her head, then made the sign of the cross with one hand, her lips moving in silent prayer. Tears sparkled in her dark eyes and trickled down her wrinkled cheeks. "I am

Luisa Ferrero, *doctora*, thank you both for coming to our village. There are now fifteen people ill. Two more were struck with the sickness just last night. One of them is my husband, Carlos.''

"Do the newest cases have the same symptoms Señor Gurza told me about. Pains in the limbs, headache, fever, weakness?''

She wiped a hand across her wet cheeks. *"Sí*, that is how it begins. One woman has been sick to her stomach, and several have also complained of being dizzy.'' Another gust of wind swirled around the corner of the house, making Luisa's full skirt flap against her legs and pulling a strand of graying hair from the loose knot at the nape of her neck. Securing her hair back in place, she stared at Sheridan, worry and fatigue obvious in her expression. "Do you know what this illness is?''

"I have several ideas, but I won't know for sure until I examine the patients. I'd like to start with your husband.''

Luisa nodded, bending to pick up the bucket at her feet. "I was just going to get Carlos more water. Let me fill this, then I'll—''

"I'll get the water,'' Shay said, stepping forward and taking the bucket from Luisa. "Take the doctor to your husband.''

"Gracias, señor,'' she replied in a low voice, then turned toward the house.

After Sheridan examined Carlos Ferrero, she went to the home of each of the others suffering from the illness. Shay accompanied her around the village, for the most part staying in the background, usually outside. He told himself he didn't go in because the houses were small, and cramming another person inside would only add to their already crowded conditions. But he also realized being present while Sheridan performed her examinations no longer seemed important. As for the reason behind his change in attitude, he refused to speculate.

Once Sheridan had checked over everyone complaining of illness, she asked Luisa to gather as many of Polvo's healthy residents as she could.

When everyone had assembled beneath a large tree in the center of the village, Sheridan said, "I've completed my examinations and I've come to the conclusion that the illness that has struck so many of your families is influenza."

"This influenza, is it serious, *doctora?*" Luisa said.

"In its severest form, yes, influenza can be extremely serious, often with a high fatality rate. But I don't believe that's the case here. The symptoms I've observed are consistent with a milder form of the disease."

"You have medicine for this disease?" Vicenta Lopez said. The sixteen-year-old girl, the only member of her family not to have fallen ill, had been caring for her parents, two brothers, and sister by herself. Her wide-set dark brown eyes were bloodshot, wisps of black hair escaped her waist-length braid, and lines of fatigue bracketed her full mouth.

"The best medicine, Vicenta, is bed rest. But, yes, I have some medicine that should help the headache and fever. The sick must all drink plenty of water, and you should try to get them to eat as much as they're able.

"We also need to take steps to make sure the disease doesn't spread. Since school has just recessed for the summer, that's one less worry. But there should be no public gatherings, inside or out. I understand there are a number of families living on farms near here." When the villagers nodded, she said, "We need to take precautions to make sure those who haven't already been exposed don't come here and risk taking the disease back to their families. If you see any of them coming into town, you must keep your distance and tell them to leave immediately." She looked from one worried brown face to another. "Does everyone understand?" Each person gave her a nod. *"Bueno.* Now I have work to do. Go back to your homes and I'll bring each of you some medicine soon."

After the villagers left, Sheridan turned to where Shay stood leaning against the tree and said, "Come with me. I'm going to the river and I need your help."

Shay straightened and followed behind Sheridan. When he caught up with her, he said, "What're you planning to do at the river?"

"Collect willow bark."

His brows knitted in a frown. "Why?"

"I'm going to make a tea."

Shay pulled up short. "What?"

Sheridan also stopped and turned toward him. "I plan to treat the sick with the quinine and aspirin powders I brought with me. But if more people come down with the disease, my entire supply of aspirin powders could be exhausted in a few days. And since willow-bark tea has been used for centuries to reduce fever and relieve pain, I'll add it to my regimen of treatment to make my supply of patent medicines last longer."

His face scrunched in a fierce scowl, he said, "Are you sure tea from tree bark will work?"

"Absolutely," she replied, flashing him a smile that caught him off guard. A bolt of desire speared through his body with lightning speed, stunning him with its intensity.

She turned toward the river and resumed walking. "Get a move on, slowpoke," she said over her shoulder. "I've got to get back to my patients."

Slowpoke? Shay's frown gradually changing to a grin, he chuckled, then started after her.

Chapter Nineteen

Orrin wrapped the reins around the buggy's brake handle, then jumped to the ground. Whistling a sprightly tune, he approached the clinic with a definite bounce in his step. He couldn't remember ever feeling so lighthearted, so enthusiastic about life, so crazy about a woman. Or so damn nervous. Pausing at the clinic's door, he took a deep breath. At forty-one years of age, he'd finally found the one woman who made him want to give up his bachelorhood. But he knew he had to tread easy with Poppy. She'd shared only a few details of her marriage, but from those scraps of information he'd learned enough to realize he had an uphill battle. If he wanted Poppy to return his love and accept his proposal, he would have to use gentle persuasion, a process he hoped to start by taking her on a picnic supper.

Poppy had just finished straightening the examination room in preparation for closing the clinic for the day, when she heard the front door open. She started into the waiting room, then came to a sudden stop. Orrin stood just inside the front door.

When he spotted her, he pulled his hat from his head, then raked a hand through his hair.

"Orrin, what a surprise," she said. Noticing how his fingers kept twisting the brim of his hat, she said, "Are you all right?"

"Fine. Fine," he replied. "Why wouldn't I be?"

Her gaze met his, a smile teasing her lips. "Well, dear man, you're fixing to mangle your hat."

"What?" Casting a quick glance at his hands, the confusion in his gray eyes suddenly cleared. "Oh, yeah." Keeping his fingers still, he cleared his throat, then said, "Guess I am a little nervous. I . . . uh . . . came by to see if you'd have a picnic supper with me."

"A picnic? You mean right now?"

He nodded, swallowed, then said, "I rented a buggy and had the dining hall pack a basket of food. I know a place not far from here, farther up in the mountains. There are lots of big trees, a spring-fed creek." He paused to steady his nerves. "Anyway, it's real pretty there, if ya'd like to go with me."

"Oh, Orrin," Poppy replied with a smile. Moving closer, she cupped the side of his square jaw with one hand. "I'd love to."

Orrin resisted the urge to give a whoop of joy but settled for pulling her hand from his face and pressing a kiss on her palm. "Are you about ready to leave? If not, I can wait. Or I can come back in a few minutes. If there's something that needs to be done, I'd be more than happy to help."

Poppy chuckled at his nervous rambling. "Thank you, but since Sheridan left three days ago there hasn't been much to do around here. And I've already done what needed doing. Actually, you arrived at the perfect time. I was just getting ready to leave." She gave him another teasing smile, her green eyes snapping with humor. "Now, if you'll let loose of my hand, I'll fetch my hat. Then we can be on our way."

The back of his neck burning with embarrassment, he pulled his hand away from hers and gave her a tight-lipped nod. He refused to open his mouth again for fear of what might come out. Since arriving at the clinic, he'd acted like a complete idiot, and he didn't want to risk repeating such behavior.

Soon Poppy sat beside Orrin in the buggy as he unwrapped the reins from the brake handle, then directed the horse down Main Street.

Several hours later she sat on a blanket beneath an enormous cottonwood, her back resting against the tree's trunk.

"This really was a wonderful idea," she said, watching him repack the picnic basket. "Thank you for asking me."

"You're welcome," he said, his earlier nervousness returning to form a lump in his throat. He reached over and picked up one of her hands. Running his thumb back and forth over her knuckles, he swallowed, then said, "Poppy, we've been seeing a lot of each other the past few weeks, and I hope you know how much I've come to care for you."

She smiled. "I know, and I care about you too."

He tried to smile, but his lips didn't want to cooperate. "Actually, caring isn't exactly what I feel. I . . . um . . ." Before he lost his nerve, he blurted out the words in a rush. "I love you, Poppy Gilbert, and I'd be honored if you'd marry me."

She blinked up at him, her smile fading, the color leaving her cheeks. "Marry you," she said in a dull voice.

"I know I've surprised you, and I'm sorry for that. But I had to get the words out before they strangled me." When she didn't say anything but continued staring up at him, her green eyes wide with shock and something else he couldn't name, fear gripped his middle. He ran his tongue over his dry lips, then said, "You don't have to answer me now. Take your time and think it through. But I want you to remember what I told you before. I'll never raise my hand to you. I'd rather die first."

She gulped down a sob, then lowered her gaze to their clasped hands. After a few moments she spoke. "Orrin, I want you to know that I've come to love you too. And I'm flattered by your

proposal, I truly am. But"—she lifted her gaze to meet his—
"I can't marry you."

Orrin waited for the initial stab of pain to ease before speaking. "Is it because of what your former husband did to you?"

"Yes, but not for the reason you think." She drew a deep breath, exhaled slowly, then began speaking in a low voice. "The beatings usually happened after he came home kneewalkin' drunk. But sometimes he hit me because I didn't do something to suit him. Or because I looked at him wrong. Or sometimes for no reason at all. I think he just liked hurting me. During the years of my marriage I must've had at least two dozen black eyes, a few broken bones, and more bruises than I can count." A shudder racked her shoulders. "I knew he had a mean streak and a weakness for liquor before I married him. But I had a young girl's starry-eyed notion that I could change him." She paused for a moment to gather her thoughts. "Anyway, I don't believe you're capable of beating a woman. You're kind and gentle and rarely drink anything stronger than coffee. You're nothing like the vicious drunk I was married to." She gave him a wobbly smile. "You'll make some woman a fine husband."

"Not *some* woman, Poppy. You. You're the woman I want to marry. To love and cherish until my last breath."

Tears sprang to her eyes. "Oh, Orrin, I wish I could say yes, but my place is with Sheridan." Blinking away her tears, she said, "I owe her my life. If I hadn't met her when I did, I never would've had the courage to leave my husband and seek a divorce. Or believe I could make it on my own. She helped me through the worst months of my life, healing my body and my spirit. After all she did for me, I swore I'd stay with her forever."

She looked up at him with pleading eyes. "Can you understand, even a little?"

"Yeah, I understand your being devoted to Dr. Kinmont.

But I think your devotion's gone a little too far, saying you'll stay with her for the rest of your life.''

"If not for Sheridan, I might not have a life. My husband might have beaten me so bad, that I—''

"Don't say it,'' he whispered. "Please don't say you might have died. I can't bear the thought.''

"But it's true. The beatings kept getting worse, so it was only a matter of time.'' Shrugging off her painful memories, she said, "In a manner of speaking, Sheridan saved my life. Now I'm repaying her the only way I know how, by devoting my life to her.''

"And there's nothing that will change your mind?''

"Only if she remarries. Then I'd just be in the way.'' Seeing his hopeful expression, she added, "Sheridan is adamant about remaining single. Her husband didn't beat her, but he still soured her on trusting a man enough to marry again. She hasn't told me, but I'm sure she's seeing Shay Bannigan. I don't put any stock in that though. 'Cause even if she fell in love with him, I can't see her changing her mind about marriage.''

"And there's no other way you'll break your vow to Sheridan?''

"No,'' she said with a sad smile. "I'm afraid not.''

Afer a few moments the knot of nervousness in Orrin's belly loosened, but not for the reason he'd hoped for: Poppy accepting his proposal. Instead, her refusal had shoved his nervousness aside and filled the space with a new emotion: resolve. He didn't want to lose her and refused to give up after only one attempt to win her hand.

Sheridan left the Ferrero house, rubbing the small of her back. A week had passed since she'd arrived in Polvo, a week of days spent tending the residents stricken with influenza and nights of getting too little sleep. But now the worst had passed. Only one other person had taken sick since her arrival, so her efforts to prevent the spreading of the disease had paid off. She planned to spend the day making one last visit to the homes of the ill and passing out the last of her medicine. Then the following morning she and Shay would head back to Shafter.

She saw Shay up the street, talking to another man, so she headed in their direction. As she approached the men, she recognized Francisco Gurza.

When Francisco glanced up and saw her, he broke off his conversation with Shay and smiled in her direction. *"Doctora* Kinmont, I am glad to see you."

"It's good seeing you as well, Señor Gurza," she said, hoping his appearance in Polvo wasn't a bad sign. "Is something wrong? Is someone in your family ill?"

"No, *doctora,* there is nothing wrong. My wife and children are well. I spoke with a man who lives near me, and he said you would be leaving soon. So I came to thank you in person for coming such a long ways."

"De nada, señor. I did only what any doctor would do."

Shay stood by quietly while Gurza and Sheridan spoke. He didn't contribute to the conversation, though he was tempted to respond to Sheridan's last comment. In spite of her claim to the contrary, he thought she'd done more than another doctor could have done under the circumstances. Being in such a remote area, with primitive living conditions and limited medical supplies, she hadn't buckled under the pressure. She'd not only found an effective substitute for the medicine she'd brought with her, but she'd also taken steps to quarantine the town and stop the influenza from spreading, then worked tirelessly to treat the ill until the crisis had passed. And all the while she remained outwardly composed, her emotions in check. There was no doubt about it, she'd done a helluva job, one any doctor would have been hard pressed to match.

He scowled. Where the hell had those thoughts come from? Not wanting to tender an answer to that question for fear his mind would conjure up more ridiculous notions, he forced himself to concentrate on the conversation between Francisco and Sheridan.

"Before I leave tomorrow," Sheridan said, "I plan to give Vicenta Lopez whatever medicine I have left. She has a natural talent for nursing the sick, and she knows how the medicine is to be given. If anyone else becomes ill after I've gone, go to Vicenta. When I visit the other residents today, I'll tell them the same thing."

"You really think the sickness is over?"

Sheridan nodded. "I can't guarantee no one else will become ill. But it's been six days since anyone showed signs of coming down with the disease, so I think we're safe to assume the danger has passed."

Francisco bobbed his head. *"Bueno.* Again, *Doctora* Kinmont, we are most grateful to both you and Señor Bannigan. As you can see, Polvo is a very poor village. We have little money to pay you. But if there's anything else we can give you as payment, you must tell me."

Sheridan smiled. "That's kind of you, señor. The people of Polvo have already done a great deal. Opening their homes to us, providing our meals, and giving us a place to sleep. But if you want to do more, we could use some food for our return trip."

"Sí. Sí," he replied. "I will make sure your saddlebags are filled before you leave." He bent his head in a formal bow. *"Muchas gracias, Doctora* Kinmont, *Vaya con Díos."*

"Adiós, Señor Gurza."

Just after daybreak the next morning Shay and Sheridan mounted their horses and rode out of the dusty little town. They traveled for a few miles before either one spoke. Then Sheridan said, "Will your being gone for more than a week create problems for you?"

Shay shrugged. "Not likely. I have good help, so they should've kept everything running smoothly. Though I'll probably have a lot of paperwork waiting for me."

"Will it take you a long time to catch up?"

"It shouldn't. I'll just work late a couple of nights, that's all."

"You seem to like being the mining company's general manager."

"Yeah, I do, even with all the bureaucratic nonsense I have to deal with."

"You just hate the location."

Shay didn't reply immediately, then finally he said, "Yeah, right." As they lapsed into silence, he wondered why his response had lacked his usual heated reaction to the mention of Shafter. Deciding the reason had to be his physical and mental exhaustion, caused by a week of helping Sheridan, doing the chores for the families whose men were ill, and getting only a few hours sleep each night, he let his thoughts drift to more interesting topics. Like Sheridan Kinmont. Glancing over at her lovely profile, he momentarily forgot his exhaustion. That night would be the first one they'd spent alone since their arrival in Polvo. Though they'd often slept side by side on the floor of one of homes in the village, there were always other people in the house. He'd managed to kiss her once or twice, a brief brush of his mouth over hers, but the coming night . . . He smiled at the possibilities.

As they worked their way to the northwest, Shay's attention shifted to focus on the surrounding scenery. On their trip to Polvo they'd passed through this area at night, the moonlight occasionally revealing a shape shrouded in deep shadow but little else. Now, under a blazing sun, what he saw came as a surprise. The craggy peaks in the distance, the mesas jutting up in the middle of an otherwise flat plain, the unnavigable canyons of steep-sided sheer rock. Even more surprising, he found the raw beauty of the desert fascinating, the silence and isolation oddly comforting.

He frowned. Dammit, he didn't want to like anything about Texas. Drawing on the hatred he'd nurtured since his arrival in Shafter the previous year, he finally managed to change the direction of his thoughts.

By late morning Sheridan told Shay they should find a place to rest the horses. When they reached a small creek, she followed the trickle of water to its source, a spring deep in one of the canyons, then pulled Molly to a halt.

"This looks like a good spot," she said, swinging off her mare's back, then removing her saddlebags. "We might as well eat something while the horses rest."

Shay nodded, then dismounted. He took the reins of Sheridan's mare, then led both horses to the edge of the spring.

While Shay watered their mounts, Sheridan moved to a spot in the lush vegetation surrounding the spring. As she pulled food from her saddlebags, she glanced up at the northern sky and frowned. She didn't like the looks of the anvil-shaped cloud, a sure sign of a thunderstorm.

When Shay joined her, she said, "We won't be staying here as long as I'd hoped. A storm's coming."

Shay accepted the food she handed him, then followed her gaze to the cloud formation to the north. "Looks like it's a long way off."

"For now. But if the wind continues to pick up, it'll get here in a hurry."

Shay had no experience with storms in Texas, so he didn't dispute her statement. As they ate a hurried meal, Sheridan kept glancing at the approaching storm. The churning clouds moved closer, blotting out the sun and turning the sky a dull gray. Hoping she wouldn't regret her decision, she waited, giving the horses as much time as she dared.

When a cold blast of wind swept down the canyon, the heavy air carrying the unmistakable scent of rain, she knew they couldn't dally any longer. As they prepared to leave, she looked over her mare's back at Shay. "I remember seeing a rocky overhang not long after we entered the canyon." Though she stood only a few feet away from him, she had to raise her voice to make herself heard above the increasing howl of the wind. "I think there's enough room for us to wait out the storm. I just hope we can get there before it breaks."

He nodded, then stepped into his stirrup and swung onto his horse's back.

They'd been back in the saddle for only a few minutes when the leading edge of the storm hit them. Shay kept his horse close behind Sheridan's, bending his head against the bite of the icy wind and the stinging slap of raindrops.

By the time they reached the overhang the rain had started in earnest, the rumble of thunder vibrating the ground. Sheridan pulled her mare to a halt and dismounted in one fluid movement. After removing her saddlebags and medical bag and pulling her rifle from its scabbard, she turned to Shay. "Grab your saddlebags and our bedrolls, then come on.

"What about the horses?"

"Even if they'd fit under the overhang, the wall's too steep for them to climb. We don't have time to find a larger shelter, so they'll have to fend for themselves."

Shay looked up at their intended destination: a shallow indentation in the canyon's wall ten feet above their heads, with an outcropping of rock for a roof.

Sheridan saw his hesitation and said, "We don't have any other choice, Shay. Now, let's get going."

He stared at her for a second, then gave her a nod. After grabbing his saddlebags and dropping them over one shoulder, he untied the bedrolls from behind their saddles, then hurried to catch up with her.

The rain-slicked rock slowed their progress, forcing them to take extra care while finding their footing. When they finally reached their destination and crawled beneath the rocky outcropping, the driving rain had soaked them to the skin.

Shay ran a hand over his face, surprised to find himself exhilarated by their adventure against Mother Nature. "What a storm," he said with a chuckle. "I've never seen anything like it."

Sheridan smiled. "Texas thunderstorms are pretty spectacular. They seem to come out of nowhere, blow across the desert at breakneck speed while dumping a torrent of water, then suddenly they're gone, the sky clear and the sun shining."

"I could use a little of that sun right now," he replied, rubbing his hands up and down his arms. "I haven't been this cold since I left San Francisco."

The deafening crack of a lightning strike and a resounding clap of thunder prevented Sheridan from replying. Wrapping her arms around her drawn-up legs, she stared at the rain falling so thick and fast, she couldn't see more than a few feet in front of their temporary refuge.

As quickly as the storm began, it ended. The rain stopped, the wind slowed, and the clouds scudded away. Sunlight returned with a blinding glare, causing steam to rise from the rocks and creating tiny rainbows in the drops of water dripping from the edge of the overhang.

"We'd better get back on the trail," Sheridan said, reaching for her gear. "If we make good time, we'll reach Shafter before dark."

"Good," Shay replied, crawling out from under the overhang. "I'm looking forward to sleeping in a real bed."

Her gaze met his, the sizzle of mutual desire crackling between them. Her lips curved in a lazy smile, she said, "Yeah, me too."

They made the descent to the canyon floor quickly, then searched the area for some sign of the horses. Finding nothing nearby, Shay said, "Which way?"

Sheridan pointed toward the mouth of the canyon. "They would've kept their backsides to the storm, moving with the wind." Adjusting her saddlebags to a more comfortable position over one shoulder, she said, "They're probably not far."

"Why don't you let me take the rifle?"

She handed over the weapon, then started walking. He tucked their bedrolls more securely under one arm, then fell into step beside her.

As they walked along, a loud rumbling noise from deeper in the canyon reached them. Sheridan stopped, cocked her head to one side, concentrating on the sound.

Shay's brow furrowed. "Do you—"

Her raised hand and the fierce look on her face prevented him from finishing his question.

The rumble continued, increasing in volume and making the ground shake.

Shay watched her face turn a chalky white. "Sheridan, what is it?"

She turned to meet his gaze, her eyes wide. "Oh, my God! Run!" She grabbed his arm and pushed him forward. "Run as fast as you can. It's a flash flood!"

Chapter Twenty

Shay opened his mouth to respond to Sheridan's shouted command, but the look on her face left no room for argument. Snapping his mouth closed, he broke into a run, shortening his stride to stay even with Sheridan. Every few seconds he glanced back over his shoulder. Though he saw no signs of a flash flood, the rumbling sound had increased to a dull roar.

Sheridan soon realized they weren't going to be able to outrun the oncoming rush of water. Spotting a pile of large rocks a few yards ahead, she made a quick decision. "There," she shouted to Shay, pointing to the rocks.

His brow furrowed, then cleared as he realized her plan. Nodding, he increased his pace and sprinted ahead of her. When he reached the rocks, he scrambled to the top, dropped the rifle, his saddlebags, and their bedrolls, then turned to help Sheridan.

"Are we high enough?" he said once she stood next to him.

"I don't know," she replied in a gasping voice. "The canyon is wider here. So the water won't be as deep, but"—she drew in a ragged breath—"maybe we should've kept going."

Shay glanced toward the mouth of the canyon, then in the opposite direction. He could see something, a brownish-colored wall working its way down the creek bed. "No," he replied. "You made the right choice. We couldn't have outrun that." Wrapping an arm around her shoulders, he pulled her against him. "Look at me, Sheridan."

He watched her chest rise and fall with another deep breath. Then she turned her head, shifting her gaze from the wall of water to stare into his eyes.

"We'll make it, Sherry," he said, then bent his head. "For luck," he whispered before pressing his mouth to hers in a quick, hard kiss. Keeping his arm wrapped around her, he moved them as far from the edge of the rocks as possible, praying the water wouldn't sweep them from their perch.

Though Sheridan had heard about flash floods her entire life and had seen the aftermath of several, she'd never been caught in one. She stared at the rapidly approaching wall of muddy water, terrified yet at the same time awed by the sheer power. Nothing in its path was spared. All rocks, all vegetation, and anything else unlucky enough to be on the canyon floor fell victim to the frothy mass of wildly churning water.

Unable to watch any longer, she closed her eyes and pressed her face into Shay's chest. Her head ringing with the deafening roar of the passing flood, water slapped against the rocks beneath them, tugging at their feet and covering them with a fine mist.

Shay tightened his hold on Sheridan, his heart pounding with fear. *God, please let this end soon.* He repeated the silent plea again and again, until Sheridan's voice penetrated his numb mind.

"Shay, I think it's over."

He lifted his head and looked around. Though the creek was swollen and filled with floating debris, the leading edge of the flood waters had passed, leaving them stranded on their pile of rocks, but alive and unharmed. "Praise God," he whispered, releasing a shaky breath.

"Amen," Sheridan said. She pushed away from Shay to check the water level. The creek rushed past just a foot below their feet. "Damn, that was close."

Shay grinned. "Exactly what I was thinking."

She turned to look at him. His cocky grin and the tiny gold flecks dancing in his dark eyes made her burst into laughter. "This is crazy. We almost get swept away by a flash flood and I'm laughing."

"A natural reaction to facing death and winning."

She sobered. "I suppose." Shaking off her momentary melancholy, she said, "Bet you never had this kind of excitement in San Francisco."

His grin disappeared. He stared at her for several seconds before responding. "No, I never did."

Sheridan wondered about the reason for his pensive look, but didn't ask. At the moment there were more pressing matters. "Well," she finally said, "Might as well make ourselves comfortable."

Shay watched her resettle herself on the rock beside him. "How long before the water goes down?"

"Hard to say. But hopefully in a few hours it'll be low enough for us to make it out of the canyon."

Shay mulled over their situation for a few moments. "If we can't leave here for a few hours, what are the chances we'll find the horses?"

She drew a deep breath and exhaled slowly before answering. "Not good. If the horses were still in the canyon when the flood hit, I just hope they got out in time. But even if they did, the storm and the flood probably scared them pretty bad. My guess is they're long gone by now. Hopefully they'll head to Shafter."

"Long gone," Shay replied in a low voice. "Great, that's just great." After a moment of silent fuming he said, "So we'll be stranded." His voice rose in volume. "On foot. In the middle of the desert."

Sheridan turned to look at him, saw the ticking of a muscle in his jaw. "Unless you suddenly sprout wings and fly us to Shafter, then, yeah, that's about it."

"This is no time for more of your smart-mouthed remarks," he said through clenched teeth. "This is serious, dammit. I don't know the first thing about surviving in the desert. I've lived through fights on the docks of San Francisco and a snow-storm once in the Sierra Nevada Mountains, so I know what it takes to survive." He was practically shouting when he added, "But not in the goddamn desert."

Laughter bubbled up in Sheridan's throat. Male pride. So fragile. So foolish. Knowing how he'd react if she let him see her amusement, she managed to stifle the urge to laugh. "Settle down. I won't let anything happen to you."

"Me? I'm concerned about something happening to you."

"Oh, I see," she replied, biting the inside of her cheek. "Well, let me put your mind at ease. I know the desert, Shay. I know how to survive here. We won't get back to Shafter today, but with luck we'll make it tomorrow. So you can stop worrying. I'll get both of us there safe and sound."

He narrowed his gaze, searching her face long and hard. Was that laughter he saw lurking in those incredible eyes? His jaw tightened. If she was laughing at him, he'd— Realizing his line of thinking would do nothing to help their situation, he managed to squash the last of his anger. Though humiliated at having to put his survival in the hands of a woman, he had no other choice. Blowing out a resigned breath, he nodded, his bruised pride prompting him to say, "And for the record, I wasn't worried. I was concerned. There's a helluva big differ-ence."

"Is there?" She pursed her lips, contemplating the I-dare-you-to-disagree expression on his face. Her heart swelling with love for this egotistical, infuriating, totally wonderful man, she finally said, "You're right. Now, would you pass me a canteen? I'm thirsty."

He blinked at her, momentarily stunned that he hadn't gotten more of an argument. Handing her one of the canteens, his mind shifted from her surprising agreement to the long walk ahead of them. He hoped like hell he'd be able to mend his tattered self-respect by doing something helpful along the way.

The sun had sunk low in the sky before the floodwaters receded enough to expose a strip of ground between the still-swollen creek and the canyon walls.

"We have a few hours before dark," Sheridan said. "So we'd better get going."

Shay nodded, then picked up most of their gear and started down the rock pile. When he reached the canyon floor, he turned and offered a hand to Sheridan. Smiling her thanks, she tightened her grip on her medical bag with her left hand, then placed her right in his and jumped to the ground.

As they left the canyon and started across the sweltering desert, Shay recalled a remark made by someone in Shafter. What had the man said? Oh, yeah. *Everything in the desert stinks, stings, or sticks.* At the time he'd laughed at the comment, but now he saw things in a different light. Though his own experience in the desert was admittedly short, he'd already learned enough to realize the remark held more truth than humor—the stink of a plant Sheridan called creosote bush, her warning about the sting of a scorpion, and the potential stick by the needle-sharp point of a cactus spine.

Yet, strangely enough, rather than dwelling on the negative aspects of the desert—perfect candidates for his list of what he hated about Texas—he found his thoughts dallying along the opposite end of the spectrum. Jolted by the notion that he might actually like the stark, unforgiving land, he quickly shoved such an absurd thought aside. Hoping to keep his mind occupied, he tried to concentrate on the work awaiting him at the mine offices.

As the last of the sunlight began to fade, casting the desert scenery in varying shades of orange, yellow, and purple, Sheridan decided to use the remaining daylight to set up camp.

After selecting a stretch of ground on a rocky slope, she said, "I'll look through our gear to see if there's something I can use to make a snare. Why don't you see if you can find something to use as firewood in case I get a rabbit."

Shay nodded, dropped everything but the rifle, then moved off into the deepening shadows.

A few minutes later Sheridan had just returned from setting a snare she'd fashioned from several narrow strips of rawhide, when she heard a loud curse coming from the direction Shay had taken. He appeared soon afterward, carrying a bundle of mesquite branches. Sheridan ran her gaze over him, frowning when she noticed the way he held his left hand.

"What happened?" she said, moving closer.

"When I reached down to pick up the last of these branches, something jabbed my hand. It hurt like hell." He gave his hand a shake. "I think it's still in there."

After a quick glance at the reddened pad of flesh at the base of his thumb, she said, "It's probably a mesquite thorn, but it's getting too dark for me to tell for sure. Let's get a fire going, then I'll look again."

Sheridan scraped a spot in the hard, rocky earth, arranged part of the mesquite branches in the shallow hole, then pulled some matches from one of her bags. When the flames blazed enough to cast a bright circle of light, Sheridan motioned for Shay to sit near the fire. She took a seat next to him.

"Yes, I'd say it's a thorn," she said, holding his left hand between both of hers. "Appears to be really deep." Reaching for her medical bag with one hand, she said, "I'll have to dig it out."

Shay jerked his hand free. "Dig it out?" His eyes went wide. "You mean with a knife?"

She looked up at him. "I told you, the thorn is deeply embedded. I'll be as gentle as I can."

He scowled at her. "I know, but, isn't there another way to get it out?"

Sheridan studied his face for a moment. "I never figured you for a baby when it comes to a little discomfort."

"Discomfort!" he replied. "Having someone digging into my flesh with a damn knife is a helluva lot more than discomfort." His neck heating with a flush, he added, "And I'm not a baby."

She bit the inside of her cheek while she considered the situation. After a moment she said, "Well, there is one other way."

"Then do it."

"Okay," she replied. Picking up several sticks from the pile of firewood, she got to her feet. "I'll be right back."

Shay watched her leave their campsite, squinting in an attempt to follow her movements, but she quickly disappeared into the darkness.

When she returned several minutes later, she held the sticks of wood like tongs, the pad of a prickly pear cactus clamped between them.

His face scrunched in a frown, he didn't speak while she removed the spines from the cactus, then used a knife to cut the pad in half. Unable to figure out what she planned, he said, "What's with the cactus?"

She reached into her medical bag and pulled out a roll of cloth bandage. "The pulp of the prickly pear will remove the thorn."

His eyes narrowed. "Is this another of your Indian remedies?"

"Yes. Now give me your hand."

He didn't move but continued to stare at the cactus. "I don't think so."

"The only alternative is for me to dig out the thorn."

He took a moment to contemplate his options. No matter which method he chose—despite her claims to the contrary—he figured he'd eventually have to submit to letting her dig into his hand. Though he still had some pain, he decided he could put up with the discomfort until morning, when she'd have better light to wield a knife. But since nothing could be done until then, maybe he should pacify her by agreeing to try the cactus hocus-pocus. Blowing out a deep breath, he extended his hand. "Okay, I'll try your magic Indian cure."

"It isn't magic."

"Sure, whatever you say," he said in a grumble, watching her lay the pulp side of half the cactus pad over his palm, then securing it in place by wrapping the bandage around his hand and tying the ends.

A while later Sheridan went to check on her snare and returned with a rabbit. Though Shay was a crack shot with a rifle, he'd never done much hunting, but when he had, he'd used a gun. So her ability to not only fashion a snare from strips of rawhide but to use it successfully were impressive. As he watched her quickly skin and clean the rabbit with quick, efficient motions, he said, "Is there no end to your list of talents?"

She glanced over at him, searching his face for a sign of sarcasm, but the shadows made reading his expression difficult. Shifting her gaze back to the rabbit, she said, "I told you I know the desert. While my mother and grandmother taught me how to heal using desert plants, they also taught me how to survive here. We used to spend days at a time in the desert, collecting plants, living off the land."

When Shay didn't respond, she hung the rabbit on a makeshift spit over the fire, then said, "Everyone has their own list of skills. I'm sure you're good at things I know nothing about."

He pondered her statement for a moment, then grinned. "I wouldn't say you know *nothing* about one thing I'm good at. In fact, I'm more than good, I'd say I'm an expert."

She looked up. "What's—" His wolfish grin ended her speculation. "You consider yourself an expert lover, hmm?"

His grin widened. "Never had any complaints."

She chuckled. "Well, as far as I'm concerned, your statement is just more proof that you haven't mastered feigning modesty."

"Hey, you're the one who said we all have talents."

"So I did," she replied, still chuckling. "So I did." Moistening a cloth from her canteen, she used the cloth to wipe off her hands, then the blade of her knife.

While using one hand to eat a meal of roasted rabbit and part of the food given to them by the Polvo villagers, Shay said, "I forgot to tell you that I spoke with Enrique Lara a few days before we left. I told him what I could remember about applying for scholarships, which wasn't much. And I said I'd write to a friend of mine in San Francisco who can give me a list of people for him to contact."

"Did you tell him why you dropped out of law school?"

"Yes, but he's still interested in becoming an attorney." He shook his head. "I don't know why anyone would want the job, but far be it from me to tell anyone else what to do with their life."

Sheridan almost responded with, "But you don't have any problems telling women they shouldn't be doctors," but she swallowed the words. Instead, she said, "Thank you for talking to Enrique."

"Sure. He's a smart kid and will probably do well in law school."

Once they finished their meal, Sheridan wrapped up the leftover food, threw the last of the mesquite branches on the fire, then spread out her bedroll and Shay's next to it.

He watched her pull off her boots, then stretch out beside him. Slipping his right arm under her shoulders, he pulled her close. "Hmm, this is nice," he said, pressing his lips to her forehead, then her nose, and finally her mouth for a long, leisurely kiss.

She wiggled to get more comfortable, her head resting on his shoulder, a forearm lying on his chest. "Yes, it is," she replied, her fingers toying with the tuft of hair peeking from the open neck of his shirt.

He moved his left hand, intent on pulling her shirtwaist from her buckskin trousers, but the bandage hampered his efforts. "Damn," he said. "I forgot about being a cripple."

Her chuckle vibrated in his chest. "Go to sleep," she murmured around a huge yawn. "We've had a long day, and tomorrow will be just as long."

Though Shay wanted to protest, wanted to touch her skin, wanted to make love to her, he knew she was right. For then he'd be content holding her close, inhaling her unique scent— a heady combination of female musk and the ever-present vanilla—and dreaming about having her naked and wildly aroused beneath him. A smile curving his lips, he drifted to sleep.

Sheridan awoke at first light, then left their camp to take care of her personal needs. When she returned, Shay sat up on his bedroll. "You going to fix coffee?"

"No, we don't have enough water. That's the first thing we need to do today. Look for a place to refill our canteens."

Though disappointed he wouldn't have his morning coffee, he nodded, then got to his feet.

Sheridan sorted through the saddlebags containing their food, then handed him something. "Here's your breakfast. It's not ham and eggs, but I'm afraid it's the best I can do."

Shay accepted the tortilla wrapped around a piece of the leftover rabbit. "This is fine. I've grown fond of tortillas during the past week." As soon as the words were out, he frowned. *Dammit, Bannigan, you're doing it again.* He wanted to continue hating Texas and everything about it, not keep finding things he liked.

After they ate, Shay put away their bedrolls and Sheridan spread out the ashes of the fire, making sure there were no hot embers remaining. As he finished the second bedroll, he said, "How do we find water?"

"We may come to a small creek, but I'll also watch for coyote tracks. Coyotes always know where to find water. So if we follow their tracks, they'll lead us to a spring or a place where they dug down and found water."

Shay's eyebrows lifted. He never would have thought to follow a coyote to water. "More of your Indian training?"

She nodded. "All native peoples observe and learn from nature. My Nde ancestors watched animals to see which plants were safe to eat, how injured animals cared for themselves, where animals find water. Then they applied what they learned to their people. Those lessons have been handed down through the generations."

He glanced around him. The heat had already started to build. "Let's hope we find coyote tracks soon."

"If we don't, there's enough moisture in prickly pears to keep us alive. But I'd rather find a source of water."

"Me too," he replied, his mouth pulled into a grimace at the idea of eating a cactus for the moisture.

When Sheridan had everything packed, she turned to Shay. "We'll leave as soon as I take the bandage off your hand."

He moved closer and held out his hand, mentally preparing himself to withstand having her dig out the thorn.

She unwrapped the cloth, then lifted the prickly pear pad and tossed it aside. Holding his hand between hers, she tipped it toward the rising sun to get a better look. She ran her fingertips over the base of his thumb, then smiled and released his hand.

"Okay, let's get going," she said, moving to pick up her bags. "It's going to be a scorcher, so I want to put as many miles behind us as possible while it's still cool."

He scowled at her. "What do you mean, let's go? I thought you were gonna dig out the thorn."

She straightened from picking up her medical bag and glanced over at him. "No need. The prickly pear worked and drew the thorn to the surface. It came out when I barely touched it.''

''What?'' His brow furrowed, he lifted his hand and studied it with narrowed eyes. He rubbed a finger over his shriveled and slightly bleached palm, paying particular attention to the base of his thumb, where the thorn had pierced his skin. The furrows in his forehead deepened.

''Well, I'll be damned,'' he murmured. The thorn was gone.

Chapter Twenty-one

As the morning wore on, the temperature continued to climb. The clumps of desert grasses bent in the hot wind. Heat rose in shimmering waves, making the mountains in the distance appear to waver in an odd sort of dance and teaching Shay another lesson: the desert distorted distance. The mountains that looked so close when they broke camp just after sunup appeared to be no closer after walking toward them for hours.

Shay tried to ignore the heat by looking at the profusion of flowers dotting the landscape—flowers that hadn't been there the day before. The recent rain, Sheridan told him, had caused the desert to burst into instant bloom. Plants she called ocotillo and cenizo, along with the creosote bush, now displayed glorious blossoms of brilliant red, deep violet, and bright yellow, a startling contrast to the otherwise monochromatic color scheme of the desert.

Near noon, as they started down another rocky slope, they came upon a small outcropping of rock. Sheridan moved into the shade provided by the rock formation, then said, "It's too hot to go on. We'll rest here during the worst of the heat."

Shay nodded, grateful for the chance to stop. He used his boot to smooth a spot in the rocky soil, then lowered himself to the ground with a sigh. Lifting his canteen, he took a sip of the tepid water. "I'm glad we found that spring earlier."

As Sheridan sat down beside him, she murmured her agreement. Reaching for a bedroll, she said, "We should try to take a nap. Conserve our energy."

After dozing for several hours, she roused and dug into her saddlebags. Their supplies extremely low, she glanced around, searching the surrounding area for something to supplement what food they had. Getting to her feet, she looked over at where Shay lay stretched out on his bedroll. "I'll be back in a minute. I'm going to find us something to eat."

He opened his eyes. "What about the food we brought from Polvo?"

"There isn't much left."

"You want the rifle?" he said around a yawn.

"No, all I need is my knife."

"Okay." His eyes closed. "Holler if you need help."

She smiled, then turned and moved down the rocky slope.

When she returned a few minutes later, she dropped her catch on her bedroll. Shay pushed himself up onto his elbows to see what she'd brought.

"I thought you went after food," he said, frowning at the collection of what looked like botanical specimens on her blanket. "Not to collect medicinal plants."

"I did. I didn't gather these for medical use. They're our lunch."

"Uh-uh." He moved his head slowly from side to side. "I don't think so."

"They're good," she replied, picking up a creamy-white yucca blossom that had just begun to open. "The fruit of the yucca is good too. Real sweet. But they aren't ripe yet. So we'll have to settle for these young buds and flower stalks.''

"No, *you'll* have to settle for that stuff. Not me."

She shrugged. "Suit yourself, but this is all we've got."

"I thought you said we still have some of the food the folks in Polvo gave us."

"Yes, but I'm saving that for tonight. I'd like to keep walking for a while after dark. By the time we stop, I might not be able to snare another rabbit or see to find other food."

Shay considered her words for a few seconds, idly stroking one side of his mustache. Dammit, why did she always have to make sense? Releasing his breath in a huff, he said, "Okay, give me one of those damn things."

She handed him a yucca bud, her lips pressed together to hold in a smile. "They're not so bad, really."

"Humph." He eyed the bud skeptically, then lifted it to his mouth.

"They're also good cooked." She bit off the end of a flower stalk. "But it's too hot for a fire." She watched him tentatively bite off a piece of the bud, then chew carefully, the expression on his face nearly making her laugh.

"Just about every part of the yucca," she said, keeping her gaze away from him, "has been used by generations of Nde. Besides eating the buds, flower stalks, and fruit, they crushed the roots to make shampoo and used the leaf fibers to make cloth and rope for mats and baskets. In fact, I can't think of a plant the Nde didn't use in one way or another."

When he didn't comment, she looked over at him. Waiting until after he swallowed, she said, "So what do you think?"

"Nothing like I expected. It's . . . actually not bad."

Sheridan smiled, resisting the urge to say "I told you so." Instead, she said, "Prickly pear isn't bad either, nor are hyacinth bulbs. I especially like mescal, which was a staple in the Nde diet for generations. That's why the Spanish gave my ancestors the name Mescalero—it means people who eat mescal. Anyway, mescal is prepared by digging up pieces of the plant's large root, then baking them in underground ovens for hours, so I don't have time to prepare it. Maybe some other time.''

"Yeah, some other time," he replied, surprised to realize he meant the words. As he reached for another yucca bud, he tried not to think about the fact that the plan he'd set into motion two months earlier meant there wouldn't be another time.

They waited until late afternoon before resuming their northwestern trek toward the Chinati Mountains. Though the sun continued to beat down with relentless intensity, the worst of the day's heat had passed.

Even after the sun slipped below the horizon, Sheridan pressed on. "I remember this part of the desert on our way to Polvo," she told Shay. "I'm pretty sure there's a creek not far ahead. That's where we'll make camp."

Too tired to speak, he nodded and concentrated on placing one foot in front of the other.

An hour later they reached the small creek Sheridan remembered crossing on their trip to Polvo. She selected the site for their camp, a level stretch of ground about forty feet from the creek bed, then took her snare and moved silently into the surrounding brush. After setting the snare, she went to the creek to rinse the dust from her face and hands, then returned to their campsite. "I wish I could wash my hair," she said, smiling wistfully over at where Shay sat on one of their bedrolls. "But it'll have to wait."

"What I wouldn't give for a bathtub and a double shot of whiskey," he said.

She sighed. "Hmm, sounds good. Those will be at the top of my list when we get back."

"Still think we'll make it by tomorrow?"

"Yes. I'd say we can't be more than six or seven miles from town. The temperature will cool as soon as we start up into the mountains, so we won't be slowed down by the heat. We should reach Shafter by midday.''

When Shay didn't respond, she said, ''Has the desert been what you expected?''

''Yes and no.''

''Really. Why's that?''

He shrugged, not sure what he wanted to tell her. Finally he said, ''After your warning a few weeks ago, I was expecting the desert to be hot.'' He flashed her a brief smile. ''And I wasn't disappointed. But I didn't expect to find anything even remotely beautiful out here.'' His voice lowered. ''Or that I'd actually like it.''

She sensed his unwillingness to accept what he'd just admitted, so she didn't question him further. Instead, she got to her feet. ''I'll go check my snare.''

He reached for the rifle, then rose. ''I'll gather some firewood.''

He didn't find much in the way of firewood close by, so he followed the creek upstream until he found enough to make an armload. On his return to their camp he heard a noise that sent an icy shiver of dread up his spine. He'd heard the sound only once before, while in the mountains of California.

He momentarily froze, then tossed the wood to the ground and broke into a run. His heart pounding in his ears, he came to a halt at the edge of the campsite. Squinting into the heavy twilight, he finally spotted the source of the sound he'd heard. A mountain lion sat crouched on a small bluff downstream, its long tail twitching with agitation. The big cat looked in his direction, then turned its attention back to its intended prey.

Shay slowly lifted the rifle to his shoulder. A knot of fear forming in his gut, he spared a glance toward the area below the bluff. His fingers tightened on the rifle, the fear inside him intensifying. Sheridan knelt along the bank of the creek, her back to the bluff. But he could tell by the way she held herself perfectly still that she knew about the mountain lion.

He took a couple of tentative steps closer. The cat didn't look at him again, but the tawny ears flattened against the animal's small head. Knowing he wouldn't get a closer shot, he sighted in his target, inhaled, released part of the air in his lungs, then held his breath. *Dear God, don't let anything happen to her.* Just as his finger squeezed the trigger, the cat rose and leapt from the bluff in one fluid motion.

Shay cursed under his breath. Keeping the rifle's sight trained on the cat, he racked in another shell and fired a second shot as quickly as he could. Unable to tell if either shot had hit its mark, he started running, his heart pounding with a terror he'd never known.

He reached the creek bank and slid to a stop, the rifle once again cocked and lifted to his shoulder. The mountain lion lay a few feet from the water, unmoving. Sheridan sat on her haunches beside the still cat.

"Good shot," she said, looking up at him with a smile. "Looks like you got him through the heart."

Relief washed through Shay, threatening to buckle his knees. He lowered the rifle, then wiped a hand over his face. "Damn, that was close. I was afraid I couldn't stop him in time."

"I wasn't totally defenseless. I had my knife."

"What?" His eyes went wide. "You think you could have saved yourself from a mountain lion with a damn knife? You might've managed a stab or two, but that's all."

She rose and moved toward him but didn't speak.

"Adult mountain lions can weigh close to a hundred fifty pounds," he said, his temper still simmering.

She remained silent but came close enough for him to see the wild beating of her pulse at the base of her throat. He glared down at her. "You wouldn't stand a chance against a cat that big. He would have ripped you"—he swallowed hard—"to shreds."

"Probably, but I still would've tried to kill him first." She took another step forward, rose onto her toes, and pressed her mouth to his in a brief kiss. "Guess you saved my life, huh?"

"You're damn right I saved your life," he replied. The heat gone from his voice, he added, "You also scared ten years off mine."

"*I* scared you?" She took a step back and thumped his chest with a fist. "I didn't ask that big cat to leave the mountains and come sniffing around our camp."

"That's not what I meant, and you know it."

"Do I?" She tipped back her head to study his face, wishing she could see him better. Remembering the hitch of emotion she'd heard in his voice, she said, "Yeah, I guess I do."

Shay spent the rest of the evening thinking about the close call with the mountain lion. He still shuddered every time he thought about what would have happened had he not heard the cat's scream or returned to camp in time to take aim and shoot the beast. Though the thought occurred to him that he'd finally done something on their trek to prove he wasn't useless, he didn't dwell on it. Compared to his mind-numbing fear when he found Sheridan in danger and the knee-weakening surge of relief when he prevented the cat from attacking her, bolstering his ego was totally insignificant.

When they finally stretched out on their bedrolls, he slipped an arm under her shoulders and pulled her close. He lowered his head to nuzzle the side of her neck, to nip the tip of her chin. Then he settled his mouth over hers for a long, lazy kiss.

He braced his weight on one forearm and looked down at her. The deep blue of her eyes looked almost black in the firelight. "Sleepy?"

"Uh-uh. You?"

"No. Guess that nap this afternoon took the edge off."

"Yeah." She lifted a hand and ran her fingers across the muscles of his chest. "So what are we going to do with our time?"

"I can think of a thing or two."

"Really?"

"Uh-huh." He bent closer and ran his tongue over her bottom lip.

Her breath caught in her throat. She swallowed, then said, "I'll give you all night to stop that."

He chuckled, then pressed his mouth to hers, pushed his tongue between her lips. She groaned, arching her back and rubbing her breasts against his chest, her belly against his aching erection. When he finally broke the kiss, he drew a steadying breath.

"I want you, Sherry," he said in a raspy whisper. "I know lying on a blanket in the middle of the desert isn't—"

She pressed a finger to his lips. "It doesn't matter where we are." She grabbed a handful of the slightly curly hair at the nape of his neck and brought his face back down to hers. "Make love to me, Shay," she said, her lips brushing his. "Here. Now."

He didn't need any more encouragement. He sat up and made quick work of stripping her naked from the waist down. Returning to a prone position, he unbuttoned his denim trousers, then reached for her. Rolling her on top of him, he wrapped his left arm around her waist and cupped the back of her head with his right hand. He applied slight pressure to her head, bringing her face down to his for a deep, mind-drugging kiss.

Before Sheridan lost what little control she had, she pulled away. "Wait." She sucked in a ragged breath. "What about a preventive?"

He bit out a vicious curse. His arms dropped away from her.

She patted his chest, then rolled off him. "Relax. I have something in my bag." Seeing his expression, she couldn't stop a blush from creeping up her cheeks. "After you insisted on making the trip with me, I wanted to be prepared, just in case we—" She glared at his twitching lips. "Be glad I did." Ignoring his chuckle, she retrieved her bag. "I'll be right back."

When she returned to their bedrolls, he hadn't moved. He

still lay on his back, one arm bent beneath his head, his trousers unbuttoned. She could see the ridge of his swollen manhood pressing against his underdrawers in the V of his gaping trousers. A quiver of excitement racked her shoulders.

Shay stared up at the mesmerizing picture she made. Hair tousled, clad in only a shirtwaist that reached the top of her thighs, she sent his desire soaring even higher. His gaze dropped to her naked feet, then skimmed up her slender, well-muscled legs, and stopped where her shirtwaist barely covered her feminine mound. He knew what the fabric hid from his view. The nest of dark chestnut curls, the pouting lips of her sex, the delicate bud of her clitoris.

A groan rumbling in his chest, he patted the blanket next to him. "Come here, Sherry. I can't wait any longer."

She didn't hesitate, dropping down beside him, letting him push her onto her back, opening her thighs to the pressure of his hand.

He stroked the damp flesh between her legs, flicking her clitoris with his thumb, using his fingers to test her readiness for him. She was hot and slick with need, her hips coming off the blanket to match each stroke of his hand. Satisfied he wouldn't hurt her, he rolled onto his back again, taking her with him.

At his instruction, she shifted position, drawing up her knees so she sat straddling his hips. "Ride me like this," he whispered, lowering one hand between them to free himself from his clothes.

Sheridan's hand replaced his, her fingers tightening around his straining organ. She moved her hand up, then down, in a slow, stroking motion. His breath hissed through clenched teeth. He closed his eyes, praying for control. No woman had ever affected him this way. Sheridan was like an opiate. Once he had her, he kept craving more and more, until he was completely—and he feared irreversibly—addicted.

"No more," he managed to say.

Instantly her hand stilled. Keeping his eyes closed, he eased out a shaky breath. Just when he thought he had regained his control, she shifted, her weight leaving his thighs. He cracked his eyes open in time to see her lower herself onto his engorged member, taking him into her body in one swift movement. He gasped, his hips bucking up at the incredible sensation of her heat surrounding him, her inner muscles clenching and pulling him deeper.

Sheridan braced her hands on either side of Shay's shoulders, lifting and lowering her hips in slow, deliberate strokes. Her position of dominance heightened her own need, intensifying the firestorm burning in her veins. When he slipped his fingers under her shirtwaist and moved upward to find her breasts, she arched into his hands. He rubbed the pads of his thumbs over her nipples, hardening them into tighter peaks, wrenching a moan of ecstasy from her throat.

He tried to maintain her lazy pace, but his need for completion was too great. Increasing the pumping action of his hips, he dug his heels into the blanket for better leverage. "Sherry, I can't wait," he managed to say between gasping breaths.

She bent forward, brushing her lips over his whisker-roughened cheeks, tasting the salt on his skin. "Then, don't," she whispered before pulling his bottom lip into her mouth and sucking.

His breath lodged in his throat, a buzzing started in his head. Jerking his mouth from hers, he lowered his hands to grasp her waist, his fingers biting into her sides while he continued his upward strokes in a near-frantic rhythm. With a primitive growl he thrust into her one last time, then froze. The pulsing of his release seemed to last forever.

After he caught his breath, he dropped his hands from her sides. "I may never recover," he said, his voice raspy.

Sheridan chuckled. Leaning forward to shift her weight to her forearms, she straightened her legs so she lay fully atop him, their bodies still joined. "The heat's taken a lot out of you."

His eyebrows rose. "Really? I could've sworn you're responsible for wringing me dry."

This time she laughed. "That's true, but I'm sure the desert has also taken its toll."

"Maybe," he replied, his strength returning enough to roll her onto her back beside him. "But not so much that I can't find the strength to pleasure you."

As his hand moved between her thighs and touched her aroused flesh, she swallowed the last of her amusement and exhaled with a sigh. "Shay, I—" She bit her lip against the words that had almost slipped out. Confessing her love would serve no useful purpose.

"You what?" he murmured, lowering his head and dipping the tip of his tongue into the tiny dimple beside her mouth.

She lifted her hips. "I don't want you to stop."

He smiled, his mustache brushing her lips. "No chance of that, Sherry."

His skilled fingers soon had her writhing on the blanket, her breathing labored, her escalating need driving her hips to a faster rhythm. The throbbing pressure continued to build between her thighs, spiraling upward toward her peak. Then she was there, sailing over the top. As wave after wave of her climax washed over her, she moaned Shay's name, pushing harder and faster against his hand. Abruptly she arched her back one last time, then went still.

She said his name again, this time with a breathless sob, and allowed her hips to drop back onto the blanket. Her entire body limp with weakness, she drew a shaky breath. "That was incredible."

"No, you're incredible," he murmured, capturing her lips for a quick, gentle kiss. "I love pleasuring you."

She smiled. "Hmm, and you do it so well."

His responding laugh looped around her heart and squeezed.

She'd never realized it was possible to love a man as much as she loved Shay. For the first time, she truly understood what her mother and grandmother had meant when they told her she would one day meet the man destined for her, the man who would steal her heart, the man who was the other half of her soul.

But just because she now understood what they meant, nothing else had changed. There was no way she and Shay could have a lasting relationship.

She pushed out of his arms, then got to her feet and gathered her clothes. "I'm going down to the creek," she said in a voice she hoped didn't sound strained. "I won't be gone long."

Shay watched her leave their campsite, then inhaled a deep breath. The night air was surprisingly cool compared to the intense daytime heat, the sky clear and filled with sparkling silvery stars. He yawned, stretching his arms over his head, his thoughts drifting to his surroundings. As hard as it was to comprehend, he realized his perspective of the desert had done an about-face. He no longer hated what he once considered to be a desolate wasteland. He now respected the desert's life-sustaining abilities, appreciated the raw beauty.

While he continued to mull over his surprising change in attitude, Sheridan returned from the creek, her lovely legs once again covered by buckskin trousers. As she bent to check the fire, he studied her through slitted eyes. His gaze moved over her profile, her long, narrow nose and slightly pointed chin backlit by the orange glow of firelight. An odd sensation gripped his chest, formed a lump in his throat.

He idly rubbed his chest, wondering at the cause of such strange sensations. The answer came as a shock and would have knocked him flat if he hadn't been lying on the ground. He squeezed his eyes closed. *No, that can't be. There's got to be another explanation.*

But when he opened his eyes and saw Sheridan lowering herself to the blanket beside him, his heart slammed against his ribs with the undeniable truth.

He loved her.

Chapter Twenty-two

As they broke camp the following morning, Shay was unusually quiet and introspective. By the time they resumed their journey, Sheridan gave up trying to draw him out of his pensive mood. Though she knew he had to be exhausted, just as she was, she also wondered if there wasn't another reason for his brooding. Recognizing his unwillingness to discuss the topic, she fell silent as well.

Shay walked behind Sheridan, outwardly calm and relaxed, but inside he churned with emotions. He still hadn't come to grips with his startling revelation from the night before. How could he have done the unthinkable and actually fallen in love? He'd loved women his entire adult life, but he'd never been *in* love with any of them. So why Sheridan Kinmont? She was entirely wrong for him—headstrong and opinionated, a divorced suffragist and a doctor. Maybe that's why he'd been attracted to her in the first place, because she was so different from the other women he'd known.

He gave his head a shake, hoping to clear the jumble of

thoughts in his mind. *You've gotten yourself into a helluva mess, Bannigan. Falling in love with the woman you're trying to get fired.* He frowned at his last thought. Somewhere over the last few weeks he'd lost the enthusiasm to prove Sheridan unfit to practice medicine. In fact, everything he'd observed about her proved she was a damn fine doctor.

Sheridan and Shay reached Shafter just past noon. As they walked down Main Street, she said, "I'll stop by the clinic to see Poppy, then I'm going home to take a long bath."

Shay nodded. "I need to let my assistant know I'm back, then I plan to do the same."

When they reached the clinic, she looked over at him. "The last few days have certainly been interesting, but I'm glad they're over."

"Yeah, me too," he replied. When she started to turn away, he reached out to grab her arm. "Wait. I . . . uh . . . there's something I have to say." He released her arm, then drew a deep breath. "I want to thank you."

Her eyebrows rose. "For what?"

"For everything these past couple a days. Saving me from the flash flood. Getting the thorn out of my hand. Knowing how to find water. Providing food." He drew another deep breath, then exhaled slowly. "You got me back here alive, and I wanted you to know I'm grateful."

Sheridan knew how much his admission must have cost him—male pride with all its quirks. She wanted to tell him he would have figured out ways to survive without her—though perhaps he would have returned looking more haggard for the experience—but decided against that idea. Even if she pointed out that he'd saved her from the mountain lion, she doubted he'd change his mind about owing her his thanks. Finally she offered him a smile and said, "You're welcome."

He tugged on his hat brim, then gave her a nod. "Well, I've gotta get to my office."

"Will I see you later?"

He shifted his weight from one foot to the other. "I'm not sure. Depends on how late I work tonight. I'll . . . uh . . . let you know."

Sheridan accepted his explanation, though she couldn't help thinking he hadn't been entirely truthful. Shoving aside her doubts for the time being, she bade him good-bye, then headed up the walk to the clinic.

After a bath, Shay went back to his office and started on the pile of work on his desk. During the hours he worked and the meeting he had with several mine employees over supper, he was able to keep thoughts of Sheridan in check. But as soon as he headed for his house, she once again filled his thoughts.

He lit a lamp, poured himself a glass of whiskey, then sprawled on the sofa to mull over his situation. By the time he'd downed the whiskey and started on a second glass, he drew some startling conclusions. He'd come up with rebuttals to each of the reasons he thought Sheridan was wrong for him. Her headstrong, opinionated nature was part of what attracted him to her in the first place, and to his amazement, he realized he enjoyed their verbal sparring. The fact that she was divorced never had bothered him, and if others thought less of her, then he'd have to set them straight. As for her devotion to woman's suffrage, he couldn't fault Sheridan's involvement. He admired people with such strong devotion to a cause they believed in. And though he'd never been actively involved in the movement to improve women's rights, he had nothing against the campaign. In fact, if the legal changes Sheridan wanted would help women as much as she claimed, then he was all for reform.

So what was left on his list of why she was wrong for him? Ah, yes, her profession. He frowned into his glass of whiskey. That was the toughest reason to refute because of his deeply embedded opinion about lady doctors. But having witnessed her work as a physician in numerous situations, he'd been forced to revise his staunch viewpoint. While he still believed some people weren't cut out to be doctors, he no longer automatically included females in that group. Sheridan had convinced him women were just as qualified as men to practice medicine.

Now that he'd rebutted all his reasons for considering her incompatible, where did that leave him? He didn't know the answer. He emptied his glass, then rose to pour another drink, hoping the whiskey would dull his mind enough to rid himself of thoughts of Sheridan and love. When the third glassful provided only minor help, he poured a fourth.

Sheridan helped Poppy with their supper dishes, then sat down to read an article in a medical journal. After finishing a sentence or two, her mind started to wander, blurring her vision and making the words run together on the page. She started over three times, then threw down the journal and got to her feet.

She meandered through the house, looking for something else to occupy her mind, but Shay continued to haunt her thoughts. Remembering how withdrawn he'd been that morning and his evasive answer when she asked about seeing him later, she wondered at the cause. Deciding she had to talk to him, she turned from her contemplation of the deepening shadows outside her bedroom window and went into the main room.

"Poppy, I'm going out for a while."

Buster leapt to his feet and gave an excited yip.

"Sorry, boy, not this time," Sheridan said, bending to scratch behind his ears.

Buster hung his head and moved back to his blanket, where he flopped down with a grunt. Resting his head on his front paws, he stared up at Sheridan, a doleful look on his face.

Poppy chuckled. "Stop pouting, you little beggar. I'll still be here with you."

Buster's tail wiggled once, then he released a long sigh and closed his eyes.

Sheridan smiled, then shifted her gaze from her dog to her friend. "You're not seeing Orrin tonight?"

"No, I've decided I should stop seeing him."

"But why? I thought you really liked him."

"I do," Poppy said with a sad smile. "But I don't want to give him false hope."

"False hope? What are you talking about?"

"While you were gone, Orrin asked me to marry him."

"Oh, Poppy, that's wonder—" The expression on Poppy's face momentarily startled her. "You turned him down, didn't you?"

Poppy nodded.

"Why? If you care about each other, you should be married."

"You know why," Poppy said, fiddling with the piece of embroidery work lying in her lap.

"Poppy Gilbert," Sheridan said, placing her hands on her hips. "I refuse to be the reason for you to miss a chance at happiness with a man who obviously loves you."

"I wish you wouldn't look at it that way, because I don't. I might not be alive if not for you." When Sheridan opened her mouth to respond, Poppy held up a hand. "Yes, I know. We've had this discussion before, so there's no need to say you don't agree. That still doesn't change anything. I'll go to my grave believing you saved my life. That's a debt I may never be able to repay, but I do intend to try. Besides, I'm already happy working as your nurse and living with you and your crazy mutt."

Sheridan blew out a long breath. "There is one way to end this so-called obligation you feel toward me."

Poppy smiled. "Yes, but we both know you'll never get married again, so that eliminates the possibility."

Sheridan stared at her friend for several moments. A few weeks ago she would have immediately voiced her whole-hearted agreement. Now, after discovering she'd fallen in love with Shay, the idea of remarrying no longer left a bitter taste in her mouth. Giving her head a shake to chase the ridiculous notions from her mind, she said, "Have you told Orrin you don't want to see him anymore?"

"No," Poppy replied in a whisper. "I know I have to, but I've been such a yellow-belly that I haven't been able to tell him."

"Maybe you should give yourself more time."

Poppy's gaze narrowed. "What are you trying to tell me?"

Sheridan shrugged. "Nothing. I just don't want you to be too hasty in making a decision." She stared at Poppy for several moments, searching for a way to lift her spirits. "You know, I just realized something. I owe you a new hat."

Poppy blinked. "What? Oh, our bet. Has it been a month?"

"Actually, it's been almost two. Guess I lost track of time with all that's been happening. Look through the catalogues you brought with you, pick out the one you want, then order it." When Poppy didn't respond, she said, "Will you do that?"

Poppy frowned, then bobbed her head in agreement.

"There's something else I'd like you to do. Promise me you'll at least think about your decision some more before you talk to Orrin."

Poppy hesitated. Exhaling with a sigh, she finally said, "All right."

"Good." Sheridan headed toward the front door. "I might be late, so don't wait up."

After Sheridan left, Poppy sat staring across the room for a long time, mulling over their conversation. Surely she'd misunderstood Sheridan's implications. Her friend couldn't actually be contemplating marriage, the only way she would consider her debt to Sheridan paid.

Poppy shook her head. No, the idea was simply too ludicrous to consider. Exhaling another sigh, she picked up her embroidery, hoping she could concentrate enough to take her usual tiny, even stitches.

* * *

Sheridan checked the mine offices first. Finding the building dark and the front door locked, she headed toward Shay's house.

He wasn't sitting on his porch as he often did, but the glow of a lamp in the main room told her he was home. When he didn't answer her knock, she moved to the front window and peered inside. Not seeing him, she went back to the door and tried the knob. The door wasn't locked and swung open without a sound.

She stepped into the room, closed the door behind her, then started toward his bedroom. She'd taken only a couple of steps, when a noise caught her attention. Turning, her gaze landed on Shay, lying on the sofa, a glass clutched in his hand.

As she approached him, she spotted the whiskey bottle sitting on the floor beside the sofa. Moving closer, she wrinkled her nose. "Whew!" Placing her fingers on his neck to check his pulse, she whispered, "Smells like you took your comment about wanting a double shot of whiskey a little too far."

"Huh?" He rolled his head toward her and opened his eyelids a crack.

Sheridan shook her head. "My God, you're soused."

"Aye, Sherry lass," he replied, letting his eyes drift closed. "But not nearly drunk enough. I can still see ye."

She frowned at both the Irish inflection in his voice and his words. "What are you talking about?"

A snore was the only response she received.

She removed the glass from his hand, picked up the whiskey bottle, and took both to the kitchen. When she returned, she stared down at him for a few moments. Had their ordeal in the desert been so difficult that he'd found it necessary to drink himself into a stupor? Or did he have other reasons for turning to whiskey? Knowing no answers would be forthcoming while he was in a liquor-induced sleep, she brushed a lock of dark hair off his face, then bent to press a light kiss to his forehead.

Even though she knew he wouldn't hear her, she whispered good night, then turned down the lamp and quietly left his house.

When Shay awoke, sunlight streamed through the window, making him squint against the glare. "What the hell?" He started to rise, then grabbed his head and fell back onto the sofa. "Christ, what happened?"

He didn't move, taking the shallowest breaths possible, afraid even the smallest movement would worsen the pounding in his head. While waiting for the pain to subside, he tried to recall how he'd ended up sleeping on his sofa, fully clothed. From the way everything above his neck throbbed—even his hair hurt—he must've been on one helluva bender.

He inched to a sitting position, groaning with the effort. God, what had possessed him to drink himself into oblivion? He hadn't gotten drunk since his twentieth birthday, when a group of friends took him on a tour of nearly every saloon in San Francisco. He paid dearly for that night, suffering through a hangover that lasted two full days—more than sufficient reason for the vow he'd made to curtail all future drinking to moderation.

He glanced around the room, looking for evidence of what he'd imbibed. There was no liquor bottle sitting around, no glass. An image of someone in his house the previous night flashed through his mind. Frowning, he tried to summon the memory, but it remained fuzzy. He remembered someone speaking to him, and he thought he'd replied, but then—had the person really been Sheridan? Rubbing his temples with his fingertips, he fought down the sudden nausea.

When his stomach settled, he got to his feet and headed for the kitchen on shaky legs. There was no way he could work in his current condition. Seeing the whiskey bottle beside the sink brought another round of nausea. When it passed, he took some headache powders, then made his way to his bedroom, where he striped off his clothes and crawled into bed.

Shay awoke the second time shortly after noon, thankfully clearheaded, a dull ache in his temples the only remnant of his overindulgence. As he bathed and dressed, he realized the foolishness of resorting to liquor to rid himself of thoughts of Sheridan and love. Nothing would change the fact that he'd fallen in love with her. But such an admission created another problem. She didn't want declarations of love or a permanent relationship, and surprisingly he did.

On his walk to the mine offices he tried to come up with a plan to change Sheridan's mind. He finally concluded his first step should be convincing her he trusted her medical abilities. Liking the idea, he decided to stop by the clinic on his way to work.

When he arrived at the clinic, he found Enrique sweeping the floor of the waiting room. He exchanged greetings with the boy, then said, "Do you know if Dr. Kinmont is seeing a patient?"

"No, señor, the *doctora* said she has some work to do in her office."

Thankful Sheridan was alone, Shay went into her office and closed the door behind him.

Sheridan looked up. At first, surprise registered on her face, then she smiled. "You're looking a little peaked, but otherwise not bad for a man who spent the night with a whiskey bottle."

"So you were at my house." At her nod he said, "I thought so, but my brain was a little fuzzy when I woke up this morning."

"I'm sure it was," she replied with a chuckle. "What can I do for you? A dose of headache powders? Something to settle a bilious stomach?"

"No, I'm fine." He smoothed one side of his mustache with a forefinger. "I . . . uh . . . came by because there's something I want to tell you."

Sheridan sat back in her chair. "What is it?"

"I wanted you to know Boyd Smith will no longer be watching the clinic. And I won't be coming here every time you have a patient.

Her brow furrowed. "And the reason for this sudden change is . . ."

"It's not entirely sudden. During the past few weeks I started to realize you didn't fit my preconceived notions about lady doctors. And then our trip to Polvo cinched it. You took excellent care of the people there, just like you've done for the mine employees you've treated."

Sheridan stared at him, stunned. Finally she said, "You're serious? You really think I'm a good doctor? Not a charlatan who relies on bogus folk remedies? Not an overemotional, irrational female who had no business becoming a doctor or practicing medicine?"

He smiled, not at all surprised to have his own words thrown back at him. "Touché," he said, the gold flecks in his eyes twinkling with amusement. "I understand your skepticism. But I assure you I have changed my mind, well, actually, you changed my mind. You've shown me that women have every right to attend medical school and practice medicine. Though I still believe some will become better doctors than others." Seeing her eyes narrow, he quickly added, "Wait. Let me finish. The same holds true for men. There are male doctors who should've chosen another occupation."

She remained silent for a moment, studying his face, trying to absorb everything he'd told her. Finding nothing in his expression to indicate he wasn't telling her the truth, she finally said, "Thank you."

"You're welcome," he replied, moving around her desk. Now, how about a kiss before I leave?"

"Hmm, sounds wonderful." She rose from her chair and stepped into his arms.

A few moments later he lifted his head and dragged in a lungful of air. "No one kisses as good as you do, Dr. Kinmont."

Sheridan wasn't sure which pleased her more, the compliment about her kissing or his calling her doctor. Smiling up at him, she said, "You'd better leave, or I might end up doing more than kissing you."

Heat flared in his eyes. "Vixen. Tempting a man like that when he has ten days of work waiting on his desk." He brushed his mouth over hers once more, then stepped away from her. "I'll see you later."

After Shay left her office, Sheridan couldn't wipe the smile off her face. She'd begun to think she'd never change his mind about lady doctors. Then out of the blue he waltzed in and announced he'd come around. What a pleasant surprise! Too bad about the timing of his change in attitude, she thought with a chuckle. *If only I'd told Poppy I needed two months, I would've saved myself the price of a new hat.*

As Shay left the clinic, he recognized Betsy Pringle coming up the street. Tipping his hat, he said, " 'Afternoon, Mrs. Pringle," then headed for the mine offices, eager to get through the day so he could spend the evening with Sheridan.

When his assistant told him he had a visitor, he nodded and crossed the room toward his office. Expecting to find the mine foreman or one of the mill supervisors waiting for him, he came to an abrupt halt in the doorway. A man with sandy-brown hair, clad in a starched dress shirt and four-in-hand tie, sat behind his desk. A suit jacket hung on the back of his chair.

Shay bit back a groan. *Damn, I forgot about Whit.* Drawing a deep breath, he stepped into the room. "Hello, Whit." He stopped in front of his desk and offered his hand. "When did you get here?"

Whit Stafford rose from behind Shay's desk and shook hands. "I came in on the morning stage." He contemplated Shay for a moment, his light blue eyes cool and piercing behind his spectacles. "After all your harping to get me here, you don't look very happy to see me."

"It's not that. I was thinking about something else, and seeing you took me by surprise, that's all."

"Your assistant said you didn't come in this morning. Are you feeling all right?"

"Yeah, fine. I've had a rough few days, so I decided to sleep late."

"I understand you've been out of town."

"That's right. Dr. Kinmont was summoned to a village downriver, and I didn't think she should go alone."

Whit accepted his explanation without comment. "I've been doing some reading since my arrival." He tapped the folder lying open on Shay's desk. "This is interesting. Very interesting."

A feeling of dread swept over Shay. "What is?"

"The notes you've compiled on Dr. Kinmont."

"You've read all of them?"

"Yes," Whit replied, dropping back into the chair. "I must admit, I was a bit hasty to dismiss your claims about her incompetence, but now . . . Well, you've done an excellent job of gathering some pretty damning evidence."

"Such as?" Shay replied, lowering himself to the guest chair in front of his desk.

"This business of using herbal remedies. Talking to patients about contraceptives. Interfering in the personal lives of mine employees. That isn't the type of behavior the owners expect from the company doctor."

Shay slumped in his chair and rubbed a hand over his face. *What have I done?* Hoping to diffuse the situation, he said, "Actually, I might have been too quick to judge Sher—uh, Dr. Kinmont for treating patients with herbs and plants. I've seen the results myself, and they're impressive."

"That's nonsense. Modern medicine is a lot more advanced than that."

"On some things, yes. But there are times when even the modern ways aren't as effective as the old methods using plants."

Whit stared at him for a moment, his fingers steepled under his chin. Finally he said, "What's going on, Shay? You sound like you're recanting your claims about Dr. Kinmont's competence."

Shay realized he'd probably already said too much, and if he told Whit the truth, his friend would likely light into him for insisting he come to Texas only to find out he'd changed his mind about wanting Sheridan replaced. Shay blew out a breath, then said, "Nothing's going on. I've just come to respect healing plants and herbs."

Another long silence passed between them before Whit said, "I'll look over your notes again tonight, then in the morning I'll send a wire to the home office. Once the rest of the owners have had a chance to review the situation, a decision will be made."

Shay nodded, silently praying the owners wouldn't find the information he'd collected about Sheridan as damning as he'd originally thought it to be.

Chapter Twenty-three

The sound of an explosion awakened Shay just past midnight. He got out of bed and fumbled for his clothes. He'd managed to jerk on a pair of trousers and pull on his boots when several rounds of gunfire echoed in the night. Cursing under his breath, he shrugged into a shirt and headed for the door.

As he ran toward Main Street, Whit caught up with him. "Is it the mill?" Whit said.

Shay shook his head. "It sounded closer than that."

Shay and Whit arrived in the main section of town a minute later and found Orrin Neilson, Ian Finlay, and several other men congregated near the front of the company store.

Shay approached the men and said, "What happened, Orrin?"

"We're just trying to find out," Orrin replied. "The explosion came from inside the store. Leonard Pringle here said he heard it and came to investigate."

Shay turned. "That right, Pringle?" When the man nodded,

Shay said, "Stay right here, I'm going to check inside the store. When I come back, I want to hear exactly what happened."

"I ain't going nowhere," Pringle replied.

"Orrin, you and Whit come with me. Ian, check around the area to see if you can find anything. The rest of you stay here with Pringle."

Whit and Orrin followed Shay into the company store. "Light a couple of lamps, Orrin," Shay said. "Then we'll have a look around."

"Might as well start with the back room," Orrin replied, touching a flame to the wick of an oil lamp. "I got a bad feeling about this."

When the three men stepped into the back room, Orrin's fears were confirmed. The safe had been blown open. Orrin swallowed. "Damn. Someone took the payroll."

"What!" Shay and Whit said in unison.

Orrin looked over at the men. "The payroll came in a couple days early. I went to your office yesterday morning, Shay, but you weren't there. And then I didn't get another chance to get back to tell ya."

"Who else knew the payroll came in early?" Whit said, wiping the smoke residue from his spectacles with his shirttail.

"Just Ed, Deputy Luján, who brought it from Marfa like he always does, myself, and—" Orrin's eyes widened. "Where's Enrique?" he said, turning to look around the room.

"Who's Enrique?" Whit said.

"Enrique Lara. His father used to work for the mine. Now Enrique works for me," Orrin replied, rubbing a hand over the back of his neck. "He was spending the night here."

"As night watchman?" Shay said.

Orrin nodded. "He knew I always stayed in the store on the nights I had that much cash in the safe. He also knew having the payroll arrive early interfered with the plans I'd made for last night, so he volunteered to take my place."

"Well," Whit said, rocking back on his heels. "Looks like we've got a suspect."

"I don't believe it," Orrin replied with a shake of his head. "Enrique wouldn't steal from the store."

"Well, you've got to admit he had plenty of opportunity. Spending the night here. Alone."

"I still don't think he did it," Orrin said.

"I agree," Shay said from where he crouched in front of the gaping safe. "Whoever blew this open used dynamite. Enrique doesn't know anything about dynamite."

"You said his father used to work in the mines," Whit replied. "Maybe the kid learned about explosives from him."

Shay frowned. "I suppose that's possible, but I still don't think the boy is responsible."

"It doesn't matter what you think. It's the evidence that counts."

Shay opened his mouth to respond, but a shout from outside halted what he'd started to say.

Before the three men got to the store's front door, Ian Finlay appeared in the doorway. "Mr. Bannigan, you'd better come see what I found."

Shay followed Finlay to a spot beneath some trees about fifty feet from the store. In the deep shadows Shay finally made out something lying on the ground. A body. Hunkering down beside the still form, he brought the lamp closer.

"Oh, Jesus," he murmured. He pressed his fingers to the boy's throat. He felt a pulse, but it was extremely weak. Looking up at Finlay, he said, "Send someone for Dr. Kinmont."

"I took care of that before I went to fetch you."

Shay moved the lamp to check Enrique for injuries, wincing when he saw the hole in the boys's back and the dark stain soaking his shirt and the ground. Even more shocking, he had a cloth bag clutched in one hand—a bag Shay recognized as one used by the bank in Marfa to transport the company payroll each month.

As Shay got to his feet, Sheridan arrived. "What happened?" she said in a breathless voice.

Shay grabbed her arm. "There's been a shooting." Unable to think of a way to soften what he had to tell her, he drew a deep breath then said, "Sheridan, it's Enrique."

"Oh, my God. Is he—"

"He's alive. Barely. He was shot in the back and it looks like he lost a lot of blood."

Sheridan absorbed what he said, then shook off his hand. "I need to examine him."

Shay handed the lamp to Finlay and said, "Stay here and hold this for her."

While Sheridan did what she could for Enrique, Shay went back to the group of men, which had increased in size during the past few minutes. Shay motioned for Whit and Orrin to join him, then said, "Pringle, I want to talk to you now."

Lenny moved away from the group to where Shay and the two other men stood.

"Okay, Pringle," Shay said, crossing his arms over his chest. "Tell us what happened."

"I was just heading home from the saloon, when I heard this explosion. I ran up the road toward the store and saw someone come running out the front door. He looked kinda suspicious, so I hollered for him to stop. When he didn't, I pulled my gun and fired."

"What do you mean, he looked suspicious?" Whit said.

Lenny turned a narrowed gaze on Whit. "Who the hell are you?"

"Whitaker Stafford. One of the mine's owners."

When Lenny just stared at Whit, Shay said, "Answer his question, Pringle."

Lenny shuffled his feet, then said, "Well, it's the middle of the night. There's an explosion. Somebody comes running outta the company store. It just didn't look right."

Shay stared at him for a moment, then said, "Did the boy have anything in his hands?"

"Yeah, a bag of money."

Shay's gaze narrowed. "You must have excellent eyes if you could tell the boy was holding a bag of money, in the dark, from fifty feet away."

"Well, I—I could see he had somethin' in his hand when he came outta the store. With the explosion and seeing him running away, I figured he must be holding a bag of money he stole from the company safe."

"That's the only bag you saw? The boy didn't drop any others when he ran from the store?"

"Nope. I saw just the one in his hand."

Shay considered everything the man had said, then finally nodded. Looking over at Whit and Orrin, he said, "Either of you have any more questions?" When the men shook their heads, Shay turned back to Pringle. "We'll want to talk to you again, but that's it for tonight. Go home and get some sleep."

After Pringle started down the street, Shay, Whit, and Orrin returned to where the other men stood talking. "Okay, fellas, let's break this up. The excitement's over."

As the men started to move away, Sheridan approached Shay. "Enrique needs to be moved to the clinic. Will you have him taken there? And I'd like someone to fetch Poppy."

Before Shay could respond, Whit stepped forward. "Shay, wait." Smiling at Sheridan, he said, "I'm sorry we have to meet under these troubling circumstances, Dr. Kinmont." He bowed formally. "Whitaker Stafford, at your service."

"I don't have time for pleasantries, Mr. Stafford," Sheridan replied in a clipped voice. "What are you doing in town?"

"I came to take care of some company business."

"Well, the company business you can take care of right now is calling some of those men back so they can take my patient to the clinic. Enrique needs immediate medical help. Help I can't adequately provide unless he's at the clinic."

"Don't bother, Dr. Kinmont," Whit replied, adjusting his glasses. "Even if the boy survives, he'll be hanged—"

"Wait a minute, Whit," Shay said. "You're making an assumption you—" Whit's raised hand halted his protest.

"Don't interfere, Shay. I know what I'm doing." Whit turned to look at Sheridan. "It's clear what happened here, so the boy will be hanged for robbery."

"That's absurd," Sheridan said. "Enrique wouldn't rob anyone."

"I'm afraid the evidence says otherwise."

"Then the evidence is wrong," she said, infuriated by his callous regard for a human life. Her voice rose sharply. "Enrique is dying, and I won't stand here, arguing with you. Get someone to move him to the clinic." She practically shouted her last statement.

Whit reached out to grab her arm. "Dr. Kinmont—"

She jerked her arm out of his reach. "Don't touch me. That boy is an employee of your company, dammit, so let me do my job and treat him."

"You're getting hysterical," Whit said, his own anger beginning to simmer. "Try to calm down so we—"

"What is the matter with you? A boy I care about is lying in the dirt, bleeding to death, and you tell me to calm down!" She drew a shuddering breath. "I want Enrique taken to the clinic. Now, or I'll see to it myself. Have I made myself clear, Mr. Stafford?"

A muscle ticked in Whit's jaw. "Perfectly, Dr. Kinmont." He turned to Orrin. "See that the boy is taken to the clinic." To Shay he said, "And I'll see you in your office first thing tomorrow morning."

Sheridan and Poppy worked feverishly to save Enrique's life. The first thing Sheridan had to do was remove the bullet. After beginning the procedure by carefully probing the wound, she glanced up at Poppy. "In spite of the amount of blood he's lost, I don't find evidence that the bullet hit a major artery."

"What about his lung?" Poppy said.

"As far as I can tell, the bullet also missed his lung. At least I didn't hear anything to indicate a problem when I listened to his lungs."

"Praise God," Poppy replied with a sigh.

"Yes."

The two fell silent while Sheridan removed the bullet, repaired a tear in a small artery, then stitched up the wound. As she applied a dressing, she said, "Do you know if word's been sent to his parents?"

"After Orrin and the others brought Enrique here, I heard Mr. Bannigan tell one of them to go to the Lara home. They should be here by now."

Sheridan nodded, then stepped away from the operating table and pulled off her rubber gloves. "Keep a close eye on him while I go see if they've arrived. I'll be back in a few minutes."

Poppy nodded, then brushed a lock of Enrique's hair off his face. "He's such a handsome boy. I sure hope he makes it."

"Yeah, me too," Sheridan replied, then turned and headed for the door.

She found Hector and Josefa Lara sitting with Shay in the waiting room. Hector's face looked drawn. Josefa's was tear-stained and pale. When they started to rise, she indicated they should remain seated.

As Sheridan pulled a chair closer, Hector said, "How is our son, *doctora?*"

"Enrique survived the surgery to remove the bullet, which is a good sign. But he lost a lot of blood and he's very weak."

"You think—" Josefa swallowed hard. "You think he will die?"

Sheridan reached over and squeezed the woman's hand. "I'll do everything in my power to see that he doesn't. He's strong and healthy, which gives him a better chance of pulling through. All we can do now is wait.''

''And pray,'' Josefa whispered.

''Yes, and pray,'' Sheridan replied. ''Would you like to see him?''

''*Sí!*'' Hector said, rubbing a hand over his eyes. ''We want to see our son.''

''He's unconscious, but I'll still allow you a few minutes with him, *bueno?*''

Hector nodded, reaching for his wife's hand.

''Let me check on him one more time,'' Sheridan said, getting to her feet. ''Then you can come in.

While the Laras looked in on their son, Sheridan joined Shay in the waiting room.

''Do you really think he has a chance?'' Shay said in a low voice.

Sheridan sighed. ''Yes, but a lot depends on whether infection sets in, and if it does, whether he's strong enough to fight it off.'' When Shay didn't reply, she said, ''Why would Orrin Neilson leave a fourteen-year-old boy alone to guard the company payroll?''

''Orrin takes his job seriously and is an overly cautious man. The first time the payroll arrived early, he told me he planned to spend the night in the store. I told him I didn't see any reason for the added security. We took care not to broadcast the fact that the payroll came in early, so keeping the money locked in the safe seemed adequate. But I couldn't talk him out of staying at the store. Even if he'd asked me about letting Enrique take his place, I wouldn't have objected. Nothing has ever happened here to indicate a need for concern.''

Sheridan fell silent for a moment, then said, ''You don't really think Enrique robbed the store, do you?''

He ran a hand over his bristled jaw. ''No, but the evidence sure points to him.''

''Did you tell his parents?''

"Under the circumstances, I didn't want to add to their worries. They have enough to deal with as it is, so all I told them is that the company store was robbed and Enrique was shot, but I didn't say he's the primary suspect."

"They need to be told. If we don't tell them, they'll hear it from someone else."

"We?"

"Yes. I want them to know we don't believe Enrique is guilty."

Shay blew out a long breath. "You're right. We should tell them. Do you want to wait until morning?"

"No. I hate to with all they've been through already, but we'd better tell them now before word gets around town."

After the difficult conversation with the Laras, Josefa, tears streaming down her anguished face, pleaded with Sheridan to let her stay near her son. Sheridan couldn't refuse the woman the chance to be near Enrique during what could be his last night. After getting Josefa's assurance that she would at least try to get some rest, Sheridan made up the cot in her office. A few minutes later a shaken Hector kissed his wife's wet cheek, then left to go home to their daughters.

When Sheridan returned to the waiting room, Shay said, "Unless there's something I can do, I think I'll head home."

Sheridan shook her head, weariness evident in her drawn face. "All we can do is wait."

"I'll see if I can find someone to stay close by in case you need to send for Mr. Lara."

Sheridan swallowed, knowing what Shay had been unwilling to say. She wished she could do more for Enrique, hated feeling so inadequate. But, as she'd told Shay, all any of them could do was wait.

Shay arrived at his office earlier than usual that morning. He hadn't slept well, the events from the previous night constantly replaying in his head and keeping him awake well into the night. After several hours of fitful sleep, he finally gave up. He rose and dressed, deciding to try to get some work done before Whit showed up.

He'd managed to get through half the stack of papers on his desk before Whit strolled into his office. Motioning to the chair in front of his desk, Shay said, "Have a seat."

Whit settled in the chair, then said, "I did a lot of thinking last night about the robbery and also about the matter we discussed yesterday. Regarding the latter, I've decided to forgo talking to the other owners. As soon as we know the fate of the Lara boy, I intend to ask Dr. Kinmont for her resignation."

Shay's back stiffened. "What?"

"Her outburst last night was the final straw. Now I understand what you meant about women being too emotional to be competent doc—"

"She loves Enrique like a younger brother, and he idolizes her. Why shouldn't she become emotional when she finds him shot and possibly dying?" Not allowing Whit to respond, he continued. "How would you expect anyone to react—man or woman—when you tell that person to let someone they care about die because they're going to hang anyway?" Narrowing his gaze, he sent his friend a fierce glare. "How would you have reacted?"

"You're too close to this, Shay," Whit said, shaking his head. "You're not seeing things clearly."

"The hell I'm not," he responded, trying to curb his growing temper. "She's a damn fine doctor and I think you're being too hasty."

"Well, I happen to disagree." Brushing a piece of lint off his trousers, he said, "How's the boy?"

Shay didn't respond immediately. He needed a minute to regain his composure. Finally he said, "I stopped by the clinic several hours ago. Sheridan said he's holding his own but it's still too soon to know for sure."

Whit stared at him for a long while. Though surprised by Shay's sudden defense of Sheridan Kinmont and wondering at its cause, he wasn't going to be swayed in the decision he'd made. Finally he said, "Well, like I said, when we know for sure whether the boy will live or not, I'll talk to her."

Shay heard the steel edge in Whit's voice and knew there was no point in trying to persuade him to change his mind. Instead, he smoothed one side of his mustache, contemplating a future without Sheridan. Whit's voice broke through his musings.

"Last night Orrin said Hector Lara used to work in the mines."

"That's right," Shay replied. "He started soon after the mines opened back in 'eighty-three. He's been ill recently, and Sheridan diagnosed his illness as miner's consumption and suggested he quit. That's how she got to know Enrique. He wanted to take his father's place in the mines, but she wouldn't hear of it. So she got him a job working for Orrin at the company store."

"A kid working a few hours a week at the store doesn't replace a man's wages from the mines."

"Of course not, but Lara recently started picking up an occasional day's work as a drayman."

"I'd venture to guess the family's still in a financial bind."

Shay shrugged. "Maybe, but that's no proof Enrique robbed the company store's safe, especially when part of the payroll is still unaccounted for. Which brings me back to the point I started to make earlier. What you said to Sheridan last night was way out of line. I never thought I'd hear you tell anyone to let a suspect die. No matter what your opinion is on Enrique's guilt or innocence, he's still entitled to due process."

Whit adjusted his spectacles. "Maybe I was a bit hasty, but the evidence seemed pretty obvious to me. Evidence, I'd wager, that would stand up in any court of law." He got to his feet.

"And you've got to admit, the boy's family's finances give him a hell of a motive."

A knot formed in Shay's gut. He didn't like the conclusion Whit had drawn, but at the moment he had to agree: The evidence continued to point to Enrique.

After Whit left, Shay tried to put the entire incident from his mind so he could finish the paperwork on his desk. By midafternoon he'd managed to get through the bulk of his work backlog. Deciding to check on Enrique, he headed for the clinic.

He found Sheridan, her face drawn and pinched with exhaustion, in the examination room with Enrique.

"How is he?"

She looked up and gave him a weak smile. "If he makes it through the first twenty-four hours, I'll be more hopeful. Right now he's slightly feverish, which is to be expected, but otherwise he's stable."

"Has he been awake at all?"

"Not completely. I've been able to get him to swallow a few sips of water, but he wasn't fully conscious when he did."

"Is his mother still here?"

"Yes." She rubbed the back of her neck, arched her back, then started toward the waiting room. "I finally got her to lie down several hours ago."

"What about you?" He followed behind her, then lifted his hands to massage her shoulders. "Have you gotten any sleep?"

She groaned. "Poppy relieved me for a few hours during the night." She dropped her chin onto her chest. "Hmm, that feels wonderful."

Shay chuckled, then bent to nuzzle the side of her neck. When he straightened, he sobered, then said, "It doesn't look good for Enrique."

Sheridan whirled around to face him. "He didn't do it, Shay."

"You don't know that for sure."

"Enrique wouldn't steal. He's too honorable to do such a thing."

Shay frowned. "Yeah, I know he seems like an honest kid, but there are too many things that point to him."

"What things?"

"Obviously he was in the store at the time. He was found clutching a bag containing part of the payroll. His family needed money. This is a mining town, so getting dynamite and learning how to use it shouldn't be a problem."

She stared up at him, her face growing even paler. "You don't really think there's a chance he'll be found guilty, do you?"

He huffed out a breath. "I don't know. But you've got to admit, at first glance the evidence against him is pretty overwhelming."

"I still don't believe Enrique would—wait a minute. You said 'part of the payroll.' What happened to the rest of it?"

"We don't know. Maybe Enrique hid it before he ran from the store."

Sheridan shook her head slowly. "No, I don't think so. There's got to be a way to find out who really broke into the safe." She grabbed Shay's arm. "Have you talked to Deputy Luján?"

"No. As soon as he delivered the payroll, Orrin said he headed back to Marfa. Something about helping the Presidio County sheriff. That's why he brought the payroll early. He's supposed to be back in a day or two, so I didn't see a need to send for him."

"Then we need to do our own investigation right away." She started pacing the waiting room. "We should start ask-ing—"

"Whoa. Hold it right there. You're using 'we' again, and I haven't agreed to do anything."

She turned back to face him. "Shay, Enrique's life may depend on this. I can't stand by and watch an innocent boy get arrested for something he didn't do." When his only response was the flattening of his lips, she said, "Maybe you can live with yourself if you don't try to help him, but I can't."

He closed his eyes, contemplating her words. After a moment he exhaled a long breath, then opened his eyes. "All right. You made your point. Where do we start?"

Chapter Twenty-four

"The company payroll came in early," Sheridan said. "Does that happen often?"

Shay shook his head. "Maybe only one other time since I've been here."

"Then, that's where we start. Finding out who knew the payroll was in the company safe ahead of schedule."

"Makes sense," he replied, smoothing his mustache while he contemplated the situation. "Orrin and Deputy Luján knew, of course, and Enrique. I would have, too, if I'd been in town. Orrin usually doesn't tell anyone else, but since I wasn't available, I'll double-check with him about that." He started pacing across the waiting room. "We also need to figure out if anyone else found out."

"I knew. Enrique told me," Sheridan said. At his surprised look, she added, "He came by yesterday to tell me he wouldn't be able to work for me today. He was so proud because he was taking Orrin's place in the store last night. His excitement was contagious, so I didn't think to ask why someone needed to stay at the store. I just told him he could work for me some other day and never thought anymore about it.''

"Did anyone overhear your conversation with him?'' When she shook her head, he continued pacing. "Okay, then, we—''

Sheridan's gasp brought him to a halt. He turned to face her and watched the color drain from her face. "What is it?''

She sank onto one of the chairs lining the wall. "I think I might have told someone about the payroll.''

"You just said you didn't know about the money arriving early.''

She nodded. "But I did say Enrique was spending the night at the company store, so they could've figured out the rest.''

Shay moved to the row of chairs and took a seat next to Sheridan. "Start from the beginning and tell me what happened.''

She took a deep breath, then began speaking. "Not long after Enrique left yesterday, I had another visitor.'' She pinched the bridge of her nose. "I guess I was still tired from our trip and preoccupied about other things, so the questions she asked didn't sink in. I just answered by rote.''

"Who are you talking about?''

She sighed. "Betsy Pringle. She comes by a couple of times a week. She's always full of questions, so I guess that part of her visit wasn't any different.''

"Can you remember what she asked?''

"Not her exact words. First she asked a lot of questions about my trip, and then because I was alone in the office, she asked about Enrique and Poppy. I don't remember specifically what I said about Enrique, but I must have mentioned he was staying at the store that night, because she suddenly got real interested. She wanted to know if he was working as a guard and why the store needed a night watchman. When I told her I didn't know, she mumbled something about it being real valuable. She asked a couple more questions, then said she had to leave.''

Sheridan lifted her chin and met Shay's gaze. "What if . . ." Her voice quivered slightly. "What if I'm the reason Enrique got shot?"

Shay grabbed her shoulders and gave her a gentle shake. "Don't start blaming yourself. You didn't know why Enrique was staying at the store that night, so you couldn't have told Betsy about the payroll."

"No, but as I said, anyone could've figured out the rest. It didn't take long for Betsy to make the connection between Enrique staying at the store and the need for a night watchman to guard something valuable. So making the next logical conclusion, that the something valuable had to be the company payroll, would be easy."

"Yeah, that's true." He released her, then got to his feet. "I'll go talk to Orrin again. Then I'll see what I can find out about Leonard Pringle and his overly curious wife."

"I'd like to talk to Betsy."

He stared down at her for a moment, then said, "If you're sure you want to."

"I'm sure."

"Okay, but why don't you try to get some sleep first?" He bent to press a kiss on her forehead. "I'll talk to you later." At her nod he turned and left the clinic.

Sheridan remained seated in the waiting room, the weight of remorse settling over her. Though Shay hadn't blamed her, she wasn't so quick to loosen the noose of guilt she'd wrapped around her own neck. Now keeping Enrique alive took on even greater importance. She not only wanted him to live to prove her worth as a doctor and because she cared about the boy; now she needed him to survive to ease her conscience.

When Poppy arrived at the clinic an hour later, Sheridan went over Enrique's condition, then said, "I have to leave for a while. There's something I need to do."

"You should go home and go to bed," Poppy replied.

"Sleep can wait." Heading for the door, she said, "I'll be back as soon as I can."

A few minutes later Sheridan approached the small stone house where the Pringles lived. Thankful she'd arrived before the day shift at the mine let out, she waited impatiently for her knock to be answered.

The door creaked open and a scowling Betsy appeared in the doorway. "What do you want?"

The hostility in the woman's voice took Sheridan by surprise. "Can I come in?"

"No, you can say yer piece from there."

"I need to ask you some questions."

"What kinda questions?"

"About our conversation at the clinic yesterday."

Betsy's face paled, but the belligerence didn't leave her expression. "What about it?"

"Did you tell your husband that Enrique would be staying at the company store last night?"

Betsy took a step back and tried to shut the door, but Sheridan moved quickly to block the attempt with her shoulder. "Did you, Betsy?"

"I don't havta answer yer questions."

"No, you don't," Sheridan replied. Then, hoping she wasn't bluffing, she said, "But you will have to answer questions from the deputy sheriff and maybe a judge."

Though Betsy's face lost even more color, she kept her lips tightly sealed. Finally Sheridan said, "Why did you start coming to the clinic? Was it really so we could become friends, or did you come to ask me about what was going on in town?"

"I ain't got nothing to say to you."

"Were you really just curious, as you tried to make me believe, or did your husband put you up to it?" When the woman just stared at her, Sheridan continued. "You never intended to leave him, did you, Betsy? You just pretended to listen to what I said so you could find out something to tell your husband. Would that keep you from getting another slap or shove?" She shook her head. "No, I doubt it did. All I wanted to do was help you, and all the time you were using—"

"I never wanted yer help," Betsy said in a near shout, two splotches of red appearing on her cheeks. "But Lenny said I should—" She drew a deep, shuddering breath. "I ain't saying no more. Now, git off my property."

Sheridan didn't reply but gave Betsy one last, pitiful glance, then turned and walked away. The door banged shut behind her, signaling the end of a relationship that had never existed.

On her walk back to town, she couldn't believe she'd been duped so easily. All she'd ever tried to do was help, and right from the start Betsy repaid her kindness by using her to gain information. The woman's betrayal was a bitter pill for Sheridan to swallow, more weight added to the burden of her already overloaded emotions.

Later that night Shay returned to the clinic. He found Sheridan in her office, head resting on an open book lying on her desk. He called her name softly.

When she roused and lifted her head, he noticed the dark circles under her eyes, the fatigue lines around her mouth.

"You should be lying on the cot," he said, coming closer.

She rubbed her eyes, then blinked up at him. "I came in here to look in one of my medical books." She managed a smile. "Guess I fell asleep."

"Guess you did," he replied, returning her smile. He stepped around the desk, then squatted next to her chair. "Any change?"

She sighed. "No. His fever hasn't gotten any worse, but he still hasn't regained consciousness."

"What did Betsy Pringle have to say?"

"Not much. After I told her why I was there, she turned downright hostile, clamming up tight. But I could tell my questions scared her. She finally lost her temper and told me she never wanted my help, then she ordered me to leave."

"You still think she told Pringle about Enrique being a night watchman?"

She nodded. "From the beginning she was using me to get information to pass on to her husband. So even though I couldn't get her to admit it, I'm sure she told him that too."

When Shay didn't respond, she lifted a hand to stroke the stubble on his jaw. "What about you? Did you learn anything we can use?"

He turned his head to press a kiss on her palm, then straightened. "As far as we can determine, no one else knew about the payroll arriving early. And as for Leonard Pringle, I'm not sure what I found out will help, but I did learn a couple of interesting things. I spoke to several men he works with, and each of them told me Pringle is heavily in debt, probably from gambling. He also constantly talked about finding a way to hit it big so he could quit his job and move to El Paso."

"Now that you mention it," she replied, "I remember Betsy telling me her husband was always saying they'd be rich someday. Stealing the company payroll would certainly qualify as hitting it big, don't you think?"

Shay nodded. "The company files don't have much on his background, so I sent a telegram to Colorado. The mine Pringle listed as a former employer closed some years back, but hopefully there's someone in town who remembers him. I'll just have to wait and see if I get a response. When I leave here, I'm going to the saloon. Maybe I'll find someone who saw Pringle there last night."

Sheridan rose, then stretched her arms over her head to get the kinks out of her back. "Let me know what you find out."

"Are you spending the night here?"

"Yes. I finally convinced Señora Lara to go home tonight, so Poppy and I will take turns watching Enrique."

He moved closer, then pulled her into his arms. Rubbing his hand in soothing circles on her back, he said, "Promise me you'll try to get some sleep?"

"Hmm, keep that up and I'll be asleep on my feet."

He chuckled, then lowered a hand to give her bottom a playful slap. "Don't fall asleep now, Sherry." He lowered his head until his breath mingled with hers. "Not before I've given you a good-night kiss."

His mouth settled over hers, at first in a gentle caress, then quickly escalating to a deeper, wilder blending of their lips. She swayed against him, her breasts pressed to his chest, her belly cradling the hardness of his instantaneous erection.

When he broke the kiss, his shoulders rippled with a shudder. Exhaling a ragged breath, he smiled down at her flushed face. "When this mess blows over, we have a lot of catching up to do."

"Uh-huh," she replied, looking up at him through passion-darkened eyes.

He stared at her intently for a moment, then said, "And there's also something I need to talk to you about."

Her brow furrowed. "Can't you tell me now?"

He shook his head, amazed he'd even suggested talking about his newly discovered feelings for her. "It'll keep. Now, what about that promise to get some sleep?"

"I'll try."

"Guess that'll have to do," he said, then pressed his mouth to her kiss-swollen lips one last time. Releasing her, he stepped back. "If anything happens, send for me. Otherwise, I'll come by in the morning."

She nodded, then watched him leave her office. She wondered briefly what he wanted to discuss with her, then pushed the thought aside. Regardless of what it was, she wouldn't take the time to speculate. She had a patient who needed her complete and undistracted concentration.

The next morning Shay pushed his breakfast dishes aside and looked up to see Whit enter the boardinghouse dining hall.

When Whit spotted him, he headed for his table. "Mind if I join you?"

Shay still hadn't gotten over Whit's directive to let Enrique die, so he nearly refused his friend's request. Shoving aside his personal feelings, he waved toward the chair across the table. "Be my guest."

After Whit ordered, he said, "I notified the home office about the robbery yesterday afternoon and asked them to contact the insurance company. Have you done anything about getting the missing payroll replaced?"

"Orrin's going to let me know how much we're short, then I'll wire the bank in Marfa for the additional funds."

When Shay didn't say any more, Whit idly stirred sugar into his coffee. "Listen, Shay, I want to apologize for the other night. I've thought about it a lot, and you were right, I was out of line." He laid down his spoon. "This is the first time I've had to deal with a robbery in the field. I've always had the buffer of being in San Francisco, getting the information as it filtered in, not viewing everything firsthand. Anyway, I know it's no excuse, but I guess the entire situation made me over-react."

Shay stared at Whit for a few seconds. Realizing the man he'd called friend for a number of years had spent little time away from the company's main office, he smiled. "Goes to show you city boys should get out into the real world more often."

Whit's eyebrows shot up. "Look who's calling me a city boy. You hate it here, remember? Always pleading to be replaced and bemoaning life in such an isolated, backward—"

Shay held up one hand. "Okay, okay. You've made your point." He saw no purpose in pointing out that he no longer thought of Shafter in those terms.

Whit smiled, then took a sip of coffee. "At least we agree about one thing. I acted like an ass the other night."

"True, but it's over and done, so let's forget it."

"Fine by me. So anything new on the investigation?"

Shay signaled the waiter for another cup of coffee. Not

wanting to tell Whit what he'd learned until he had something stronger than speculation, he said, "Nothing concrete."

"Have you spoken to the police?"

"Deputy Luján is out of town," Shay replied. "As soon as he delivered the payroll to Orrin the other day, he headed back to Marfa. He's been helping out at the county sheriff's office."

"Have you notified him about the robbery?"

He lifted his cup and sipped the steaming coffee. Choosing his words carefully, he said, "Not yet. He thought the sheriff needed him for just a couple of days. If he doesn't get back by noon today, I'll send him a telegram."

Before they could continue their conversation, the waiter brought Whit's breakfast. Shay used the opportunity to make his exit. Murmuring an excuse about a meeting, he took one last drink of coffee, then rose and left the dining hall.

By the time Shay arrived at the clinic, morning had nearly slipped by. Relieved by Sheridan's smile of greeting, her face no longer pale with exhaustion, he brushed his mouth over hers in a brief kiss.

" 'Morning," he whispered. He ran the pad of his thumb over one of the less prominent circles beneath her eyes. "Looks like you kept your promise. You're looking more rested today. Does this mean Enrique is improving?"

She smiled again. "Poppy let me sleep several hours longer than she was supposed to. And yes, Enrique has improved slightly. His mother's sitting with him now. He's still feverish, but his color is much better and his pulse is stronger."

"Are you concerned about the fever?"

"Not yet. A fever is normal when the body suffers extreme trauma and often lingers for a few days. It doesn't become dangerous unless it rises drastically and remains high for a long period of time. I'm more concerned because he hasn't regained consciousness."

Shay nodded, pulled a piece of paper from his shirt pocket, then sat on the edge of Poppy's desk. "I received a response to my telegram about Pringle. The man who responded was the foreman for an Aspen mining company when Pringle worked there. Seems Pringle had money problems before he came to Texas. Always trying to look like a big spender but never having the heavy purse to pull it off. He left Aspen in a cloud of suspicion about a number of robberies in the area. He was suspected of being involved, but the authorities couldn't find enough evidence to link him to the crimes. Then, after he left, the robberies suddenly stopped."

"Isn't that coincidental?" Sheridan murmured. Looking over at Shay, she said, "I haven't heard of any robberies around here since I arrived in town. Have there been others?"

"Not that I'm aware of. Maybe Pringle changed his methods, decided to bide his time and wait for his one big opportunity."

"And I helped him."

"You don't know that."

"Yes, I do. I'm convinced Leonard got Betsy to pretend to be my friend so she could get information he could use. She practically begged me to go to the Shannon party, asking me to look at everything in their house so I could tell her about it. She had an excuse for asking, but now I see what she was really trying to do. Find out if the Shannons have anything worth stealing."

Shay stroked one side of his mustache. "Could be. I wonder if she really knew what he was up to, or if she did what he asked just so she wouldn't get knocked around."

"She claims they love each other," Sheridan replied with a sad shake of her head. "As pitiful as it seems, there are people who believe hitting and getting hit is part of loving someone. Once they get caught in that vicious cycle, they can't stop it."

After a moment Shay said, "I can see why working for women's rights is so important to you. Trying to help women in those circumstances is a worthy cause."

She glanced over at him and blinked. "Thanks."

"I hope you haven't decided to give up your work just because you couldn't help Betsy Pringle."

She shook her head. "It'll take a while to get over the way she used me, but I intend to continue fighting for my beliefs."

"Attagirl," he said with a smile. He suddenly sobered. "There's something else in this telegram that's interesting. A close friend of Pringle's was one of the best dynamiters in Aspen. Apparently Leonard learned how to use dynamite by listening to his friend and asking questions."

Sheridan pursed her lips thoughtfully. "So, we know Leonard needed money. He knew how to use dynamite. And he guessed, thanks to Betsy, the reason the company store needed a guard was because the payroll arrived early."

"None of which proves he blew open the safe or shot Enrique."

"That's one thing I don't understand. If Leonard knew the store was guarded, how did Enrique end up outside, shot, holding a bag of money?"

Shay shrugged. "The robbery must've gone bad somehow. That's the only thing that makes sense." He fell silent for a moment, then said, "I picked up another interesting bit of information last night. The men who were in the saloon when Pringle was there said he was usually a heavy drinker. That night he barely touched the one drink he ordered."

"As if he had plans and wanted to keep a clear head."

"Exactly what I was—"

"*Doctora,* come quick."

Sheridan started at Josefa's excited voice. After exchanging an anxious look with Shay, she hurried into the examination room. Seeing Josefa's beaming smile, her gaze snapped to her patient. When Enrique stared back at her, his eyes clear and alert, she released the breath she'd been holding.

The boy shifted his gaze back and forth between his mother and Sheridan. "Mama," he said, his voice low and raspy. "*Doctora* Kinmont. What happened?"

"You do not remember, Rique?" his mother said.

He rolled his head from side to side on the pillow.

Shay, who stood just inside the door, said, "You were spend-ing the night in the company store. Orrin had plans, so you volunteered to take his place. Do you remember that?"

"*Sí*. And I remember Señor Neilson leaving the store." His brow furrowed. "But after that everything is a blur." He lifted a hand to rub his temple, wincing with the movement.

"Don't worry, Enrique," Sheridan said. "That's normal. With time, your memory should come back."

Sheridan and Shay exchanged another glance. Both knew if Enrique's memory didn't return, they might never have the evidence they needed against Leonard Pringle.

Before Shay left the clinic, he and Sheridan agreed not to make the truth about Enrique's recovery common knowledge. They thought a smarter course of action would be to let Pringle continue thinking the boy remained unconscious, otherwise their primary suspect might panic and leave town.

That afternoon Shay received a response to the telegram he had sent to Marfa. Deputy Sheriff Luján would be returning the following morning. With time for his own investigation running out, Shay spent the afternoon trying to come up with a way to prove Enrique's innocence. The evidence he'd gathered pointed to Pringle, but there were still missing pieces. Such as, if Pringle suspected the company store's safe contained the payroll and he planned to steal the money, why did he try to set up Enrique for the robbery? Why didn't he just kill the boy while they were both in the store? Why didn't he take off with the rest of the payroll after he shot the supposed thief? And where was the missing payroll?

The clock on his office wall struck six, ending his musing about those questions. He cleaned off his desk, then rose, grabbed his hat, and left. Though he wasn't particularly hungry, he decided to head to the boardinghouse to see if Whit wanted to join him for supper. But first he'd stop by the clinic again.

When Sheridan told him Enrique's memory was returning and he remembered more about the night of the robbery, Shay prayed whatever the boy had to say would provide some needed answers.

Chapter Twenty-five

Later that night Shay tracked down Leonard Pringle at the town saloon. When the man sitting with Pringle saw Shay approach, he shoved his chair away from the table, rose, and hurried toward the door.

"Pringle," Shay said, nodding a greeting. "Mind if I have a seat?"

"It's a free country."

"Yes, it is," Shay replied with a smile. He called for the barkeep to bring him a beer, then sat down in the chair vacated by Pringle's previous companion. "I want to talk to you about the other night."

Pringle tensed, his muddy brown eyes narrowing to slits. "Yeah?"

"I've been thinking how fortunate the company was. You being so close to the store after the explosion, then seeing the boy run out the door and—uh—stopping him from getting away."

The tension left Pringle's heavily muscled shoulders and

arms. "You offering me a reward for saving the company payroll?

"That's the thing. Only part of the payroll has been recovered. The bag Enrique took from the store. The other two bags are still missing. Any idea where they might be?"

Pringle shifted in his chair, his gaze darting toward the door. "How the hell would I know? That Mex kid probably did something with them."

"Maybe," Shay replied, lifting his glass to take a sip of beer. "I need to clear up some of the details about what happened that night."

"Like what?"

"Like how come you were practically outside the company store when the safe was blown open?"

Pringle flashed a toothy grin. "Just lucky, I reckon."

Shay nodded, then took another long sip of beer. "There's something else I've been wondering about. How come you had only one drink in here that night? One drink you barely touched."

Pringle shot an angry glance at the barkeep, then at the other men in the saloon. Finally he said, "I . . . uh . . . wasn't feelin' too good. Yeah, it was my . . . uh . . . stomach. That's why I left when I did and headed for home."

"Really?" Shay replied, tapping his fingertips on the table. "Isn't your house in the opposite direction?"

"Uh, yeah. But I needed some air, so I decided to take a walk through town first."

"Let me get this straight. You order a drink but don't touch it because you aren't feeling well. Then you leave the saloon to go home. But first you decide to take a stroll through town. Is that how it went?"

Pringle nodded. "Yeah, that's right."

Shay sat back in his chair, staring at the man across from him with hooded eyes. "You sure you didn't drink that night because you wanted to make sure you had a steady hand to light the dynamite?''

Pringle's entire body went rigid. "I don't know what yer talking about?''

"Here's something else I find interesting. How come you never told anyone you're an expert with dynamite? I hear you learned while you were up in Aspen—from one of the best.''

Pringle's fist came down on the table so hard, their glasses bounced. "That don't prove nothing," he said in a roar. His insolent gaze scoured the barroom. "Don't matter what any of ya say"—he swung his gaze back to Shay—"you ain't gonna pin this on me.''

"Oh, but I am, Pringle," Shay replied in a deceptively calm voice. "Because I have an eyewitness.'' When he saw Pringle's startled expression, he said, "That's right, Enrique Lara not only survived you back-shooting him, but he regained consciousness today.'' He waited a heartbeat to add the final blow. "And remembers everything.''

Fear leapt into Pringle's eyes. When he didn't speak, Shay continued. "You knew Enrique would be in the store, thanks to your wife, so you had to take care of him before blowing the safe. But the boy surprised you, didn't he? Clever kid, freeing himself from the rope you used to tie his hands, then trying to keep you from leaving the store until help arrived.'' Shay chuckled. "I bet that was something to see, you dodging those tins of fruit he threw at you. That's when the bandanna slipped off your face, right?''

Pringle's jaw tightened, but he still didn't reply.

"Is that when your plans changed, when you realized he could recognize you? Is that when you decided to set up Enrique by handing him a bag of money and forcing him to run from the store at gunpoint?''

The only response he got was a look of pure hatred leveled at him. Shay leaned closer. "You took the other bags of money outside when you told Enrique to run, didn't you? Then, after you shot him, you used the minute or two before someone came to investigate to hide those bags. Once all of this blew over, you planned to go back and get the hidden money, then leave town."

Pringle's face flushed a dark red, and a muscle jumped in his jaw. Hoping to use the man's rising anger to his advantage, Shay said, "That has to be a big disappointment. All that work to finally get your hands on that much money, but you can't spend one red cent. Must be tough waiting around, itching to go back and get—"

Pringle got to his feet so fast, he overturned his chair. "Damn Mex kid! He spoiled everything." His voice shook with rage. "If he hadn't gotten in the way, I'd be in El Paso right now. I thought sure one bullet would kill his sorry ass, but I musta waited too long to pull the—" Awareness of what he'd just said passed over his face in a split second. He bolted for the door.

"Stop him!" Shay shouted to the other men in the barroom.

Pringle barreled into the three men who tried to block the door. One man went sprawling, but the other two grabbed hold of his arms and held on. He cursed loudly, struggling in desperation to free himself. With one final curse he gave up.

"Lock him up," Shay said to Pringle's captors. "And post a guard until Deputy Luján gets back in the morning."

The men nodded, then hustled Pringle out the door. Shay spoke with several of the men in the saloon, taking down a list of those who would testify against Pringle. A few minutes later he stepped outside and drew in a deep breath of the cool night air, relieved the crime had been solved. With the number of witnesses who'd agreed to tell the judge they heard Pringle's confession, he could see no reason why the man wouldn't be sentenced to a long prison term. The only task remaining was finding the missing payroll bags. That shouldn't be difficult since Pringle had had little time to find a hiding place. Shay made a mental note to have some men check around the company store first thing in the morning.

As he started down the street, he contemplated going to Sheridan's house. He knew she'd want to know about his confrontation with Pringle, especially since the ugly scene confirmed Enrique's innocence. Imagining how her beautiful eyes would darken with pleasure, her bright smile giving way to a burst of delighted laughter, he grinned in anticipation. But then he decided against the idea. When he spoke with her earlier, after Enrique told them about Pringle's attempted robbery of the company payroll, she planned to go home for her first real night's sleep in several days. So regardless of how much he wanted to witness her reaction, he couldn't bring himself to disturb her much-needed rest. The news would keep until morning.

However, he had no such compunction about disturbing Whit, who hadn't spent nearly every hour since the robbery working to save a boy's life. Delaying going home to his own bed a few more minutes, he headed for the boardinghouse.

Whit hadn't turned in yet and offered to buy Shay a drink to celebrate.

"I'll pass, Whit. I'm really beat. Deputy Luján sent word he'll be here first thing in the morning, and I need to meet with him as soon as he arrives."

"Another time, then."

"Sure thing." Shay lifted a hand to cover a yawn. "I'm heading home. I'll talk to you tomorrow."

Whit nodded, then extended his hand. "Good work tonight, Shay."

Shay clasped his friend's hand. "I was just doing my job."

"Maybe, but I want you to know how much the owners, myself included, appreciate your efforts on the company's behalf. We're lucky to have you." Whit's voice took on an icy edge when he added, "Not all our employees have the best interest of the company in mind when they act."

"Uh, thanks," Shay replied, surprised and embarrassed by Whit's comments.

After the two said good night, Shay left for his house. Recalling his conversation with Whit and his friend's words of praise, he smiled. Then, when he remembered Whit's last statement and how his voice had changed, his smile slipped. Had Whit been trying to tell him something? Or were the events of the past several days making him look for hidden meanings in everything? Frowning, he rubbed the back of his neck. *I'm too tired to think about it tonight.*

When he reached his house, he headed straight for the bedroom, then stripped off his clothes and crawled into bed. In minutes he'd pushed all thoughts from his mind and fell into a deep sleep.

The next morning Shay spent more than an hour with Deputy Luján, going over the events of the past several days and providing a list of people the man needed to speak with. As soon as he could, he excused himself.

At the clinic Poppy told him Sheridan had arrived not long after sunup. An hour later Mr. Stafford came in. He spoke privately to Sheridan for a moment, then the two of them left. Sheridan hadn't returned.

Shay checked everywhere he could think of, but no one had seen Sheridan. As he started back to the clinic, he glanced toward the cottonwoods lining the creek and caught a glimpse of something moving between the huge tree trunks. Watching until he saw the brief flash of white and brown again, he suddenly smiled. Buster.

He found the dog romping on the creek bank. Sheridan stood nearby, head bowed, shoulders hunched forward as if she were in pain.

He made no effort to hide his approach, and yet she appeared to be unaware of his presence. "Sheridan," he said in a soft voice, not wanting to startle her. When she didn't respond, he raised his voice slightly and called her name again. This time her head came up and her shoulders straightened, but she kept her back to him.

He stepped around in front of her. When she didn't meet his gaze, he lifted a hand to cup her chin. She jerked her head to the side.

"Don't touch me."

The chill in her voice struck him like a physical blow. "What is it, Sheridan? I thought Enrique was doing fine."

"He is," she replied.

"Then, what's wrong?"

She slowly lifted her face and met his gaze. "Why are you pretending you don't know?"

The pain Shay saw reflected in her eyes shocked him. "Pretending? I don't know what you're talking about."

"Of course you do. You're the one who kept a file on me, recording everything I did that you didn't agree with, collecting evidence to give to Mr. Stafford."

"Whit?" Shay's eyes narrowed. What had his friend done? A feeling of dread increasing his heart rate, he grasped her shoulders. "Why did Whit come to the clinic this morning?"

She glared up at him. "Do I have to say it? Is that what you want?" When Shay tried to speak, she cut him off. "Mr. Stafford came to tell me I'm being relieved of my duties. As soon as the replacement he's sent for arrives, I'll no longer be the company doctor." Before Shay could respond, she added, "He would have insisted on terminating my contract immediately, but out of deference to Enrique he's letting me stay until the new doctor arrives. Was that your idea, or was such concern for a patient his doing?"

Shay squeezed his eyes closed for a moment, temporarily tucking away his anger at Whit. In a gentle voice he said, "Sheridan, let me explain."

She shook off his hands and moved away from him. "There's

nothing to explain. Mr. Stafford's visit put everything in the proper perspective. From the moment I arrived, you made it your personal crusade to get me replaced. First you tried to get me to resign, but I refused. Then you tried to get Mr. Stafford to fire me, and when that didn't work, you came up with your own plan." Her lips curved into a smile that held no humor. "I knew you didn't have any faith in lady doctors. You made that clear from the moment we met. And I knew you were watching my every move, hoping you'd catch me making a mistake, waiting for a reason to get me fired. But I thought things had changed after we—" She swallowed, then lifted her chin and sent him a chilling glance. "Obviously I was wrong. Give yourself a pat on the back, Mr. Bannigan. Your plan was a rousing success."

When she turned to leave, he blocked her departure. "You've got to listen to me. I admit, when you first arrived and for a while afterward, I did make it a priority to find reasons to get you replaced. But after I told you about my sister's death and why I believed women shouldn't become doctors, what you said to me made sense. That's when I began to see things differently. And as I watched you these past weeks, I came to realize I was wrong to condemn you for being a doctor. I told you that just a few days ago. Don't you remember?"

"Yes, I remember," she replied, her gaze as icy as an Arctic wind. "And I also remember you told me you'd called off your watchdog. Now I understand why. You hoped by feeding me those lines that I'd let down my guard and provide you with more information to give Mr. Stafford."

"Dammit, that isn't true!" He removed his hat and ran an unsteady hand through his hair. Settling his hat back on his head, he said, "I want you to listen to me, because this is the God's honest truth. I stopped making notes about you weeks ago, but I wasn't in my office when Whit arrived, and he found them. Now I wish I'd destroyed the damn things. Whit thought the information I'd collected was sufficient to get you fired and intended to present my findings to the other owners. I objected, but he wouldn't listen. He still planned to let the owners decide about your future here. Then, after your argument with him about Enrique, he changed his mind and decided to take matters into his own hands. But he said he'd wait to take action until we knew Enrique's fate. I thought he'd cool down in a day or two and forget about acting on his own." He paused to collect his thoughts. "If I'd known Whit planned to see you today, I swear to you, I would have done everything possible to stop him."

"That's easy to say now, isn't it?" she replied, the pain in her chest making speech nearly impossible. She'd been such a fool for allowing herself to think she could trust this man, and even more of a fool for falling in love with him.

"Dammit, Sheridan, you've got to believe me. I didn't mean for this to happen." He drew a shaky breath, then lowered his voice to a quavering whisper. "I love you."

She closed her eyes, wishing he'd said anything but those last three words. There couldn't have been a worse time for making a declaration that should have filled her with joy. But it was too late. His betrayal erased all happiness and left only bitterness in its wake.

"I need to get back to the clinic," she said in a voice devoid of emotion. She turned, called for Buster, then walked away.

"Sheridan," Shay said, starting after her. "Wait."

"Just leave me alone, Shay," she said, never breaking stride.

He jerked to a halt, a horrible numbness settling over him. How could he have been such an idiot? He should have destroyed his notes about Sheridan. Then Whit wouldn't have found them or taken it upon himself to fire her. Blowing out a weary breath, he turned back to the creek. He stared at the rippling surface for a long time, watching his future rush downstream with the water's current.

* * *

Sheridan managed to get through the next several days by willing herself not to think about Shay's betrayal. Calling upon all the inner strength she possessed, she managed to keep him from niggling into her thoughts—at least most of the time. Once in a while a memory slipped through the barrier she'd erected in her mind. Like the night of the Shannon party and her first sight of him in more formal clothing, or the long hours he worked by her side to help the residents of Polvo, or when they were in the desert and he saved her life by shooting the mountain lion.

Early one afternoon she left Poppy in charge of the clinic and went home to begin packing. Her replacement would be arriving any day, and she didn't want to wait until the last minute to pack.

She dragged her steamer trunk into her bedroom and lifted the lid. Another memory stirred. Her arrival in Shafter, Shay's less than cordial greeting, and his outrage over the amount of luggage she and Poppy brought with them. In spite of the pain clutching her heart, she smiled. He'd been so irritated when he found out she was the new company doctor, and she'd reacted with a flare of temper at his outdated views. Yet at the same time, from the first moment she saw him there had been something strongly appealing about Shay Bannigan.

As she began the tedious process of emptying the chest of drawers in her bedroom and filling the opened trunk, she wondered if she'd been wrong not to believe him. Was he really sorry he'd kept his notes about her? Had he really tried to talk Whitaker Stafford out of firing her? Did he really believe her to be a competent doctor? And the question that plagued her most—did he really love her?

Possible answers swirled in her head, making her dizzy with the effort to sort them out and confusing her even more. She finally forced herself to concentrate on the one bright spot in her otherwise gloomy life: Enrique. The boy's recovery had been astounding, progressing much faster than she'd hoped. He'd bounced back so quickly that the previous day she'd allowed him to finish his recuperation at home. At least she wouldn't be leaving town with the added burden of Enrique's death increasing the ache in her heart.

She sorted out a few pieces of clothing, the articles she'd need before the new doctor arrived, then packed the rest in her trunk for her trip to— She squeezed her eyes closed, wondering where she was going to go. Back to Baltimore? Or Boston or New York? Or maybe she'd stay in Tex— Pounding on the front door ended her musing about her destination.

She opened the door to find Boyd Smith on the other side. Arching her eyebrows, she said, "Did Mr. Bannigan send you to do more spying on me, Mr. Smith?"

He jerked his hat from his head, a dull flush of color creeping up his weathered cheeks. "No, ma'am. And I was only doin' what Mr. Bannigan paid me to do."

Sheridan's irritation cooled. "I know that," she replied with a sigh. "And I'm sorry I sounded so cross. Now, what can I do for you?"

"There's been an accident. Mr. Bannigan sent me to fetch you."

Her gaze narrowed. "He did? Are you sure?" At his nod she said, "What kind of accident?"

"I was sitting outside the boardinghouse, when a man come riding inta town, shouting for a doctor. Said an ore-wagon driver got hisself hurt near the south mine. Mr. Bannigan heard the shout from inside the dining hall and came out to see what was going on. Then he sent me to fetch ya."

She hesitated long enough to decide she couldn't refuse to go with him. Even if the story Boyd Smith just recited proved to be a selfish ruse on Shay's part, she couldn't take the risk that a patient's life might be at stake. "Did they bring the man into town?"

"No, ma'am. I reckon he's still by the mine."

"The south mine's more than a mile from town. Have you got a horse I can borrow?"

Smith nodded. "He's right outside. Just leave him at the stable when you get back."

"Thanks. I'll go change."

A few minutes later Sheridan arrived at the mine. Whit Stafford, several mine workers she didn't recognize, and Shay stood in a circle near an ore wagon. She dismounted, then pushed through the group of men, keeping her gaze averted from Shay's.

"What happened?" she said, dropping onto her knees beside the slender young man lying unconscious on the ground.

Shay stepped closer and crouched on the opposite side of the prone wagon driver. "His name's Miguel Suarez. The others said he was in line to have his wagon loaded with ore, when one of his mules started acting up. He got down to check, something spooked the rest of the team, and they bolted. He got knocked under his wagon. Near as we can tell, one of the wheels ran over his right leg, and he took a pretty good bump on the head."

Sheridan nodded, still not making eye contact with Shay. "There's a lump on the side of his head, which explains why he's unconscious." She moved to examine his leg. "His thighbone's broken. But it's a clean break. Good thing his wagon was empty. Otherwise it would've been a lot worse." She sat back on her heels and looked around. "Is there someplace we can take him that's close by? I don't want to risk jarring his leg by making the long trip into town."

Shay rose and spoke to the other men. He turned back to her and said, "Some of the miners have homes near here. We can take Miguel to one of them."

Sheridan also got to her feet. "We'll need something to use as a stretcher. I want to keep his leg as immobile as possible while we move him."

Shay gave instructions to have Sheridan's request carried out, then swung his gaze back to her. She looked as tired and miserable as he'd been these past few days. He knew the moment she realized he was staring at her. Her back suddenly stiffened, her lips flattened to a thin line, and her fingers tightened on the handles of her medical bag. The ache in his chest intensified. Since their scene at the creek, she'd refused to speak to him. He had to make her understand, had to convince her he loved her.

But as each day slipped by, he feared his time was quickly running out.

Chapter Twenty-six

Shay insisted on helping Sheridan care for the injured driver, his closeness adding to her already frayed nerves. By calling on her training as a doctor, she managed to remain focused on the needs of her patient and pushed everything else from her mind.

After getting Miguel transported to a one-room miner's shack built against a hill, Sheridan helped the men carefully move him from the makeshift stretcher onto the bed.

After the others filed out of the house, she glanced over at Shay, then looked back at Miguel. "I need to get his trousers off."

"I'll help you," Shay said, moving to her side.

She nodded, then explained what they would do. After they accomplished the task, she forced Miguel's thighbone back into alignment, then placed a light blanket over his torso for modesty's sake. Sorting through her medical bag, she removed a roll of tape and a length of cloth bandage.

Shay stood a few feet away, watching her run the tape down

each side of Miguel's right leg then under his foot. Then she slipped the bandage beneath the tape on the bottom of his foot, letting the ends dangle off the end of the bed. Shay tugged on one side of his mustache, trying to figure out what she planned to do.

"I need some kind of weight," she said, pulling him from his musing. "See if you can find something heavy."

Shay turned to follow her instructions. A moment later he returned with a flatiron. "How about this?"

She glanced up. "Perfect," she said, flashing him a smile. As soon as she realized what she'd done, the smile vanished.

As he watched her attach the flatiron to the bandage, he finally realized her intentions. "Ah, now I see. You're using the flatiron for traction."

"Yes. This is pretty primitive, but it should work. When the femur, the thighbone, breaks, the leg muscles pull the ends of the bone apart and keep it from healing. By creating continuous traction on the leg, the muscles will eventually stop pulling on the bone, allowing the broken ends to stay aligned and heal properly."

"Ingenious," Shay said in a low voice.

Sheridan's gaze snapped to his, surprised to see admiration in his expression. "I didn't invent the procedure," she replied with a shrug. "I just improvised with what was available."

"You still did a damn fine job," he replied.

She needed all her powers of concentration to squash the pride his words caused. Remembering the day he told her he'd changed his mind about women having no business becoming doctors, the comments he just made totally supported that claim. She blinked, startled to realize he really did sound sincere. Was everything he told her the truth? Were her accusations against him wrong? She gave her head a shake. No, that couldn't be. She was right to— Miguel's moan snapped her back to the present.

The man murmured something in Spanish, then, as Sheridan's fingers probed the lump on his scalp, he sucked in a sharp breath. When he opened his deep brown eyes and focused on Sheridan, he said, "What happened?"

"You were hurt when your team of mules bolted," Sheridan replied. Seeing the confusion in his eyes give way to remembrance, she said, "Other than this lump on your head, you have a broken leg." When he tried to sit up, she grabbed his arm to halt his efforts.

"No, Miguel, don't try to move. I set the bone in your leg and I tied a weight to your foot to keep the bone in place. You must remain as still as possible, *bueno?*"

"*Sí.* My head hurts too much to move anyway," he replied with a sigh. "You will let Dulcina know I have been hurt?"

"Dulcina?"

"My wife. We live with her parents. Her father grows vegetables on land near the creek, a few miles north of town."

"I'll make sure she's notified as soon as I get you something for your pain and to help you sleep."

"*Gracias, doctora.*"

"*De nada,*" she replied, adjusting his blanket.

After giving Miguel his medication, she waited until he fell asleep, then decided to go outside for some fresh air. When she turned toward the door, Whitaker Stafford stood leaning against the doorframe. As she approached him, he didn't speak but stared at her, something she couldn't name reflected in his light blue eyes. When she stood directly in front of him, he gave her a nod, then moved aside to let her pass through the door.

When she stepped outside, Shay was waiting for her.

"Sheridan, I'd like to talk to you."

"What about?" she said, keeping her back to him.

"I want to talk about us."

"Us?" Though his earlier words had planted a seed of doubt in her mind, nothing had changed. "I think you've said all there is to say on the subject."

He grabbed her arm and swung her around to face him. "No, I haven't said all there is—"

"And I say you have," she said through gritted teeth. "I told you before, but I'll tell you again. I don't want to hear it. Now, let go of me."

His hand dropped from her arm. "You're sure this is how you want it?"

At her curt nod he turned and walked away without another word.

After her confrontation with Shay she stayed away from both him and Whit as much as possible, preferring to remain inside the small house near her patient. A short time later the man Shay had sent to notify Miguel's wife returned, escorting Dulcina Suarez, who insisted her place was with her husband, and her two sisters.

The three women fussed over Miguel, especially his pretty, young wife, who pressed kisses all over her husband's face, tears streaming down her pale brown cheeks.

Several hours later, when Dulcina walked outside to bid Sheridan good-bye, her enormous dark eyes glittered with the threat of another round of tears.

"How can I thank you," she said with a sniffle, "for all you have done, *Doctora* Kinmont?"

"The only thanks I want is for you and your sisters to take good care of Miguel."

"*Sí*, we will do everything you told us."

Sheridan smiled at Dulcina. "He is lucky to have you."

The woman's cheeks darkened with a blush. "I am lucky to have such a fine man as my husband."

After Sheridan gave some last-minute instructions and said her good-byes, she started toward the sorrel gelding she'd borrowed from Boyd Smith. As she secured her medical bag to the saddle, she looked up and down the row of small houses. There were several men from the mines standing nearby, but she didn't see Shay. Refusing to acknowledge her disappointment at not seeing him, she mounted, then swung the sorrel around toward town. Using more force than necessary, she jabbed her heels into the gelding's sides.

Sheridan arrived in Shafter covered with dust from the hard ride. After leaving the horse at the stable where Smith boarded him, she headed home. The afternoon and early evening had been trying, both professionally and personally, and she looked forward to a hot bath, something to eat, and the cool sheets of her bed.

As she approached the house, she saw the front door open and Orrin Neilson step outside. He turned toward Poppy, who stood in the doorway. They appeared to exchange words before Orrin took a step closer, bent to kiss Poppy's cheek, then spun on his heel and left.

As Orrin walked toward Sheridan, she opened her mouth to greet him. But he kept his head bowed and moved past her as if she were invisible. Snapping her mouth shut, she shifted her gaze back to the now-closed front door. Her brow furrowed, she hurried toward the house.

She entered the front door a few seconds later, calling a hello. When she didn't get an answer, Sheridan went looking for Poppy. She found her staring out the kitchen window.

"What's the matter with Orrin?" Sheridan said, moving to stand beside her friend. "He acted like he—" The sight of Poppy's tear-stained face caught Sheridan by surprise. "Poppy, what is it?"

Poppy drew a deep, shuddering breath, then said, "I finally worked up the nerve to tell Orrin that you and I will be leaving Shafter soon." She gulped down more tears. "He . . . um . . . didn't take it well."

"Oh, Poppy. You should've listened to me and accepted his proposal. Just because the man I love proved to be another snake in the grass, that's no reason for you to give up the man you love."

Poppy blew her nose, then said, "So you're finally admitting you love Shay?"

Her mouth quirked in a sheepish smile. "For all the good it'll do me now."

"Have you told him?" When Sheridan shook her head, Poppy said, "I think he deserves to know how you feel."

Sheridan sighed. "Poppy, our relationship was an arrangement. We agreed to enjoy each other's company for whatever time we had together. With no promises. No expectations. And no confessions of love." Then, in a lower voice, she added, "I never thought I'd have anything to confess."

"But he loves you."

"That's what he told me."

"Why would he lie?"

Sheridan didn't know how to respond. The reasons she'd previously come up with to explain his confession no longer seemed valid. To add to her confusion, her earlier doubts resurfaced. Had Shay told her the truth, as he claimed? Had she made false accusations against him? Still not certain of the correct answers, she finally said, "I'm going to take a bath."

As she soaked in the tub, she considered where she and Poppy would go and what her future held. Though some of the eastern cities she considered had possibilities, none of them really appealed to her. And as for her future, all she could see was an eternity of boring, lonely days looming in front of her.

She rested her head against the back of the tub and closed her eyes. For a few moments she considered the pathetic scenario she'd just pictured for herself. How would she survive such a— Her eyes popped open, the truth hitting her square in the face. She jerked to a sitting position, sending water sloshing over the edge of the tub.

Her future wasn't back east in a fancy hospital. She didn't need that kind of environment to attain professional satisfaction. She could work as a doctor anywhere. But she wouldn't have a future at all without one important element—Shay Bannigan.

She slid back down in the tub, wondering what she should do about the discovery she'd just made. Was it possible she and Shay could make a life together? She remembered once thinking that she would have to change his opinion about her profession if their relationship was meant to be. He told her he'd changed his opinion, and the more she thought about his claim, the more she was convinced he hadn't lied. Shay was an honorable man. He hadn't hidden his distrust of lady doctors, nor the fact that he'd hired someone to watch the clinic. As she'd told her mother, she suspected he was trying to get her replaced—she even understood how he'd acquired his cock-eyed prejudice once he explained about his sister. So having Mr. Stafford inform her that her suspicions were correct shouldn't have come as a surprise. Then, when Shay tried to explain, saying he regretted the notes he'd made and would have fought for her job had he known Whit's plans, she refused to believe him. She frowned, realizing something she'd been too angry and too hurt to realize sooner. If Shay still wanted to get her replaced, he had no reason to tell her those things. His goal had been accomplished, so why would he lie?

Her frown slowly transformed into a smile. Shay had told her the truth—about everything. Yet the most important question remained. What should she do about it? Her smile fading, she mulled over everything she'd learned, searching for an answer. Her bathwater had gone cold by the time she forced herself to crawl out of the tub.

She lay awake a long time that night, contemplating her future. After finally deciding upon a course of action, she closed her eyes and soon fell asleep.

"Poppy," she said, breezing into the kitchen the following morning. "Don't pack another thing."

Poppy looked up from pouring their coffee, surprised to see Sheridan in such fine humor. She studied her friend through a narrowed gaze. "You haven't been nipping the whiskey already this morning, have you?"

Sheridan chuckled, then held up her right hand. "I swear. Nary a drop." She accepted the cup Poppy handed her, then took a sip of the steaming coffee. "I did a lot of thinking last night, and I finally decided you were right."

"I was?"

"Absolutely. That's why I'm in such a good mood."

"Are you going to tell me what you're talking about?"

"Later." She took several more sips of coffee, then set the cup on the table. "I overslept, so I've got to get going."

"But—"

"See you at the clinic."

The front door banged shut a few seconds later, leaving Poppy to ponder her friend's strange behavior.

Sheridan arrived at the mine offices and went directly to Shay's office. She knocked on the door and entered at the direction of a muffled voice. Stepping into the room, her smile of greeting faded. Whitaker Stafford sat behind Shay's desk.

"Dr. Kinmont," Whit said, getting to his feet. "Just the person I wanted to see. Please, come in and have a seat. There's something I need to tell you."

"I can stay only a minute," she finally said, sitting where he indicated, then watching him resettle in his chair.

"Dr. Kinmont, let me begin by saying I owe you an apology. I had no right to speak to you the way I did a few days ago, for which I'm truly sorry." He paused a moment to let his words sink in, then said, "I'm withdrawing my termination of your contract, and I'd like you to consider staying on as our company doctor." When her only response was the arching of her eyebrows, he said, "You're a truly fine physician, and I was wrong to ever think otherwise."

"And my reaction the night Enrique got shot?"

"Totally understandable under the circumstances." His lips curved in a weak smile. "Shay gave me hell for what I did, but at the time my stubbornness prevented me from realizing he was right. Again you have my humble apology for what I said to you. I was completely out of line.''

She didn't reply for a moment, then finally said, "I accept your apology, Mr. Stafford. I'm flattered you want me to stay. But before I give you my answer, I'd like to talk to Shay.''

Whit glanced at the clock. "You'd better hurry, then. He's planning on taking today's stage.''

"Stage? Where's he going?''

"Back to San Francisco, I imagine. He finally convinced me to accept his resignation last night.'' He nodded to the pile of papers on the desk. "In a moment of weakness I agreed to stay on until I can get someone here to take his place.''

Sheridan got to her feet. "If you'll excuse me, I have to be going.''

He waved her toward the door. "Sure. Go on. I'll be here whenever you want to give me your answer.''

Sheridan raced down Main Street, her heart thumping wildly against her ribs. The stage line office was empty and no passengers waited outside. Hoping the stage hadn't arrived and already left on the return run, she started toward Shay's house.

Not bothering to knock, she opened the front door and burst inside. "Shay? Shay, where are—''

"Sheridan!'' Shay said, entering the room carrying a leather satchel. "What are you doing here? Is something wrong?''

She drew a ragged breath, her anxiety easing now that she knew she hadn't missed him. Her relief abruptly changing to fear-driven pique, she closed the distance between them. "Yes, something's wrong,'' she said, glaring up at him. "You're a coward.''

He scowled. "What are you talking about?''

She poked his chest with a finger. "You know good and well what I'm talking about. How could you be such a coward and leave town after telling me you love me? Haven't you ever heard of fighting for the woman you love?''

Shay dropped the satchel onto the floor, then crossed his arms over his chest. "That's what I've been trying to do these past few days. But the woman in question wouldn't talk to me."

Her burst of temper fizzled out. "Well, she had her reasons," she replied, her face burning with a blush. "She was hurt. Angry. Confused." She inhaled, then released the air slowly. "But none of that matters anymore, because she finally realized her love for you is more important."

"Love?" His eyebrows knitted in a frown. "Are you saying she—you love me?"

She nodded, then swallowed. "I love you, Shay."

He blinked, then hauled her into his arms. "Oh, God, Sherry," he said with a groan. "I never thought I'd hear you say that." He pressed his mouth to hers in a heated kiss.

When he finally released her, she gulped in a lungful of air, then said, "Why did you resign?"

"After you refused to talk to me yesterday, I realized I couldn't stay here once you left. Memories of you would probably kill me, so I told Whit he had to accept my resignation or I'd quit."

She swallowed the lump in her throat. "Will you reconsider staying in Shafter if I stay?" Before he could answer, she said, "I know you don't care for Shafter much, but maybe with more time, it'll grow on you."

He stared down at her for several seconds. "It's already grown on me. And yes, I'll stay. But, you realize, neither one of us has a job."

She smiled. "Mr. Stafford just asked me to stay as company doctor, and I don't think it would take much persuasion for him to forget about your resignation."

"You're probably right," he replied with a grin. "Whit saw the amount of paperwork on my desk." He suddenly sobered. "But before I go see him, there's something else we need to discuss."

She looked up at him with wide eyes. "What?"

"Whether we stay here or not, I want us to get married." When she opened her mouth, he pressed his fingers against her lips to halt whatever she started to say. "I know you weren't planning to remarry. You made that plain from the beginning. And I certainly wasn't planning on falling in love. I imagine that wasn't in your plans either. Am I right?"

When she bobbed her head in agreement, he said, "But now that we've done the unthinkable"—he flashed her a smile—"I think getting married is the right choice. So whatdaya say? Will you marry me?"

She stared up at him, stunned by his proposal but more shocked to realize she wanted to shout yes at the top of her lungs. Instead, she forced herself to think everything through. As the thoughts tumbled around in her head, she made several more startling discoveries about herself. What she'd felt for Winston hadn't been love at all—infatuation maybe, but she definitely hadn't been in love with him. And her adamant claims to never marry again had been nothing more than a defense mechanism. A smoke screen to protect herself from more heartache.

Satisfied she had cleared up the last of her own misgivings, she needed to make sure he'd done the same. "As I recall, you said marriage wasn't for you. You love your freedom too much. And variety is what gives life its flavor. Are you saying you've changed your convictions?"

He chuckled. "Are you always going to throw my words back at me?"

"Probably. Now, answer the question."

"From the moment I met you, my life began to change. My ideas about female doctors, Texas, love, marriage. Guess I just had to find the right woman to make me see the error in my thinking."

She swallowed the lump in her throat, her heart swelling with more love than she could have imagined. If only she'd placed more faith in what her mother and grandmother told her about meeting the right man and finding the love of a lifetime. They were right; she'd finally found that man. Smiling up at him, she said, "Ask me again."

"Sheridan Kinmont, will you marry me?"

She rose on her toes and pressed a quick kiss on his mouth. "Yes," she whispered against his lips. "I'd be proud to be your wife."

Shay groaned, then wrapped her in his arms and held her close. A day that had started out so depressing had suddenly transformed into the happiest day of his life. Pressing his cheek to the top of her head, he realized how much he'd changed since arriving in Shafter. Not only had his opinion about both the town and Texas undergone a major change, so had his opinion of the woman in his arms. He once thought Sheridan totally wrong for him but now knew he'd found his perfect mate—a beautiful lady doctor with incredible Texas indigo eyes.

Epilogue

The following year

Shay pulled his horse to a halt beside Sheridan's in front of the adobe ranch house belonging to her grandparents. This would be Shay's second visit to the home of Rafe and Karina Tucker, a family gathering to celebrate Rafe's eightieth birthday. Shay's first visit came shortly after he and Sheridan were married in a double ceremony with Poppy and Orrin a month after Sheridan accepted his proposal. Following a brief wedding trip to San Francisco, they stopped at the Tucker ranch on the way back to Shafter to resume their respective jobs.

Shay glanced with appreciation at the sprawling house beneath several large cottonwood trees, whose thick canopy of leaves provided the relief of cool shade on even the hottest days. Sheridan's grandparents had certainly chosen a beautiful setting to make their home. He smiled, thinking of Sheridan as a child, running barefoot along the creek bank, listening to her grandmother teach her the ways of the Nde and undoubtedly being a real pistol. His smile widened. Sheridan could still be a pistol—impetuous and headstrong, as her mother told him the first time they met—but he wouldn't want his wife any other way.

He inhaled a deep breath of the late summer air, realizing how much he already loved the Tucker ranch. He also loved the surrounding desert and the nearby mountains. As he dismounted, he glanced over at the source of his greatest love and gave Sheridan a wink and a grin. He still found the events of the past year hard to believe. Not only had he come to love living in the desert of far West Texas and remained the mining company's general manger, he'd also fallen in love and gotten married.

"What are you thinking about?" Sheridan said, moving close and rising to tiptoe to peck a quick kiss on his mouth.

He looped his arms around her waist and held her in a loose embrace. "You. Us. The past year."

"Hmm," she replied, running her tongue over his bottom lip. "It has been pretty spectacular, hasn't it?"

"Yeah," he said, lifting one hand to tuck a lock of hair back into the loose knot at her nape. He wished she'd worn her hair down, which now reached nearly the center of her back in a glorious tangle of chestnut silk. He smiled at the memory of their first conversation about her hair, grateful she hadn't changed her mind about letting it grow long. Leaning down to nibble on her mouth, he said, "Next year will be even—"

"Hey, you two." Eli Kinmont's voice reached them from the front door. "There's time for that later. Get in here and say hello to everyone."

Sheridan and Shay exchanged another smile, then turned to walk hand in hand toward the house. When they reached Eli, Sheridan kissed her father's cheek, then said, "You've got no room to talk, Daddy. You and Mama are always kissing."

Eli chuckled, offering his hand to Shay. "Guilty as charged. Can't get too much of a good thing, can we, Shay?"

Shay clasped his father-in-law's hand, then glanced down at Sheridan. "No, sir, we certainly can't."

Eli smiled, pleased his daughter had found such a good man. When Sheridan was a child, he'd often told Jade he took pity on the man who fell in love with their daughter. But no longer. Shay could handle Sheridan without crushing her independent spirit. Holding the door open, he said, "Rafe and Karina are in the parlor. Go say hello while I gather the rest of the clan."

Sheridan entered the parlor and immediately went to where her grandparents sat on a sofa. "Happy birthday, Granddad," she said, bending to brush a kiss on his cheek. Though his once-tawny hair had turned silver and his tanned, angular face sported a network of fine lines, Sheridan still thought him handsome. "You're looking as healthy as always."

Rafe smiled up at her, his grass-green eyes sparkling. "Thank your grandmother for that," he replied, turning his gaze on his wife. "It doesn't seem possible that more than fifty years have passed since I first laid eyes on you. Seems only yesterday I saw this beautiful young woman arguing with a wagon master on a San Antonio street."

Karina returned her husband's smile. "And I met a rude, infuriating White-Eyes"—the laughter shining in her silver eyes took the sting out of her words—"who the spirits predicted would be in my future."

Rafe reached up to finger a strand of Karina's hair, the long black tresses now heavily streaked with white but no less appealing to him. "It took a while to convince me," he replied. "But now I never question what the spirits tell you or Jade."

Sheridan watched her grandparents, saw the love in the look they exchanged, and hoped her own marriage would have the same longevity.

Soon the entire family assembled around the dining room table for Rafe's birthday dinner. As the meal progressed, the room echoed with the din of boisterous conversation and frequent bursts of laughter.

When everyone finished eating, Rafe rose from his place at the head of the table. The room immediately quieted. "I want to thank all of you for coming. You've made this a special day not only for me, but for Karina as well." Moving to pull out his wife's chair, he said, "Now, who'd like to join me for a glass of peach brandy?"

"Wait," Karina said, halting the shoving of chairs away from the table. "I believe Sheridan has an announcement she wants to make. Don't you, dear?"

All heads turned in Sheridan's direction. Through narrowed eyes she looked over at her mother, then back to her grandmother. Other than the sparkle in their eyes, their faces revealed nothing. Stealing a quick glance at Shay, she saw surprise reflected in his dark eyes. She gave him a shrug and a smile, then turned to meet her grandmother's gaze. "Yes, Gran, I do." Reaching for Shay's hand, she laced her fingers with his. "Shay and I want you to know that we're going to become parents."

The room erupted in more laughter and congratulations from everyone. As the group moved into the parlor, Sheridan stood in the doorway, waiting to talk to her mother and grandmother.

"Gran, I didn't tell anyone I wanted to make an announcement," Sheridan said in a low voice.

Karina and Jade exchanged a knowing look and a twitch of their lips. "We know, dear," Karina replied. "I hope you're not angry with me, but I was afraid you'd think sharing your wonderful news would be intruding on your grandfather's day."

Sheridan looked back and forth at the two women. "How long have you known?"

"A couple of weeks." Karina took Sheridan's arm and led her into the parlor. "That's when the spirits sent me a vision about you being with child."

Sheridan frowned, casting an accusatory gaze at her mother. "What about you, Mama? Did the spirits also send you a vision?"

Jade shook her head. "I'm afraid not, honey. The spirits spoke only to your grandmother."

Eli crossed the room to join the women. "Everything okay, *roja?*" he said, wrapping an arm around his wife. "Our daughter doesn't look happy about becoming a mother."

"Daddy, that's ridiculous," Sheridan replied, a smile replacing her frown. "I'm thrilled. I just didn't expect to find out Gran already knew about the baby." She looked at Karina again. "Did the spirits reveal if I'm going to have a boy or a girl?"

"No, they didn't tell me that. Come sit with me and I'll tell you about my vision."

"Of course, Gran," Sheridan replied, turning and walking with her toward one of the room's sofas.

Later that night Shay and Sheridan lay cuddled in one of the guest rooms, his palm resting on her belly. "Your grandmother had a vision about our baby," he said with a chuckle. "I still find it hard to believe."

"Yes, I do too."

"I thought you believed in the psychic abilities of your mother and grandmother."

"I do."

"Then why is it hard to believe this time?"

Sheridan pushed herself up onto one elbow. Looking down into her husband's face, she said, "Shay, Gran told me everything she saw in her vision."

His brow furrowed. "And?"

She took a deep breath, then said, "We're having twins."

Shay's jaw went slack. Blinking up at her, he said, "What?"

"Twins. That's two babies."

"I know how many, but are you sure we're going to have twins."

"Gran's vision confirmed it."

He just stared at her for several seconds, then finally his lips curved in a smile. "Twins! Well, I'll be damned."

"I say we'll both be damned if they're as arrogant and domineering as their father."

"Arrogant and domineering!" Shay grabbed her shoulders and rolled her onto her back in one quick motion. "Is that what you think I am?"

"I used to," she replied, wrapping her arms around his neck and tugging him closer. "Along with a few other things, but not anymore." Before he could reply, she added, "Now that I think about it, maybe you are still arrogant, especially about your sexual prowess, but that's—"

"Enough," he said in a raspy whisper. "I'm about to show you why I have every right to be arrogant."

Her eyes went wide with mock innocence. "Really? And how are you going to do that?"

A groan rumbling in his chest, he lowered his mouth to hers. "Lie still, darlin'," he whispered against her lips. "And you'll soon find out."

"What if I don't want to lie still?"

He chuckled, then gave her a quick kiss. "Then what would you like to do?"

She whispered a suggestion in his ear.

His eyebrows shot up. "You're sure?" At her nod he rolled onto his back. "Okay, darlin', I'm all yours."

Sheridan rose onto her forearm and smiled down at her husband, her heart nearly bursting. "I love you, Shay," she said in a hushed voice.

"I love you too," he replied, lifting a hand to run the backs of his knuckles down her cheek. "You're the best thing that's ever happened to me."

She leaned closer, her breasts pressing against his chest, one hand exploring the planes and angles of his body. "Yes," she said, moving her hand down his flat belly. "And don't you ever forget it."

Shay's sudden bark of laughter changed to a moan. "No, never."

Author's Note

I hope you enjoyed *Texas Indigo,* the final book in my Texas Healing Women Trilogy. I truly loved writing the stories of Karina, Jade, and Sheridan, three strong, independent women whose love of healing helped me show how medicine advanced during the fifty-year span of my trilogy.

Shafter, once a silver-mining boom town, died when the mine shut down permanently in 1942. Without its economic reason for being, there was nothing to keep the town afloat, forcing most residents to move in order to find work. Today a handful of residents keep Shafter from being a true ghost town. But the adobe ruins of the stamp mill, the mine tailings, and the crumbling walls of homes and businesses along the banks of Cibolo Creek remain, reminders of what the town was like during another era.

As Sheridan demonstrated, the women involved in woman's suffrage worked for more than the right to vote. The movement, which officially began in 1848, was originally a political campaign to address problems regarding women's limited rights.

The early leaders of the movement sought to change the status of women in specific ways. In addition to suffrage, their goals included securing women the right to speak in public and testify in court, access to equal education and professions, control their own personal wages and property, and legal custody of their children after divorce. All these rights were previously denied them. As reforms on some of those issues were accomplished, the focus eventually centered on the most difficult right to obtain: suffrage. By 1900 only four states had granted women full suffrage. Then finally in 1920 the long battle to win women the right to vote ended with the adoption of the Nineteenth Amendment to the Constitution.

I love hearing from readers. If you have a comment about *Texas Indigo* or would like to be added to my mailing list, I invite you to write to me. I always respond to reader mail, plus I'll send you a bookmark and my current newsletter—a legal-size SASE is always appreciated. Please write to Arlene Hodapp aka Holly Harte, P.O. Box 563, Comstock, MI 49041-0563. For my on-line readers, visit my Web page at: http://www.net-link.net/~hharte or send an E-mail to: hharte@net-link.net.

BOOK YOUR PLACE ON OUR WEBSITE AND MAKE THE READING CONNECTION!

We've created a customized website just for our very special readers, where you can get the inside scoop on everything that's going on with Zebra, Pinnacle and Kensington books.

When you come online, you'll have the exciting opportunity to:

- View covers of upcoming books
- Read sample chapters
- Learn about our future publishing schedule (listed by publication month *and author*)
- Find out when your favorite authors will be visiting a city near you
- Search for and order backlist books from our online catalog
- Check out author bios and background information
- Send e-mail to your favorite authors
- Meet the Kensington staff online
- Join us in weekly chats with authors, readers and other guests
- Get writing guidelines
- AND MUCH MORE!

**Visit our website at
http://www.zebrabooks.com**

ROMANCE FROM FERN MICHAELS

DEAR EMILY   (0-8217-4952-8, $5.99)

WISH LIST   (0-8217-5228-6, $6.99)

AND IN HARDCOVER:

VEGAS RICH   (1-57566-057-1, $25.00)